This Cruel Fate

The Cruel Ascension Trilogy
Book 1

Maddi Bluhme

To everyone who found themselves on the gifted and talented kids to burned out twenty-somethings pipeline.

Author Note

All my life, I've struggled to wrap my head around the fact that the most evil person I could think of probably experienced soul-crushing, earth-shattering diarrhea at least once in their lives which is a very gross way of saying they were still human. To me, that is scarier than any monster under the bed or threat from above.

I don't believe that anyone who has committed evil against others is ever owed forgiveness or understanding, because they hurt real people, but I've always found fiction to be a safe place to explore what it means to be good or evil, or the many multitudes of space between the two.

Does our moral compass change, or are we always pointing north and the change comes from the morals themselves? Can we understand what drives people to act the way they do, even if it's reprehensible?

I know these are heavy topics, and I know that this book covers darker themes and topics, so thank you to all the readers of this story. Thank you for taking a chance, not only on a debut novel, but one that presents you with a main character that is, perhaps, unsympathetic in her actions and thoughts. And while Xolia was not created with the intent of anyone looking up to her, I do hope that she is someone you can understand. And somewhere throughout the trilogy you find that the line of understanding was blurred with the line of being right and wrong.

Maddi Bluhme

Chapter One

City of Atalia, Ris. 1011 years into human rule.

THE WAVING OF THE WHITE FLAG DIDN'T SIGNAL THE END of the war to Xolia so much as it heralded the start of her new life. What once seemed inescapable, a barrage of bodies against another, ceased, a brief respite between revolution and governing. Her battered body understood the implication of the Risian Congressional Party's surrender before her brain did. It sent her running through the confused and decimated enemy soldiers and scrambling over leveled buildings as she searched for her mentor, Silas, so they could forge their new government together.

Xolia slipped on a body that was too covered in mud and blood to tell what color their uniform was and by extension, which side of the war they were on. Whether it was the slate blue of the Risian armed forces or the black of her own side, the ragtag rebellion of variants who had just fought for their freedom—a freedom won.

Summer heat rolled through the demolished ten block

radius. Structures of some buildings near the outskirts of the war zone remained, while everything in the middle of the radius was rubble. It created a bowl of suffering, a clear line between where things still looked okay, and a place where nothing could be okay ever again.

Sweat dripped down Xolia's mud-stained face. With a huff, she ripped out her broken earpiece, the one thing that was supposed to keep her in contact with other variant leaders. There was no telling now how the siege on the Presidential Palace was faring or where Silas was.

Another variant, a gaping wound on his right arm, met Xolia's intense glare. "You," she barked at him. "Where's Silas?" Blood poured down his uniform while the tendons, muscles, and skin slowly knitted themselves back together.

"I... I don't know," he said through gritted teeth. Variants healed at an accelerated rate compared to humans, but it wasn't painless. The gashes ran deep, muscle and bone exposed to the blinding sun.

While Xolia could sympathize with his pain, they had known what was expected of them after the fighting ended. There was no time to let the country of Ris falter without a strong governing body to rule them. There was no time to waste in the battleground before another party or group would try to swoop in and make their claim to the highest seat of power in the country. "Find him."

"Of course, Lieutenant," he said, dipping his chin deferentially. He clutched his arm to his chest and stumbled off in the haze of smoke and bodies. Beyond him, and beyond the worst of the wreckage, a pristine white van rolled to a stop. It was labeled with Freedom for ALL Risians in black block letters, and a dozen other vans pulled in right behind the first.

Men and women rushed from the vans, carrying medical equipment and handcuffs. Xolia nodded. Everything was going exactly as planned. They all wore identical pure white uniforms. The newcomers' dress contrasted starkly with the rough chaos of everyone else, but it was all by design. Silas's design. He had told Xolia that Peter Bellevue, and his small fringe political party, needed to be unscathed by the war. It would be easier for FAR to cement their political authority if they took on the role of a helping hand rather than of the aggressors in the violent rebellion that Silas had started.

With practiced precision, FAR personnel erected white tents around the perimeter of the leveled cityscape, all bearing the four-pointed-star-and-halo flag of FAR. If Atlas had survived the onslaught, which he most likely had, he should be at the tents, rounding up variants and soldiers alike, getting them food and water. While she wouldn't be upset if Atlas was a casualty of war, she had seen him at various points, a force of wind and fire against bullets. He rained water and flung earth around him in an impenetrable vortex, tearing into enemy lines. There was a reason she and Atlas were held in equal esteem under Silas, and it wasn't because they were likely to die in battle.

Thoughts of other survivors pulled her mind away from her objective. Whether her friends had survived. Whether Adonis and his team had managed to secure the Presidential Palace as property of FAR.

A shock of red hair on the ground dashed all other thoughts from Xolia's mind. Silas's hair was red. Red like the fire he commanded. Dropping to her knees she gripped the corpse's limp shoulders. It wasn't Silas's lifeless eyes staring at her. Though, they were the eyes of a comrade. Blood seeped from the twin wounds in his head and chest.

Xolia fought to keep the relief at bay and instead focused on how this was someone who had fought for freedom. Someone who would now never get to see it. Gently, she laid his head back on the ground, sliding two fingers over his eyelids. Her gloved hands were covered in blood, but she tried to clean his face as best as she could. It was the least she could do to give his body some dignity.

She was still crouched over the body when someone grabbed her shoulder. Without a thought, she clutched at the wrist, whipping herself around and standing up. The offending hand only belonged to Marshall, the scrawny boy who was one of her oldest friends and under her direct command. "You're alive," she remarked as she released him from her grasp.

"Were you expecting me not to be?" he asked, mouth askew with a small and forced smile. He embodied everything she knew of seventeen-year-old boys, and while he showed more restraint than she would've preferred with his powers, she was still relieved to see him. So much so that she pulled him in for a hug. He was stiff against her at first before wrapping his arms around her. "The worst of it is over now."

"If I expected you to die, I wouldn't have kept you around all these years," she said, pulling away. Although she was only seventeen herself, there had never been any question about her position directly under Silas's leadership. "Have you seen Silas? I don't want to see Peter without him."

Marshall squared his shoulders. Xolia tensed, he wasn't going to have anything good to say. "People saw him heading toward the tents already," he admitted.

"What?" Xolia took a step back, as if distancing herself from him would distance herself from his words. "That wasn't part of the plan."

"What do you want to do, then?"

Xolia bit the inside of her cheek, considering. There had to be a reason Silas went to FAR leadership without her. "Let's go to Peter."

With Xolia leading a half step in front of Marshall, they made their way towards the beckoning white tents. Around them, variants nursed a multitude of garish wounds, all slowly knitting themselves back together. She ignored the haggard and bitter faces of the enemy, their wounds open and festering. All she could do now was forge her path ahead, hoping that Silas and Peter were waiting for her.

Armed guards stood at the entrance of the largest tent. They let Xolia inside, but she paused at the opening when they directed Marshall to one of the smaller tents, citing his lack of rank. Xolia gave him a nod to listen and stepped inside the sweltering tent. A dozen men and women stood around a rectangular folding table, their voices melding together. With the others all dressed in the simple white uniforms, Xolia felt self-conscious in her state of dress. She wiped her blood-covered gloves on her legs, but it did little to help.

Peter, the older man at the head of the table, snapped his head up, finding Xolia. He smiled, small wrinkles forming at the corners of his warm, brown eyes. He held his hand up to the group, and everyone fell silent around him. One by one, all the other pairs of eyes turned to Xolia. A new round of murmurs broke out amongst FAR's leadership. Of the group, she only recognized a few of the faces. General DuBois, who'd left President Gornne to start fighting with them almost six months ago, and Treasurer Davenport, who'd been sympathetic to their cause from the beginning.

Xolia paused. None of this was right.

Peter walked around the table until there was barely any space between him and Xolia. Before this, they had never communicated directly, everything went through Silas. "Xolia, I've been eager to meet you. We have much to talk about." While his tone was light, his posture was just as still and rigid as Xolia's.

"Where's Silas?" she found herself asking while looking surreptitiously around for any signs of suspicious movement.

"That's what I need to talk to you about," he whispered.

Xolia's stomach dropped. *Is he okay?* "What happened?"

"Not here." Peter shook his head slightly. "Somewhere more private." He looked over his shoulder and waved someone over to their small group. "Please help Xolia get cleaned up and in a new uniform."

"Right away," the woman answered.

Protests from Xolia fell on deaf ears, and she had no choice but to follow the woman out of the main tent and into a smaller one where she showered in cold water behind a flimsy partition before slipping into the shapeless white uniforms that everyone else in FAR wore.

Once she was ready, her attendant led her to another tent, one that was farther back from the relatively organized row of medical tents. The interior was outfitted with a small folding table and two chairs. A large water bottle sat on the left side of the table.

"Please, drink some water and sit down. Peter will join you shortly," the woman said and left Xolia alone.

She couldn't deny how nice the chair looked, even if it was a simple metal folding chair. Xolia settled into it and tapped her fingers against her thigh. Silas was poised to take over the presidency. If he had died... Xolia shook her head, not wanting to follow that line of thinking. There had been no contingencies for the death of Silas, or Peter, who was in line for the vice presidency. The untouched water sloshed around the plastic barrier, responding to Xolia's mounting anxieties. Inhaling and exhaling, she willed herself to let go of the water—to quell the pull in her body that constantly sought it out.

Once it had settled Xolia took a measured sip. Peter stepped into the tent, two armed guards trailing behind him.

Xolia made to stand, but Peter shook his head and sat down in the chair opposite hers. The guards took up positions on either side of him. "I'm sorry about them," Peter said. "It's just a precaution."

A precaution? "So, Silas is dead then?"

Peter pursed his lips and glanced at his guards. Xolia's heart rate picked up. *This isn't right.* The hairs on the back of Xolia's neck stood up. Peter looked at her, with the saddest smile she had ever seen. "Look, Silas betrayed us."

"He wouldn't do that." Xolia didn't even think before defending him. She'd known him practically her whole life. He was the only father figure she had, and he wouldn't have betrayed them, wouldn't have betrayed *her.* "This is what he wanted, what he planned for. It must be a miscommunication."

"And what was his plan, Xolia?" Peter crossed his arms, those warm eyes hardening.

"Is this an interrogation?" Xolia asked, scraping her chair backwards. Once again, her frazzled nerves reached out to the water, something she *could* control, and sent it swirling around the cup.

Both guards shifted their guns, their fingers inching nearer to the trigger.

Peter held up his hands. "Stop, please," he said to the two

men. To Xolia he said, "I know this doesn't make sense, but it happened. He tried to kill me. We have him secured right now."

"Let me see him," she demanded. Silas hadn't told her of any plan to fight against FAR. The whole point of this final fight was to merge their two factions into one. It was why they had decided on a variant and a human for the highest political offices. It was supposed to be unification.

"We can't do that," Peter said, and as much as Xolia wanted to believe he was lying to her, he sounded contrite. "No one can see him until we figure out what's going on."

"But I'm telling you that Silas wasn't planning anything," Xolia said, splaying both hands on the tabletop and leaning into Peter's space. "If I can talk to him, we can figure it out."

"It's not just my decision," Peter said, words terse. "They've named me acting-chancellor. Everything's changed."

Xolia shook her head. "No, no I don't understand. This isn't what we planned."

"Then tell me why he would do something like that," Peter all but begged of her.

Peter was different from Silas in so many ways, and this vulnerable demeanor was one of them. Xolia didn't know if she could trust it, she certainly couldn't trust it more than she trusted Silas. He wouldn't lie to her.

She leapt up, sending the chair flying backwards and held out an open palm. She called to the water, and it answered her by flying out of the cup in a long spiral. It was just enough for her to fashion it into a dagger, its tip sharp and deadly.

"You must have betrayed Silas." Xolia lunged across the table and swung the blade without precision. It swiped across Peter's cheek, leaving a trail of blood. "What did you do to him?"

Peter paled as he lifted a shaking hand to touch the gaping wound on his face. A loud bang filled the tent.

Then there was only burning, screaming pain in Xolia's abdomen. Her body shifted from an intense warmth to a freezing cold and her extremities tingled before feeling faded away. She dropped her head; her white uniform was now red. *Blood.* Her blood was all over the front of the simple shirt.

The guard on Peter's right still held his gun out, the barrel smoking. Xolia tried to draw in a breath, but something was in her lungs.

Peter slammed the gun out of his guard's hand. "She's just a child. One that we are trying to save."

If he said anything more, Xolia didn't have the consciousness to catch it. Instead, she was focused on the feeling of free falling to the ground, her body crumpling and beyond her control. She coughed, thick and bloody, and that was all she knew.

Chapter Two

Seven years later — Year 1018

Tᴵᴄᴋ, ᴛɪᴄᴋ, ᴛɪᴄᴋ. Tʜᴇ sᴇᴄᴏɴᴅ ʜᴀɴᴅ ɪɴ ᴛʜᴇ ᴏʟᴅ grandfather clock moved forward with a distracting loudness that Xolia clung to. The steady tick pushed out the oncoming dread of never seeing her therapist, Krista, again.

For her part, Krista appeared unperturbed by the repetitive noise and said, "I'm so proud of you. You've grown so much since our first session."

A half-smile tugged at the corner of Xolia's mouth. "You're sure I don't need at least four more sessions?" She took in the pale-pink chair that Krista sat in, the coffee table between them, and the simple but cluttered desk behind Krista. It was familiar, safe.

"We've been over this," Krista said. It was true, the ending date for Xolia's court-mandated therapy had been set a year ago during her last rehabilitation check. "And you don't want me to recommend more sessions. Your random checks are ending, so you are no longer under an obligation to take your suppressants so long as you don't use your powers illegally."

There is that. "Still, I'm just not ready for things to change again." Xolia shifted in her seat. Even after talking to Krista for the past seven years, there were still barriers that were hard for Xolia to break down. A side effect of trauma, as Krista had explained to her.

Krista smiled and pushed her graying hair behind her ears. While she glanced at her notepad, Xolia noticed how deep the lines and wrinkles were around Krista's soft brown eyes. Her therapist had gone and gotten old while Xolia looked more or less the same. Xolia would live three of Krista's lifetimes before succumbing to old age.

"Not all change is bad, though. You had your interview two, three days ago?"

Xolia nodded.

"And how did it go?"

"I think it went really well," Xolia said. "But even if I don't get it, I enjoy what I do." Her insides squeezed at the words. Xolia desperately wanted that promotion, but happy people didn't get sad if things didn't go their way. And that was what these past seven years had been about—being happy.

Krista quirked an eyebrow. "What, you still aren't harboring hope of being a senator someday?"

"Those were Silas's plans for me." Xolia shrugged. "These are the plans I'm making for myself." That had become her mantra once she was able to grapple with the fact that Silas betrayed her and FAR. That he had only ever acted out of his own self-interests rather than for the freedom of variants.

At the mention of Silas's name, that easy smile dropped

from Krista's face. "Speaking of Silas, there's something I think we should talk about together before parting ways."

"What?" Xolia's heart stuttered. She thought they had laid conversations about Silas to rest years ago.

"This information isn't public yet, but I want you to be prepared when it breaks," Krista said. "Silas was killed in prison a few days ago."

Everything in the room stilled. The clock ceased ticking and Xolia stopped breathing. Xolia found herself nodding, though she didn't know why. There was a difference between understanding his betrayal and expecting him to go through a trial for his crimes than to hear he was dead. It was easier to hate him when he was alive, easier to remember every cruel and callous thing he had ever done to her. But dead? All the good memories surfaced. His paternal role in her childhood.

Closing her eyes, Xolia focused on her breathing. *In. Out. Repeat. I am living my own life now. Not Silas's.* Finding some semblance of calm, Xolia opened her eyes.

"I know it's a pretty heavy topic to bring up on our last day together, but I'd rather you hear it from me than the news. You're safe here," Krista assured her. For Krista to offer her that olive branch of acceptance, that knowledge that despite of who Silas had been, he was still important to Xolia, eased some of the sharp hurt.

That was enough for her. Rubbing her eyes of unshed tears, Xolia shook her head. "I'm fine."

"Should you choose to continue therapy you could always get specialized grief counseling. It won't hurt forever," Krista said, sympathy softening the edges of her mouth.

Xolia said nothing, did nothing.

Krista shifted in her seat. "We still have some time together. Is there anything else you want to talk about?"

"Thank you." The words were out of Xolia's mouth before she knew what she was saying. "For everything, I mean. I wouldn't have gotten this far without you."

"Give yourself some more credit. You put in the work to change your mind and your life."

It's my life, it's my life, Xolia repeated to herself. "I guess." She was powerless to stop change, just like she had been powerless to stop Silas. But she could control her emotions. Losing Krista wouldn't break her, she was still going to be happy for this new life that she had created for herself.

"Are you sure you don't want to talk more about Silas?" Krista asked.

"I'm sure."

By the end of the session, Xolia had managed to lock away lingering sadness about Silas's death and the fear of an unknown future without Krista. Xolia thanked her again before leaving the simple office that had so integrally defined her first years in a post-rebellion world.

Making her way to the nearest subway stop, Xolia shouldered past the throngs of people that were always present in the downtown business district of Atalia. A long and stuffy subway ride later, she emerged to a less crowded side of the city.

The Bureau of Variant Integration and Wellness stood in one of the blocks where the Variants' Revolution had occurred. It was far from the well-manicured lawns with rows of neatly trimmed hedges and austere, ancient buildings that made up the government district.

The bureau was one of the ten commercial buildings that had been rebuilt or restored in the past seven years. The three-by-ten-city-block radius that suffered the brunt of the battle was still devastated. And wholly deserted.

While there were days when the work felt meaningless, and the view of their past burdened their present, Xolia loved her work at the bureau. She was fortunate to even have a job in the government. After her initial attack on Peter and refusal to side against Silas, there had been talks of charging her with treason. Until Krista had stepped in. Thinking about Krista sent a pang through her chest. Krista had been her first stepping stone to a potential life without violence. And now she had been ripped from Xolia's life like it was nothing. Xolia scoffed at herself. *So, it's going to be one of* those *days*. One of those days when the work was more taxing than inspiring.

The glass doors, which were supposed to be locked, opened with the smallest of pushes. Only employees of the bureau ever came to this part of town. Security was so lax that neither of the two security guards looked up from their computers when she stepped into the lobby.

Bypassing the broken elevator, Xolia went up a flight of stairs to her floor of poorly constructed cubicles. Rumors of a remodel had died out long ago; there was always too much work to be done for the bureau to close.

Despite the war being over, variants needed help, and the integration of variants into human society carried more problems than Xolia had ever anticipated.

Rowan, the first friend she had ever made in the barracks, was already seated on her side of their adjoined cubicle. Staring intently at the screen, Rowan didn't so much as move a muscle when Xolia stood directly behind her, peering over her shoulder.

"The Ollmann's still aren't receiving their Good Faith

checks?" Xolia asked, skimming through the report illuminating Rowan's screen. "Make sure to send that to Risian Financial." When the war had ended, FAR instituted a ten-year program in which variants received monthly Good Faith checks to aid in everyday expenses and in finding their footing in society, much to the outrage of the human population.

Rowan turned around, revealing a thin pair of wire-framed glasses. It was a new habit for Rowan—to try human things like wearing glasses. But it only made her look ridiculous since Xolia knew there was no prescription in the lenses. "It may come as a surprise, but I do know how to do my job," she responded drily.

Xolia shrugged and sat down at her desk. "I just hope they respond to you this time."

"Me too," admitted Rowan, with a sigh. She pushed her glasses up the bridge of her nose. Her movement looked natural, effortless—like it was something she had done her whole life. Xolia had always been secretly jealous of how naturally assimilation came to her friend.

"Are you ready for the gala?" Xolia asked.

"As I'll ever be," Rowan said, fully abandoning her work for the time being. "Are you actually going to show up with Marshall this time?"

Xolia pursed her lips. In her opinion, that wasn't a fair shot. Three years after the rebellion, Marshall and Xolia had been reacquainted through Rowan. Like Rowan, Marshall was a paragon of seamless assimilation. He exemplified everything that Xolia had learned happiness was supposed to be. He fit all the boxes of living a fulfilled, ordinary life. And Xolia had nearly ruined their relationship at the last FAR sponsored event when she had insisted they arrive separately.

"I had to be there early, it just didn't make sense for him to be there, too," Xolia defended herself.

"Right. And you have to be there early this week as well?" Rowan asked, sarcasm blatant.

"That is part of the requirement for speaking at these events." Tired of the conversation, Xolia turned to her computer, clicking on the internal messaging software that connected all employees in the building. She tapped her finger against the right button on the mouse, waiting for any news from Grant Howard, the bureau's director, about the promotion for the vice director position. Directly underneath Howard, it would give Xolia more reach and influence to help the nation's variants. And with the nation's first election since the rebellion cresting over the horizon, it was more important than ever to make sure variants were protected.

Finding no new correspondence from Howard, Xolia sighed and opened the rest of her work software. She managed to focus on work for all of three minutes before she spun her chair around to Rowan. "Do you think Howard will announce the next Vice Director before the gala?"

Rowan froze. "I don't think there was a deadline for the announcement. Why?"

"It would be nice to have good news to tell Peter," Xolia said.

"You act like you've already gotten the promotion. And Peter would be proud of you for just showing up to the event." Rowan's words were terse.

Xolia opted to ignore the slight nudge of jealousy. "You don't think I'll get it?"

"I didn't say that. I just don't think you should act like it's a sure thing before it's done, you know?"

"Right." With a curt tone, Xolia effectively ended the conversation, and she turned back to her desk, perturbed by Rowan's lack of enthusiastic response. Xolia had the most leadership experience out of everyone, barring Director Howard. And she really wanted to impress Peter, a man whose idealism was second to none. Even after her haphazard assault, he never gave up on her. It was he who had insisted she speak every year during FAR's annual state of the country dinner about her experience going from being Silas's protégé to living a well-adjusted life, where they celebrated another successful year of peace. If the news about Silas had hit Xolia harder than anticipated, seeing Peter again would fill that parent-sized hole in her heart.

"Hey, I'm sorry, I didn't mean it that way," Rowan said.

Xolia shook her head, of course Rowan wouldn't mean it that way. "It's okay."

Xolia focused on her computer, steeling herself for an uneventful day at work.

Chapter Three

Friday morning found Xolia staring intently at herself in the mirror as she applied makeup. A luxury that never had been allowed in the past, it was one of the best parts of post-war life. The pile of unfolded laundry she sat next to on her bed was the worst.

The spray of the shower turned off in the adjoining bathroom; Marshall was done showering. She paused in her mascara application to sigh in the direction of the door. He would be joining her the entire day while they ran through the evening's agenda before the official start of the dinner.

While these dinners happened every year, this one was especially important. All the pundits and journalists speculated that this would be the day Peter announced his plans for re-election in the first official election since the rebellion, or Variants' Revolution as it was colloquially known. Tensions ran high as new political parties sharpened their sights on the chancellor's position and unseating FAR.

Xolia glanced down at her phone, the screen opened to the most recent news coverage about other potential candidates. No one had announced yet, it was as if the entire country was caught up in a bubble that was about to burst. The door handle turned, and Xolia hurried to swipe away the incriminating evidence of her addiction. She wasn't supposed to watch the news; she'd been re-admitted to rehab three years ago when a rogue human militia group killed the first variant couple to conceive a child post-rebellion. Krista had, in no uncertain terms, told her to protect her mental health and stay away from upsetting news coverage from then on.

Marshall entered the bedroom with a towel slung around his hips. His body had filled out since their younger days. He smiled and dropped the towel, his eyebrows raised suggestively. Xolia swiftly turned back to the mirror, trying to hide her eye roll.

"You really don't have to come if you don't want to," she said, giving him yet another opportunity to drop out of the pre-gala activities. "It's never any fun."

"I want to spend time with you," Marshall said, stepping into the pressed trousers of his suit. "Unless you really don't want me to go."

"That's not what I said. You can come, I just don't think you'll enjoy it."

Marshall pushed the laundry to another part of the bed and sat next to her. Now in the process of pulling on his white button-down shirt, he leaned over and pressed a kiss against her temple. "Look at it this way—I'll be your bodyguard against Atlas. You won't have to talk to him at all."

She waited until she was done with her makeup to exhale. "I don't know how many times I have to say this, but I don't hate Atlas."

Marshall snorted, not even bothering to hide his disbelief. "You don't have to lie to me, Xo."

"Don't call me that," Xolia snapped and got up. She clasped a simple teardrop necklace that had been a gift from Marshall a year into their relationship around her neck. "Are you ready?"

Marshall nodded. "Actually, you can start heading out. I'll be right behind you; I need to grab something."

What could you possibly need? "Yeah, fine." Xolia didn't stop to see what he was rummaging around in his dresser drawer for and walked to the front door of their small one-bedroom apartment. She grabbed her coat. Even though autumn was only starting, the weather was unpredictable and they had a long walk ahead of them.

THE PRESIDENTIAL PALACE was one of the oldest buildings in Atalia, gothic in appearance with spires and gargoyles looming overhead. Its use as the heart of the Risian government dated back to when monarchical rulers had governed the land, all of whom had been variants. One thousand years ago, the humans had rebelled and installed a quasi-democracy that revered humans and reduced variants to little more than fighting and killing machines. One thousand years of human presidents presided over the country, until the Variants' Revolution opened the doors for FAR to install a chancellorship. Rebellion was the way of change in Ris. Xolia wondered who would instigate the next upheaval or if the election would pass by them in peace, with Peter presiding over the country for another seven years.

Xolia and Marshall walked past the main gates, which would be open in the evening to allow for the influx of esteemed guests, and went to a small wrought-iron gate where a pair of guards waited for them. Once their identities had been vetted, the taller of the two guards led them through the doors to the main hall.

The ballroom, which hadn't changed much in two thousand years, was adorned in soft green and white. FAR's four-pointed-star-and-halo was emblazoned on a flag on the right wall. A long table, dressed for ten people, and a podium were placed in front of the flag. Thirty smaller tables, these ones round, filled the rest of the room. The room's balcony doors on the left wall were propped open while staff bustled in and out of various doors and hallways to finish preparing the room for the evening's festivities.

Peter, surrounded by numerous staff members, assistants, and guards, entered the room. Even after all these years, the first thing Xolia noticed about him was the faint white scar that went from the corner of his mouth to the bottom of his ear lobe. Her mark. Her reminder of her past and the forgiveness he had extended to her. She owed it to Peter to do all she could to make sure he was re-elected. His brows were creased, his salt-and-pepper hair grayer, and his frame thinner than Xolia remembered. His head was bent as he listened to what a sharply dressed woman to his right was saying. She held a clipboard and pointed to various places in the room.

Xolia's shoulders relaxed slightly at the sight of Peter sans Atlas, and she strode over to him. At the click of Xolia's heel against the polished marble flooring, Peter looked up and broke out into a wide smile. "You look beautiful," he said, opening his arms for an embrace.

She walked into his waiting arms and gingerly hugged him back. It was safe, comforting, a reminder that he was real and alive and still in her life. "It's good to see you," she said as she pulled away.

"Same to you," Peter said. He looked over her shoulder. "It looks like you've brought a guest with you."

"Yes, I hope that was okay," Xolia said. She stepped to the side to allow Marshall to join the conversation.

Peter shook Marshall's hand. "Of course. I'm happy to see you settling down. You look good together. What's your name again?"

"Marshall," he supplied.

"That's right. The years haven't been as kind to me as they've been to you all."

The same woman who had been talking to Peter earlier motioned for him to come back.

"It looks like we're needed. Atlas should be here any minute, and we'll run through the speech order. I proposed a small change," Peter said. "I want you to be our closing speaker."

Peter's words alarmed Xolia. She never followed Atlas. He was Peter's vice-chancellor. "We've never done it that way."

"There's a first for everything." Peter winked, already walking back to the waiting gaggle of people. Without making sure Marshall was following, Xolia stepped in line behind Peter. A coughing fit stopped Peter in his tracks.

"Are you okay?" Xolia froze. Should she help him somehow? Was he choking? Peter recovered and shook his head at her, smiling though his eyes were tense.

"Xolia, you've brought someone with you," came a loud tenor that grated on Xolia's nerves.

She tensed her shoulders and breathed in deeply. *I don't hate him, I don't hate him, I don't hate him.* "Atlas, so kind of you to show up."

Golden-haired Atlas held himself with an easy confidence that almost overwhelmed Peter's sense of authority. Atlas was always Silas's perfect successor in that way—they both acted as if no one could tell them what to do, and anyone rarely ever did. He scoffed at Xolia and opted to fully ignore her as Peter and the apparent party planner pulled him in for a hushed conversation.

Marshall gently grabbed her elbow, perhaps in a show of solidarity or understanding, but Xolia jolted away from his touch.

"What?" exclaimed Atlas, ending the whispered conversation that Xolia and Marshall had been pointedly excluded from.

"The order change is final," Peter said, all grim seriousness. He embodied the chancellor role in that moment, his pressed suit perfectly tailored, and his wizened face drawn up in a severe frown that brooked no arguments. "Now, are you ready to go over the rest of the night?"

Atlas glared at Xolia before nodding stiffly at Peter. "Go ahead."

BY THE TIME GUESTS ARRIVED, Xolia was ready to go home. The tension between Atlas and Peter never quite went away, and Marshall was little more than an unhelpful distraction. He was acting clingier than normal, and Xolia wasn't sure how to respond. Since the beginning of their romantic relationship, he had been the initiator, and Xolia was fine with that, but the way he clung to her arm and side, while she was trying to run through her speech and make sure it held up to Atlas's, angered her. Not that she mentioned anything to Marshall.

Instead, she grabbed the first flute of sparkling wine as the servers handed drinks to the guests milling about the empty half of the room. Dinner would start as soon as all the guests had arrived with speeches following.

The acidic burn slid down her throat. Too late, she remembered the drink was wasted on her. Since her last meeting with Krista, she had forgone her suppressants and relished the return of her powers and quick healing rate. However, the downside was that, without the suppressants taking hold of her digestive system, she was unable to feel the effects of alcohol.

She sighed and swirled around the remaining liquid.

"What's wrong?" Marshall asked.

"Nothing," Xolia said. She hadn't told him yet that she was off her suppressants. He would worry too much about the side effects, ones that had hit him hard when he was cleared to stop taking his. "Rowan should be here soon." She took a slight detour to the open bar in the back of the room and placed the drink on the bar top.

Marshall pulled her hand into his, and they threaded through the growing number of people, offering polite hellos and shaking hands before getting close to the entrance. Outside, the dark sky contrasted with the glimmer of lights surrounding the walkway and manicured grounds. Politicians and notable variants from the rebellion comprised the majority of attendees. Journalists and celebrities made up the rest.

Rowan made her way inside, wearing a simple floor-length purple dress and glasses. Xolia started towards her when Rowan's attention was snagged. Director Howard stood tall and proud in his black-and-white suit, talking intently to Rowan.

"Why is she speaking to Director Howard?" Xolia mused aloud.

"Where is she?" Marshall craned his neck to try and get a good look.

Xolia pointed them out. "She's with Director Howard. I didn't think she liked him."

"I mean, you don't either," Marshall said.

"If I'm going to be vice director, I have to at least be friendly with him." Xolia debated between letting Rowan find her or butting into their conversation. Whether it was indecision or some lurking anxiety, she stayed still, staring at their indecipherable conversation.

"Maybe she wants to move up as well."

Of all the things that made up Rowan, ambition was not one of them. And she had been that way since Xolia first met her. It was what made their friendship work so well. Xolia was inclined to lead, and Rowan was content to follow. Still, it was strange to see her and the director talking, laughing even. Something soured in Xolia's stomach. "You wait for her; I'm going to get something else to drink." Xolia pulled free from Marshall's touch and pursed her lips once her back was to him.

Keeping her head down, she barely focused on the world around her. *What would they have to talk about?* So consumed with mapping out the possibilities, Xolia didn't even notice when someone stepped directly in her path and the two collided. Cold wine spilled down her chest. Her golden dress was marred with an egregious red stain.

"What the hell is—" The rest of her words sputtered out when she saw who had run into her.

"Xo?" asked a silky voice.

"Adonis." His name rolled off her tongue. He was like a ghost before her, all lean muscle, and hazy memories of who they had been together during the rebellion. His hair was as dark and looked as soft as it had been back then; however, now it was artfully tousled instead of wild and unconfined.

His eyes roved over her, setting Xolia on edge. They were practically strangers now, and he was taking her in like no time had passed between them. She crossed her arms in a futile attempt to cover the stain.

"I'm sorry. Here." He shrugged out of his tailored suit jacket and held it out to her. Hesitating, she kept her arms crossed, before deciding to take it. It was the least he could do, and his shirt was the deepest black. She couldn't even tell where, or whether, the wine had spilled on him.

Enveloped in warmth and lingering notes of cedarwood cologne, she struggled to find the right words to say to him, keenly aware of just how little distance stood between them. "I've never seen you at one of these before," Xolia said.

He shrugged, a laid-back gesture that was so reminiscent of who he had been during the rebellion. "I've been busy in the past, but I wouldn't miss the last one."

All warmth disappeared. "The last one? Peter is running again. He's going to win." There was no other feasible outcome that she had heard about.

"Right, I'm sure all the protestors agree with you."

Shame at her own ignorance flooded Xolia. She hadn't seen anything about that. *And whose fault is that?* No biting retorts came to mind, and there was no way she could feasibly deny the claim. "Change won't make everyone happy, but they will see that FAR is trying to make things better."

"Please." Adonis rolled his eyes, and dark hair fell into his face. "Peter hasn't made any meaningful progress. He chose his own Senate and they still manage to stall every radical reform proposed. No idealism can overcome high taxes and zero follow-through. He needs a new campaign to win the election next year."

No one had ever disparaged FAR so blatantly to Xolia before. She didn't think anyone could feel that way about them. Not after all the work FAR *had done* for the country. Any dissent that made it to her was trivial. Individual. Easy to fix. Not everyone would be happy with change. "What are *you* doing for Ris?" She turned the tables back on him.

"I'm trying to bring it into the future," he shot back, and though she wanted to, Xolia couldn't deny the earnestness in his eyes.

Without her suppressants, and after the lost years of maintaining control over her powers, Xolia was nearly overwhelmed. Her body longed to reach out and find water or to give into her more unsavory powers. In their youth, Adonis had been a rebel and poked fun, but there had never been this outright hostility. He had led the assault on the Presidential Palace. It unnerved her to see his allegiances so twisted.

Someone tapped her on the shoulder. She whirled around and bit out a strained, "What?"

It was only Marshall. Supportive Marshall. Unchallenging Marshall. She forced herself to relax a fraction, still aware of Adonis behind her. Xolia tried to relay that she was fine in response to Marshall's worried gaze.

"It's time for dinner to begin," Marshall said. "Atlas is looking for you."

She nodded and turned back to try and get in one last cutting remark to Adonis. Even though he was one of the few people dressed in all black, he had already disappeared into the sea of people making their way to the tables.

Chapter Four

Xolia sat to Peter's right at the long table. Atlas sat on his left, and they ate their food in relative silence. She hunched in on herself, all too aware of the oversized suit jacket she wore and how she was in prime position to be scrutinized. Marshall hadn't asked her about it, though there really hadn't been the time.

She pushed her food around her plate. The podium loomed in front of the table. Its upright position kept Xolia's attention while the murmur of conversation was at an all-time low. Her heartbeat wouldn't settle, everything Adonis had said unnerved her more than she wanted to admit. *I just have to say the same things I do every year, and then I can go home.*

Peter smiled at her, the unscarred side of his face visible to her. She didn't even attempt to smile back. There was no way she could fake it well enough to convince him. All she could do was continue to eat in silence and wait for Peter to start the speeches.

Her plate was a precarious mess of uneaten food when Peter finally cleared his throat and stood up. He smiled at the crowd, the crow's feet in the corners of his eyes more pronounced than usual under the glare of lights. He took his time walking around the table and to the podium. The rest of the dinner's attendees quieted and even the music halted when Peter drew in a deep breath. A deep cough tore through him for several moments before he managed to stifle it and smile at the room of attendees.

"Seven years," he began. "It's been seven years since the end of the Variants' Revolution. While I can't say things are perfect, I will say that things are better for everyone. And that has only been possible through the dedication and sacrifice from everyone in this room."

Thoughts of Silas entered Xolia's mind uninvited. *Even if he lost his way in the end, no one would have sacrificed anything without his initial vision.* She shook her head, now of all times was not the time to think about him. *I am who I am in spite of Silas, not because of him.* She tried to refocus on Peter.

"Progress is not a destination, but rather the journey of our people. Every one of us is making a better decision today than we made yesterday. I know that there is still distrust between humans and variants. The fight to fully integrate schools has only begun, but it's a fight I won't give up. I haven't in seven years, and I will continue to fight for the next seven years should this great nation re-elect me as chancellor."

Applause erupted, and Peter paused his speech. Xolia clapped politely. Two seats over, Atlas remained stoic, his face a neutral mask. Perhaps Atlas was still angry at Peter for changing the speech order. Either way, it gave Xolia a small jolt of excitement. Peter was choosing her over Atlas, even if it was just for tonight.

Once the clapping receded, Peter closed out his speech.

"My competition will tell you we are in tumultuous and unstable times. That aggressors on both sides grow bolder by the day. But has it not been the history of Ris to find its most peaceful days after the bloodiest ones? These dissenters are afraid of the change we are enacting. They forget they are the minority. Allow me and my party to bring us into a new era of unprecedented peace and prosperity." Peter bowed his head, and Xolia found herself standing while she applauded. Soon, much of the room was standing in ovation for him. As the first person to announce his candidacy, he had set the example for everyone to follow.

Peter introduced Atlas, who had noticeably remained sitting the entire time, and the two men shook hands before Peter returned to Xolia's side. She longed to ask about the awkwardness between them, but they were too visible to the rest of the room.

Atlas's face was stoic, the perfect mask of a politician, but Xolia was close enough to see the small tremor in his hand as he clutched the side of the podium. "Thank you, Chancellor Bellevue, for your courageous words tonight. I think we are all in agreement that the betterment of Ris and its peoples are our main priority. Variants have much to thank FAR for, and I know that, should Chancellor Bellevue's reign continue, variants will continue to progress." He abruptly announced Xolia and turned away from the podium, his back rigid and movement stiff. Xolia turned, sending a questioning look to Peter, whose features were drawn back, seemingly in resignation.

As Atlas was sitting down, he turned to her. "You're up."

What the hell? Like her, he was supposed to repeat his usual annual speech; she had expected him to announce his campaign to reprise his role as vice chancellor tonight. When they had rehearsed earlier in the day, he flew through the words smoothly, like always. She didn't know what had changed between then and now.

Xolia stood and smoothed out the skirt of her golden dress, her borrowed jacket mostly hiding the stain. It wasn't her ideal look, but it was better than anything she had ever worn to rebellion meetings. Each step toward the podium was another turn of her thoughts. *What did Rowan and Director Howard talk about earlier? What made Adonis so cynical? What is Atlas playing at?*

By the time she stood behind the podium and grasped at the sides, all of her well-rehearsed lines floated just out of reach. Her throat was dry. Too dry. Near the front, Marshall sat, leaning forward. He smiled; he was always trying to be the encouragement she needed. She took a long, steadying breath and brought her hands down to her sides.

"FAR is not the party of variants. It's not the party of humans. It's the party of Risians," she stated. They were the same words she had said to Adonis. Despite his lackluster response, she spoke the truth. *Right?*

"FAR is the party of progress. I've known Pet—Chancellor Bellevue since the days of the rebel—Revolution, and never once has he wavered in his beliefs that all Risians should be treated equally. He was the first human to treat me as more than brute protection. *FAR* remained infallible even when..." She trailed off, unable to say Silas's name. For some reason, knowing that he was dead made it harder to talk about his transgressions. She hadn't even gotten to say goodbye, which was far from the thoughts she should have concerning him, but she couldn't drop it.

Everyone looked at her expectantly. Their full attention stayed on her, which normally she reveled in, but tonight?

Tonight, it was unbearable. Tonight, their stares weighed on her chest and the walls shrunk, drawing everyone in closer. Could they see her troubled thoughts, dangling for escape on the tip of her tongue? Did they see that no matter how hard she tried, no matter how much work she put into her job, there were still people like Adonis who didn't believe in her words? Did they know she doubted her words?

She focused on Marshall again, but that sense of security she needed from him escaped her. People grew restless and murmured amongst themselves. Xolia looked back at Peter, all the exhaustion of his position was clear in the way he sagged in his seat. She didn't want to disappoint him in the same way Atlas most assuredly had.

No matter how much she tried to get the rest of the words out, they were blocked by a lump in her throat. Once again, she turned to Peter. "I'm sorry," she rasped out before running from the table. The murmur grew to confused conversation, but she didn't stop to listen. Didn't stop to see whether Marshall was running after her or whether Rowan had decided to check on her. She reached the open balcony doors and slammed them shut behind her.

———

The early-autumn air ruffled her hair as she leaned against the stone railing. She pulled the suit jacket closer around her body, hating the way it brought her comfort.

"Fuck," Xolia shouted over the quiet grounds. She rested her head against one arm and let the other fall over the side, dipping into the inky pools of shadow. Things weren't supposed to go this way. *I am happy. I'm* supposed *to be happy.* Supposed to be and actually being were two entirely different things. Xolia feared she related to the former more often than the latter. She needed to let Silas go, for real this time. She had thought she had done it, but now he wouldn't leave her alone. Just as she was about to let the tears fall, the soft clicking of the door made her tense. Conversation filled the night air before it was closed off again.

"I'm really not in the mood," she said, quickly wiping away any evidence that she had been about to cry.

Rather than some worried questions or well-intentioned platitudes from Marshall or Rowan, she was greeted with Atlas's caustic voice. "But you don't even know what I'm about to say."

Xolia sighed. This was the last thing she wanted. Telling him off would only spur him on, so she steeled her nerves and stood up straight. "What do you want?"

"From one disappointment of the night to another, do you have a minute to talk?"

Chapter Five

Despite feeling like a disappointment, she didn't think she had missed the mark quite as much as Atlas. "I don't feel like commiserating with you."

Apparently, that was enough of an invitation for him, and he walked right up to the railing, leaning his elbows against the ancient granite. He didn't speak right away; instead, he stared off into the dark grounds. If Xolia hadn't been waiting for the inevitable arguing, she might've let herself relax into the peace the night offered. No one else dared to come to the balcony, leaving them isolated from the rest of the gala. She hated that, in this moment, they were one and the same.

"Did you hear the news?" he finally asked.

"Yeah." It shouldn't hurt—shouldn't leave her with a void in her heart.

"Did you see him before?" Atlas asked, turning to face her.

"No." She scoffed. "I haven't seen him since the day the rebellion ended."

Atlas nodded. "I saw him a week before."

Xolia stopped breathing. "What?"

"It was normal for me to see him about once a month," Atlas said, his tone remaining casual despite the life-altering words he was smacking Xolia with.

She briefly shut her eyes. *I am who I am in spite of Silas. He does not define me. I create my own happiness.* Every single phrase that she and Krista had worked on ran at full speed through her head. Silas had not been an ally. She hadn't needed to see him, hadn't needed his harmful ideology in her life. She was happy. And happiness was the important thing.

Still. . . "How was he?"

"Eh." Atlas shrugged. "A miserable bastard. He wasn't built for prison. Or isolation."

The conversation lapsed. A million questions danced on the tip of Xolia's tongue, chief among them was *did he ever ask about me?*

Before she could pluck up the courage to ask, Atlas changed topics. "Why didn't you pursue politics? Peter still wants you in his Senate."

Xolia arched a suspicious brow at him. "Why are you asking this now?"

"Indulge me."

Sighing, Xolia thought about her life over the past seven years. And how it had been before that. "I wasn't happy then. I did my part, and now I can focus on my own life."

"And you're happy now?" he asked, disbelief clear in his voice.

I don't know. "Of course." Xolia inwardly congratulated herself when her voice didn't waver. Whatever these feelings meant, she wasn't going to wade through them in front of Atlas. "What about you?" If he was going to probe into her life, she would return the favor.

"What about me?"

"Are you happy, Vice Chancellor?"

"I've never cared about something that trivial," he said. Tapping his fingers against the railing, he stared at her. Much as she wanted to shrink away from his gaze, she didn't. "I really came out here to proposition you."

Xolia narrowed her eyes. He couldn't seriously be offering what she thought he was.

"To blow off some tension," he elaborated. He ran a hand through his short hair, and Xolia thought she could still see a slight tremble.

"That explains nothing." Xolia leaned away from him.

He rolled his eyes at her. "Did you know there's an organization that runs fights? Like the same kind we used to run for training?"

"There's no way that's legal."

"Of course it's not," Atlas snorted. "But you can't deny that nothing else compares to sparring."

His words were absurd. Juvenile. "Is this some sort of trick?"

"How is it a trick if I'm going to ask you to come with me?" Atlas asked. "I would also be doing something illegal."

"Look, I don't know what restrictions you're under, but I just got my suppressant checks waived. I'm not jeopardizing that, and I'm not stressed. My life is going exactly how I want it." She laughed in a slightly crazed way at the end. Nothing was how she wanted it, but nothing would ever drive her to willingly do anything with Atlas.

Atlas leaned into her, closing the space she kept putting between them. "You don't want to go for old times' sake? Afraid I'll still beat you?" he taunted.

It was laughable, really, if he thought that would be enough to goad her into changing her mind. "I'm not falling for this, and I don't know if this is some weird way to get back at Peter for changing the speech order, but that wasn't my call. I don't want anything to do with you."

Finished with the ultimately pointless conversation, Xolia made her way back to the door. Atlas yelled after her, "You're so boring now, Xo. You used to be interesting at least."

Xolia froze. Her breaths came out heavy, and that pit in her stomach that controlled her powers yearned for release. How she longed to give in, to drag him to his knees. *I hate—No. I don't.* She clenched her fists so tight that her nails dug into the base of her palms. "Don't fucking call me that." She went inside.

With dinner and the lackluster speeches over, people were back to milling about the open half of the room. She shouldered her way past politicians and other notable guests without so much as an apology. When she found Marshall, she stomped up to him and grabbed his elbow. "I want to go home."

"Xolia," Rowan exclaimed, her face rosy and smiling. When Xolia faced her, the smile dropped. "Are you okay?"

"I'm fine," she snapped. She leaned in close to Marshall. "We need to leave."

"Okay, just give me a minute," Marshall said, caressing the back of her hand with his thumb. Rather than being a comfort, it was just pressure. She pulled her hand out from under his. "Peter recovered the evening after you ran. I was going to go after you, but everyone saw Atlas follow you."

"Is Peter upset?"

"He just announced his candidacy, and neither his vice chancellor nor his favorite civilian couldn't even fill their times," Marshall said. "He might be a little upset."

Of course he would be upset with her, it was childish for her to have thought anything else. Xolia sighed. "Thanks."

"I'm back," announced an entirely too-cheery voice—one that Xolia didn't immediately recognize.

Xolia turned to see a woman with mousy brown hair pulled back into a low bun. Her dress was gray, utterly devoid of shape and style. And because she wore no makeup or jewelry, nor anything else to hide away the memory of the past, Xolia knew exactly who she was looking at. Semele. The overly zealous girl she and Marshall and Rowan had spent countless hours making fun of in the past. Semele had the unfortunate habit of believing everyone and everything, with her entire soul. Nothing was too outlandish; no matter how many times she had been tricked by her fellow variants, she had kept on believing the next person in line.

Semele handed a glass to Marshall, who accepted with an apologetic glance towards Xolia. "Xolia, it's so good to see you. Marshall, Rowan, and I were just catching up."

"Likewise," Xolia responded, voice monotone. "Anyway, Marshall and I have to head out."

"Why?" Rowan asked, her brows furrowed and her nose scrunched.

"We'll stay for a few minutes longer, right, Xolia?" Marshall levied her with a pleading look.

Xolia crossed her arms over her chest. "Just a few minutes."

"What are you wearing anyway?" Marshall asked, sipping from his drink.

Xolia hesitated. Marshall didn't like Adonis, and while Xolia wasn't sure how she felt about him, it was different. Everyone looked at her, waiting with bated breath. Just like at dinner, though this time her words were arguably more devastating.

"I ran into Adonis." She opened the jacket up to reveal the stain. "Or, he ran into me."

As she expected, Marshall clammed up. The slight popping of his jaw was evidence enough of his discomfort. Either unaware or determined to keep the mood light, Rowan interjected, "Sel, I haven't thought of Adonis in forever."

"It was kind of him to lend you his jacket," Semele said with a small and demure smile.

Xolia nodded once, not wanting to spend longer on this topic than needed. "So, Semele, what have you been doing these past few years?"

Tactfully, Rowan turned to listen to Semele and Marshall followed. "I'm so glad you asked," she gushed, "because I've actually devoted my life to Sel and the Church of Rheatha. They gave me a purpose after the Revolution ended."

"Oh." Xolia didn't know how else to respond. Religion wasn't really her thing, and Semele's answer was too rehearsed to be anything other than a desperate ploy to get others to convert.

"That's incredible," Rowan responded. "I think the church has done a lot to help with the integration of schools; Marshall teaches at one."

Semele turned to him in wide-eyed wonder. At the mention of Marshall's job, Xolia further retreated from the conversation. Just like religion, she wasn't much one for children either. With slow, shuffled steps, Xolia found herself at the edge of the small circle; no one stopped to invite her back in.

Listless and tired, Xolia took in a quick sweep of the room, hoping she might catch Peter to apologize. She stopped when she spotted Adonis, his dark gaze homed in on her. And for one brief moment, it was just the two of them in the room, drinking the other in like all their secrets might be spilled if they just looked hard enough.

Behind her, Marshall scoffed and broke whatever trance held them both. "Good job, he's headed over this way now."

"Don't be so immature," Xolia snapped.

Adonis met Xolia and her small party with a slight nod and an even smaller smile. "Marshall, Rowan, Semele."

"Adonis," Rowan said. "How are you?"

He lifted a shoulder. "Can't complain." He stopped and leaned forward slightly. "But, I have to ask, why are you wearing glasses?"

Rowan defensively adjusted the aforementioned object over the bridge of her nose. Xolia suppressed a laugh. "I like them," Rowan said. "And maybe there is something helpful in them; I haven't run into a single person tonight."

"Fair," Adonis ceded.

"Adonis." A clear voice rang out over the dim chatter.

A beautiful woman stepped up to them, and while Xolia was sure she had never met her before, there was something familiar about her. Something about the jut of her prominent cheekbones and the strong nose. "This is Helen DuBois," Adonis said, introducing her.

"Like General DuBois?" Marshall beat Xolia to the punch.

The woman, who was now draped across Adonis's arm, looked exactly like her father. If he was more feminine and younger. Irrational jealousy swept through Xolia.

Helen nodded. "Xolia, it's an honor to meet you. My father spoke of little else during the Revolution."

Xolia blanched. While her run-ins with General DuBois had been few and far between, neither had ever managed too fully best the other. And then he had betrayed the Gornne

Administration for FAR before they could ever fully parse out who was the better strategist between the two. "I'm not sure that's a compliment."

"If you knew my father, you'd know it's the highest compliment."

Jealousy turned to exasperation. She couldn't hate someone who talked her up like that. The importance that Xolia used to feel bubbled up inside her. A warm feeling that promised more. That hungered for more.

"Well, it was nice to meet you, but Xolia and I were planning to leave," Marshall said, an ingenuine smile stretching across his face. Xolia grimaced, he really was a horrible liar.

Rowan and Semele said their goodbyes, and Xolia answered in kind, though she kept glancing back at Adonis. It was impossible not to when he kept staring at her. She wanted to say more to him, to ask him about what he had said earlier, but there was no time. She was pulled along by Marshall to the front doors, stolen suit jacket and all.

THE BRISK NIGHT air cleared Xolia's mind. She and Marshall walked down the twinkling drive, their breaths barely visible puffs. Her mind raced with the events of the day, and her body sighed at the prospect of making it home. All she wanted to do was to curl up in a ball and find the refuge of sleep. Exhaustion cloaked her, as thick and heavy as the jacket she wore. The coat that smelled like Adonis. Xolia sped up.

"Slow down," Marshall lamented from a few paces behind her. He jogged to catch up when she stopped under a lone streetlamp, its neighbors on either side broken and dark. He caught his breath with his hands resting on his thighs. "Xolia, I'm sorry I didn't leave when you wanted to."

She arched an eyebrow. "Are you sorry because you made me stay or because you had to talk to Adonis?"

He scoffed and stood straight, allowing her to start for home again. "Next time I'll be more excited to see your ex."

The last thing Xolia wanted to do was talk about Adonis. He was immaterial to her at the moment. For Marshall to be so fixated on him made the whole situation that much more unbearable. She couldn't coddle Marshall's ego when she already had to carry the guilt for letting Peter down and had to think about Atlas's weird behavior. And she had to figure out a way to learn more about the protests against Peter. They didn't have a television. And with Marshall home for the weekend, she wouldn't have much time to herself.

"You're walking too fast again," Marshall shouted.

Xolia stopped. She didn't have time for this. "I just want to go to sleep. Today wasn't great for me." She started walking again.

"Xolia."

"Oh Sel, what?" Xolia whipped around to find Marshall on one knee, the tips of his ears pink under the street lamps and his chest heaving. "You're slowing us down, Marshall. Just push through, and then we can lay in bed."

He looked confused. "What?"

"Get up and let's get home. I just want to sleep."

Marshall shook his head and pulled something from his pants pocket. "There's something I wanted to ask you."

"I'm sure it can wait." Xolia inched onward, determined to get home to bed.

Not hearing his footsteps, she turned around. From his position on the ground, he gaped at her for a few minutes. "But— you're right. It can wait." He staggered back up and fell into stride next to her.

Marshall posed no more interruptions, and Xolia flung open their apartment door when they finally made it home. She kicked off her shoes in the small foyer and dropped the suit jacket on the floor of their bedroom in an undignified heap. The dress was stained irreparably. Sighing, she reached for the back zipper, but Marshall's hands stopped her.

"Allow me," he whispered and slowly dragged the zipper. He moved the straps off her shoulders and kissed her neck. No sparks. Only pressure. She wanted him to stop, there was too much on her mind to even muster up the energy to act inter- ested in his advances Instead of telling him to stop, she let him lay her down against the stiff mattress as he looked at her with half-lidded eyes. He was all over her, touching, prodding. Kissing her neck, he breathed out a soft, "I love you."

It was her turn to say it back. Just three words. But, in that moment, she didn't. And she couldn't say it. She pushed him off her. "Stop."

"What's wrong?" he asked, shifting to sit.

What's wrong? She wanted to scream at him. *I told you I had a bad day and all you want is to grope me.* But she didn't say that. She just mumbled out a gruff, "I don't know," and crawled to her side of the bed where she pulled the covers up to her chin. The mattress shifted as Marshall got up and left. *I'm happy. I'm happy.*

Chapter Six

THE WEEKEND ALLOWED XOLIA TO PUSH BACK ALL THE negative thoughts to the small corner of her mind reserved for things that needed to be ignored. Her and Marshall's relationship had repaired itself by way of ignoring that night. Routine was re-established when Marshall left for work at six on Monday morning to catch up on grading before the students got in.

There was no way Director Howard wouldn't announce her promotion to vice director today. Not after Peter's candidacy announcement. As something Peter founded, the bureau would have to be running efficiently during his campaign.

With Xolia at the helm, she could ensure Peter was re-elected. This was her purpose. Her reason. Nothing, not even rumors about protests rocking the country, could dissuade her from supporting Peter.

As soon as she crossed the threshold to the bureau, security greeted her. "Xolia Stone," the burliest one said, "you're to report directly to Director Howard's office."

One side of Xolia's mouth quirked up. *This is it.* Nodding

her thanks, Xolia bypassed the broken elevator for the stairs. She stopped at the second floor to drop off her bag and tell Rowan the good news before meeting with Howard, but Rowan wasn't sitting at her desk. Xolia shrugged it off; Xolia had made it in earlier than usual. There was no need to dwell on it. Rowan would just have to settle for being surprised whenever she did show up.

The third floor consisted of several large offices. Full-length windows revealed the, admittedly, depressing surroundings, but they let in natural light, which was more than could be said for the lower two floors. The third floor was where the important work was done. It was where real change happened for the betterment of variants.

Director Howard's office was the last one on the left. She knocked once against the dark door. He yelled for her to enter, and she took a deep breath before opening the door. Grant Howard was one of the oldest variants alive in all Ris. His strong features showed the beginning signs of aging; his hair was gray, and wrinkles marred the corner of his eyes. It was a testament to everything he had lived through. Xolia may have had her disagreements with the man, but he was to be respected.

"Good morning, Director Howard," she said, adopting the same tone of voice that she usually reserved for Peter, and before him, Silas.

"Ms. Stone," he replied. Xolia winced at the use of her last name. It wasn't her familial surname; those had all been stripped away during their time in the barracks. After the rebellion FAR managed to declassify old, archived documents that listed out families and relatives for all variants. It had allowed displaced variants to choose whether to reconnect with their biological families or not. Xolia had opted not to. Stone was a government-provided name, and while it didn't suit her, she thought her biological name would suit her even less.

When Howard wasn't any more forthcoming with the reason for her arrival, Xolia took the reins of the conversation. "You asked to see me?"

"I did." He gestured to the open seat across from his and the rough-hewn desk that was as imposing as he was. Both were old and indomitable. She sat.

"Is this about the vice director position?"

He nodded and steepled his fingers. "Xolia, I've known you a long time. I was there when Silas singled you out. And I was there throughout the war. You were just a child charged with leading people into battle." He scoffed. "You were a child, by human standards even, and pushed into something no child should go through. Unlike Silas, I've been able to watch you since the war's end. Seeing both sides of you made my decision easy."

Xolia nodded, waiting to be given the title of Vice Director Stone.

"Despite Peter's comforting words the other night, we are in tumultuous times, and I need someone I can depend on. This bureau, and this country, needs someone who knows when to stop and when to push, and I don't see that in you, Xolia. I'm sorry, but you won't be getting the promotion."

What? She blinked, struggling to make sense of what he had said. If not her, then who? She was supposed to get the job. She had the experience. His mouth kept moving, but she heard nothing. Her heart pounded in staccato beats.

"Who got the job?" It was like talking over sandpaper.

"Good morning, Director Howard."

The world fell out from beneath Xolia. If she wasn't sitting, she would be falling. Slowly, so slowly, she swiveled in the chair. Rowan stood in the doorway, dressed in a casual suit that was perfectly tailored to her body. It was nicer than anything Xolia had ever seen her wear before. Like a bullet, the memory of the two of them laughing at the gala struck her.

"You." It was quiet, but Rowan still reacted, shrinking back. Xolia turned back to Director Howard. "I don't understand. She didn't even apply." *Why is it so hard to breathe?* The office walls closed in around her, caging her in.

Either deliberately ignoring Xolia's obvious distress or trying to cut through the tension, Rowan joked, "I did. It's my turn to boss you around now, Xolia."

The compression snapped. Numbness spread over Xolia's extremities. She glared at Director Howard, then Rowan. Her best friend. Her friend who knew more than anyone how important this position had been for Xolia. She stood up. *Release, release, release,* her powers begged of her. She could do it, too. It had been almost a full week of no longer taking suppressants, it would be so easy.

"I'm leaving," she said instead. Director Howard didn't say anything to stop her, and Rowan finally had the decency to look apologetic. It was too late for that, though. Xolia brushed past her. She didn't pause, didn't even breathe until she collected her things and was out of the building. The warm day mocked her and her misery. A scream hung in her throat, waiting for her to lose control. The decimated city block invited her to hide away in its neglect and yell and throw rubble until the feelings were gone.

This isn't how it's supposed to be. Xolia raked her fingers through her hair. *What am I supposed to do?* Silas wouldn't have let that happen; he wouldn't have done it to her in the first place. Silas. . . Xolia slammed her fist into the side of the dilapidated building. She held her hand up to watch as the scratched skin pieced itself back together, burning the whole time.

Perhaps, she should talk to Peter. There was no way he would stand for such an obvious snub. Unless he was still upset with her for the gala. *The gala.* One person came to mind, he might not fix the situation, but he had offered distraction.

<hr>

Xolia was sweating under her extra layers of clothes by the time she had stomped her way to the gates of the Presidential Palace. The severity of the building loomed over her, its jagged outcroppings and twisted spires spoke of a time long past.

The job? Out of her control. Almost everything was out of control as she hurtled forward. She couldn't help but feel it was her fault. If she just had one thing, one choice, she could go back to how things were supposed to be. Marshall and she would be happy again; he loved her enough for the both of them. Rowan wasn't a leader and would find out soon enough that she hated the job. Those responsibilities and extra hours weren't for her. Rowan would respectfully leave the position, and Xolia would graciously accept. Order would be restored.

Heavily armed security greeted her. Their deep-green uniforms carried the star-and-halo sigil that had become so familiar to her. "I'm here to speak to Atlas Campion," she said.

"Do you have a meeting with him?" asked the female guard. Her short hair was tucked behind her ears.

"No," Xolia answered. "But I'm an old friend. He'll want to talk to me."

"I'm sorry, ma'am, but it really doesn't work that way," said the male guard.

"It's okay," the woman said. "Ms. Stone was just here the other night. I'll have someone call Vice Chancellor Campion while we vet you."

"Thank you," Xolia said.

"Wait here," she instructed and nudged her companion back to the small security booth. Xolia crossed her arms, trying to come up with the right words to say to Atlas. It was already humiliating enough that she would be backtracking her earlier words and all but begging to accompany him to the fight.

Shit, this is such a bad idea. Xolia stepped back from the gate, ready to flee, but Rowan's sarcastic quip reared its head and settled on her chest. Xolia hated that Rowan had been chosen over her, and she hated even more that Rowan had lied to her face and ignored all the hard work Xolia had put into preparing for the role. Rowan had never shown any inclination for moving up in the bureau. If Xolia hadn't known Rowan as well as she did, she would've called it spite.

What would Silas do in my place? He would face Atlas and go to the fight. Just one night of blissful escape. There, she wouldn't have to be the Xolia who was paranoid to the point of paralysis, but, instead, could be the Xolia who had fought a war. That Xolia didn't bend for anyone or anything. One night. That's all she needed. To get to that, she needed Atlas. She tapped her fingers against her elbow.

Her savior left the booth and unlocked the small gate in front of it. Next to the main gates, it was completely hidden from the street side of the palace. Xolia slipped through, and it was locked behind her. A tremor of guilt wracked her at the thought of being here and avoiding Peter entirely. Once she had been vetted and cleared, the female guard led her past the main entrance to the building.

"Where are we going?" Xolia asked, redirecting her step to follow.

"Vice Chancellor Campion requested to meet you at his residence. It's behind the palace."

Xolia had never gone behind the palace before. She hadn't even known there were more buildings on the grounds. The palace was so large and vast that there was surely enough space for both the chancellor and vice chancellor to live inside its ancient halls.

The walk was beautiful in the early stages autumn. Leaves were turning from rich green to bright gold and yellow. They rustled like flames against the wind.

Behind a hedge of densely packed bushes and sweeping willow trees, a grand house sat. Atlas stood outside on a small gravel path, arms crossed and body tense. He raised a hand, not in greeting but in dismissal.

Her escort stopped short. "I have to go back; it was my honor to assist you, Ms. Stone."

"Thank you," Xolia responded, and the other woman began the trek back through the grounds.

Xolia and Atlas stared at one another, positions mirrored with their arms crossed and expressions blank. The silence stretched between them, unbearable in its oppressiveness.

"Why are you here?" Atlas finally asked.

She took in the autumn air and the house she assumed to be his home, and shrugged. "Because you refused to meet me in the palace?"

"That's not what I meant, and you know it."

"Fine." Xolia steeled herself for Atlas's ridicule. "I changed my mind."

Atlas remained still, his eyebrow quirking up slightly.

"About your. . ." What he had suggested was illegal; it didn't seem right to blurt it out. "About the proposition."

Atlas's eyes widened, and he looked suspiciously around the grounds, as if searching for prying ears. "Come inside."

He and Xolia walked up the narrow pathway to the front door of the house. The inside of Atlas's home was impersonal. She could no more tell Atlas lived there than anyone lived there at all. It was dressed like something from a museum, all outdated furniture and ornate paintings from past presidencies. Atlas descended into the living area of the house, but Xolia was so struck by the sheer unbelievability of the home that she lingered in the foyer, a much grander space than she would have expected of such an inconsequential building. Portraits of past vice presidents and their families lined the walls.

Xolia perused the portraits until she stopped short at a black-and-white photograph. It was smaller than all the paintings. It was Atlas. With Silas. From the rebellion. Atlas was still a teenager, and Silas had a protective arm over his shoulder. They looked like a real family; their hair looked the same color in black and white, and their facial structures were eerily similar with square jaws. Their smiles were nearly identical to one another too.

Xolia knew there was no way for Atlas to be Silas's biological son, but looking at that photo, she became aware of how different she looked from Silas. She became aware of how much Silas wasn't her father and had never been her father. Tears welled in her eyes, and she turned away from the offending picture before they could spill down her cheeks.

Atlas stood right behind her, which jolted Xolia into stillness. "That picture was taken right before the final siege."

Xolia had no pictures with Silas. Not like that, at least.

"I was surprised when I found it in FAR's Revolution archives. I thought it might fit here." Atlas shrugged. "I hate him, but he's the closest thing any of us had to a father, right?"

How can you hate him and have more of him than I do? "I'm not here to talk about Silas," she said, hating the way her voice broke on his name. How weak was she?

"What made you change your mind?"

Xolia sighed. It was inescapable, that dejected exhaling of air. She looked at the couches, seemingly untouched, but Atlas gestured to the smaller of the two. Xolia sat down on the stiff cushion, deliberating on what to say.

"Does it matter?"

Atlas sat on the adjacent couch and nodded.

"Maybe I'm just feeling nostalgic," she said. "I want to blow off some steam."

"Wrong answer."

"Why do you want to go?"

Atlas scoffed at her, clearly uninterested in her constant deflections. "We're coming up on an election year. And if I've learned anything in the past seven years, Peter is a dreamer, but there is too much conflict in the Senate and amongst the country for any of his dreams to be carried out. I'm going to lose my position and my job by next year."

Xolia narrowed her eyes. Atlas had never been this forthcoming with her, and the whole thing reeked of some insincere excuse. It wasn't like she had any way to refute it, though. Besides, it might feel better to be honest for once in her life.

"Rowan got the vice director position. I didn't even know she'd applied for it."

Atlas raised an invisible glass. "Cheers to losing our jobs, then."

Xolia nodded, lifting her own unseen cup.

"The fights are huge, I don't know how they've evaded official detection for so long," Atlas said, leaning back against the couch. "Humans and variants bet on winners; I don't even know the extent of the money that gets traded around those places."

"How did you find out about it?"

"What? Do you think my job is following Peter around all day?" Atlas asked.

Xolia didn't, but she thought that maybe his immediate defensiveness had something to do with whatever tensions lay between them. She shrugged, hoping to irk him.

"Senators see a lot of interesting things, and not many of them can keep quiet."

"But you haven't managed to track the money or find any specific people to connect to the fights?" Xolia guessed.

Atlas's frustrated *hmph* confirmed her guess.

"I'm not going to run any surveillance for you," Xolia said.

"Of course not. We're just blowing off steam. That's what I said at the gala isn't it?"

"Fine. What else do I need to know?"

Atlas smiled like he always did right before he was about to go in for the kill. For whatever reason he was so desperate to have Xolia join him, he had succeeded.

"This Friday at six, meet me at the old meat-packing plant—"

"The one—"

Atlas nodded. If a variant was talking about a meat-packing

plant, there was only one they were referring to. The historic one that lay smack dab in the middle of the pocket of devastation of the rebellion. It was a fixture of Atalia, one of the first major businesses, which had provided beef to nearly half of Ris. The smell of rotting cow carcasses when it had been blown apart on that fateful day was seared into Xolia's memory.

"Meet me there. Wear a mask, and don't bring your phone or anything that could connect your identity back to you. Unless you want to spend a year in rehab and be on suppressants the rest of your life."

Xolia nodded. Standard rules for illicit activities. "Any other rules?"

"Just yours."

Xolia glared at him. He sounded so much like Silas. Those were the exact words that Silas used to say to her too. It was a punch to the gut. There was one thing Silas resented about her. One thing he forbade her to do. And rather than ever voicing it out loud, rather than calling attention to it, he just called it 'her rule.' Just one thing that she needed to follow that no one else ever did. "You don't have to tell me that."

"I thought this whole thing was for old times' sake." Atlas shrugged. "If that's all, let me escort you out."

He led her to the front door, leaving her to pick her way across the grounds and through the front gate. By the time she reached her apartment, a small smile tugged at her lips as she thought about hashing out her feelings in a good old-fashioned spar.

Chapter Seven

Thoughts of sparring and finally loosening her restraint on her powers became all-encompassing for Xolia. She woke up to lingering dreams about the exertion of fighting. The dance of two bodies locked onto the same goal. She sat in her cubicle, still painfully aware of Rowan's absence, dreaming about defensive blocks and maneuvers she hadn't tried in seven years. At home, Marshall would detail his days of separating volatile children from one another, and she imagined standing triumphant for all to see.

By Thursday, she had formed a steady routine of leaving work early for extra training time before Marshall would get home. She unlocked the front door to her apartment, dropped her coat and bag unceremoniously on the floor of the foyer, and ran to change out of her semi-formal wear.

After slipping into a more comfortable change of clothes, Xolia made her way to the bathroom and turned on the bath faucet. She filled the tub halfway before turning the water off. Drawing in a deep breath, she closed her eyes and cast out her awareness to the water, holding out open palms. Years of suppressants had eroded the mastery she used to have with her powers. What once had been second nature now only peeked its head out during times of emotional distress.

The still water in the tub connected to her, the water gently swaying in her mind. She called to it, and when she opened her eyes, the water was siphoning itself into a contained stream around her. Holding the water was imperative, at the slightest break in control the water would splash to the ground, and there was no way she could dry the floor without using all the towels and alerting Marshall to her actions.

She pushed the water back into the tub where it sloshed around, a few drops falling over the side. Holding onto a smaller amount, she tightened that metaphysical grasp with a small twist of her wrist and reached out to touch the shapeless form with her hand. At the touch of her fingertips, the water solidified into a wickedly sharp knife, solid as steel in her hand. After learning to establish contact with their elements, all variant children had been taught how to form weapons in the barracks. It's what had made them such efficient killers and bodyguards.

Leaving the rest of the water in the tub, she left the bathroom for the living room, which had more open space to work through old forms. She slashed and parried imagined enemies, holding onto the knife with a vise grip. Terror gripped her in a way it never had before. If she failed at this, the one thing that had vaulted her above her peers in her youth, it would irrevocably change the way she saw herself. Choosing not to use her powers and being unable to do so made the difference between knowing she could do better and fearing she'd already done the best she ever could.

She moved with the push and pull of this newfound anxiety, pushing herself harder than she had all week. Her body was drenched with sweat by the time the click of the key turning in the lock reached her.

Shit. What time was it? Xolia whipped around to find the time on the clock above the stove, and she broke her concentration, sending a large splash of water to the linoleum flooring. *Fuck.*

Marshall opened the door, the small smile on his face dropping when he looked at her, shiny with sweat and hair plastered to her face. "What are you doing?"

Xolia stared back with wide eyes. He wasn't supposed to be home yet. The water pooled around her, and she hoped that the couch blocked his view of the floor. "You're home early."

"Right, because we have to leave in an hour," he said slowly.

What's today? Xolia wracked her brain, trying to remember what she had clearly forgotten while she kept a neutral expression so that Marshall wouldn't grow suspicious of her.

"I was just getting ready to shower," she said. "I'll be ready in time."

"For what?" he asked.

An anxious chill made her shiver. How was she supposed to know for what? "What do you mean, 'for what?'" Shame heated her face; this was pathetic of her.

"Dammit, Xolia. Did you really forget our anniversary?"

Our anniversary. She had forgotten. "No, just the time. I swear I'm getting ready now." She bolted to the bathroom, ignoring the muttering under his breath, and slammed the door shut behind her. She turned on the shower, hoping the spray of water would drown out the sound of the tub draining.

AN HOUR AND A HALF LATER, Xolia had her arm hooked through Marshall's as they walked to a small diner. Their anniversary dinner was to be a replica of their first date—the small restaurant they had gone to three years ago when Rowan reintroduced them.

Xolia had just ended an extended stay at a rehab center, where she went through the program's schooling and daily therapy appointments with Krista. She had been so desperate to finally experience the normal existence she fought for, a date with Marshall had been one of the most exciting things she had to look forward to. Marshall had looked up to her during the rebellion, and in a post-rebellion life, he had continued to hold her up on that pedestal. It had been a nice feeling.

Now, they were both tense. Marshall probably still thought —correctly—that she had forgotten the occasion, and Xolia was more focused on tomorrow night than the present.

The restaurant was small, a local place run by a human family that spanned back to the earliest days of human-led government. During a normal summer it was beautiful, flowering vines hiding away a small courtyard. It had been over dry that season and the vines were dried and dying with the black bars of the fence looking more imposing rather than gifting privacy. They were seated inside, by a large window that offered an unobstructed view of the courtyard. It was the same booth they had sat in three years ago.

When they first sat in these seats, Marshall had spent the evening looking at her in wide-eyed wonder. He had told her she was a fantasy made reality. Now, his eyes were downturned in exhaustion and his knee wouldn't stop bouncing. Xolia didn't know if it was from agitation or an effort to stay awake. She was sure she looked no better; all of her energy was devoted to keeping tomorrow a secret. It wasn't that she was worried he would turn her in, but he *would* be disappointed. Upset. Angry. She would further fall from that pedestal he used to place her on. Even if she didn't want to admit it, much of what endeared Marshall to her was his opinion of her. It was there lingering in every kiss and conversation, that Marshall was the smallest bit more engaged than her.

Those aren't good thoughts. Xolia pushed them down. He made her happy, and she did love him. *She did.* This relationship was what she had fought for. "How was work today?"

Marshall pontificated about the finer points of teaching in one of the city's first variant-and-human integrated schools since the rebellion. Children tended to self-segregate, and it was a constant battle to work through their parent-given prejudices about what was right and wrong. It was nothing Xolia hadn't heard before, and the longer he droned on about the smaller details of the day, the more Xolia's strayed to tomorrow. What should she expect? Would there be a lot of people? Would she fight Atlas? Or someone else?

"Xolia?" Marshall asked.

Xolia blinked, her unfocused gaze snapping to his concerned face. "What were you saying?"

"I was asking how you were feeling about Rowan being promoted and everything." Love and sympathy poured from every word; though it bordered too closely to pity for Xolia's liking. That ugly, gaping wound of Rowan's betrayal made itself known. The escape the fight offered wasn't entirely foolproof.

On the other hand, this was her opening to supply a lie. A tiny white lie that would cover her tracks and explain her prolonged absence tomorrow night. "I'm sorry," Xolia said. *For what I'm about to do.* "She didn't tell me she also applied, so that was a shock. But I'm going to her apartment tomorrow after work."

"I'm glad." Marshall smiled. "I knew you two would work things out. Rowan told me how guilty she felt when she got the job. She just didn't know how to tell you."

"You knew?"

The cutting tone of her voice contorted Marshall's expression from one of relief to apprehension. He nodded. "She made me promise not to tell you."

A secret. One that she had been excluded from. The emotional wound tore open even further. Marshall reached across the table and grabbed her hands. She moved to pull away, but he tightened his grip. "I'm sorry, I didn't want to interfere in your friendship."

You mean you didn't want to take sides because... because you can't choose between us. Xolia was supposed to be his first priority. *She* was the one dating him. Not Rowan. Rowan and Xolia shouldn't have even been on the same level. The belief she had clung to, the one where Marshall exalted her above all others, crumbled. She was just like everyone else.

"We're not here to talk about Rowan, though," Marshall said. "Tonight is about us."

Xolia stiffened. He was the one who brought up Rowan. It was his fault their night was completely ruined now instead of just tense. It was his fault she hurt so bad. "Then, what should we talk about?" she asked without much vigor.

"Well." Marshall pulled his hands back, wringing them together. "There is something I've been meaning to ask you."

Xolia waited.

He shoved his right hand into his jeans pocket. "Xolia, I've loved you since the day I met you."

Xolia's breath hitched. She couldn't say the same of him. And right now, with the betrayal of his allegiances, she didn't want to say she loved him at all.

"I loved who you were, but I love who you are now even more."

The excitement of tomorrow made Xolia doubt if she liked herself more now than she had in the past.

"The life we are building together is the best part about me. And there is nothing I wish for more than to continue building our family."

Did either of them know what family meant? *Wait—* "Building a family?"

Marshall nodded curtly, not breaking his speech. "Xolia Stone"—he slipped from his chair and dropped to one knee— "would you do me the honor of being my wife and becoming Xolia Williams?" Without much grandeur, he opened a white ring box. Nestled inside the pale velvet was a thin band, affixed with a small diamond glinting under the warm lights.

Marriage. His family name. Children. Distress short-circuited Xolia's brain. They didn't even talk to his family, and she still couldn't comprehend why he took their surname after they abandoned him. She couldn't breathe. *I don't want this.*

But isn't this exactly what she fought for? This was what regular people did. This was the next step in being happy. Nausea assaulted Xolia. Her mind warred between saying yes, like she knew she should, and the fear that this was wrong. *This is what I'm supposed to want.* Wanting to want something would have to be enough. She nodded, body numb, and held out her left hand.

Marshall broke out into a wide and unrestrained smile. He slipped the ring onto her third finger, kissed the back of her hand, and continued to kiss up her arm until he could reach her face and kiss her on the lips. She returned none of the affection.

The rest of dinner passed in fast motion. Other patrons of the restaurant congratulated them. Marshall was exuberant in his thanks while Xolia merely nodded in silence. They walked home, hands intertwined.

At home, when Marshall initiated sex, she gave in. She lay there, mind far away with the trajectory of this change. *What am I doing?* That thought replayed through her mind long after Marshall had finished, slipped out of her, and rolled onto his side. She fell asleep trying to pretend she was happy about her day, trying to convince herself that everything was blissful joy. She *was* happy. This was always the plan.

Chapter Eight

An empty backpack lay on Xolia's bed. She rummaged through her sparse closet for a reasonable change of clothes to maintain the façade that she would be with Rowan all night. Finding something nondescript, she shoved it into the backpack. Marshall had clung to her during the early morning hours. Surrounded by the warmth of their room, he had whispered sweet nothings into her hair before he left for work. All the while, she pretended to be asleep. Xolia called out of work, citing illness, something which only accosted variants if they were on their suppressants. She had been sick all of once in her life, when she was first put on heavy doses of the power-suppressing medication.

Now, as the evening drew nearer, she was dressed as inconspicuously as possible. Tight black pants and a formfitting black long-sleeved shirt. There was nothing for an opponent to easily grab onto should the fight devolve into something as unsophisticated as hand-to-hand combat. She plaited her black hair into two braids—her favored style back in the rebellion days.

She appraised herself in the mirror, seeing herself as who she used to be rather than who she was. Half-feral, ready to fight her way through hell to get what she wanted. Now she had what she'd thought she wanted, and it wasn't what she'd pictured at all.

She shut her eyes. That was the doubt talking. This fear of living in the known. *I am happy. This is what I want.*

She opened her eyes. The doubt was still there.

Sighing, she went back to the closet, and she reached for an old shoebox, shoved behind other boxes. It was dented and bruised, but it wasn't the box that was important but what was inside. A pair of worn but well-made black combat boots stared up at her. The ends of the laces were frayed slightly, but she could always tuck them into the band that buckled around her ankles.

Slipping her socked feet into the boots felt like coming home. In all the years of disuse, they hadn't lost their memory of the contours of her feet. She stood up, shouldering the back-pack, and rolled her shoulders. This was her last moment to back out, to stay home and fully commit to the belief that every-thing was fine.

She took in her small bedroom and the clothes strewn about the bed. Marshall's presence drenched the place, leaving little of her. Absent-mindedly, she thumbed at the small band on her left hand. *The ring.* She slipped it off and tucked it into the top drawer of her nightstand. *I just need one night away from it all. Then I can be happy.*

Finally ready, she left the room and was almost to the front door when Marshall walked in. They both froze, not expecting the other. Movement returned to Xolia first, and she clasped her hands behind her back, hoping Marshall didn't see the lack of gold around her finger.

"You're home early," she said.

"Yeah, I finished all my grading." He stared at her. The braids, the clothes, the boots. *The fucking boots.* There was no way he didn't recognize them. "You look like you did back then."

"Rowan and I are going to a martial arts class," Xolia lied.

"I thought you were getting dinner."

Shit. "We are. After." Xolia smiled unconvincingly. Her heart felt like it was going to break through her breastbone. "I'll see you later tonight." She stepped past him to the waiting and open front door. If she could just make it out—

"Xolia."

She turned. "Yes?"

He crushed her in a hug, holding her close to him, like she was the only solid thing in the world. Xolia's chest tightened. It was suffocating. He kissed the top of her head. "I love you."

Xolia extricated herself from him but not without giving him a chaste kiss on the lips, hoping he wouldn't notice how she didn't say anything back to him. Before he could comment or protest, she was out the door, almost sprinting towards the abandoned meat-packing plant.

It was nearing 6:30 p.m. when Xolia made it to the partially cleaned wreckage. The acidic smell of burning oil and gas lingered in the air, remnants of broken machinery. Xolia could have sworn the air still smelled of rotting cow.

Atlas leaned against an inconspicuous black SUV, arms crossed and a guarded expression on his face. He was dressed in a similar fashion to her—all utility. Even in such a broken place, and with the last drops of sun dipping below the horizon, he was golden. Any available light haloed around his golden hair. A spitting image of Silas, other than the hair. She never hated Atlas more than she did in that moment.

"I thought you chickened out," Atlas said by way of greeting.

"But you waited," Xolia pointed out.

He smirked but didn't respond. Xolia walked to the passenger side and got in the car. She pulled her phone from her pocket and carefully placed it into her backpack and set the bag down at her feet. Atlas didn't comment on the phone, which was a relief. She wouldn't have been able to leave it at home without rousing Marshall's suspicions.

Atlas took his place in the driver's seat and drove through the barren wastelands to the outskirts of the city. "So, how is it working under Rowan?"

Xolia rested her head against the headrest and turned toward the window. Small commercial strips and dilapidated houses made up her vision. Why did she have to admit that to him? "I've gotten used to it."

He scoffed. "I know you don't expect me to believe that."

"Why shouldn't you?" Xolia argued, hating that he saw through her so easily. "She's my friend."

"Not a good one if she lied to you."

That stopped Xolia short. If she thought about Rowan's lies, she would have to think about her own. "Shouldn't you be focused on your re-election campaign?"

Atlas's hands tightened around the steering wheel, his knuckles turning white. "That's not important to me."

Xolia's jaw dropped, but before she could ask a question or even mock him, he continued with a small shrug that was too controlled to be genuine. "Anyway, I'm glad that you came out here with me. I know we've never been friends, but we are the only people who understand each other."

It was her turn to scoff. He was referring to the fact that they were the only two variants who could wield more than one element, but Atlas's abilities had been celebrated by Silas while Xolia's second element had been forbidden. She may as well just have control over water. What weirded her out more was the almost amicable disposition from Atlas. Other than the apparent tenseness about his future, he had been almost cordial. She regarded him warily. "I don't think anyone would think we were similar."

At that, Atlas glanced at her before turning onto the highway, taking them out of the city proper. "I'm just stating facts. Who else could relate to you about your powers?"

"You were allowed to use all of yours," she retorted. Bitterness that had been long buried surfaced. He would never understand what it had been like for her.

"So it's not exactly the same, but we're still different from the rest of them."

"I don't want to talk about this anymore."

Atlas didn't push the issue, not that Xolia would've listened to anything else he said. He turned off the highway to a road that was still familiar after all this time. There was a brief stretch of agricultural land they passed through before turning left to a walled-off complex. The Atalian Variant Barracks. Her old home.

Her heart thundered harder in her chest the closer Atlas brought them to the rusted gates. Memories washed over her. She had never thought she would step back on the property. Involuntarily, she leaned forward in her seat.

He braked and shifted the car into park. "Wait here."

She narrowed her eyes at the command but remained in her seat. Atlas got out and opened the gate, the rusted hinges creaked loud enough to reach Xolia through the closed doors. Many of the streetlamps that used to illuminate the microcity were broken and dark. Atlas disappeared past the car's light as he opened the gate all the way. He hopped back into the car to pull through and stopped to close the gates behind him.

"How has this stayed a secret?" Xolia couldn't stop herself from asking.

"With the amount of people that know about it? It's not kept a secret."

She hummed, but he didn't elaborate, and she wouldn't give him the satisfaction of telling him he was right. They pulled into the main part of the city; the parts that were illuminated revealed plant life reclaiming the sidewalks and streets. What was once a hive of activity and variants running to and fro was now derelict and deserted.

They parked near the old housing barracks. The same building that Xolia had lived in from the time she was twelve to seventeen. Silas had managed to take over the barracks from the government and had used it as his base of operations up until that final day. That seemed a lifetime ago now.

Atlas was quick to grab a reflective helmet and jumped out of the car while Xolia hesitated. The past slammed into her. All the tiny moments she had laid to rest when she went into rehab wormed their way back up. Things hadn't been simpler, but they had been straightforward. There had been a comfort and consistency in her past that Xolia missed. She could stand to admit that to herself.

Pulling herself into action, she followed Atlas to the center of the complex, a large arena that was once the training epicenter of the whole space. She had fought Atlas many times within the walls. Two lights by a side door showed two guards. Their arms were crossed, allowing them to flex their muscles. When they caught sight of the pair approaching, they flexed even more, bulbous veins popping out of their necks. Xolia was no stranger to variants like these; they spent all their time building muscle mass, to the point where their veins were popping and healing in a never-ending cycle. They were growing out of their bodies and continually being pushed back inside their skin.

She curled her lips in disgust but didn't say anything. Instead, she pulled her mask from her back pocket and tied it around the back of her head. It covered her nose and mouth, dropping down below her chin. Atlas had a full-face-covering, it was hard and reflective and completely obscured his face.

Atlas took the lead, stepping in front of her, and brought his index finger to his forehead and dragged it down to his neck. Once he made it to the soft and exposed skin of his neck, he dragged his finger across it. It was said to have been the last gesture of the final variant king before his public execution at the directive of the Risian Democratic Congressional party when they had started their reign. It was a well-known story amongst variants, but Xolia had never seen it used.

The guard on the left nodded. Their password was correct. "Numbers?"

Atlas shook his head. "Newcomers."

The guard on the right smirked. "Fresh meat? Inside and to your right." He pounded a heavy fist against the door, and metal scraped as the bolt slid across the lock. A masked figure opened the door and ushered the two of them into the dimly lit hallway. There was no going back now.

Chapter Nine

Both Atlas and Xolia were silent as the usher pointed them down to the right, the direction of the old locker rooms. Peeled paint revealed dull-gray cinder blocks. A cloying smell of sweat permeated the hall, and it only got stronger the closer they got to the locker rooms.

"Here." Atlas stopped and entered through a break in the long wall. She rolled her eyes; he spoke to her as if she wasn't acutely aware of where everything was. But she had no other choice but to follow him.

In her time away, the rows of lockers had been stripped away, leaving the room bare. It was stuffed full of other masked figures, all fighters, she presumed. Another employee, or whatever the people who ran the fights were called, sat at a small folding table. He waved them over and handed them each a numbered adhesive.

"Here, this will be your number; if you come back to the next fight, the number remains the same."

They each took their numbers. Xolia's was 8540.

"Domains?"

"What?" Atlas lifted his head from where he was affixing his number.

"What's your element?"

"Why does it matter?"

Xolia smirked. It gave her some satisfaction to see him flounder, even if it was over something small.

"Guests like to make bets. This helps them make their decisions. First-timers don't normally get too much audience support without a history of wins, though."

"How long have these been going on?" Xolia asked. The whole thing was well organized and efficient, nothing like the backwoods skirmishes she had imagined.

The man regarded her with narrowed eyes and his mouth set in a thin line. "What's it matter?"

"It doesn't," Atlas intervened. "Earth. Hers is water." Atlas turned his head, and again, it was up to Xolia to guess how he looked at her. Disdain, she supposed.

The organizer made a note on his tablet and nodded at them. "Stay in here. Your numbers will be called when they're ready for you." His tone was guarded, on edge. Xolia winced; she was so out of her element here, so clearly an outsider.

Atlas shoulder-checked her on his way to join the twenty other fighters lounging around the room in varying degrees of silence. *This is the stupidest thing I've ever done.*

She didn't bother to follow Atlas further, their brief camaraderie over and done with, and she slid down the cold and dirty wall until she was sitting against the floor. With only glimpses of exposed skin and facial features, she didn't see any people she recognized. She leaned her head back and waited.

Though she didn't have her phone and there were no clocks in the locker room, Xolia estimated she had been sitting there for two hours by the time half the room had cleared out. Atlas wasn't in the remaining group of people.

Her number was called alongside another woman's. They appraised each other, her opponent was broad-shouldered, with corded muscles running down her arms. Her face was entirely obscured by a flesh-colored, transparent mask that took away all defining features. It was unsettling. Both remained silent as they walked through an exit on the other side of the locker room. Xolia tried to formulate a plan of attack, but without knowing the other woman's element, it was all conjecture.

She remembered the training arena well enough; however walking into it revealed it had been transformed into a theater of sorts. Stands and rows of seats surrounded a large wire cage in the center of the room. The upper level of the building still had its windows intact in what was once a viewing room for high-profile military and political officials to watch the progress of their youthful and nigh unstoppable soldiers. Lights shone from behind the slightly smudged windows, and Xolia wondered who was up there now, watching the chaos and carnage unfold.

A pair of organizers ushered Xolia and her opponent into the cage and locked it from the outside. Lights shone down on them, making it nearly impossible to see anyone who might be watching. Briefly, she wondered where Atlas was, whether he had won his fight or not. Limited to only one element, he would have been severely disadvantaged against people whose experiences were built around using just one. She hoped he had lost.

The announcer introduced them and their elements; if the cheers were anything to go by, her opponent was a crowd favorite. While she was not. She bristled under the weight of their heckling. It made her blood sing with desire for revenge. The announcer gave them their fighting style: a melee fight. A small mercy for Xolia, it was easier to maintain the shape of an element when she was in contact with it.

A loud ding sounded over the roar of the crowd.

Xolia hesitated a moment, reeling between the crowd, and their adverse reaction to her, and to her competition. *What's your domain?*

The other woman, whose number was 513, crouched as if waiting to see what Xolia would call to. Xolia remained still, calling back all of her training and fighting exercises. 513 lunged for the rocks, lumped in a corner of the cage, and formed a hammer, swinging it over her shoulder.

Xolia stepped back and called the water, all resting in a tub in the opposite corner. After a brief hesitation from the water, it flew gracefully to her fingertips. Once the first few drops dripped down her skin, she shaped it into a long spear, the tip sharp and hard as diamond.

The extra reach the long handle provided would, hopefully, compensate for the brute strength of her opponent and the hammer she wielded. As long as Xolia could retain a grip on the spear, she considered them evenly matched. In her week of practice, she had managed no more than a few seconds of holding a shape without direct contact with water.

Armed, they circled each other. Xolia fell back into an old defensive pose, stepping back from the advancing woman. The crowd fell into a hushed pause.

Xolia considered the merits of a full-frontal attack; if she was quick, she might surprise 513 enough to get the upper hand. A loud shriek pierced her ear drums, pulling Xolia's attention to the audience.

The cold hit of the stone hammer slammed its full weight into Xolia's left shoulder. Xolia collapsed, the pain sending her brain into overdrive.

She let go of the spear, and the water trickled between the boards of the floor. How long had it been since she felt like this? Her shoulder was probably broken. It needed time to heal, time she didn't have.

513 advanced again. The raucous cheers and screams from the audience almost made Xolia angrier than getting knocked on her ass. She scooted back and swiped 513's feet out from under her. Her adversary fell, and the cheers turned to leering shouts.

It was a cowardly move, but it gave Xolia time to scramble to her feet and command more water into her waiting right hand.

New spear in hand, she lunged forward and jabbed 513 in the calf. A red blossom darkened the flesh-colored bodysuit, which only further incentivized the crowd against Xolia.

With first blood drawn, tension between Xolia and 513 increased. 513 had managed to hold the shape of her hammer, and she swung a volley of swings as soon as she was on her feet.

Xolia narrowly avoided having her face smashed in, then countered. The blow glanced off the side of the hammer.

She was forced to slow down. To calculate each move and parry. What once came reflexively now came at the cost of precious seconds. They danced around each other, neither inflicting enough damage for the fight to end.

The more Xolia dodged and parried, the more she remembered, though it still wasn't enough. Sweat dripped into her eyes, blurring her vision. She feigned right. Another blow landed on her hip, a sharp edge on the rock slicing through fabric and skin.

Crimson sprayed and pooled on various spots on the splintering floors.

She clutched her side, ignoring the strain in her healing shoulder, when she heard it. The chanting.

"Kill. Kill. Kill."

Xolia looked up. 513 towered above her, heaving the hammer over her head, preparing for the death blow. Even with her mind fuzzy from pain, she wasn't going to go down so soon. She lifted her spear at the same time the hammer swung down.

The shaft, and Xolia's mental hold, wasn't enough against the full force of 513. The spear shattered into thousands of water droplets.

Without any hesitation, 513 lifted the hammer and swung at Xolia's knee. It bent the wrong way, shattering bone and sending more blood flying across the cage.

White fogged the edges of Xolia's vision. She should have fallen to the ground, yelling in pain and resetting the bone to accelerate healing, but some things overrode her logic.

Her injuries hurt, but the thought of losing a fight? Unbearable. Pulling together all of her strength, she stood up.

It was a white-hot anger that told her she wouldn't allow 513 to disrespect her and make her look so weak in front of everyone else. And she certainly wasn't going to lose to a nobody.

Tendrils of Xolia's blood solidified and wrapped around her wounds to keep her standing. More tendrils braced against the floor and lifted her higher. This was something no one else could do. And she was just getting started.

Xolia trained her bloodshot eyes on the other woman in the cage. 513's hammer hung at her side, and her featureless head was tilted upwards, up to Xolia.

Blood discolored the mask, right where her opponent's nose was. 513's body clenched and crumpled into an unnatural bow with a few thoughts and hand movements from Xolia. The woman's movements were jerky, a result of her fighting against Xolia's invisible hold.

At her domination over the other woman's movement, the corners of Xolia's lips rose in a wicked grin. Power and ecstasy raced through her veins. It was freeing, to use this forbidden ability, and to use it well. Silas may have hated her ability to control hers and other people's blood, but she relished every moment. Nothing compared to this feeling.

Xolia compressed and tightened her grip. The other woman shook, trying to fight against the complete stopping of her blood circulation. At the exertion, Xolia's control over her own blood diminished, the tendrils failing to hold her up.

She was falling.

Something struck Xolia in the back of the neck so violently that she didn't feel the initial impact. She jerked forward before the pain hit. She screamed, releasing the last dredges of control over herself and 513.

Collapsing on her bad knee only added to the pounding, overwhelming pain that engulfed her body in a flaming hell.

Xolia had only been shot once before, but she recognized the sensation. Light faded; everything went dark. She struggled to maintain her grip on consciousness, what little she had left. Her last few frames of vision were of a dark figure stooping to where she lay.

Chapter Ten

XOLIA WOKE TO THE STEADY DRIP OF AN IV. AS HER MIND sluggishly regained consciousness, she kept her eyes closed, trying to discern her surroundings. An IV meant professional medical care. Her body was free of the aches and pains that normally accompanied such an expansive heal, another sign of professional care.

Did Atlas take me? She sighed, the only other sound aside from the IV. That gave her pause, silence wasn't a feature with hospitals. There was no use putting it off any longer. She cracked open her eyes, which were crusted by sleep. Her mouth burned like she hadn't drunk anything in days. And she wasn't in a hospital.

She was in a bedroom. A stunning bedroom. Silk sheets cocooned her, and vague, shapeless art hung on the wall. Floor-to-ceiling windows provided a breathtaking view of downtown Atalia, far from the destitution of the barracks.

To her right was a mobile IV drip and a machine that monitored her vitals. There was a heart rate clamp on her left index finger, and behind the portable medical setup, a tall glass of water sat atop a mahogany nightstand. A fluffy towel and folded clothes sat neatly beside the water.

Sitting up, Xolia pushed the covers down and examined herself. Dried sweat and blood were smeared over her skin and clothes. The sheets were ruined. *Good.* No amount of kindness from Atlas would take away the petty satisfaction of inconveniencing him. Her stomach gurgled in protest at her movement. She needed food, but first, she needed to find Atlas and demand to know who had shot her. She removed the clamp from her finger and took a deep breath before pulling out the IV from her right forearm and staunching the blood flow.

When she withdrew her hand from her arm, the small puncture had already healed. She was inspecting the towel—the promise of a shower was almost too much to resist—when her blood ran cold.

Shit, shit, shit. She cursed her sluggish mind for having ignored major problems in her initial guess as to whose house she was in. Atlas's house was on the grounds of the Presidential Palace, and the impersonal modern art was far from the historical accuracy he kept. *Where am I?*

The only solace she found was in the fact that whomever her mystery benefactor was, they didn't want her dead. Which meant they weren't associated with whomever had tried to kill her. Maybe they knew who did it. Calling the water that sat in the glass, she formed a small knife, grasping it with stiff fingers.

Slowly opening the door, she peeked into the darkened hallway. No one. She took one cautious step into the hall and then another. To her left was a large living area, and to the right the hallway continued.

Which way? She lowered the dagger, considering her best

chance for a successful confrontation. She settled for the hallway and turned right.

"I was wondering when you would wake up," a deep, and regrettably familiar voice rumbled from behind her. Xolia jumped.

"Adonis?" She spun.

Standing in the entryway to the living area, Adonis flicked on a warm light and gestured to a sleek couch. Xolia bypassed him, but not without remaining wary every second her back was to him. Earlier, she had been so sure she was in relative safety, but she didn't know Adonis anymore. She picked up her pace to the wall of windows, an exact mirror to the bedroom. While she wanted to press her nose to the glass and take in the city she had spent a lifetime in, she turned and rested her back on the glass.

Adonis hadn't moved from the entryway, but his eyes had followed her. The hair on the back of her neck rose. His hands were shoved into the pockets of a pair of black joggers.

He broke the silence. "What the hell were you doing at the fights?"

Xolia bristled. Who was he to talk to her like that? And, really, what would she even say? *Sometimes I hate my life?* That was too blunt and saying it out loud would mean she believed it. She couldn't afford to believe it. "I don't have to tell you."

"Please." Adonis waved off her paltry retort and joined her by the windows, finally focusing on something other than her. "I'm not FAR's poster child. And I didn't get shot."

Her cheeks burned, and she was thankful she was turned away from him enough to shield her vulnerable expression. She leaned her head back against the glass, finally facing Adonis. Moonlight cascaded over his face, casting shadows that pronounced the sharp lines of his cheekbones and nose. He cut an imposing figure, even in casual attire.

"I don't know who shot you," Adonis admitted. "But I'll find out."

She scoffed, though it carried no malice. He talked like he still cared about her, like he would've back in the old days. How different he was from Marshall. *Shit. Marshall. He's probably tried to call me.* Her phone was tucked away in Atlas's car. Which could be anywhere.

"That's not my biggest worry," she said, pushing off the windows and pacing around the unfamiliar room, her water dagger still clutched in her hand. "How long have I been here?"

"It's Sunday night."

"No, that can't be right."

Adonis shrugged. "You had a bullet wound to the neck, a shattered knee, and countless other injuries." He grabbed a half-full cup of water and drained it before holding it to Xolia. She sent the water into the cup, only a few drops splashing over the side. "I wouldn't be surprised if you're still healing internally."

"Sel, I'm so fucked." Xolia grabbed her head, drumming her fingers against her skull. "Uh, did you happen to see Atlas?"

Adonis's expression hardened. "Why do you ask?"

Of course it had been stupid to ask. Everything she had done since the gala was stupid. It all proved why happiness, even fake happiness, was better than whatever chaos she found herself in now. "We went together," she said on an exasperated exhale.

"Together?"

Despite the stress and panic flooding through her, Xolia rolled her eyes at his repetition. "He invited me at the gala. Just to relive the old days for a night. It was stupid of me to go."

Even now, with the years and distance between them, Xolia knew Adonis was thinking of something by the slight furrowing of his brows. He pushed his dark hair out of his face. "I didn't say that," he muttered. He cleared his throat.

Before things could get any more awkward between the two of them, Xolia changed course. "Where are we? I need to leave."

"I'll drive you home, and you're more than welcome to shower and change before we go," Adonis said. The suggestion sounded more like a plea.

Xolia opened her mouth to protest, she needed to be home two days ago. But Adonis must have anticipated what she was going to say. "You've already been missing two days, what's another hour?"

Logic like that couldn't be argued with. She gave him a curt nod and wandered back to the bedroom, where she grabbed the towel and the clothes—a pair of joggers and a sweatshirt, made of the softest material she had ever felt in her life. On the front of both items was twining snakes embroidered in deep red against the black fabric. She knew the logo despite owning nothing from them. The snakes represented Persion, one of the oldest fashion houses in the country. And one of the most expensive. *Who is this man?*

***

CLEAN AND DRESSED in the soft clothes, she made her way back to the living room. Adonis had moved to the couch and sat hunched over with his elbows resting on his knees. Hunger still gnawed at her, but she was more determined to get Adonis to answer all the questions she had prepared in the shower.

Apparently, he had his own questions. "If you wanted to relive the old days, why didn't you go with Rowan or Marshall? You all looked like great friends at the gala."

Friends. A convenient half-truth. She was engaged to one and barely speaking to the other. Some friends. "They aren't like that. They'll probably kill me when they find out."

"Just don't tell them where you were."

Xolia crossed her arms. "Do you make it a habit to disappear from your friends lives for an entire weekend?" *Why didn't I tell him about Marshall and me?*

"You don't?" Adonis countered.

A smile almost landed on Xolia's face. Her stomach growled. Adonis stood and led her to the foyer, where he grabbed a jacket and a pair of car keys. He opened the front door to a spacious elevator. Xolia stepped in and Adonis followed, pressing the bottom button. There were only three; the basement, the lobby, and the top floor. *A private elevator.*

"What do you do?" she asked.

"My parents took me back in. I joined the family business."

She was happy for him. In her work experience, more than half of all variants from the barracks were still estranged from or unclaimed by their families. It wasn't an easy thing to reconcile, especially when many of the families had human children they loved dearly. "What do they do?"

"They're Persions."

Xolia looked down. "The clothes."

"It was good PR to accept their variant son," Adonis said bitterly. The elevator reached the basement, and they stepped out to a parking garage with half a dozen luxury cars. He unlocked a sleek black sports car with windows so darkly tinted she couldn't see inside. "When they found out I had a knack for business, it turned into a financially beneficial arrangement." And there it was. It wasn't a happy story of a broken family healing.

"I'm sorry." It wasn't the right thing to say, but Xolia had nothing else to offer. She refrained from ever reaching out to her family for fear of the same thing happening to her.

"Don't be." Adonis opened the passenger door and waited until Xolia was seated in the soft leather seat before walking around to the driver's side.

Xolia didn't have a license; there had never been any reason for her to drive once the war ended. The ease with which he maneuvered the car out of the garage and onto the relatively peaceful street fascinated her. It was short-lived as her thoughts strayed to Marshall. And what he would be thinking. How worried he would be. Or angry.

Her stomach growled. She needed a distraction. "Why were you at the fights?"

Adonis side-eyed her before refocusing on the road ahead of them. "It's something of a business venture for me. You would have made me a lot of money on Friday."

Xolia huffed. It didn't really answer her question. "So, was Helen upset you had your ex in your apartment all weekend, or did you just not tell her?" She hadn't needed to ask about Helen. She *shouldn't* have asked about Helen. She lied to herself that she'd asked because Adonis having an angry partner would lessen the guilt she felt about Marshall.

"Helen?" Adonis furrowed his brows. "We're not—she's not important." He closed himself off, his knuckles turning white around the steering wheel. "What are you doing for work?"

A stilted question and a clear deflection. Xolia sighed. This distraction wasn't doing anything to quell the tumult inside of her. Talking about work only made it worse. Her job was the main reason for her lapse in judgement. "I work at the bureau."

Adonis pulled into a drive-thru, where they paused their conversation to order fried foods that made Xolia's mouth water. Food like that had been unheard of in their early years, anything they had been given to eat was fully utilitarian. Nothing sweet or fried or having the least bit of flavor.

She savored the warm, salty crunch of a fry before giving Adonis her apartment address. She gave him the unit number, too, though it was unnecessary.

"So, is Grant Howard still a hard-ass?" Adonis asked once they pulled out of the drive-thru.

Xolia pictured Director Howard, austere behind his desk and telling her that he wouldn't give her the one thing she wanted—needed. And Rowan's guilt at being caught. And how nothing had been right since that meeting. She couldn't say any of that to Adonis, not now, when he must already think her pathetic and a shell of who she used to be. *I'm not who I used to be.* It was the first time she thought that in so many words. It was the first time she realized that for the past seven years of her life she hadn't been in control of who she was or what she was doing. She had let everyone tell her what to do, let them convince her of the best way to be happy. And none of it had worked.

"Xo?" Adonis asked.

Xolia turned to him, and their eyes met for a single second. A second that stretched out beyond them and into the future. A promise of who she could be if she only dared to take it. Xolia broke contact first, nausea roiling around her gut. She shut the bag of fast food, unable to stomach the grease any longer. "I'm sorry." She dropped her head into her hands, threading her fingers through the still-damp strands.

"For what?"

I don't know. Abruptly, Xolia lifted her head. "I did look for you. After. I was kept in solitary confinement for the first few years, and you had no record of being in a rehab center."

Adonis's jaw clenched, and he tapped his fingers against the steering wheel. "I looked for you too, but things were hard at first. With my parents."

"You don't have to tell me if you don't want to," Xolia said, resting a hand on his leg. He looked at her, and her breath caught.

"Not tonight," he said, his voice half an octave lower.

She yanked her hand back and nodded. *Stop. Stop. Stop.*

"I'm sorry." This time it was Adonis who was apologizing. Xolia could have laughed. They were the last two people one would associate with a willingness to apologize, and now they had each said sorry within five minutes of talking.

He turned left down a familiar street. They were almost at her apartment. And it was with a bitter, sinking feeling that Xolia realized she didn't want to lose Adonis again. She frantically searched for anything else to ask him, to keep that connection open. "At the gala, you said there were countrywide protests, but the bureau hasn't dealt with anything like that."

"Atalia's in a bubble. If you think Peter has the best shot at winning, you haven't been paying enough attention," he said as he pulled up to her apartment building.

Panic coursed through Xolia. She wasn't ready to step out of the car. "Thank you. For everything."

"I'd do it all again for you, Xo."

They stared at each other. Underneath the shadows and the missing years, with the faint tinge of cedarwood cologne in the air, Xolia felt out of her depth. "Don't say things like that, Adonis."

He leaned towards her, into her space. She screamed at herself to put more space between them, but she found herself falling. Their noses nearly touched, just a hair's breadth away from each other. Their breaths mingled in that heady space between them.

"I need to leave." She hadn't realized she had spoken out loud. Not until Adonis pulled back and grabbed at the cuff of her sleeve. He pulled a pen out of his pocket.

"Let me see your arm."

She held out her forearm to him, all pale and unmarred skin. In clear print, he wrote out a phone number. His phone number. It was so childish, so like the time he wrote down the encrypted radio wave they had used to talk to each other without anyone else listening in back in the barracks. "Until next time," he said, his voice no more than a whisper.

"Goodnight."

Staying in the car any longer would be a bad idea. Xolia forced herself out of the car and refused to look back. She tugged the sweatshirt sleeve down her arm. Marshall couldn't find out. Not that she had done anything wrong, with Adonis at least. Or had she? She didn't notice men like she noticed Adonis. She didn't even look at Marshall like that, finding their connection to be based more in their shared history than in physical attraction.

She pinched the bridge of her nose. With each step she took towards the apartment door, the entire weekend washed further away until it felt like no more than a fever dream, and those hard-line thoughts about living for herself were reduced to half-baked ideas about asking for compromises. With an immeasurable amount of shame, she knocked on her third-story apartment door.

Chapter Eleven

Marshall opened the door, his face haggard, the bags under his eyes suggesting he hadn't been sleeping well. His eyes lit up the moment he saw her, and he pulled her into a hug she didn't deserve. A hug she didn't want. She tolerated it for a few brief moments before gently pushing away from him.

"I'm sorry," she whispered. Because that was the truth. Whatever else she might be feeling, she was sorry to have hurt him.

He lowered his eyes, taking in the clothes that weren't hers and touched the ends of her still-damp hair. "Where were you?"

All the words she should say lodged in her throat. She couldn't tell him if she tried. Had Atlas reached out to him? Would Marshall tell Krista? She'd be back on her daily suppressant checks in a heartbeat. She'd lose her job.

She shook her head, pulling back from him even more. "I can't tell you."

He grabbed her hands, pulling them up between their chests. "Why not?" His thumb stroked the fingers on her left hand. A left hand that was ringless.

Tension froze Xolia, and her jaw was set so hard she was afraid she'd break her teeth. She prayed that Marshall wouldn't notice, it was such a new thing, maybe he had forgotten.

He lowered his hands. Xolia started to exhale before his next words shattered what little hope she had. "Where's your ring?"

"I kept it here, where it would be safe," she answered, unsure if that truth would help or hurt her case.

Marshall backed away from her, his features all drawn up. "Tell me where you were."

"Marshall, I already told you—"

"Right, you won't say anything," Marshall seethed.

"It's not that I won't." *It was.* "It's that I *can't.*"

"Can't? What do you think I'm going to do, Xolia? Turn you in? Did you do something illegal?" Marshall ran a hand through his short hair. "We're supposed to be a team."

That ignited Xolia's own indignation and hang-ups with Marshall. "A team? Right, and that's why you wouldn't leave the gala when I asked you to. That's why Rowan told you she applied for that stupid job and you never told me. You don't listen to me anymore. Some teammate you are."

Marshall had the gall to look stricken, as if she had hit him. "I didn't know you felt that way."

"Well, I do."

Xolia crossed her arms, frustratingly aware of Adonis's number resting on her skin. Marshall stepped into her space, a hand reaching out to rest on her shoulder before he let his arm fall limply to his side.

"Do you think we can fix us?" he whispered. It was so soft Xolia almost didn't catch it. Almost.

"I don't know." There was no end. Marshall wasn't happy

with her anymore. Peter wasn't happy with her anymore. Sel only knew where Atlas was and what had happened to her stuff. She had no phone. She barely had a job. "I don't know," she reiterated. As if Marshall needed any more confirmation.

Marshall left the apartment, though the tension between them remained. It was cloying. Xolia sat down on their small and faded couch. She hung her head in her hands. Guilt gnawed at her. Nothing was happening like it was supposed to. But she had felt so alive at the fights. And Adonis. . . No. She pushed all thoughts of him deep down.

With a furtive glance at the front door, Xolia got up, went to the kitchen, and turned on the faucet. She rolled up her sleeve and stared at the number. *Just do it.* She shoved her arm under the water and scrubbed at her skin until there was no reminder of him. Just pink skin.

Good. Xolia moved to her bedroom, where she could change into clothes that were hers. A pen and a pad of paper lay on Marshall's nightstand. The temptation was too great; she scribbled down Adonis's number, which she had *not* memorized on purpose, and tore off the paper. She collapsed onto her side of the bed, tired even after having been unconscious for two days. Tenderly, she stared at the number. She dropped her arm over the side of the bed, finding that small tear in the mattress that neither she nor Marshall ever bothered to fix. She slipped the paper inside, hoping she could forget about it.

XOLIA WAS NEARLY asleep by the time the front door clicked and multiple sets of footsteps entered the apartment. Xolia jumped out of bed, wondering if Atlas had finally decided to confront her. She left the room and found Marshall and Rowan. They exchanged a few hushed words, but it was too quiet for Xolia to make out anything specific. Her stomach dropped when Rowan turned her head and they made eye contact.

It grew hard to breathe. Rowan was the last person she wanted to see, and she didn't know why Marshall thought it would be okay, in any way, to bring her to their home. Rowan just greeted her with her lips pressed in a thin line, neither comforting nor condemning. All carefully calculated and laced with pity. Xolia set her jaw.

"What are you doing here?" she asked.

"You need to talk to someone, Xo."

Xolia *tsked*. "Don't call me that. And I don't know why you think I would talk to you." Despite her words, she moved to the living room, and stood by the couch with her arms crossed. "I won't tell you where I went."

"Can you at least tell us why?" Rowan asked.

Us. Why. Rowan asked it like there was one simple answer. Maybe it wouldn't be so hard to tell them where she went. Xolia's breathing constricted more. Why was it so hard to breathe?

"Xolia, are you okay?" Marshall was across the room in an instant, clutching her shoulders. Rowan stood close behind him.

How had they gotten so close? They were too close. She was going to suffocate.

Ripping free from Marshall's worried grip, Xolia paced the length of their small living room. "I just—" *I want things to go back to normal. I hate normal, though. But normal is what we fought for. I don't actually know what I want. I don't think I want you, though.* "I want to not feel this way anymore," Xolia cried out. She didn't want to be pulled in opposite directions.

She wanted one path. Right now, she was falling apart. Normal was so boring. Happy wasn't fulfilling, not in the way the fight had been. But that was illegal. A threat to what FAR—what Peter—was trying to accomplish. And while she was dealing with all of that, there were Rowan and Marshall, both of whom were so assured in who they were. Never once had she heard them talk about the old days positively. Or at all, really. Those days were behind them.

How could she tell them everything when they were so content in the now? Running a clammy hand through her hair, she turned wild eyes on them, hoping they could see past the lump in her throat. All she needed was their understanding. She could forgive and forget if she just had that.

"What are you feeling?" Marshall asked. His features were drawn up tight, his eyes trained on her empty ring finger.

Xolia wanted to shout at him. Of course he would immediately assume it was about their relationship. "I don't know," she answered, putting all she felt into the words. "I feel..." She looked at Rowan's glasses, useless lenses of glass. She thought about Marshall's arm cast the first year they had reconnected, so inundated with suppressants that she had been sure they were healing slower than humans. ". . . human." She slumped onto the couch.

Rowan frowned. "And that upsets you?"

"We're not human," Xolia said. She didn't hate humans, but she wasn't one. "And I hate that you applied for the vice director position without telling me."

"I should've told you," Rowan said, sitting next to Xolia.

Xolia scoffed. Like the admission did anything to heal the rift between them.

Rowan kept talking. "I was upset with you for applying at all, I think."

"Why?"

Rowan shifted away from Xolia on the couch. Despite their knees still touching, there was an insurmountable gulf between them. "You were really mean, by the end of everything. I like the way we're friends now. If you had gotten that position, we wouldn't be friends anymore."

Xolia looked at Marshall.

At least he had the decency to look sheepish, but he still shrugged at her. Xolia hadn't been mean to them. They had been in a war, how was she supposed to have treated them?

"If my friendship is such a burden to you," Xolia said slowly, "you don't have to bother with me anymore."

"Wait," Rowan said, "that's not what I—"

"It is," Xolia interrupted. There was no hesitation. All the hurt and lingering confusion swirled around Xolia. "You knew what that position meant to me, and you went behind my back. Get the fuck out of my house."

All Rowan did was swivel to look at Marshall. That was the tipping point. Xolia grabbed Rowan's arm and pushed her from the couch. "You don't need to look at him, *I'm* telling you to leave." Venom dripped from each word in an ugly reveal of Xolia's deepest truths. Rowan's eyes went wide and even Marshall stepped away from Xolia. Her muscles shook. *It's not supposed to be happening this way.*

"I'll walk you to the door," Marshall whispered to Rowan.

Xolia seethed. While it had been some years since she was a child, she was instantly transported back into her earliest memories, when the barrack caretakers had talked down to her in an effort to quell her burgeoning feelings and power.

They continued their whispered conversation up until Marshall shut the door behind Rowan.

"That wasn't okay, Xolia," Marshall said.

She didn't care for the slight drawl of exasperation, like she was in the wrong. Like she hadn't been betrayed by Rowan. "She knew how badly I wanted that job," Xolia said, her voice sounding foreign to her own ears. It was a broken desperation that she hadn't heard from herself in years, not since she let go of her dreams to be in the Senate.

Marshall lifted the inner corners of his eyebrows. *Pity.* "She wanted the job too."

"Why are you defending her?" Xolia couldn't calm down, her emotions wouldn't settle. "All I wanted was for one thing in my life to matter."

"Don't I matter?"

She scoffed. Was he willfully missing the point? "This has nothing to do with you," Xolia shouted at him. It maybe had a small thing to do with him. Probably. It did.

Marshall drew in a deep breath, his entire upper body inhaling and exhaling. "I don't know what you want."

Neither do I. Xolia wanted to scream. She wanted to run. To change something. She kicked at the couch, ignoring the small flare of pain in her toe. "I just want to go to bed. Please don't bring anyone else here." She walked away from him.

"Do you want me to call Krista?"

She stopped but didn't turn. "No." Krista had been so proud of her; the next time they spoke, she couldn't be like this. She couldn't let Krista down, not when she had such high hopes for Xolia.

Xolia slammed the bedroom door shut behind her, and crawled underneath the covers and pulled them over her head.

As the minutes dragged out, heavy exhaustion settled over her. Once the emotions ebbed, she was left feeling empty. Her outburst hadn't fixed anything, it had just made it all worse. *How am I supposed to make things go back to normal after this?* That was the last thought on her mind when she slipped into a fitful and restless sleep.

Chapter Twelve

THREE DAYS AFTER THE ARGUMENT, AS SHE HAD DUBBED it, found Xolia finally setting up a new phone. Atlas never had shown up at her apartment to demand answers or provide any of his own. He never had returned her things, nor ridiculed her for getting shot, nor bragged about his own escapades that night. It was as if it had never happened. That unnerved Xolia more than the lingering quiet between her and Marshall or the indefinite leave of absence Rowan had insisted she take at work. All she'd had was three days of sitting around the house, questioning if there would be any consequences she would have to face.

Eventually, the lack of answers drove her to the store where she got herself a new phone, rather than wallowing and waiting for Atlas to remember her. Without Marshall to offer his brand of unhelpful advice or remind her of Krista's maxims, Xolia purchased the newest model the store carried. It had internet access, the very thing she had denied herself for so long. The promise of unguarded information was so tantalizing that Xolia forgot why she had ever denied herself in the first place.

At home, she turned on the device, staring noncommittally at the dark screen as she made her way to her bedroom. She flopped onto the bed, one arm hanging off the side and the other clutching the phone. Her dangling arm fiddled with the side of her mattress that sported a small tear. She grasped a small slip of paper inside. Her eyes widened and she pulled it out. It was Adonis's number that had been hidden and quickly forgotten in the chaos that had been the rest of that night.

She sat up, staring at the ten digits in one hand. And a new phone in the other. Before The Argument, she had told herself she wouldn't talk to Adonis. Now though. . . *I still need to return his jacket.*

The borrowed suit jacket still hung in the back of their shared closet, shoved to the farthest corner of Xolia's side. She hoped Marshall had forgotten about it. If she could return it to Adonis, she would have the chance to say thank you and then they could go their separate ways. She could forget about him again, leaving him to the anecdotes of her memories.

The thought of letting Adonis go sent a strangely hollow pang through her heart. Not that he was really in her life now, but he offered her the promise of something more. *I wouldn't be doing anything wrong by just talking to him.*

Xolia groaned. If she had to argue with herself, she was already in the wrong. Krista had told her that once, when Xolia had her sights set on a senate seat. She tucked Adonis's number back into its hidden nook. Regardless of the state of their relationship now, she and Marshall shared too much for her to leave him.

Hadn't she and Rowan shared just as much, though? More even, from their earliest memories in the barracks. What was to become of them now? Were they doomed to be echoes of each other, each carrying a piece of the other, always there and always known, but never to see each other again? Xolia's breath quickened. If she was losing Rowan, she couldn't also lose Marshall.

As Xolia was about to toss the phone to the other side of the bed, it chimed. A message from an unknown number. Lingering anxiety was quick to transmute itself to dread. Was it Atlas?

She tapped on it. *Xolia,* it read, *I've been trying to reach you for some time now. Please respond at your earliest convenience. Regards, Peter.*

Her throat had constricted by the end of the message. Why would Peter want to talk to her? Had Atlas told him where they had gone? Was Peter upset about the gala still? He was the ulti-mate authority in the country, he could put her back through a rehab center or have her back on daily suppressant checks with a single breath. Having just made it to no checks, she wasn't ready to give up that taste of freedom. It was the most she had felt like herself in years.

She considered not responding, but the fear of not knowing outweighed the fear of talking to him. *He won't do those things.* Barely reassured, she messaged him back.

The call came immediately.

One deep breath. A second. She answered the call. "Hello?"

Peter's voice carried no malice. No resentment. "Xolia, I was worried something happened to you, are you okay?"

"Yeah," she said. "My phone was just broken, but it's fixed now."

"Oh good. I'm glad to hear that." A pause. "I need to talk to you urgently, is now a good time?"

"Of course." Her response was immediate. All she had was time. "What did you want to talk about?"

"Not on the phone. I'll have a car sent to you right away."

Before Xolia could offer her address, he hung up, leaving Xolia dumbfounded. *What the hell just happened?*

A quick peek at the clock confirmed it was nearing late afternoon. Marshall had been staying late at work the past few days, Xolia hoped he would do so today. She stretched her cramped limbs and got up to put on something worthy of a direct meeting with the chancellor.

Half an hour later, a black SUV pulled up outside of her apartment building—Xolia spotted the SUV from her vantage point on the fire escape. Cold wind whipped her hair around while the vehicle rolled to a stop, and a well-dressed man stepped out of the driver's side door.

Xolia's phone chimed. A notification that the car was ready for her. She slipped back into the apartment and grabbed a coat before running out the front door.

She slowed down to a self-assured walk by the time she left the lobby. The driver was still standing by the front door and offered her a small nod before opening the back driver's side door.

"Thank you," she said and got into the dark interior. The driver closed the door behind her and quickly took his own spot.

"Are you ready, Ms. Stone?" he asked, voice a tenor monotone.

She nodded, heart beating too quickly for more than that. *What does Peter want to talk to me about?* Xolia needed to amend her earlier feelings; this was worse than an eternal not knowing. This was a slow reckoning—the end too near and too far for her to do more than be stuck in a limbo of guesses.

An eternity had passed by the time the car was ushered past the iron gates of the Presidential Palace. The gargoyles loomed with harsh and judging expressions. Sweat beaded along Xolia's forehead.

The driver pulled around the back of the castle, down a gravel pathway to the chancellor's private wing. The wing was not open to the public and Xolia had never seen it before. The immense gardens and trees blocked any visibility of Atlas's house despite Xolia craning to catch a glimpse.

She wondered if Atlas would be in the meeting. Her heart stuttered. *Sel, please let him not be there.* If she was forced to wait any longer, she might explode in a ball of shame and anxiety.

The driver pulled up to a back entrance. It was small and unassuming, very much the opposite of the grand front entrance.

A woman in a blue pantsuit stood by the door. The driver parked and hurried to open the door for Xolia. She stepped out with a small nod of thanks in his direction. The woman shook Xolia's hand. "Hello, Ms. Stone. My name is Lana, I'll escort you to Chancellor Bellevue."

"Thank you."

Lana opened the door, revealing a simple hallway with a lush carpet. There weren't any motifs of war or variants, or humans for that matter, just photographs of various places in the country, ranging from wild spaces to cities, most of which Xolia had never seen in her life. It was strange to think about the variants who lived in those parts of the country. They were living better lives because of what she had done.

Eventually, they turned right through a doorway to a small sitting room, the furniture reminiscent of an earlier time. It was so unlike what she associated Peter with. It was all light floral patterns and motifs, even the wallpaper was adorned with small purple roses, creating busy lines that were broken by cherry-red bookshelves and coffee tables.

Peter sat in an egregiously patterned chair, his eyes downcast and the scar even more prominent than normal.

This was her moment of reckoning. Peter turned and smiled when his eyes met hers. "Xolia, I'm so glad you're here."

He stood up and walked slowly, like his joints were stiff and another kind of fear tickled at Xolia's scalp. Humans aged so much faster than variants, and Peter had already been old when they met.

"Thank you for escorting Ms. Stone, Lana. You're dismissed." He waved a hand in the woman's direction, something Xolia had watched him do countless times. Silas had done the same thing, but no one ever cowered or ran from Peter like they would have from Silas. Lana left the room on quiet feet, leaving the two of them alone.

Xolia's body was rigid, and Peter seemed to take note. "Please, sit."

He gestured to a small couch adjacent to his chair, where he sat back down. A deep sigh escaped him. Xolia hesitantly perched on the edge of the couch.

Having not found any signs of Atlas, Xolia decided to take charge. "Did Atlas tell you?"

Peter furrowed his brows. "Tell me what?"

"That we..." Xolia stuttered. Nothing in Peter's face suggested he had any idea what she was talking about. "We met up, I just wondered if you knew."

Peter looked like he wanted to press the issue of Atlas but decided against it. "Do you keep up with the news lately?"

Xolia could lie to most anyone if the past week had proved anything. She was exceptional at lying to herself, even if she always shoved that unbidden thought deep down as soon as it surfaced. She could lie to Marshall until the sun went dark if it meant saving herself, but she couldn't lie to Peter. Not to the man who had protected her and offered her the world even after she had tried to kill him. She shook her head.

"I envy you," Peter said.

Envy. No one had ever told her they *envied* her life before. Before the rebellion she had been little more than a useful pest. During the rebellion she had been constantly compared to Atlas, and after she had chosen her pursuit of quiet happiness, she'd faded into the background of society's collective awareness. There never had been any room for envy before.

"You don't mean that," Xolia said. She didn't envy her life, he shouldn't either. Not when he had the highest seat of power in the country and she couldn't even get a mid-level management position.

He smiled, wrinkles crinkling at the corners of his eyes. Xolia once thought she'd work with him, be the one next to him rather than Atlas before her life took another turn. The exhaustion in his frame reminded her that she chose her life because she already had given what she needed to. She had done the work, and it was time to reap the benefits. But with the first election coming up, those benefits were precariously hanging in everyone else's hands.

"I do. Things aren't good, Xolia. Seven years isn't a lot of time for old prejudices to be washed away. And now these rumors that John Clemont is going to announce his candidacy?" Peter shook his head. "It's all going to shit."

Xolia blinked. Peter never swore. "There's no way you won't win the election; you brought unprecedented peace and freedom to the country."

He scoffed, another unnatural sound coming from him. "You're one of the few people left who still believes in me. A lot of humans aren't happy with these changes, and variants are still displaced. Surely that is not news to you."

It wasn't. Families were still broken; variants were unable to get work. Since variants got pregnant so rarely, the few all-variant families had negligible access to prenatal care.

"You'll fix it."

"It'll take a century to fix," Peter said. "Speed is the cost of democracy. At least you'll still get to see it."

The words of a dying man. "Why am I here, Peter?"

This time when he looked at her, there was no smile, no gentle reminder of paternal care. It was just exhaustion. "This current administration isn't working. All my promises have yet to be fulfilled, and at every point, I'm stalled by the Senate. All they do is argue themselves into circles."

Peter dropped his head into his hands. Xolia wanted to cry at his state. "How can I help?" she asked.

"I want you to run as my vice chancellor."

"Atlas is okay with that?" It was a stupid thing to ask, but she hadn't been thinking when she blurted it out. How could she have been when she was still processing what he'd said?

Peter scoffed again; this time the sound was steeped in malice. "He is not my superior. I make my own decisions."

"Right," Xolia conceded. She leaned forward from her seat. "Why me, though?"

"There are so many humans who believe that variants are innately violent. They don't trust them. Who better to show them the truth?"

A weight settled on Xolia's chest. The guilt of the fight still sat on her mind, though that paled in comparison to the unyielding memory of how much she loved it. Xolia didn't think variants carried some innate volatility, but she worried *she* did. That if she let herself free of these rigid constraints, she would burn through everything. Happiness had to come in small packages, or else.

"I know you're done with war and politics, but they didn't end," Peter said, seemingly mistaking her silence as uncertainty. "The battleground is just different now. And there are fewer people to trust than ever."

"I wouldn't know what to do," she said, voice quiet. This was everything she shouldn't want, but thinking about standing next to Peter, enacting real change, thrilled her more than anything else. Being the vice chancellor was power. And maybe, *maybe*, power wasn't the antithesis to happiness.

This was important to Peter. The most important person in her life. So it was important to her.

"Do you think anyone else wants me to lead them?"

He nodded. "I see so much of myself in you. We're both idealists, and that is not a kind thing in these times. Especially when we are getting reports of variants causing an uptick in violent crimes; it's easy fodder for the Clemont campaign. We need to show a peaceful and united front."

This is what you've been waiting for. Just take it.

But I'm not who he thinks I am.

Peter let the silence linger for a few more moments. "I can give you time to decide, if you need. I would like to announce my pick for VC when the Museum of Variant History opens."

Her heart beat erratically. "Okay."

Chapter Thirteen

Xolia couldn't stop herself from imagining herself sitting in the Presidential Palace, surrounded by other important people, doing important work. She wouldn't have to slog through bureaucratic red tape, trying to make sure a single person was getting their Good Faith check. She wouldn't have to sit in a cubicle alone, Rowan's empty seat taunting her the entire day. If she still had a job to go back to. This might be her one shot at employment, and what a promotion it would be.

"Xolia?" Marshall's voice distantly filtered through the haze of imaginings.

"Yes?" Her food slid off her fork and back onto her full plate. She had forgotten they were in the middle of dinner.

He stared at her. Exhausted. Defeated. She still wasn't wearing her ring, and he hadn't pushed the issue. She didn't know if she wanted to broach the topic.

"I was trying to ask you if you wanted to get some help?"

Xolia bristled. "What do you mean?"

"For us," Marshall was quick to clarify. "To fix us."

Why do you want to fix us? "What did you have in mind?" *Do I want to fix us?*

"Well, we were all talking to Semele during the gala, she was at our table, and she was talking about the Rheathian church. I looked into it, and they offer counseling services to their congregation."

She almost laughed. "You want us to go to church to get help for our relationship?"

"I don't know what else to do, Xolia," he rasped, voice breaking over her name. "I love you."

All she needed to do was say the words back. I. Love. You. Three words. It would ease Marshall's frantic worrying over them. Maybe it would save her from church. But they got tangled up in her throat until there was a lump she couldn't speak past. She could barely breathe past it.

She nodded. *Breathe in. Breathe out.* "We can go to church." It was the best she could do. Abruptly, she got up, leaving Marshall alone at the kitchen table, and walked into their bedroom. *Sel, what would Silas think of me right now?* She was a coward, but she couldn't let go of Marshall. Not yet. He loved her, and that was worth something. *Is it worth enough?*

She sank into bed, wondering if Marshall would be quick to follow her. One minute passed. Then another. The door didn't open, nor did the noise of soft foot-falls signal his approach.

Would she be ready to give up Marshall if she took the vice chancellor job? Would he even want to stay with her? Rowan certainly wouldn't want anything to do with her. What if Marshall and Rowan became better friends with each other than they were with her? It was an irrational spark of jealousy, why should she care? But she did. She cared a lot.

Xolia groaned. Everything was supposed to have gone back

to normal after the fight, but it all just had become so much worse. That was ignoring the apparent disappearance of Atlas. All she needed was for one thing to make sense.

Without thinking, she grabbed Adonis's number from the tear in the mattress. She glanced surreptitiously at the door. Still no Marshall. Unfolding the paper, she justified giving his suit jacket back to him, at the very least. If she was going to accept Peter's offer, she would need clothes fitting her new position. Adonis could help with that too. Talking to him wouldn't have to mean anything. It *wouldn't* mean anything.

Her hands betrayed her anxiety as they shook while she entered his number into her phone. Before she could change her mind, she typed out her message: *It's me. Xo. Thank you for all your help. Care to help me with another favor?*

Sent.

Once it was done, panic flooded her. She was so stupid, if Marshall found out she had talked to Adonis behind his back, he would never forgive her. *Would that be so bad though?*

Xolia crinkled the paper in her hand, nearly tripping over her own feet in her haste to get to the bathroom trash can.

Adonis responded: *Of course. Care to discuss the favor over dinner?*

She bit her lip. This was her chance to set clear boundaries. No matter what path she chose, Adonis didn't fit in. The only correct response was to deny dinner and suggest a quick and impersonal meetup.

She hated herself as she typed out a counteroffer of lunch the following day. In a final act of doing the wrong thing, she deleted the messages before getting ready for bed.

The constant hum of anxiety had just started to settle when Marshall came into their room. All of her breathing exercises and self-delusion shattered when he slid into bed next to her, an arm circling her midsection. "We'll get through this," he whispered into the loose tresses of her hair.

Xolia nodded against him, bringing her hand to rest over his, whether as a comfort for herself or for him, she didn't know.

Xolia waited outside her apartment building for Adonis. He pulled up in a glittering black sports car, different to the one he had driven her home in. She raised an eyebrow at the superfluous show of wealth.

Adonis stepped out. Dressed in all black, except for the red embroidered Persion snakes on his left breast pocket, he cut an intimidating figure compared to her sweater and dark jeans.

"Afternoon." He opened the door for her. Xolia narrowed her eyes slightly. Another aberration from the irreverent boy so emblazoned in her memories.

Still, she got into the passenger side. The interior was blood red with the dashboard matching the ebony exterior. Adonis got into the driver's seat, and the engine purred as they joined the lunch-hour rush.

The silence stretched out a beat too long before Adonis spoke. "I was glad you texted me."

He didn't need to say *finally* for Xolia to pick up on it. "I lost my phone. It took a few days to get another one."

Adonis didn't respond. For the first time since they had reconnected, all the awkwardness of the lost years separated them. She felt it was too soon to ask him about clothes for the VC announcement, seeing as she hadn't even formally accepted yet.

She snuck a glance at him, his dark eyes were focused on the road, and he was gripping the steering wheel tight enough to turn his knuckles white. "You know," she said, "I haven't driven since the war ended."

"Seriously?" He side-eyed her, the corner of his mouth quirking up. "You taught me how to drive."

"Because you were unteachable," Xolia said, smiling. They had been fourteen, Silas had taught her how to drive, and Adonis had burned through all available tutors. It was up to her and the barracks' oldest van in the dead of night to teach him. The night he had successfully driven them through the abandoned roads at the edge of the complex without hitting a post or a rock, he had kissed her for the first time. It had been an innocent thing, full of joy in a time when Xolia had had little. Her heart fluttered at the memory— at how beautiful and unsullied it still was.

Adonis was smiling, too, a real smile and not some sly smirk. She wondered if he was thinking about that night, if it was as memorable for him as it was for her. "Maybe I just didn't care about impressing any of the other instructors."

"Really? Not even Irina?" Xolia shot at him.

He rolled his eyes. Irina had been old, almost three hundred, when they were in the barracks. There were none alive today as old as she had been. The oldest variant alive was 189. Irina hadn't been good for much else other than terrorizing the younger generations, rehashing the stories of her great-grandparents, who had lived during the days of the variant monarchy, and teaching the youngsters how to drive. In essence, she was everything Xolia and the rest of her generation had been terrified of in those early days when the rebellion was just whispers in the wind.

"I mean, she was my first choice. You were just the rebound," Adonis said. They made eye contact, and it was like no time had passed between them. Xolia parted her lips, whether to speak or not, she couldn't say. They couldn't stay in the moment, though. Adonis pulled his attention back to the road, where they drove closer to Juthian Heights.

Xolia looked down at the tops of her thighs. *What am I doing? This is crossing a line.*

"Well"—Adonis's voice pulled her from her own thoughts—"you can drive on the way back to your apartment."

"I can't do that," she said.

"Why not?" Adonis turned right down a street filled with high-end shops, and the traffic thinned out to reveal well-dressed people walking up and down the clean sidewalks.

"Your car has to cost more than my annual salary," Xolia said, exasperated. "I don't think I even remember how to drive."

Adonis waved off her concerns but didn't say anything more. Instead, he focused on pulling up to a restaurant, where the valet waited outside of the front door.

The restaurant was dark and intimate, with each table in its own alcove, creating a maze of rows and tables. The host sat them in a particularly secluded spot in the back of the restaurant, away from the other patrons and the kitchens. After he handed them menus, he left them to their own devices.

Xolia couldn't stop herself from glancing around, trying to find a hint of another person. Soft music drowned out the low conversation. The effect was isolating in the best way; they were utterly alone. They could let their guards down. Not even that niggling voice of reason had much to say. No one could see them, and it wasn't like she was planning on doing anything wrong.

"So, we're at lunch now." Adonis crossed his arms and rested them on the table.

"We are."

"What does the indomitable Xolia need me for?" he asked.

Xolia hesitated. Maybe the whole thing was stupid. She hadn't even said yes to Peter yet. *But you want to say yes.* Was it smart to say yes when she was still so uninformed? She settled on, "You told me that Atalia is in a bubble. I want you to show me the truth."

"Why now?"

I didn't realize how much I was lying to myself. I woke up one day and realized how unhappy with my life I am. I can't pretend anymore. "The only reason I went to that fight was because my life. . ." Could she actually say the words she thought all day, every day? "It isn't what I want all the time."

"Xo."

She made eye contact with him, relishing the way he said her nickname. He was, after all, the person who had given it to her and the only person with permission to call her by it. They didn't break eye contact with each other, even as the server poured two glasses of wine.

"What do you want?" he whispered.

It was infuriatingly intimate, the softness of his voice, his deep eyes locked in on her, the seclusion of it all.

And the question. What did she want? Rowan's job? Rowan's friendship? Marshall's love? His judgement?

Or did she want the vice chancellorship? The thought of political office both excited and terrified her. Would Silas think she was suited for the job? *He's not here anymore.* "I don't know."

Their waiter returned to take their food order. Too wrapped

up in her thoughts, Xolia deferred to Adonis to order, not that she was really hungry anymore.

Once they were alone again, Adonis leaned back in his seat, almost an invitation for Xolia to lean forward. "I'll show you the truth about Ris, Xo. You can figure the rest out later. In fact, I have a truth for you now."

She raised an eyebrow.

"About who had you shot at the fight."

"How'd you figure that out?"

He sipped his glass of wine. "I'm good at getting information."

Xolia leaned back, not wanting to play into his game. "Spill."

"Vice Chancellor Campion."

"Atlas?" It couldn't be him. She shook her head. They weren't friends, but they had a shared history. A bond like that couldn't be thrown away. Why would he even want to kill her?

But Adonis nodded. "It was easy enough to track down the shooter. All of his communication was done through encrypted digital channels, and there were multiple dummy accounts, but they eventually led back to Atlas."

Xolia's head spun. Peter just offered her the vice chancellorship, but if he had been planning on offering it to her, why hadn't he done so at the gala? *He might've if you hadn't embarrassed him.*

That could've led to the tension between Peter and Atlas that day. It wasn't substantial evidence, but it was a start. "Could I talk to him?"

Adonis paused. "The shooter?"

Xolia nodded.

Adonis shook his head. "He can't really talk anymore."

It wasn't a huge leap to imagine what Adonis had done to him. Even though he was more put together, dressed in finer clothes, he still carried with him that edge of danger he'd had when they were younger. He hadn't gone soft like Marshall, or like Xolia herself. There was no doubt in her mind that Adonis was still capable of casual violence. If such a thing could be casual.

She didn't know what it said about her that she wasn't all that bent up about it. She rested her head against the palm of her hand, her fingers curling protectively around her cheek. If Atlas had tried to kill her once, would he try again? If she said yes to Peter, would that only further enrage him?

The waiter returned with their first course. A simple puréed soup that melted against Xolia's mouth. For a brief moment, she forgot about everything else to focus on the taste. Of course, the ignorance couldn't last. She rested her spoon against the bowl.

"What's wrong?" Adonis asked, resting his own spoon on the table.

"Peter offered me the vice chancellorship," she said, unable to hold onto the information any longer. Someone else needed to know, and if anyone else could understand, she hoped it'd be him.

He looked up at her. "He did?"

"I haven't accepted yet," she said.

"Why not?" he asked.

Xolia leaned back. "It's a huge responsibility."

"Xo, this could change everything for Ris." Adonis leaned forward, earnestness dripping from his voice. "You have to take it."

"You don't get to tell me what to do." Xolia crossed her arms over her chest.

"We can really work with this," Adonis said, his eyes flicking back and forth. Xolia furrowed her brows. Who did he think he was, to already start mapping out her future for her?

She put her hands on the table, startling him out of his thoughts. "We?" There might've been a 'we' years ago, but things had changed.

"I'm sorry," Adonis said. He didn't sound sorry at all. "But variants are still struggling. Peter is failing, and neither Atlas nor the Senate seem too worried about fixing things anytime soon. Other parties are circling. If you don't care, then you aren't—"

"Don't care?" Xolia interjected. "I care a lot. Or have you forgotten what I gave in the war?"

"But the war's not over," Adonis said, exasperation spilling into his tone.

"Fuck you." She was speaking too loudly for the restaurant, but she couldn't handle listening to him anymore. She couldn't handle him talking like he knew her more than she knew herself. "My life ended the day the war did. Nothing has worked out since then."

Her voice broke. Was she really going to admit it?

"I'm *unhappy*, Adonis. I haven't been happy in a long time, and I'm tired of pretending I know what will work." It was out there, in the world. The words couldn't be taken back, and there was some underlying freedom in that thought.

She shook her head and looked up at the ceiling, willing tears away. She wouldn't cry in front of Adonis. Not again.

"Sel, I don't know what the hell I'm doing anymore."

"Xo."

He always said her name so reverently, no one else could make a single syllable carry so much weight. It never sounded right in anyone else's mouth. But when Adonis said it, it was like she mattered.

A warm hand closed over her left hand, and Xolia looked down. "Let me help you. I can make you happy."

Heat rose to her cheeks. Why did he have to say things like that?

"Okay," she whispered. She didn't trust herself to say anything more. An inkling of guilt wormed its way to the forefront of her mind. This was crossing every line she had told herself she wouldn't cross when she reached out to Adonis. Marshall would hate her if he knew. *That's why he doesn't know.*

Xolia yanked her hands back, busying herself with going back to eating the soup. Adonis took the rejection in stride and went back to his meal.

"You want to know more about Ris," he eventually said. "General DuBois is having a small get-together for John Clemont. Come with me. I think we could be good partners. If you take the position, I could help you."

It would be a good strategic move. If she was going to support Peter, she needed to know his competition. *What's the worst that could happen?* "Partners."

Chapter Fourteen

Sunday rolled around to blustery winds and an overcast sky. She and Marshall had barely talked the second half of the week, but today was church day. Today was *pretend they were going to fix their relationship* day. *Try and forget about Adonis and Peter and politics* day.

Xolia sifted through the clothes on her side of the closet. She pulled out jeans and a black long-sleeved shirt. The color would always remind her of her old uniform, and for that reason, she had stayed away from it the past seven years. It called to her now, though. That sense of strength and power she always had derived from her uniform slipped around her as she put her arms and head through the holes of the cloth. Pulling her hair free, she appraised herself in the mirror. Slight bags had made a home under her eyes; she hadn't been sleeping well. She had agreed to a public outing with Adonis, and she still didn't know how she would tell Marshall.

She had been texting Adonis throughout the week, and it was stressful enough to hide the messages and pretend she wasn't talking to anyone in particular with Marshall's cautious eyes tracking her every move while he was at home. Xolia finished getting ready, wondering how they were supposed to fix anything. She ignored the part of her that yelled at her to end it rather than keep dragging it along.

"Are you ready?" Marshall called through the closed bedroom door. "If we don't leave now, we'll be late."

"Coming," she called out. She wiggled her left ring finger, the one that was still bereft of the engagement ring she had worn all of a week. The ring was still tucked into her nightstand, hidden at the very bottom.

She stepped out of the sanctuary of her bedroom and smiled at Marshall. He responded in kind. It felt like a small truce between the two of them; things would be okay, even if it was just for a moment.

***

The First Rheathian Church was consisted of stone and stained-glass windows. While the entire building, from the windows to the double oak doors, was as it had been originally constructed, the property was well maintained. There was not a weed on the grounds.

People filtered into the building. Xolia tensed. They were really doing this.

Marshall stopped beside her, as if he too needed a moment to take in everything around him. "Ready?" he asked.

It was oddly reassuring that he asked with things so muddy between them. She wasn't ready, and she didn't want to go in, but she nodded all the same. They crossed the street as soon as there was a break in the traffic. Marshall pushed the doors, which opened silently on well-oiled hinges.

Candles, along with the slightly distorted natural light from the stained-glass windows lit the foyer, leaving the room well lit but also unsettling. It was so far removed from modernity that Xolia half-worried they had stepped backward in time. Paintings of variants in various acts of war decorated the walls. They were brutal, and the strategically placed candles added an additional element of drama to the visceral images.

Marshall held onto her elbow and tried to pull her forward, but she was drawn to the antique paintings. Small plaques with the years they had been painted were stationed just below the deep-brown frames. While the artists were different, and there was a thousand-year range as far as Xolia could tell, all the images were unified in heavy usage of moths. They always surrounded one variant more than the other, and that variant was almost always the perceived victor.

Xolia zeroed in on one image in particular. She swore something in the air pulled her to it, whispering unintelligible promises. In the painting a dark-haired man stood on the offensive. His arms were up, obscuring most of his face except for his eyes. And even though it was dried paint from a thousand years ago, the absolute rage he felt burned through Xolia. He carried it in his eyes. In his arms he held a flaming sword pointed at the neck of some blond-haired opponent. The moths surrounded the dark-haired man, and Xolia felt a deep kinship with him, as if they were one and the same. She didn't know what he was going through, or what his quarrel with the blond was, but she understood him on a level that didn't require context. It was just fact—they were the same.

"We need to go inside," Marshall said. He sounded far away, too far for her to reach, when something pulled on her elbow again the connection between her and painting was broken. She blinked at Marshall, who was standing closer to her than they had been all morning.

"Are you okay?"

She nodded. "I'm fine. Let's go in." She spared one final glance for the man she couldn't help but see herself in, before facing the doors that led into the church's main chamber where services were held. Stained glass lined the walls of the chamber, with a large circular window adorned in red glass above a raised dais. A podium placed directly under the light from the window was atop the dais. Pews lined the remaining two-thirds of the room.

The front rows were densely packed, while the farther back ones were more sparsely populated. They ensconced themselves near the back, far away from everyone else. The seat was uncomfortable, the thin cushion offering little relief from the harsh angle of the wood. She made eye contact with another congregant, who gave her a small smile and nod, before she took her own seat. A fissure of embarrassment ran through Xolia. *What are we doing here?*

Why had she ever thought that church would solve their problems? Marshall sat with his back straight and stared straight ahead. Xolia tried to pull up the reasons she had fallen in love with him at the beginning of their relationship, but she fell short. She could only resent the man who sat beside her.

Her heart beat erratically. The air grew thicker. *I can't fucking do this.* "I'll be right back," she whispered to Marshall. She tried to keep the panic from her voice, and either she succeeded, or Marshall didn't care as he gave her a quick nod.

Xolia got up from the pew on unsteady feet and marched to the antechamber. Wanting to avoid contact with anyone, she opted not to stay in the room and took a left down a hallway that was entirely lit by oil lamps on the walls. Assured she was alone, she pinched the bridge of her nose, half-praying to the church for answers while chiding herself for such nonsensical thoughts.

"A lost soul wanders into our church," said an airy voice from deeper in the hall. "Can I offer you any guidance?"

Xolia's eyes snapped open, looking for the source of the voice. A man dressed in gray robes, like someone from a long-forgotten time, walked toward her. He was covered from the neck down, with pristine white gloves covering his hands. He was bald and clean-shaven, including his eyebrows. It was a stark look that left Xolia on edge.

"Who are you?" she asked.

He stopped a few feet away from her. "Someone who listens. Someone who occasionally has answers. What troubles you?"

Xolia scoffed. "What doesn't trouble me?"

"Life can never offer any simple answers, can it, Xolia Stone?"

"How do you know me?"

The man laughed softly. "Rheathism is an old religion, one that nearly died out after the last king's death. But we were there during the years of servitude. And we were here during the Revolution."

"Lots of variants fought in the rebellion, do you know all of them?"

He shook his head. "Not all of them have the abilities you or Vice Chancellor Campion have."

Despite the mention of Atlas's name, it was nice to be singled out above her other comrades. It had been so long since she received any glory for herself rather than for FAR as a whole. She stepped closer to the man, hungry for more.

Xolia studied the unmarred glimpse of visible skin. "Are you a variant?"

He nodded.

"Did you fight?"

"I've belonged to the church since birth. I have been given special exemptions to act as head priest for the church for almost a century now. But that doesn't mean I don't know what you gave for us."

Xolia turned away from him, looking back to the antechamber. *Is what I got worth what I gave?* She still had her life; she was given her happy ending. Or at least, *someone's* happy ending. "I gave less than some."

"And more than others. Though it's not a competition." The priest folded his hands into the sleeves of his robe. "Do you want to share what troubles you?"

She didn't even know his name. And yet, the thought of unburdening herself to this stranger was tempting.

He must have seen the shift in her emotions because he gestured further down the hall. "We can talk in private if you wish."

"I told Mar—my. . ." She stuttered over the word *fiancé.* "I left someone in there." She gestured behind her.

"I'm sure they won't mind your absence. Today's sermon is about to start, and it's a good one."

"Shouldn't I be there to hear it?"

The priest smiled. "I believe we have more important things to discuss."

Another fork in the road. Xolia glanced behind her, back to where Marshall waited. Turning back to him would be choosing what she had been chasing for seven years. Maybe she wasn't meant to find her happiness that way, with Marshall. With a job that didn't appreciate her. She turned back to the priest. "Lead the way."

He led her deeper into the seemingly never-ending hall and past multiple doors until they turned right into a space which housed a single red door. The priest opened it and waited by the door until Xolia stepped inside. It was a spacious office with a large bookshelf full of old tomes and books that were most likely first printings and hundreds of years old. On another set of shelves, reliquaries and trinkets took up all the available space. Xolia was drawn to a chain with a moth dangling at the end of it. Rather than a body, a dagger bisected the insect, with bloodred wings unfurling around it.

It held her attention in the same way the dark-haired man had in the antechamber. There was a oneness between the two, though they were wildly different. The door clicked shut behind her and soft footsteps signaled the priest's approach. "That's the mark of the Selermine."

Xolia turned to him. "The Selermine?"

He nodded. "Sit, please, and share your troubles with me."

"Right." They didn't come in here to look at old religious artifacts, though that was preferable to spilling her guts. Still, she sat down and waited until the priest was sitting in front of the old bookcase. His hands were folded in his lap, and he remained perfectly still.

There were so many places to start, problems that she never dealt with, but she settled on the one thing that encompassed them all. "I'm not happy."

"Not happy with what?"

"With anything." Xolia furrowed her brows. "With my life. With this freedom that I fought for, and I can't seem to figure out what it means."

"And that's why you came here today?"

"Well, Marshall said it might help. Things aren't going well between us"—what a relief it was to admit that— "and we really came here for the counseling." She huffed out a laugh. "He'd be mad if he knew I was here without him."

The priest hummed. "Well, now I know why Marshall came here. But why did *you* come here?"

"I didn't want to," she admitted, unable to stop this compulsion to tell this man everything. "But I'm tired of pretending this is what I want. I was happier in the war than I am now." She stopped abruptly. She hadn't ever said that before. Not even to Adonis.

"The church may be able to help you, child. Do you really know what Rheathism is? Who Sel is to us?"

Xolia shook her head. She had gone into this without much piety or respect. Seeing someone, an elder, who had devoted four of her lifetimes to the religion made her feel guilty for her blasé attitude.

"I can teach you, because I do believe the church offers guidance to those who need it. We are Sel's dearest creation, and they wish for their creation to be happy. Maybe you need to look for happiness in other places. What was it about the war that made you happy?"

"Well." Xolia paused. "I mattered then."

"And you don't now?"

Xolia couldn't answer. It was hard enough to admit to having been happy during a time people had died to end. Everyone she knew bore unseen scars from the rebellion, it was depraved to admit she was happy then, even more so to admit to it for such selfish reasons.

The priest didn't push or pry for an answer. When it

became clear to him that she would not be offering one, he cleared his throat. "I think there is freedom in admitting what we want, and in what makes us happy."

He stood up and pulled a small book from the shelf behind him and handed it to her. "Here is a book of our history. Your history. Read it and we'll talk again, Xolia Stone."

The book was simply titled *The Rheathistic Way*. Xolia ran her thumb over the gold lettering. "Thank you."

"Until next time." He led her out of the office, and she walked on her own through the door to the service chamber, but something stayed Xolia. Instead of joining the rest of the congregation, she walked back to the painting of the enraged man. She swore fire burned and writhed in his eyes and the corded muscles of his arm bulged and moved in front of his face.

She stood there until she heard Marshall's uncertain call. "Xolia?"

"Marshall." They faced each other, surrounded by candles and glass and paintings. *Freedom is admitting to what you want.* It was time she admitted the truth. "We need to take a break."

Chapter Fifteen

The entire walk home was punctuated with Marshall's protests and begging for her to change her mind. "We're just going through a rough patch. We're going to be okay," he pleaded with her as they stepped out of the subway car and onto the dingy platform.

"Can we just wait to talk about this until we get home?" Xolia asked. She could practically feel the judgement from onlookers.

Marshall sighed. "Fine."

They spent the rest of the way home in silence. Marshall slowly slid the key into the old lock of their front door. Xolia squared her shoulders. *I'm admitting to what I want. I'm admitting to the truth.* She stepped inside.

Marshall was ready for their confrontation. He stood by the dining room table, arms crossed and eyes red. "I know things have been hard, but I didn't think they were this bad."

"You didn't think things were this bad?" she asked, her voice rising. "You don't even know where I was last weekend. I haven't worn my ring since you gave it to me. I thought we were done that night I came home. You left."

"I didn't," Marshall argued. "I was upset, but leaving you never crossed my mind. I love you."

She couldn't say it back. "Do you? Or do you just love this version of myself I've been pretending to be? I tried so hard to be happy, but I hate my life." The more she said it, the more fully realized it became, the more she saw all those small details in her memory that told her she was unhappy. All those quick fixes and lies she told herself fell apart.

"What do you mean?" The fight was gone from Marshall, all the power had left his voice.

"I was..." Xolia's ears rang, her heart beat fast. Could she actually admit her darkest feelings to Marshall? "I was happier during the war than I am now."

Marshall's jaw dropped. He stared at her; green eyes turned to an endless void. Internally, Xolia screamed at herself. *Why did I think saying that was a good idea?*

Some other part of her, one that she'd long thought had disappeared, spoke over that scared and tremulous voice. *Because you know it's true. You've known it was true since you turned down Peter's offer of a seat in the Senate. You've known it was true since the first date Marshall took you on. You knew it was true when he proposed, and you didn't care. You aren't who you say you are.*

"Shut up," Xolia whispered to herself. She was blowing her life up, and for what? Some bald guy told her to? Adonis made her feel special?

It was too much. That pit in her stomach writhed and reached out, searching for water. For blood. She couldn't control it.

"You need to leave," she told Marshall, who was staring at her with wide eyes. Concern overshadowed the hurt, but there was no fear. "Go."

"What the hell is happening to you?" he asked. "Do you need me to call Krista?"

"I need you to get the hell out," she yelled at him. The surge in her emotions caused her to lash out. Marshall was the closest being to her, and his blood called gloriously to her. She grabbed ahold of it and yanked it toward her, sending Marshall falling to his knees.

"I'm sorry, I'm sorry," she kept repeating as she tore through her mind, searching for all the old breathing exercises and practices that they'd learned as children to control their powers when their emotions went astray.

Finally, she was able to let go of Marshall, who was still on the ground, defenseless against her since she knew he still took his suppressants every day, after a bad emotional outburst at work. When he looked up at her, not only was there the hurt from her words but also betrayal. She had never used her powers on him, it was looked down upon even in the old days. Their powers had been only meant to be used during sparring sessions or real fighting, never amongst their peers.

"I'll go to Rowan's," Marshall said. He offered her no acceptances or comfort. He left her in the living room and was ready to leave within the hour. By the time Marshall left their apartment, Xolia had calmed down enough to sit on the couch. The door slammed behind him, closed with the finality of a relationship ending. *What do I do now?*

Xolia wallowed in her apartment for four days, varying from self-pity to celebratory moments for taking charge of her own life. The celebratory moments tended to be short-lived, as she realized she had no discernible plan for her life. If she accepted Peter's offer, they would have to campaign, and she wouldn't know if she had the job for months. The immediate nothingness of her life sent her into deep spirals that left her unable to get out of bed for hours at a time, no matter what time of day.

Rowan never reached out to her. Not about Marshall showing up at her apartment or Xolia going back to work. Not a text or a call. Not even an angry pounding on the door. Xolia wouldn't have abandoned Rowan like that if their situations were reversed.

By the fifth day, Xolia dragged herself out of bed and into the shower. Adonis would come to her apartment by noon to take her to Dresden Bay to watch as John Clemont attempted to rally support Risian Allied Party. She wondered if he would use the event to announce his candidacy.

Xolia had spent some of her abundant free time reading up about the presidential-era party that was full of fear-mongering ideology about variants plotting another violent uprising to claim absolute power over humans again. Many of the party's edicts would see variants under much harsher social restrictions, with them all but reduced to finding work as mercenaries and bodyguards again. She had also dedicated some time to reading through the Rheatha book, finding herself sucked into the long history of variant monarchies and the human consorts they took to keep the bloodlines flowing. Their long lifespans came at the cost of incredibly difficult conception between two variants. There were few, if any, humans who didn't carry variant blood in their genes. It was all by design of Sel, who wanted their two creations to live in harmony according to each of their unique strengths and weaknesses.

Out of the shower, Xolia braided her hair out of her face and threw on simple clothes to meet with Adonis. Black, as was becoming a preferred choice. She paced around her living room, waiting for Adonis to message her. She didn't have to choke on the guilt of interacting with him now that she had extricated herself from Marshall.

The knock at the door startled her, she was expecting a message that he was waiting in his car. She opened the door and Adonis stood in the doorway, his hands shoved into the pockets of his suit pants. He peered inside, his eyes moving slowly and missing nothing.

"Come in," she said, backing away from the door. She was acutely aware of how different their homes were. The view of the city he had compared to the dismal view of her street. She clenched her jaw. What right did he have to invade her space like this?

"Hey, Xo," he said. "Are you ready?"

His eyes roved over every inch of the apartment, and Xolia was painfully aware of the faded upholstery of the couch. The dining table and its mismatched chairs. Her own simple clothes and the simple bag that carried her toiletries.

"I am, let's go," she said, trying to herd him back through the front doorway.

Adonis *tsked* at her, holding out an arm to bar her from the door.

"Excuse me?" Xolia asked him, glaring up at him.

"I believe you owe me something," Adonis said. A small smile played on his lips.

She didn't know what he was talking about.

Before she could say as much, he spoke again. "My suit jacket."

"Oh. Right." Xolia managed a small laugh. "If you wanted to see my room that badly all you had to do was ask."

"I didn't think you'd be that easy," he quipped.

She shoved him but led him to her room all the same. As soon as she opened the door, she realized her mistake. The rest of the apartment might've been ambiguous as to its occupants, but the room was littered with the evidence of Marshall.

His side of the bed was still unmade, the pillow dented where he rested his head. His clothes were scattered around the floor, and a picture of him and Xolia sat on his nightstand.

"Shit," she whispered to herself. She stopped in the doorway, but it was too late. Adonis was already cataloging every item that didn't belong to her.

He stepped into the room, his jaw tensing slightly. Xolia winced.

"I didn't realize—"

"We're broken up," Xolia interjected.

"It doesn't look like it," Adonis said while pointedly looking at a pair of boxers on the floor.

Xolia ran her tongue along her teeth. "You saw me leave with Marshall at the gala. Surely you thought—"

"I did, but then you never mentioned him again," said Adonis, whirling around to look at her. There was something almost vulnerable in his eyes. Hurt, maybe. "I kind of thought..."

He trailed off and it was more than Xolia could bear. *Why, why, why?* She felt like an idiot. An idiot for talking to Adonis, an idiot for staying with Marshall so long. For all the premature growing up she'd done, she felt woefully immature and naïve when it came to relationships. They hadn't had any examples of romance or family in their lives. It wasn't fair, the way her feelings hadn't faded for Adonis; they were just buried under years of forgetting. As soon as he'd come back, they'd been there again, to remind her of every bad decision and lackluster kiss and touch from Marshall.

"I was with him," Xolia said, voice brittle, "but we broke up. I left him."

Adonis worked his jaw. "Why didn't you tell me?"

"Because. . ."

"Because why?"

Xolia groaned. "Because I didn't want you to know, okay? When I saw you for the first time again—I guess I just... He never made me feel like you did. And it wasn't that I didn't try to make things work, I mean, Marshall is so good at assimilating, and that's what I was supposed to want, right? But it's not and you came back—"

Adonis cut off her word vomit with a bruising kiss. It was far from the soft and tentative kisses of their teenage years. His lips were insistent against hers, and as soon as her shocked mind caught up with what was happening, she gave as good as she got. Electricity sparked through her; her brain short-circuited on the simple pleasure of a kiss. She forgot it could feel like that.

He licked along the seam of her lips, and she opened her mouth for him. He greedily deepened the kiss, wrapping a hand around the back of her neck.

A low moan escaped her, and she placed her arms around him, pulling herself closer to him. Adonis broke the kiss to look at her with darkened eyes. "Does he kiss you like this?" His mouth was back on her, biting and sucking at her neck.

"No." She whined—something she had never done for Marshall.

The ringing of the phone jolted them apart. His lips were swollen, and his hair was thoroughly mussed. She was sure she looked no better. "I'm sorry, I'm sorry," he muttered before drawing his phone from his pocket. He left the room and the soft sound of his greeting, still slightly breathless, faded the farther he walked away.

Xolia didn't know if he was sorry about the kiss or the call. She focused on her breathing, trying to calm the erratic beating of her heart. Once she had calmed down enough to form logical thoughts, she made her way to the closet and pulled out the suit jacket, still safely tucked in the far back on Xolia's side. She gently folded it over her arm and left the bedroom.

Adonis was slipping his phone back in his pocket. They made eye contact, it was heavy. The kiss had done nothing to diminish the tension between them if anything it was only denser. A tangible thing she would have to work around.

She held out the jacket to him. "I think this is yours."

"Thank you." He took it from her and slipped it free of the plastic hanger. Nonchalantly, he threw the jacket over his shoulder and held out his right arm for her. "Are you ready?"

"Yeah."

"Let's go."

Chapter Sixteen

THE DRIVE FROM XOLIA'S APARTMENT TO DRESDEN BAY was articulated with a peaceful silence. As soon as they left the city limits, Xolia's face was pressed against the window. The city-scape fell away to an open expanse of trees and fields. Xolia had never left the city limits. At least, not in her memory, as she didn't know which part of the country she had been born in.

Adonis pulled off the highway for old winding roads that led them among the dense trees. Houses were nestled among the foliage. The small towns they drove through were so unlike the concrete swathe of Atalia.

He rolled down the windows halfway, inviting in the oceanic breeze. Xolia shivered despite the heater running at full speed. It was colder here than in the city. Three hours into the drive, Adonis turned into an especially secluded stretch of road, the salt of the ocean rich in the air and the houses more hidden than the others she'd seen.

"General DuBois's estate is to the right," Adonis explained at an intersection. "My parents' house is down this way." He turned left and took an immediate right before they came to an ornate estate. The driveway turned from asphalt to gravel. The house wasn't as large as the Presidential Palace, but it had a similar gothic appearance. There were no fewer than three turrets, and the stone exterior had a weathered look with browning vines clinging to the walls.

"It's more impressive in the summer," Adonis said. He drove behind the house, where a six-car garage loomed over the landscape.

"Because it's so disappointing now," Xolia said, unable to hold back the awe from her sarcastic quip.

One of the doors was already lifted, and Adonis parked easily. Lights flickered to life the moment the car crossed the threshold of the garage. They got out and made their way to the door. "It was jarring to start living like this after the way we were brought up," Adonis said.

"Have you gotten used to it?"

Adonis opened the door for her. It revealed a large mudroom, which was kept meticulously clean. Adonis flicked on the light from behind her and shut the door. "None of it's really mine. So no matter how much I want to get used to it, I'll always feel like an outsider."

Xolia stopped. There were so many things she wanted to say, chief among them *I feel like an outsider too*. Nothing came out though, she only nodded at him and turned away.

"Anyway"—Adonis cleared his throat—"I'll show you up to your room. Your dress is waiting inside."

They walked through a plain kitchen, though it contained a staggering number of cabinets, before they walked into the main foyer of the house. The foyer was painted a rich maroon, and all the wood accents were dark. A spiral staircase led to the second floor, while hints of a second kitchen, more aesthetically aligned with the rest of the house, peeked through the back hallway.

"Welcome to the Persions's ancestral estate," Adonis said without much vigor.

"How long?"

"Since the days of the monarchy." Adonis scoffed. "The Person family rose to fame when they dressed the royal family, and many of their daughters were married off to various high-ranking variants in the court. I'm sure not all those marriages were wanted, and I used to wonder why my parents were so disgusted by me." He walked up the stairs, his hand trailing along the railing.

"Hey." Xolia ran up behind him and placed a hand over his. "You didn't ask to be born a variant."

He shook his head. "It's not that," he lamented. "I'm the proof the Persions only got what they did because they whored themselves out for generations."

His words were ice in Xolia's bones. While it was true that most humans carried variant genes due to centuries of needing the virility of humans to maintain bloodlines, she'd never thought of it like that. "Is that what you think?"

Adonis refused to meet her gaze; his head was bowed in an uncharacteristically subservient way. Xolia felt like she was looking at what she had been like for the past seven years. But she didn't have to live that way anymore, and neither did he.

"You're the proof of your family's strength," Xolia said. She moved her hand to his chin, turning him around so he would look at her. "Your family should be bowing to you. They should be thankful that their blood produced such a strong variant. They can't do what you can do, Adonis."

A small smile grew across his face. "These almost sound like anti-human sentiments." He *tsked*. "And to think they are coming from *FAR*'s future vice chancellor?"

"That's not what I meant," Xolia rushed to say. "I just meant that you're not your family. And if they can't see what you're worth, that's their problem."

His eyes softened. Something skittered down Xolia's spine. Marshall had never broken down like that. She had never been able to comfort him, to pull him out of his darkest thoughts.

"Xo, I—" He cut himself off and dragged his hands over his face. When he dropped his hands to his side again, he smiled at her. "Thank you. Let me show you your room."

XOLIA HADN'T KNOWN what to expect of the dress, but the deep crimson and soft, shiny material exceeded any expectations. The neckline ended in a deep v, with two thin straps holding the dress to her body. It was more angular than anything she'd worn in the past, but it suited her more than any of the soft sloping dresses had. She carefully pinned her hair into an updo, one of the many skills she had picked up on regarding her vanity since the end of the war. Looking nice was its own kind of power that she reveled in.

Satisfied with herself, she left the bathroom in the guest room. When she reached the wide corridor full of bedrooms, she realized she wasn't sure which one belonged to Adonis. Maybe he was in a different part of the house entirely.

She teetered on the edge of action and inaction when the sound of soft footfalls made her turn around. Adonis was in a, predictably, black suit, though the pocket square tucked into his breast pocket was the same shade of red as her dress.

"You look beautiful," he said. "You're beautiful."

The blush rose to her cheeks, unbidden, and she was grateful for the light dusting of makeup to hide her reaction to such simple words. It was like they were fifteen again, struggling to parse out feelings in the midst of so much uncertainty.

"You don't look so bad yourself," she commented, reaching out for his arm. She placed her hand in the crook of his elbow, which he covered with his hand. The touch was innocent enough, though electricity sparked through Xolia. It was an echo of their kiss and a promise of what was to come. It was a reminder of what they were both too stubborn to say but were desperate enough to show through their actions. Without Marshall to steep Xolia's feelings in shame, she could admit so much more to herself. She *wanted*. She wanted Adonis and the opportunities he provided. She liked the nice clothes, the encouragement to join Peter, the headfirst dive into Ris. Nothing was covering her eyes anymore. With Adonis she didn't have to pretend at happiness and pretend that she could be like Marshall.

"Are you ready?"

She nodded. "Do you think John Clemont has a chance?"

Adonis shrugged against her as they made their way downstairs, arm in arm. "It's hard to say since the race hasn't officially started yet. And we don't really have a precedent for what the voters want. But FAR had big goals that haven't really come to fruition yet. It's a dangerous spot for Peter to be in."

They released each other's arms, and Adonis led her back through the mudroom. He opened the passenger door of the car for Xolia, who slid into the seat. They were off to the general's home.

A GILDED WHITE manor lit up with sparkling lights, emerged from the darkened expanse of foliage. Xolia leaned forward to take in all the scenery.

"I didn't know being a general came with such a high salary."

Adonis snorted. "It does when you control more than half of the nation's military."

Xolia imagined that sort of power. The power that could start or end wars with a shift in mood, a misplaced comment. That an entire country would lay down their lives at the behest of one person, and do so with honor, boggled her mind. She didn't have that during the rebellion. Sure, Silas gave her a command of her own, but that never expanded to anything substantial. Even he only commanded a fraction of all the variants in Ris, which was a fraction of all the people in Ris.

The wheels of the sports car crunched over the gravel driveway as Adonis pulled up to stop in front of the valet. Xolia and Adonis stepped into the chill of the night. Adonis came around the car to join her after providing his keys to the attendant.

Rather than offering his arm, Adonis grabbed her hand, lacing their fingers together. The simple touch settled her. A tremor of anxiety threatened to throw her off her axis as she stared up at the palatial estate. This would be her first interaction with people who weren't beholden to FAR or Peter.

If she wanted to help Peter, to be his vice chancellor, she would need to understand the country. Not just him. She tugged at Adonis's hand, and together they climbed the stairs and stepped into the grand foyer of the house. Waitstaff greeted them, and other guests milled through the open space. *Does Peter know this is happening?*

Adonis lowered his head to her ear and started to say something when the night's host, General DuBois, stepped down the grand staircase. He nodded once at Adonis, though his eyes narrowed when they homed in on Xolia.

Xolia didn't know what to make of Adonis's apparent camaraderie with the general. DuBois had backed the Gornne Administration during the rebellion until it became clear they were losing. Peter hadn't had any military strategists as competent as DuBois, and in an ever-changing world, inside and outside of their country's borders, Peter couldn't take his chances with replacing him. At least, that was always as much as Xolia could gather.

"It's good to see you, Adonis," General DuBois said. "I am surprised to see your companion, though."

Xolia was so taken aback by being talked about rather than talked to that she couldn't muster up some pithy retort to throw in the older man's face. He did look old now, his hair entirely gray, rather than the salt and pepper it had been during the war.

"Xolia and I had the good luck to become reacquainted at FAR's annual gala last month." Adonis brushed his thumb reassuringly over her hand.

"Naturally," the general answered. He held Xolia's gaze. "It's nice to meet you under less contentious circumstances, Xolia."

"Likewise," she replied, unsure if she meant it. Hearing his daughter admit he respected her was different than them behaving civilly toward one another.

"Well, Adonis, Xolia, enjoy your evening," he dismissed the two of them, walking around them to greet the other guests.

"Is Helen here? I'd like to talk to her again," Xolia said. They turned left to enter the main ballroom, or at least that's what Xolia deduced from the music filtering in through the room.

Pressed against him, she felt Adonis tense. "I'm sure she'll turn up at some point tonight."

She stopped them before they could disappear into the crowd of notable politicians and pundits. "What's wrong? I thought you were. . .friends."

He smiled at her, but it was tight, forced. "We're more like business partners. It's nothing. Let's just enjoy the party." They entered the room. People milled about, only sparing them the occasional glance and nod.

"Why is Peter's highest-ranking general hosting a party for his political rival?" Xolia asked. That had to be a huge conflict of interest for the upcoming political season.

"It's all part of the game, Xo. Who's to say Peter doesn't know this is happening? Maybe he suggested it—keep your enemy close and all that."

"I know that." But she had forgotten it. Xolia sank into herself. What happy memories she had accrued since the end of the rebellion were all hazy with the obliviousness of willful ignorance. Even if it had made her happy in that moment, she wasn't happy now. The rich smell of food pulled her attention away from Adonis. "I'll be right back." She walked away from him, hating the way the loss of his warmth was palpable.

His dark head of hair disappeared into the crowd, an echo of their interaction at the gala. She had been so angry at his presence then, how things had changed in such a short amount of time.

Still, the promise of food dampened any sadness. Small finger foods were spread out in abundance over the table, and she helped herself to a small, sweet pastry that melted on her tongue when she took the first bite.

"Excuse me," a short, middle-aged man said to her right. He reached out to grab a pastry from right in front of Xolia.

She didn't grace him with a response, instead stepping away from him to give him space. Whether from obliviousness or malice, he stepped closer to her, shoving the entire thing into his mouth and chewing loudly.

It grated on Xolia's nerves. She exhaled loudly, hoping that was enough of a hint for him. It wasn't. Instead, he inched closer to her, and the fountain of running water behind her splashed precariously out of its pool.

Damn. It had been so long since someone had gotten under her skin for such a petty reason. However, it was more pathetic that she hadn't been able to control her external response.

The man's ice-blue eyes lit up, and his sly smile grew. "You're a variant."

She nodded, turning away to look for Adonis.

He held out a hand when she turned back to him. "John Clemont."

A slight gasp escaped her. What an unsettling coincidence. "Xolia. . .Stone." The awkwardness of her last name had never really gone away since it was given to her. It never felt right or fit her in any way.

Recognition sparked across John's face. "Your reputation

precedes you, though I am embarrassed to admit I didn't recognize you from your Presidential Palace addresses."

Despite the seemingly transparent words, there was something guarded about him. The way he had sidled up to her at the table lingered in the back of Xolia's mind.

"I didn't think anyone really watched them on PAN," she said with a forced smile. The Public Access Network always televised the yearly dinner and speeches; however, it was a far cry from having any real public notoriety.

"It pays to stay informed," John said. He wiped his hands on a napkin, which he left discarded on the table. "Could I convince you to walk with me around the grounds?"

"It's cold," she objected, but already curiosity was telling her to say yes.

John shrugged. "I'm sure you've lived through worse."

Xolia narrowed her eyes but still matched his purposeful stride through the main room. A live band played music next to the open bar which was set up on the eastern wall. Adonis was still hidden somewhere amongst the partygoers. Her chest tightened; the whole thing felt off.

The tempo of the music changed in time with her heart, the sound of the music overwhelming her senses until it quieted as they walked through a set of double doors, leading to a terrace and a walkway that was enshrined in dying vines. There was a wildness here that didn't exist behind the property lines of the Presidential Palace.

"How are things at the bureau?"

Her heart stopped. How did he know where she worked? It's not that it was a secret, but she had never publicized it before.

Before she could ask him about it, he kept talking. "That

good, huh? The bureau is a huge waste of Risian taxpayer money. FAR's spent more funding the bureau than they have on rebuilding efforts."

All those fallen buildings around her work were certainly a testament to that. However, the inside of the bureau was a mess of underfunding and overworked employees. "That's not a good comparison. Nothing has been put toward the rebuilding efforts." She didn't know if anything would ever replace the catastrophe that ate away at Atalia's eastern border.

"It should be. Don't you think the city—this country—deserves something better than devastation?"

Xolia snorted. As if she wanted the country to stay the same forever. "I don't have the power to change any of that." Even if she accepted Peter's offer, she couldn't just wave a hand and rebuild city blocks of infrastructure.

John started walking down the quiet and darkened path, giving Xolia no choice but to walk with him. "Wouldn't you like to?"

"I'm not really interested in construction," she retorted, tiring of his aimless wandering and meaningless words.

She was resolutely ignored. "I've heard whispers that Peter isn't asking Atlas to be his vice chancellor again. Early polls aren't in Peter's favor. He's too much of an optimist for this country." John stopped and stepped in front of Xolia, sending her to an awkward stop, her heels scuffing against the gravel. "Did you know this past year law enforcement agencies saw a 30 percent increase in human-and-variant violence across the country? Do you want to know how many variants died in those skirmishes?"

Xolia was sure she could figure out the answer, but shook her head no.

"None." He had no problem answering his own question. "Variants are made for violence, Xolia. Are you content sitting behind a desk and emailing someone to get another variant a Good Faith check?"

Air. She needed air but couldn't breathe. She wasn't only made for violence. *But you love violence.* No, she didn't. *You do. You never feel as powerful as when you are fighting—when you're using your powers.*

She clenched her fists to her sides. *Shut up.* That inner voice that wasn't logical, the one that spoke to her worst fears subsided, at least for now. She took a deep breath, held it for four measured seconds, and exhaled. "If I knew you were going to come out here and insult my people, I wouldn't have joined you."

"It's not meant to be an insult," he said. "I'm trying to offer you a job."

"What?"

"Endorse me. I'll be making my official announcement at the end of the month. Give me your influence, your vote. I'll make you the head general of the new Risian army—an army of variants."

"You offer me General DuBois's job in his own home?" Xolia crossed her arms. "And you'd have me be exactly who I was during the rebellion?"

"No." John leaned forward. Xolia took a step back. "You're misunderstanding me. Peter wastes the potential of variants. I'm not trying to force anyone. I want variants to embrace their true nature and fight for the country. Keep the peace in our borders and beyond. Get paid for it."

Maybe Xolia couldn't parse out her feelings about violence and her relation to it, but just one thought about Marshall or

Rowan was enough to know variants were not inherently drawn to violence. She was broken—by war, circumstance, or some misfire in her brain. His proposal was no better than her past, salary or not. Nor would it be true power.

Even though his words left her on edge, she laughed. Right in his face. "If you think any variant will vote for that, you're an idiot."

He just shrugged, an entirely relaxed gesture. "Maybe so. Lucky for me I don't need the whole population's vote, just the majority. And humans are pretty united in their regard for your people. If your little bureau hasn't had to deal with the Human Rights Initiative yet, they'll have to soon."

For the first time since she had started talking to him, fear lanced through her. She didn't know how united humans were, or much of anything about their opinions. She couldn't let him know any of that. Not here. Not now. She wanted to laugh at him again, with all the confidence of a minute ago, but nothing happened. "Humans are fractured in their beliefs. You'll never win."

"Maybe. Maybe not." John stuffed his hands into his pockets. "Fear has a way of uniting people." He left her with that, disappearing under the canopy of vines back up to the party.

Xolia shivered; her arms were covered in goosebumps, but she couldn't bring herself to go back inside. Instead, she continued further down the path, the gravel shifting under her feet. At the base of the small hill that the house was perched on, there came a fork in the path. Xolia went left to a trail that wrapped close to the house. A covered veranda with a fire came into view. Two figures were huddled closely together on one of the seats facing her.

Some forgotten instinct tugged at her. This was a private

moment, and yet, she couldn't tear herself away from watching them. Careful to slip her heels from her feet, she walked barefoot on the frigid gravel to hear the pair. Xolia stopped when she made out the dark head of hair and the beautiful blonde draped across a chaise. The woman was leaning over into the man's space. Adonis was hiding out in the cold with Helen.

Chapter Seventeen

It took every ounce of Xolia's self-control to stay hidden amongst the shadows of the path. She had thought that Helen was more of a nuisance to him, but this tete-a-tete was far too familiar.

She tried to keep her breathing even, she didn't want to betray her presence to the two of them. What she focused on instead was quietly inching forward, crouching to hide close enough to listen in on their whispered conversation.

A conversation, she found out, that was very one-sided. "I can send the twins with you if you want," came Helen's low and frustratingly melodic voice.

"Fine," came his short reply.

The twins? Xolia hadn't thought about them in years; they had been Adonis's closest friends during the rebellion. Why were they working under Helen?

"I want everything ready by the next fight," Helen continued. "Now that Peter's announced his campaign, everybody else is going to follow. Clemont is mobilizing all of his support, it's time we do the same."

Adonis leaned away from her, his silhouette nodding along at her words. *Support? For her?*

"Sel, there's so much we need to get done." Reproach crept into Helen's voice. "And you've been impossible to get ahold of. My dad has started asking questions, you know."

"He's probably asking where you are now," Adonis said. "You should go back inside."

She scoffed. "The bastard's probably getting drunk and sharing all of his favorite war stories. I can't believe you came here with Xolia."

Xolia stopped breathing at the mention of her name. She hadn't hated Helen before, but now?

"You don't own who I spend my time with," he retorted.

"I own you," she answered. "Isn't that the same thing?"

"Go back to the party, Helen."

Helen sighed but stood up. Xolia froze, unsure if she should hide or act like she had just stumbled upon them. In the end, she moved off the path and crouched amongst the lingering vines. Helen didn't look away from the path. When she was gone, Xolia turned back to Adonis.

He had stood up while she was looking away. He stuck his hand into the red flames, pulling all the tendrils up along his arm. Fire had always been a point of interest for Xolia. It was the hardest element to master. Air was everywhere. The earth was everywhere. Even water was always near. But fire was elusive. Short-lived. Adonis always wielded it with a feral grace. He was fast and deadly, a good combination, especially when confronted with the more brutal and stocky earth wielders.

Once all the flames were wrapped around Adonis, he snuffed them out, leaving him shrouded in darkness. "Dammit."

He kicked at the fire ring, the metal clang ringing out over the quiet of the night.

"Rough night?" Xolia asked, stepping up to the small patio area.

"Xo. What are you doing here?" he asked.

She scoffed. "Oh, just listening to Helen order you around for her political aspirations."

"How much did you hear?" he asked in a drawn voice.

Xolia made her way up the freezing stones until she was standing in front of him. Even in the dim lighting he looked wan, a far cry from the easy confidence he normally espoused. "What game are you playing? You tell me you want to help me. You want me to run as Peter's vice chancellor, then I come out here and Helen seems to be under the impression that you want her in office."

"It's not like that," he said.

"Then explain it," Xolia demanded. "Because all I saw was a bitch on a leash."

He shouldered past her, checking her harder than strictly necessary. "You don't know what you're talking about."

"Then tell me, Adonis."

Adonis gripped the back of an outdoor chair. "I don't know where to start."

"Find someplace."

"I made a bad deal. With Helen. I'm trying to get out of it."

Xolia pushed at his shoulder, goading him into looking at her. "So you're using me to fix your own mistakes?"

At that, Adonis sneered at her. "Please, like you haven't been using me this whole time too. The victim look isn't a good one for you, Xo."

She recoiled. "I haven't been using you."

Adonis titled his head. "You lied to me about being in a relationship, and you've jumped at every opportunity I've given you to fix your own pathetic life. We need each other."

"I'm the pathetic one?" Xolia snarled. "I didn't ask for any of this."

"Fuck, Xolia." Adonis ran a hand through his hair. "I saw you at the gala. I know you, and I know you want more than what you've been telling people. I do too. I'm a renter in my own life. All my money belongs to my parents or it's tied up in the fights. Which, surprise, are controlled by Helen. She could ruin me. You were gone, and I met her when things were really bad."

He deflated, sinking into one of the chairs. "All I wanted when the war ended was to be my own person. I mean, isn't that what we all wanted? But my parents barely tolerated me. The only variants I had any contact with were the twins. Then I met Helen."

Xolia sat down on the chair opposite his, her back rigid against the cold wicker.

"She's a variant too. Unregistered. Her father would've lost everything if President Gornne had found out. He saved her from the barracks, but that doesn't mean the general was a good father. She hates him just as much as I hate mine. It was perhaps the only thing we have in common, but at the time it seemed like enough."

"So you started the fights with her?" she asked.

Adonis shook his head. "The fights were already there. I just organized them, made things better for the variants who were fighting. Weeded out the traffickers. Helen funded everything. So all the money the fights bring in, most of it goes to her."

"Am I just a means to an end to you?" Xolia asked, her voice pitched low. It wasn't the point of his words, and she knew that, but it was really the only question that mattered to her.

Adonis looked at her, his face exasperated under a cold sliver of moonlight. "You're not *just* a means to an end."

She exhaled heavily. "What changed with Helen?"

He leaned back against the chair, closing his eyes. "It started when she took the twins from me. My closest friends. And now they'd kill me if she asked them too. Her idea of government is just as bad as Clemont's."

"I talked to him tonight," Xolia said, letting the conversation stray from him for the moment.

"How'd that go?"

She shrugged. "About as well as could be expected from someone who still harbors the same beliefs as the Gornne Administration."

"Helen would see humans subjugated. We'd be in a civil war if either of them win, surely you can see that."

Xolia arched an eyebrow at him. "I haven't accepted Peter's offer yet."

"But you want to," he argued. "We want the same things for Ris, Xo. Use me. I can help you and you can help me. I was serious about us being partners."

"Why should I listen to you?"

Adonis sat up. He leaned forward until he was in her space. His warm puffs of breath against her face reminded her of how cold she was, now numb her skin was from sitting in the empty pre-winter air. "We've always worked well together, haven't we?"

He has money. He has opportunity. He has what I want.

He trailed his nose along her jaw, eliciting a soft hiss of breath from Xolia. "Let me convince you."

Adonis tugged her chin up, and his lips met hers in a rough kiss. She reciprocated briefly before pulling away. "Not here."

He heaved in a heavy breath, the rise and fall of his chest jerky. "Let's go home, then."

"Fine."

With stiff joints, Xolia laced her fingers with Adonis's, and they crept around the manor until they reached the valet at the front. Adonis accepted the keys, and Xolia was more than happy to find warmth in the lush interior of the car, her body finally able to relax enough to focus on the adrenaline of what she and Adonis were about to do.

***

STRONG HANDS HELPED her from the car. Adonis had lurched to a stop and was out of the car and opening the door for her before she could unbuckle her seatbelt.

"Come with me," he said huskily. There was no mistaking the meaning behind his words, nor was there any hiding the thrill that ran through her when he said them.

As soon as she nodded, Adonis acted. He grabbed her hand, and they raced from the cold garage to the door. In an uncharacteristic act of clumsiness, he fumbled with the door handle before getting it open.

He tugged her through the undecorated kitchen and the foyer of the house. *Maybe we did use each other*, she mused. *But it came from necessity. Maybe it's not bad. We just aren't like other people.*

Adonis gripped her wrist, desperately, and she thought about how willing he had been, whatever she asked for, he gave. It wasn't like he had ever lied to her; she did want to accept

Peter's offer, and if it worked out for them both, so what? She needed to do something to save the floundering country.

Adonis pulled her closer to his room, his actions only betraying a hint of apprehension. It gave her a shameful sense of satisfaction, to see him so undone before her.

"Do you really want me to be vice chancellor?"

He paused and gave her a quizzical look before understanding crossed over his features. "There's no one better." He kissed her hand, the heat from his lips melting into her skin, and he opened the door to his bedroom.

She followed him into the room, and he was on top of her, groping at the straps of her dress and lavishing kisses on her neck. Teeth made contact with her skin, and after every bite was a conciliatory lapping at the stinging area with his tongue. Her hands were far from idle, and she guided his hands to the dress's side zipper.

With the dress unzipped, Adonis stepped back and watched it fall in a crimson puddle of silk around her feet. Soft moonlight filtered in through the sheer curtains of the windows, caressing her breasts in the pale light. The chill of exposed flesh, combined with her excitement, left her nipples in hardened peaks. Adonis grabbed her and lifted her. She wrapped her legs around his midsection, and their lips met again, their tongues tangled. This kiss was slower, re-tracking once well-known territory.

"Will you follow me?" she asked once they parted for breath.

"Yes."

"Will you worship me?"

"That's what I'm trying to do," he whispered furiously.

His impassioned words amped up her desire. She pushed at

his jacket but couldn't take it off while wrapped around him. She huffed, and he laughed. He walked them until they reached the bed, gently depositing her on the cool cotton sheets.

With her safely ensconced on the mattress, Adonis took the time to divest himself of his clothes. First was the jacket, then the tie and shirt. He unbuckled his belt and stripped himself of everything except his boxers.

Anticipation spurred Xolia into action. As beautiful as he was in the moonlight, standing over her with all hard planes of muscle and smooth skin, she wanted more. She reached up, grabbing at him and pulling him on top of her. He wrapped her up in his arms, caging her body with his.

Adonis peppered kisses over her body. Her jawbone, her neck, her shoulders. His breath came out in warm puffs over her breasts, and in one swift motion, he sucked on her right nipple.

She gasped, arching her body closer to him. "Adonis," she whined. He moaned and pressed down onto her; the length of his erection only added to the gaping void of want spilling from her.

She gave in. "You were right, you know."

"Occasionally." Adonis switched to the other nipple, giving it a quick bite. "What was I right about?" He swirled his tongue around, her skin left feeling hot and cool, and then repeated. She moaned, a pathetic, submissive mewling that drove her mad. She was losing control, and it was thrilling and debasing all at once. She fisted both hands into his hair, pushing him down her body, needing him to supplicate to her.

"I am using you," she ground out.

Adonis leaned back on his knees, pulling her panties down her legs. "Our childhoods were fucked up, Xolia. What do any of us know about healthy relationships?"

So rarely did he call her by her full name; it did a funny thing to her heart. The sincerity of his voice sobered her partially of the lust-driven madness. "But I went to therapy. I'm not supposed to be broken anymore. I thought I was past this."

He eased a finger into her with a sigh. "You're not broken. I think you spent too long convincing yourself that there was only one way to be free of the past. Only one way to be happy."

His words and ministrations wracked her body and soul. All she could manage in response was a hitch in her breath.

"If that version of freedom wasn't making you happy, maybe you should change your definition of freedom." With his free hand, he freed his cock from the confines of his boxers.

"But—"

He slid into her with one smooth thrust. "Xolia. Stop talking. Please." His voice was strained.

She nodded in response. They moved in unison, setting a steady pace. Xolia canted her hips to meet his. He kissed her thoroughly. The sounds of smacking skin filled the air.

Sweat pooled on their skin, and Adonis wrapped his arms around Xolia and rolled them over so Xolia was on top. She took the control he so willingly offered and relished the way all of his attention was on her.

He gripped her hips, his eyes tracking each bounce of her breasts. Fire coursed through her. This was what she needed.

Adonis used his left hand to rub small circles against her clit, bringing a new wave of arousal from Xolia. She shuddered against him, driving him to pump wildly into her. It was frenzied, the culmination of all the chaos of their reunion since the gala—the lies and truths between them.

She broke against him, his name falling from her lips. Adonis followed suit, emptying himself into her.

They remained connected while they gathered their breaths and composure. Once the chill of the room crept over her again, she slid off Adonis and collapsed onto the bed. He wrapped her up in his arms, head resting on her chest. Xolia threaded her fingers through his hair.

"I'm going to do it."

"Do what?"

"Take the job. I want to help Peter, and..." Xolia shifted closer to Adonis, unsure of how to finish the sentence.

"And?" he prompted.

"And I miss it," she said. "Feeling powerful. Like my life mattered."

Adonis shifted to his side, resting on an elbow. "Then take it. I'll help you."

"I'll help you, too."

He smiled, leaving Xolia to wonder about the nature of their partnership. It was better than an apology or an empty promise that they wouldn't use each other anymore. They would. They would have to if they wanted to accomplish anything. It was a security that Xolia hadn't felt in all the years since the rebellion. Neither Marshall, Rowan, nor Krista had any stakes in Xolia's life other than their feelings. Or court mandates.

Mutually assured ascension and destruction was so much better. It mattered more. Xolia hummed, seeking warmth under the covers. Adonis pulled the comforter over them, and she rested her head against his chest until sleep pulled her in.

Chapter Eighteen

Xolia awoke in the dead of night. Even the light of the moon had waned since she'd fallen asleep. Adonis had an arm slung over his face and the other around her midsection. Carefully, she moved his arm and left the cover of the sheets. She shivered, and she immediately searched the dark and drafty room for clothes of any sort. She found his closet, which was sparsely stocked but she was able to find a soft T-shirt that she slipped into. The door next to the closet was a bathroom, which she went to next. Feeling slightly refreshed, but still groggy, she padded out of his room to the guest room she had used earlier.

Her phone rested on the nightstand, plugged in and charging. Xolia pulled it from the charger and went through the notifications. Marshall had called and texted her, asking if they could talk and where she was. He told her how much she hurt him, and that she should've told him sooner that there was no hope for their relationship. While they would need to talk, he wasn't quite ready to see her again.

She didn't bother responding to him and ignored hollowness in her chest and instead went to Peter's contact information. *I accept,* was all she typed out and sent to him. He had been so secretive about talking to her that she didn't want to send any potentially damning information, in any form, that could be traced.

Xolia sighed, thinking about what life as the vice chancellor of Ris would look like. She would oversee the small Senate, ruling over the decisions they couldn't come to an agreement on. Peter would consult her over any choice he had to make. The possibilities made her giddy. It would be better than being a lieutenant in the war. It would be exponentially better than wasting her life away in the decrepit office building that housed the Bureau. Rowan would have no control over her.

Xolia found herself smiling at her phone screen like an idiot. Peter hadn't even responded yet. They still had an entire campaign to run. There was an election to win, but just the prospect of it was enough to fill her with a lightness she hadn't felt in years. Domesticity and anonymity weren't for her, and it was time to stop pretending they were.

What will Atlas do when he finds out? Does he already know? Why else would he try to kill her? It would explain why he and Peter were so tense the night of the gala, Xolia reasoned. She would have to keep her guard up. Although he had backed off for now, he was too tenacious not to try anything again. *If that's what his plan is.*

She took her phone and went back to Adonis's room. He hadn't moved from his sprawl on the left side of the bed. As quietly as she could, Xolia slipped back under the covers. Adonis molded himself around her like it was second nature, instinct. Warm skin met cold skin, and he stirred. "You're freezing."

"This house is freezing," she huffed in response.

He hummed. "This house is old. The central heating isn't reliable."

"Well, that's hardly my fault," she grumbled.

Adonis slowly blinked his eyes open. "Do you want it to be warmer?"

Xolia nodded.

He stretched out and slowly full consciousness filtered back into him. Xolia couldn't tear her eyes away from him. She couldn't look away as his muscles shifted when he rolled his shoulders. "I wanted to show you something anyway, now is as good a time as any." He pulled the covers away from his body.

"I think I've seen it," Xolia said with a pointed stare below his abdomen.

"Not that," he said, gently pushing her back against the mattress. "Something else." He leaned over the side of the bed, pulled his boxers back on, and went to the cold fireplace on the eastern wall. Though logs were already inside it, Adonis grabbed a fresh one from the pile beside the fireplace and placed it strategically on the other logs. His shoulders rose and fell with a deep breath.

Xolia tilted her head to the side, wondering what he could possibly have to show her in the dominating darkness of the room with only the briefest echoes of starlight to illuminate him. Then flames sparked to life across his hand.

Xolia gasped. He hadn't grabbed a lighter, or anything, that she had seen. The flames steadily grew until they covered his entire hand, and he thrust his burning hand into the fireplace. After a few seconds the licks of flame ate away at the dry logs, crackling and lighting up the room.

"That's impossible," she breathed out. Variants could only control their element, not create it from nothing.

Adonis took his hand from the flame, letting the lingering flames around his hand die out. He smiled at her, something so proud and boyish that Xolia smiled back at him. "Who says it's impossible?"

"Everyone." Warmth spread into the room as Adonis crawled back into bed with her. She grabbed at his hand, turning it over to investigate. "But you did it."

All sleepiness was forgotten in favor of the starved-for-information student who lived hidden in Xolia. It was the same part of her that had pushed herself to her limits in the barracks, repeating every offensive and defensive stance with her powers until she perfected them. The same tenacious pupil that had committed to passing the secondary schooling FAR had instituted for variants who had only achieved primary schooling before the rebellion. This was perhaps the most interesting thing she had seen since her childhood. This was unprecedented.

"How?"

He smiled again, but this time his features were pulled tight at the edges. *Exhaustion.* "It's really fucking hard. I haven't been able to hold onto it much longer than that, but I read about it in some old Rheathian texts. Back from the days of the monarchy. I don't know how to explain it, I only figured it out through trial and error."

"Rheathian archives? Like the religion?"

Adonis nodded, falling back against his pillow. "There was a brief stint when my parents and I thought to mend our relationship, and as Rheathism is supposed to be the religion for humans and variants, we started going."

Xolia got back under the covers, waiting for him to finish talking. Her mind raced with her interactions with the Rheathistic priest. Did he know that was possible? What secrets did the church have hiding away in their ancient building?

"Of course once they learned about the creation story, they decided it wasn't for them." Adonis turned to face her, gently pushing a loose lock of Xolia's hair behind her ear. "I don't really know if I believe it, but there is some amount of peace in the church that I can't find anywhere else. And after I donated a sizable sum to help with the construction of a new food pantry for them, they were more than happy to let me look at their archives."

"But anything from the monarchy must be thousands of years old."

He nodded. "Many of the priests are trying to digitize everything so their record keeping is meticulous. Everything is kept in climate-controlled rooms,and you have to wear gloves to even touch the parchment."

"How did you know what to look for?" Xolia asked. Surely, if this was open information, it would have spread like wildfire amongst variants. "I mean, why would the church keep this a secret?"

"I didn't, I was just curious and taking every perk they offered me. And"—he shrugged—"I like their creation story. I was looking for more about it. The lines about variants creating their element were brief. Just two."

"That's incredible," she said, because it really was. Not only had he stumbled onto one of the most important and forgotten secrets of variants in a millennium, but he had taught himself. "Will you teach me?"

"Of course." He closed his eyes. "I just can't help but to wonder how much of ourselves we don't know. How much did we lose when the monarchy ended?" His speech was slower, his breathing evening out. But there was no way Xolia could fall asleep. Not on the heels of such a discovery. Could she learn to create water from nothing? How much more could they do with control like that? What were variants capable of that humans had so ruthlessly taken from them when they rebelled against the monarchy? She already worried she had lost so much of herself following the rebellion; now she had to worry she didn't size up to the variants of old.

Xolia thought back to the painting of the variants in the antechamber of the church. Did they create their weapons from nothing? She thought about the angry-looking one, holding his sword aloft and hate burning in his eyes. In that moment, she could understand the depth of that hate. Why had she been reduced to this helpless shell of a being that was removed from what slivers of culture she had? How was it fair that she had been blessed with her abilities, twice blessed at that, and at every turn, she had been shunned or told to hide that part of herself? She had endured forced military service, a war, and faltering peace, and for what?

She sighed. Adonis would teach her, once she could master that she'd be unstoppable. Even Atlas would cower before her. Then he could not deny her superiority over him. Nothing would stand in her way, not with Peter and Adonis at her side. At some point the crackling of the fire and the comforting pressure of Adonis's body next to hers lulled her back to sleep, dreaming of unprecedented power springing from her fingertips.

XOLIA AND ADONIS ate a comfortable breakfast in the nice kitchen. The kitchen closer to the garage door was for staff to use when making food for parties and events that his parents hosted, Adonis explained. She marveled at the impracticality of it. That people had enough to hide away the help. Of course, it was similar to how she had been reduced to a dimorphous shadow before the rebellion. Back in the days of shadowing politicians and business tycoons to protect them from any real or imagined threats lurking in the streets of the city.

Would her life be like his parents' if Peter was re-elected? Surely her time would be of too much value to be wasted on menial domestic labor. Everyone had a role to play, and there was no shame in supporting the lead players. Those roles weren't for her, she would be best used at the top. There was no shame in admitting to that either.

They hadn't discussed the previous night. Not what they had done nor Adonis's revelation. Even with their proximity in his car as they sped back to the city, they remained quiet. Xolia couldn't stop turning it over in her mind, the possibilities that Rheathism had opened. The priest had been so certain they would meet again, and now Xolia believed that too.

"What's the creation story?" she asked, turning away from the window to face Adonis. He stared ahead at the road, eyes only looking at her for a brief lingering moment.

"Sel was expelled from the heavens after arguing with their siblings. There were no stewards for the animals. The land. The planet was in chaos. While their siblings delighted in watching the untamed wildness from up above, Sel couldn't bear it. They value control and order most of all. So they made humans in secret. While their siblings slept, Sel fashioned humans from earth and different parts of animals, molding all the pieces together until humans existed. Sel offered a piece of themselves to give the humans sentience. Weary of their immortal life, Sel gifted humans a brief life span but endless curiosity." Adonis looked at her again. "You've not heard this before?"

She shook her head. "I've gone to the church once. Marshall —" She cut herself off at the mention of his name, but Adonis didn't appear perturbed, so she continued, "Marshall thought they could counsel our failing relationship or something. I talked with one of the priests, but that was it. So no, I haven't heard it before. Continue with the history lesson."

He readjusted his grip on the wheel. "Well, it might not be history. Just a story."

Xolia scoffed. "You go to church but have no faith?"

"It's hard to come by," he said, shrugging. "Anyway, Sel hid them amongst the trees and caves. For a time, they taught the small population how to shepherd over the animals and how to tend to the earth in an orderly fashion, all set in cadence with the seasons. Sel returned to the heavens, satisfied with the growing order of the land. Humans celebrated Sel, and they flourished. Their population grew until they could no longer hide. The wild spaces disappeared, and the curiosity in humans brought them running out of hiding, seeking new places to settle. Naturally, Sel's siblings found out they were the culprit. They expelled them down to Ris, where they would be forced to live amongst their own creation.

"For a time, Sel relished the worship and bounty laid at their feet. But the years dragged on. Humans grew. Prospered. Surpassed the simple teachings of Sel. They grew haughty. Unappreciative. The offerings stopped."

"I imagine it made Sel unhappy," Xolia said. As much as she was loath to admit it, she understood Sel. Everyone had deferred to her during the war. She'd had Silas's influence, and thus, everyone had fallen in line around her. Other than Atlas, there'd been no pushback. No questions. No sooner had the war ended than everyone had started to question Xolia. No one listened to her, they all just wanted to make her into something else. They wanted to tell her what to do. That made her unhappy.

Adonis nodded. "The humans owed everything to them. Sel made up their mind to destroy humanity. But they were their own creation. How could they? Sel was not so barbaric as that, and above all, they believe in order. Sel ran back to the cover of the caves, snatching humans and animals and making all sorts of sacrifices to the heavens to lure one of their siblings down to Ris. Eventually, one answered. Lamina. Perhaps the only sibling sympathetic to Sel. Lamina came down to Sel's cave under the cover of a thunderstorm."

Unease prickled along Xolia's scalp. Unconsciously, she found herself leaning closer to Adonis.

"You can't kill a god. They are without beginning, without ending. Somehow, Sel managed it. They killed Lamina and mixed their godly remains in with the human and the animal and the earth until the first of the variants were created. Created in likeness to humans but, of course, longer lived, harder to hurt or kill. Quick to heal. In control of the elements. Humans were made to be stewards of the land and animals. Variants were created to be stewards of humanity."

"What happened to Sel?"

Adonis gave her a rueful smile. "Not even a god can kill another god without consequences. Sel's corporeal body was destroyed, melted from the inside out. In their last moments of consciousness, they latched onto a variant who was the steward over all. He became known as the Selermine, the direct mouthpiece of Sel."

"The priest mentioned the Selermine."

Adonis nodded. "The order is extremely tight-lipped about them. If their history is to be believed, the first Selermine was the first king of Ris. While there was not consistently a Selermine, if one appeared while another king was on the throne, the king was immediately removed for the Selermine."

"And there hasn't been one since the last king," Xolia said.

"Rheatha's popularity dwindled once humans took over," Adonis said.

Xolia chewed on her bottom lip. "Only the church can find the Selermine?"

He nodded. "Do you think it's fate or circumstance that finds them, Xo?"

"Faith is hard to come by."

"Exactly."

A sigh escaped Xolia. She leaned her head back against the headrest. "I guess I can see why humans haven't declared Rheathism the official religion of the country."

"I don't know. From what I can tell, they have a dedicated human congregation." Adonis tapped his fingers on the steering wheel. "I think there's almost something freeing in their beliefs. If you don't have to be in control of yourself, you don't have to worry. Someone else can worry."

"Unless you're the Selermine."

"But I'm not," he said. "Besides, even the Selermine is merely the mouthpiece of Sel."

Xolia hummed. She couldn't relate to Adonis's sentiments, but she supposed she could understand them. "And you don't know how they choose, or find, the Selermine?"

"Those secrets are kept under lock and key. I wasn't allowed to read any texts about the process," he said. Adonis turned off the highway, taking them back to familiar city streets. It comforted Xolia to be back amongst the crowds and noises that had been so conspicuously absent from Dresden Bay.

"Religion doesn't have as much sway over people anymore. But surely, if the Rheathian church, the oldest remaining institution in the country, crowned a Selermine, variants would be likely to follow them," Xolia mused. She tried to remember every word the priest had spoken to her, turning over his turns of phrase for any hidden meanings.

"That's true," Adonis said.

Xolia's thoughts ran wild with possibilities. Hopes and fantasies. Hadn't the priest told her they'd meet again? What if he meant something more by it? What if he wanted her to be something more? What if, what if?

"Do you think. . ." Xolia paused. What if this was her purpose? She wasn't religious, but she could be. She could listen to Sel, and she could direct the country. Who else wanted a fair and equal Ris more than her or Peter? "How do you think they find them?"

Adonis shook his head, swerving out of his way to avoid hitting an elderly woman who was crossing the street. "I'm not sure."

"I think we should figure it out."

"Why?"

Xolia bit the inside of her cheek. "If FAR really is crumbling, and John Clemont is able to unite humans, we won't stand a chance. I need to do everything I can to get Peter elected."

"What are you saying?" Adonis whipped his head to look at

her, and Xolia got the impression that he knew exactly what she was implying.

"What if it's me?"

Adonis gaped at her. "Xolia. I don't think it's real." He turned back to the steering wheel, his brows furrowed. "Though it doesn't matter, I suppose, whether it's real or not. Not if people believe it is. Maybe I could make another donation to the church."

Xolia's heart sank. It probably wasn't real. What had gods ever done for anyone, anyway? But she wanted it to be real. She wanted to be special, truly special, like she had once believed herself to be. She wanted to be that girl again, the one who was unstoppable. "It's a plan."

"Good. This is good," Adonis said. He pulled up in front of Xolia's building, but rather than idling, he put the car into park. "If you want to come back to my apartment, you can."

Xolia attempted a small smile. "Thank you, Adonis." *Do you really believe in me? Are we just using each other, or is this something more?* "But there are some things I need to do here. Conversations I need to finish."

Adonis's jaw ticked. "You told me you broke up with him."

"I did." Xolia winced. Had she really? "But I just need to handle this first."

"If we're going to be. . ."—Adonis moved his mouth, but couldn't seem to settle on the right word—"partners, then we need to trust each other."

"I do," Xolia said. *Do I?* She locked eyes with him. "Do you trust me, Adonis?"

A beat passed.

He nodded. *Do you?* Because she could, and because she wanted to, she kissed him. He responded immediately, wrapping his hand around the back of her neck, pulling them even closer together. At the very least, she could trust in this. When he ended the kiss, he rested his forehead against hers. "Tell me what Peter says."

"I will."

"Can I take you to dinner tomorrow?"

"Yes."

"Good."

With a final burning kiss, Xolia gathered up her bag and left the warm car. She waved back at Adonis, though his windows were too tinted to see if he returned the gesture, and she walked inside her building. Even though it had scarcely been twenty-four hours since she had been there last, she had the distinct feeling that she no longer belonged. The third-floor button didn't work, forcing her to leave the elevator and go to the drafty stairwell.

Her dread only grew the closer she got to her door. Was Marshall home? Would they try to talk? Finally, the brass 3H on her door came into view. She shoved her hand into her pocket and withdrew her keys. All she had to do was unlock the door. *Do it,* she begged herself, but her arms didn't want to cooperate.

Kicking at the door, she forced her limbs to listen to her, and she jammed the key into the lock. It turned, and in one swift movement, she opened the door. No Marshall. Everything looked the same as it had when she left. Nothing was out of place or touched. It was like stepping back in time.

Carefully, Xolia closed and locked the door behind her. Silence permeated the air, oppressive and heavy over her. "Hello?" she called out, mostly to break the quiet of the place.

No one answered. Xolia let out a sigh of relief, and she dropped her bag onto the kitchen counter. She took her phone from her pocket to check if Peter had messaged her. He had. Just once. Him asking to meet at the Presidential Palace the following day for lunch. *Good.* Xolia grabbed a glass from a cabinet and was about to turn on the faucet when the door handle turned.

Chapter Nineteen

Xolia froze. Her hand was still on the faucet handle when Rowan's voice filtered through the opening door. "Don't worry about it," she said. "I'll be in and out."

Rowan had her phone up to her ear in one hand and a suitcase in the other. As soon as Rowan caught sight of Xolia, her face dropped into an impassive mask. "I'll call you back." She shoved her phone into her pocket and dropped the suitcase. "What are you doing here?"

Xolia, who had been afraid and then angry that she'd been afraid, was now just angry. "I live here," she said, jaw ticking. "What are you doing here?"

"Picking up clothes so that the other person who lives here doesn't have to run into you," Rowan said scathingly.

"How mature of him." She didn't want to be angry. She had felt bad when she hurt him, but everything about Marshall and Rowan just seemed so trivial. Xolia was about to be thrust into the limelight of politics and take her seat next to Peter, and here she, was playing at avoiding an ex? It was beneath her and pathetic for all of them.

"You hurt him," Rowan said.

"I told him to leave," Xolia defended. "It's not my fault he didn't listen."

Rowan looked at her with pure unbridled derision. There was no other word for it. Her lips were curled up and her eyes were hard. "You are supposed to be in control of yourself."

"I would've been if I hadn't been on suppressants for seven years," Xolia shot back.

"No one told you to stop taking them. It's a privilege to no longer be tested, not the okay to do whatever the hell you want."

Xolia slammed her empty cup down on the table. "Right. Just get what you need and get out of here."

Rowan pushed past the fallen suitcase until she stood in the kitchen, facing down Xolia, righteous anger curling around her. "Let me make something very clear to you—you don't get to tell me what to do anymore."

Oh, how Xolia wanted to yell at her, wanted to reveal that should FAR win the re-election Xolia very much *would* get to tell Rowan what to do, wanted to mock her for being so defensive over a situation she knew nothing about, but it didn't matter. Rowan didn't matter. Not anymore. If they ever had been friends, it had been conditional. Neither met those conditions any longer. "Whatever. Tell Marshall that he'll need to stop hiding behind you so we can break the lease."

"He's not hiding. I wouldn't talk to you anymore either. He was trying to make things work, Xolia. We were all just trying to help you."

Godsdammit. Why were they both so insistent on getting under Xolia's skin? Xolia chewed the inside of her cheek. It was clear that Rowan had her mind made up. Power coursed through Xolia. She was better than these people and their trite dreams and meaningless lives.

Xolia reached out and caught onto the thread of Rowan's bloodstream. She would give her and Marshall something to commiserate about together. She yanked on it, pulling Rowan to the ground. Her nose hit the linoleum flooring harder than Xolia had intended, and a wretched crack filled the air. *Shit.* "Let *me* make something clear, Rowan. I'm not interested in your help. I'm not interested in anything you have to offer. So get Marshall's shit and get out of here." She released Rowan, who curled into the fetal position and gripped her nose.

"Sel, what did you do?" Rowan groaned, her voice strained and partially muffled by her hands.

"Move," Xolia snapped.

A broken nose shouldn't have taken long to heal for a variant free of suppressants, but as the seconds dragged on, and Rowan remained prostrate on the floor with no visible signs of healing, it dawned on Xolia that Rowan still took her suppressants. Eventually, Rowan looked up at Xolia, her eyes were bloodshot and streaked with hate. Xolia clenched her jaw and mirrored the disdain. "Why are you still taking suppressants?"

Rowan struggled to get back up to her feet, one hand still clenched around her nose. Already, the skin under her eyes was darkening into a deep purple. "It's my choice to take them."

"You wouldn't be in this position if you didn't."

"It's not your choice to make, Xolia." Rowan winced. "Get out of my way."

Xolia stepped to the side, tracking each shallow breath Rowan made as she picked up the suitcase and walked over to the cramped bedroom. Because she could, she followed Rowan. She offered no help as Rowan only used one hand to open drawers and throw clothes haphazardly into the quickly filling case. Once it was full, Rowan had to let go of her nose, red and sticky with blood, to shut the thing. Xolia backed out of the bedroom doorway, but not so far that she could avoid Rowan shoulder-checking her on her way out.

Rowan left without a word, dropping the suitcase long enough to slam the door shut behind her. Xolia walked over to the front door and pressed her hand against the painted wood grain. *I shouldn't have done that.* She dropped her head against the door, castigating herself for resorting to violence so quickly.

She clenched her jaw. For the first time that day, she was glad to be alone. Adonis couldn't see her like this; she didn't even want to know what he would think about the situation. Xolia slid down to the floor, dropping her head into her hands, hiding away from the day. One moment she had been so powerless and a moment later, the most powerful person in the room. It wasn't fair that no other feeling came close to the euphoric rush of bending people to her will. *Is that how you will handle all your opposition as vice chancellor?* Xolia rocked back and forth. *I don't want this. I don't want to feel this way.*

That other voice whispered in her mind. *You do want to feel this way. That's why you keep doing these things. It's who you are.*

"No, it's not," Xolia said. She repeated it to herself, aloud, over and over again until all the voices in her head quieted down. Trying to maintain her fractured sense of calm, Xolia got up and went to her bedroom, pulled out pajamas, and shed her sweats and sweatshirt to get into the shower.

As the hot water burned trails into her skin, Xolia tried to work out her thoughts. Something about Rowan and Marshall made her forget everything except violence. It was hardly her fault that she pushed back when provoked. It was just like the fights; if she didn't defend herself, she would be hit. All of her actions were simply self-defense.

Satisfied with her self-justifications, she crawled into bed. The sheets were freezing, and the bed swallowed her up whole, her wet hair clinging to the sides of her neck and face. She was about to give up on sleep entirely when, finally, she was able to relax enough to slip away.

Xolia stared at herself in the mirror. There were no imperfections or blemishes on her skin, and her hair was pulled back and out of her face. Dressed in a soft sheath dress, she felt mostly appropriate for a meeting with the chancellor of the country.

She had debated asking Adonis for something that was suitable to wear, but their relationship felt fragile to her despite their declarations of trust. Slightly dissatisfied, but unable to do anything more to herself, she got up and slipped into a pair of shoes. The car would be at her apartment any minute to chauffeur her to the Presidential Palace.

Her phone chimed with a notification from the driver, and Xolia made her way down through the three flights of stairs and the lobby, the driver greeted her and opened the back passenger door for her.

Xolia tried to relax against the leather seats. She was excited to finally work with Peter, but the whole scene with Rowan still left her rattled. Underneath that, she missed Krista. So much of her life had changed, and without the constant guiding hand of

Krista, Xolia was unmoored, floating from one person to the next. One opportunity to the next.

Xolia had had all the confidence in the world when she told Adonis she would advocate for herself to be the next Selermine, but they didn't know what it would entail. What if the gods were actually real and they sensed her disbelief? What if the priests wouldn't entertain the idea of buying the title of Selermine? It was something she couldn't afford to mess up.

Just focus on lunch. Just lunch. She could do lunch. The drive to the Presidential Palace, while it probably took the same amount of time as always, felt like it was over in a minute. All too soon, they were ushered in through the iron gates, and the driver wound his way to the back of the building to Peter's private entrance.

Lana, dressed in another impeccable navy pantsuit, waited just outside with a cheery smile. "Ms. Stone," she said as soon as Xolia stepped down from the SUV. "Welcome. The chancellor is excited to have lunch with you, please come with me."

"Lead the way," Xolia said, stepping right behind Lana. They walked through the hallways of paintings and along the plush carpeting of the Presidential Palace.

Rather than going into the parlor on the right, they walked deeper into the wing than Xolia had ever gone, and Lana led her into an ornate dining room. The carpet gave way to rich and freshly lacquered wood flooring. A dining table set for eight took up the majority of the room, with Peter already seated at the head.

"Xolia," he exclaimed, standing up to greet her. His movements were just as stiff as when they had met in the parlor, and Xolia rushed past Lana to meet him. Out of the corner of her eye, Xolia could see even cheerful Lana had adopted a more somber expression, her mouth set in a grim line.

Worry lanced through Xolia as she hugged Peter. He felt ephemeral next to her, like she might look away and he'd disappear. "Please, sit. The food will be brought out shortly."

Peter sat back down, and he gestured to the other head of the table. Xolia was hesitant to sit so far from him, but she made her way with lead feet to the other end of the table and sat down in the high-back chair.

"Thank you for bringing her to me, Lana," Peter said.

"It's my pleasure, Chancellor," Lana said, smiling. This time it was forced, brittle. "Enjoy your lunch." She left and it was just Xolia and Peter. Unbidden tears threatened to spill down Xolia's face. What a far cry this was from their first actual meeting seven years ago. He had been surrounded by guards and she had been prepared to kill him. Now, she was prepared to do anything to save him. To keep him in power.

"Xolia, I can't tell you how relieved I was to wake up to your message the other day," he said. "I'm sure it wasn't an easy decision. I know how badly you wanted to be done with all this."

"All of this would continue whether I did something or not," Xolia said. "I wouldn't be upholding what I fought for if I ignored it now."

Peter smiled at her, and it felt like understanding. Despite their rocky start, he had never given up on her. He'd visited her when she had been in solitary confinement. It was he who had stopped the fledgling *FAR* from charging her with treason. Peter had always seen the best in her, even when Xolia was sure there was nothing 'best' in her.

"As you know, all of my policies aim to put variants and humans on equal footing. We will review specific laws and propositions I'm working on so we can present a united front. Once word breaks that you're running as my VC, it's going to be an endless media cycle."

"I understand," Xolia said. "I'm ready." If she could push Rowan out of her mind, Xolia would be ready. She could be fighting again, albeit in a different way than she was used to, and this time, everyone would be looking to her. She wouldn't have to work in the shadows. It was thrilling to think about.

A door behind Xolia opened, and staff brought out an array of plates and set them down on the table. They remained long enough to put portions on both Peter's and Xolia's plates, which was mildly discomfiting, and then left back through the door. "We employ some of the best chefs in all of Ris," Peter said, wasting no time in digging into his food, though his bites were small and he took double the normal amount of time to chew.

He coughed, sending his whole body into a shaking mess. Xolia, having little experience with the ailments of humans, was rooted to her seat watching in unrestrained fear. Once the fit finally subsided, he took a small sip of water and went back to his food.

"Are you sick, Peter?" she asked, already anticipating, and dreading, the answer.

Peter swallowed. He nodded. Xolia's stomach dropped. "Cancer," Peter said. "And old age."

An errant tear rolled down her cheek. "Will you get better?"

She didn't know much, but she had heard the word cancer tossed around in the past. It was never good, especially not at his age. Why did humans have to die so young?

Peter shrugged. It was the worst thing she had ever seen. "All I can do is have faith that I will."

Faith. How could he rely on something so fickle, something

so easily manipulated by circumstance and money? "If you're sick, why aren't you keeping Atlas as your VC?"

"I could die any day, Xolia. I hope I don't. There's still so much that has to be done before Ris sees true peace and equity among its citizens." Peter templed his fingers. "I want to hope for the best, but I do have to be realistic. Atlas and I don't see eye to eye on much of anything these days. But I've always seen myself in you, child. If I die, the vice chancellor takes over. You're the only one I trust."

Xolia's mouth dropped open. "Surely there are others with more experience."

"Sure, there are. But they don't have your heart. You care about your people. You were Silas's staunchest defender. Ris needs someone who believes in her. Someone who can make Ris something to believe in."

His words warmed her though the circumstances in which he told her them still left the tips of her fingers numb. Would Rowan agree with Peter's words? Probably not. But that had just been one mistake. The country was still fractured. It would take a strong arm to bring order and justice. Xolia could be that, even if it wouldn't be pretty. Rowan didn't understand that. That wasn't Xolia's fault.

"I know it's a lot to take in," Peter said. "But I'm not planning on dying anytime soon. I won't leave you alone in this."

What else could Xolia do but trust him? She nodded and tried to relax enough to eat. "What do we do?"

Peter smiled at her. "As soon as we announce you as my running mate, I want you to move into the Presidential Palace. You'll need twenty-four-seven security, being here will be the safest place for you."

Xolia furrowed her brows. "I won't be able to leave?"

"Of course you will," Peter said. "You'll just need protection."

"I am capable of taking care of myself."

"I know you are, but as a figurehead of order and justice, you won't be able to use your powers. Atlas always has security with him, we can't be seen as both the mouth and the arm of justice."

But Atlas goes anywhere he wants. I've never seen him with security. Xolia choked down a bite as she processed everything else Peter was saying. It made sense, sure, but it wasn't fair. Still, it wouldn't do to let Peter down again. He needed to trust her more than he trusted Atlas. "I understand."

"Good," Peter said. "We also must find you a chief of staff to help coordinate your schedule and, later, hire the rest of a staff. I'd like you to come here weekly for lunch so we can review policy. Everyone will be asking you questions; we need to make sure we are united in our answers." Peter broke off to have another concerning coughing fit.

Xolia clenched the fork in her hand, her glass of water vibrating against the crystal. He calmed down, but his features were drawn tight and all the color was gone from his face. "I'm sorry, my dear, but I think I need to rest now. I'll have Lana show you out."

He tapped against his phone, and a minute later, Lana popped in through the door, her smile back to its cheery, chipper curve.

"Goodbye, Peter," Xolia stuttered out before she was ushered from the room, Peter back to coughing.

Once the door was closed, Lana gave her a sympathetic, if awkward, pat on the back. "Some days are better than others, but we're optimistic."

"Right," Xolia said absentmindedly. Her mind was swimming with everything she had just witnessed and heard. If Peter got his way, she had just under a month until her sense of freedom, of anonymity, disappeared completely. Lana talked aimlessly about the different hallways and rooms they walked past. *Because I'm going to live here soon.* It was a strange thought.

They were almost back to the main hallway when Atlas walked by. His head downturned as he focused on a stack of papers in his hands. He was dressed in a slate-gray suit with a starched white shirt and burgundy tie. The perfect image of an important politician.

"Xolia," he said in surprise when he looked up.

Xolia blanched. They hadn't seen each other since the fight. The night that Atlas tried to have her killed. He stood before her, his face pleasantly neutral like he'd just run into an old friend.

"We have to get Ms. Stone home, Vice Chancellor Campion," Lana said.

"Of course." Atlas smiled. "I assume you've accepted Peter's job offer. Let me buy you a drink to celebrate."

Xolia was taken aback. Did he think she would ever trust another word he said again? "I have plans already."

Atlas took it in stride, much unlike his insistence that she join him for the fight. "With Marshall?"

Did he know somehow?

He spared her from having to respond. "If for any reason your plans fall through, I'll be at the Armistice tonight. First round's on me."

"I'll keep that in mind," Xolia said, already committing herself to forgetting it.

"Let's go, Ms. Stone," Lana said, pushing the small group apart. "The car is waiting for you."

There were no more incidents with any other staff in Peter's wing of the palace. The car was waiting by the door when they walked outside, and Lana stayed long enough to see Xolia inside and driven around the side of the building, before Xolia lost sight of her.

She stomped up the two flights of stairs, pulling out her phone to ask Adonis when he would pick her up for dinner. There was so much she needed to tell him, and his input would be much appreciated.

His replay was both delayed and disappointing. *Have to do something for Helen. Will make it up to you tomorrow.*

She wasn't hurt, or at least that's what she told herself. She had rejected his offer to stay at his apartment. They hadn't decided they were anything more than partners, even if they had slept together.

You naïve girl. Never before had she guessed about what a boy was thinking. Her relationship with Marshall was all but pre-arranged and she had been too caught up in learning a new life to question it. The barracks and the war hadn't allowed for much time to question feelings or plan for the future. Now, all she had was time to think about was the possibility of Peter dying. What, if anything, Atlas was planning. And the worst thought of all: what if being vice chancellor didn't make her happy either? From what Peter had said, it still wouldn't be true freedom. *But it is power.* Which was more important?

Chapter Twenty

Xolia shouldered her way through the cold and crowded streets of the government district at peak rush hour. The government district was three blocks away from the sprawling grounds of the Presidential Palace, but the buildings were just as stately and lined with uniform trees along the impeccably kept sidewalks. Amongst the court buildings and other municipal governing institutions sat an old bar by the name of The Armistice.

Founded back during the days of the monarchy, it had managed to stay open after humans came into power by way of the building's reputation for discrete backroom politics and the rumored passageways from the bar to the Sovereign Court building. While Xolia had no doubt that most of the people on the streets were tourists, curious as to how the country ran, none of them would be allowed into the bar. One had to be a government employee or have an invitation from one. Xolia hoped that Atlas had been mostly sincere in his offer. Though watching her be turned away from an elite bar as she was on the cusp of getting the second-most coveted seat of power in the country had a certain level of pettiness that she wasn't sure he was above.

Still, spending the night around useless alcohol with Atlas sounded better than wallowing in her shitty apartment, wondering what errands Helen had Adonis running. Security teemed around the building, and the bouncer was wide and brawny, his sharp gaze missing nothing. He lifted his chin up at Xolia's arrival.

"I'm here to see Atlas Campion," she said, purposefully forgoing his title.

The bouncer didn't comment on it. "Name?"

"Xolia Stone."

He grabbed a leather binder and flipped it open, scanning the list. "ID?"

She pulled it from her bag and handed it over, the bright red of her card signaling to everyone looking that she was a variant. Satisfied with her identity, he nodded her through.

The inside was all dark wood and warm lighting. Leather seats formed small circles around low tables, where various groups of men and women in suits sat, talking in hushed tones. The bar itself showcased an impressive array of alcohol, none of it the low-brow bottles Xolia had tried with Rowan when they first started their suppressants. Truthfully, Xolia didn't know the difference between those bottles and the ones in front of her, other than their price tag.

"Xolia, you showed up," Atlas said from behind her.

She tensed at his voice, her only reassurance that he wouldn't try anything was that they were in such a heavily guarded place. This wasn't the lawlessness of the fights. Besides, she'd already accepted the job. If Atlas wanted her out of the way, he'd have a harder time now. Forcing herself to relax, she turned around to greet him. She hoped that her smile didn't look too forced.

"You expected that, though," she quipped. "I was on the list."

He shrugged, motioning towards the bar. "I like to make educated guesses." They sat down at the far end of the bar, partially obscured by shadow. "What'll you have?"

"Nothing," Xolia said. Why would she waste her time?

Atlas gave her a funny look. "Why not?"

She returned his incredulous look. "What's the point?"

His mouth dropped into a surprised *o* before he threw his head back and laughed. "I forget how sheltered you are sometimes. Here."

Again, that sinking feeling of naïveté rocked through Xolia. She had fought in a war, killed people. Yet she couldn't stop from fumbling her way through connecting with people nor from always missing the point or some key context. While twenty-four was incredibly young by variant standards, she had always imagined her future full of freedom and certainty. There had been no room for uncertainty in the past, it wasn't really fair that it appeared as she got older.

Something cylindrical poked into her thigh. She looked down. "What's that?"

"Sel, Xolia, I'm trying to be discrete." Atlas clapped his free hand over his face.

Because that's subtle. She mentally rolled her eyes at him but glanced around surreptitiously before grabbing the small canister from him. Glancing at the object, she couldn't figure what was so special about it. It was gold and looked like it screwed at the top.

"It's powdered obruo." Atlas leaned in close to her to whisper. "You'll have to go to the bathroom and snort it."

Xolia blanched. "Why would I do that?"

Atlas turned to give her a more straight-forward look. "Don't you want to get drunk? You just got your victory after all. Celebrate my misery with me."

"I don't know what obruo is, though," Xolia said. Did he think she was completely stupid?

Perhaps he did. He rolled his eyes at her continued hesitance. "It was the first iteration of rimere." Rimere was the widest-used suppressant on the market for variants. It was what Xolia had taken daily for seven years. "It slows down healing time, which is what allows you to get drunk, but doesn't take away your ability to use your powers. It's a great, albeit hard to get ahold of, party drug."

"For whom?" The majority of variants weren't well paid enough to buy out-of-date prescription drugs.

"We didn't all choose some moral high road upon the war ending to work in some under-funded government offshoot," Atlas said. "Some variants do well for themselves and want to enjoy the spoils of war, simple pleasures like getting drunk and lounging around all night."

Xolia spun the vial around. "I would think you'd be busy writing policy and overseeing the Senate."

He shrugged. "Maybe I was bad at my job. That's why Peter offered it to you instead."

That comment was enough to set her on edge. Her hand clenched around the vial. "I thought the news would've made you angrier."

"I am angry," he said.

Xolia stilled. If he had said anything else, she would've

assumed he was lying. This couldn't be anything other than the truth.

"Less angry now," he continued. "Besides"—he leaned in close to Xolia, his mouth hovering near her ear—"with Peter on his deathbed, FAR is a sinking ship. The party is nothing without him." He straightened. "So I should be thanking you."

"You tried to—" Xolia cut herself off and lowered her voice so only Atlas could hear it. "You tried to kill me."

Surprise overtook his features before they settled back into that infuriating neutral mask. "And it obviously didn't work, so I fail to see the issue. Have you ever been drunk?"

She shook her head, surprising herself by answering his question when he had so calmly admitted to an attempt on her life.

"You should try it; it would make this conversation much less painful." Atlas waved over the bartender, who so far had been content to let them wallow in their secluded corner.

Did she trust him? No. Did she want to understand the loss of inhibition that so enthralled humans? Yes. *You're in a public space, Atlas can't hurt you.*

Slipping the vial into her pocket, Xolia stood up. She'd made up her mind. If she hadn't been allowed to be stupid in her teen years, then twenty-four was as good a time as any to let loose. To be free. She deserved it, after all. "Order me a drink," she commanded before making her way to the dark doors of the restrooms.

Once she had the door closed behind her, she pulled the vial from her pocket. An illicit thrill ran through her. This was different from the fights. Lower stakes. Unknown. But it carried that same sense of freedom. The same sense of reckless abandon that made

Xolia think of Adonis's words about finding comfort in a loss of control. It both terrified and excited her. She unscrewed the top and nearly spilled half the drug onto the floor when she realized the lid extended down into the vial and curved to hold the powder.

Thoughts of Adonis ran through her mind when she moved the tray of powder up to her nose. She hesitated. Surely it shouldn't be too difficult to breathe it in. She lowered her nose. *Do it.*

After four failed attempts and an embarrassing mishap where she bumped her nose into the tray, she was finally able to snort the entirety of its contents. It seared the inside of her nostril, her eyes widening as she shoved the empty container into her pocket, and she stumbled to the sink to wash it off her face. *You fucking idiot.*

After a painful minute the burning subsided and she chanced a look up at the mirror. Her skin was wan, with red splotches around her nose where she had scrubbed. Her eyes were bloodshot, thin tendrils of red streaking across the milky white. It wasn't unlike the first time she had ever taken rimere suppressants, though that faded as soon as the drugs were regularly in her system.

Xolia turned the water back on, going within herself to find that ephemeral part of her that controlled water. It answered her call, and with minimal effort, small water moths danced around the room. She hadn't been able to do that on rimere. *Interesting.*

Curiosity overwhelmed the initial fear, and she made her way back to Atlas, where a glass of amber liquid waited for her. Sweat had formed around the glass in her absence. Atlas didn't say anything, he just raised his glass to hers in a wordless toast.

Steeling her nerves for the uncomfortable burn of alcohol, she grabbed the glass and chugged.

MIND FUZZY, limbs unstable, and voice utterly slurred and sluggish, Xolia teetered dangerously on the edge of consciousness. Once that first cup had been emptied, Atlas was all too happy to keep a steady stream of alcohol flowing between them. Conversation had drifted in and out though Xolia was sure she had forgotten a few words spoken between them. She didn't think they'd said anything important or worth remembering.

Drunkenness was a strange feeling. She understood why humans gravitated to it for leisure. She understood why Adonis relished a loss of control. It was weightless. She could run for miles without a care for what anyone would say. Her mind buzzed with endless possibilities, and she worked hard to keep her phone tucked away in her pocket when all she wanted to do was yell at Adonis for having stood her up and yell at Marshall for being a coward. Yelling sounded fun. Since Adonis and Marshall were out of the question, she focused her attention back on Atlas. The man who tried to kill her. The man who'd looked down on her at every opportunity. The man who'd won Silas's affection from the moment they met, while she'd had to fight and constantly prove her worth.

Tears burned along the bottom of her eyes, but she would be damned before a single one fell in the presence of Atlas. This wasn't fun anymore, and that weightlessness crashed into her. All of her fear and anxiety crushed her breastbone. Peter would be so disappointed in her if he found out she'd let herself get so drunk, and he would be more insistent than ever on her being constantly surveilled.

No one surrounded Atlas. Nothing bad ever happened to Atlas. *It's just not fair.* "I want to go home now," she said. Her words were mangled, and she half-worried that Atlas wouldn't be able to understand her. Had he been talking? She couldn't remember and decided she didn't care.

"Let's go," Atlas said. While he settled the tab, Xolia stewed in her emotions. Why did everything come so easily to Atlas? Why hadn't she tried harder to get what she wanted when the war ended? Belatedly, she realized she was angry. She was so angry at Atlas. Why should she continue to hide that from him? What was the point of sitting around and pretending at being friends when they both knew they hated each other?

Even with the drugs and alcohol impairing her judgement, she knew it would only turn out badly if she attacked him in the bar. She'd have to wait until they were outside, then. She nodded to herself, that was a good plan.

Atlas offered his arm to her, but she refused, instead choosing to walk on unsteady legs out of the bar. She could feel the eyes of multiple patrons on her, but she refused to look anywhere other than directly ahead of herself. One step. Then another.

Cold air hit her face, mildly sobering her up. There was a moment of clarity before the warm haze settled over her again. *I don't think I'll drink again.* "Did you bring a car?" she asked, suddenly aware of how far she was from home and how much she didn't want to walk.

"I did," Atlas said. "I'll drive you home if you let me show you the Museum of Variant History first. Think of it as a tour before you announce your vice chancellorship."

Sober Xolia would have struggled to piece together Atlas's intentions, drunk Xolia didn't consider them at all. Them being alone and hidden on the museum grounds would be perfect for her planned assault. She could punch him, hard enough to break his nose. Hard enough to prove that he wasn't infallible. Hard enough to convince herself that she wasn't just a second choice. Hard enough to be able to move on with her life. "Let's go," she said, her mouth stretching into an unnaturally wide smile, completely against her wishes.

A black, compact car pulled around the corner, and Atlas opened the back door. Xolia slid in and he followed her. Heat enveloped her, and she slipped further into an inebriated sense of peace. This night was turning out better with each passing minute.

The Museum of Variant History was being built inside an old building for a defunct newspaper. It was a block away from the Natural History Museum—which, in the years following the war, had taken down all their incorrect and outdated exhibits about variants. Now, less than a month from the grand opening, the building was shrouded in scaffolding and surrounded by large construction vehicles. The grounds were torn up. Xolia didn't know how it was going to be fixed by the grand opening. She strained her eyes to see more in the dark, but with two broken street lamps, the block of the museum was ominously darker than its surroundings.

The hair on the back of Xolia's neck stood up, some latent self-preservation despite her impaired state. *This is the perfect opportunity for me.* The thrill of getting even with Atlas was enough to make her overlook just how disadvantaged she really was. It hardly mattered.

Xolia and Atlas got out of the car, which remained running

with the mysterious driver hiding behind the wheel. The car pulled away, just up the block, leaving them even more alone. This would be her chance. Anticipation bubbled up inside her, and her blood rushed through her body. She clenched her hand into a fist—

"Xolia," Atlas said. "I really brought you to come here because I need to ask you something."

"Yes?" She teetered on the edge of her patience.

"You need to step aside from the VC nomination," he said, his mask firmly in place.

Xolia blinked. "I don't understand. You wouldn't be getting it even if I declined." Her brain couldn't make a single clear thought.

"I know." His voice had a hard edge to it. "That's not why I'm asking. I'm trying to do what's best for Ris, and you're a loose cannon."

"I'm doing what's best for Ris too." Her fist was still clenched, and Atlas took a step toward her. It would be so easy to hit him. Quickly, he reached out and yanked her arm. Xolia startled but didn't fight back as he dragged her past the temporary fencing around the museum and led her into the grounds.

"I've been working too hard for the past seven years for you to mess things up. Just listen to me, I'm doing what is best for variants," he said. They didn't stop until he opened a side door that had been left unlocked. That felt like an important detail. Xolia promised herself she would remember it.

Lights flickered on to reveal a warehouse, boxes stacked in precarious towers. They were all marked though the writing was too small to parse out any details. Not that Xolia was much up to reading at the moment anyway.

"Just tell me you'll back off," he pleaded with her. Xolia

struggled to remain standing upright. "I thought you were happy with Marshall and your little bureau job."

At the mention of Marshall's name, Xolia laughed. "Happy? I haven't been happy in a long time, Atlas." How easily the words tumbled out of her mouth once she was no longer inhibited by herself. How easy it was to let the truth come out. "And why should I listen to you? You tried to kill me."

His jaw twitched. "Because I was afraid this would happen." At his sides, his hands shook.

She narrowed her eyes. "Why can't you let me have anything? You had to be Silas's favorite. Peter's favorite."

"I was never Silas's favorite because I wanted to be," Atlas snapped. "He just didn't like you."

Consciousness flickered in and out. When Xolia found some lucidity, Atlas was pacing back and forth. "That's not true. He told me I had a great role to play when the war was over. Something only I could do." She slapped a hand over her mouth. She was too conversational.

"And you believed it?" Atlas stopped his pacing. "You still believe it?"

She shook her head because it was supposed to be a lie. Krista had told her it was a lie, a manipulation tactic. *But I am special. I want to be meant for more.*

"You're not drunk," she realized aloud.

He barked out a laugh. "Of course not. Then, I wouldn't have the advantage."

The sleepy tune fizzled out. She wanted her opening. She'd been stupid and let Atlas get the better of her again, and now he thought he could wheedle something else from her. No more. With a clenched fist, she threw a punch against the square of his jaw.

The contact made a resounding and satisfying crack. He stumbled back and adrenaline coursed through Xolia. She was ready. This was it.

Atlas cradled his jaw, but when he looked up at her, his eyes flashed with pure hatred. It sparked Xolia's own animosity. She went to throw another punch, but Atlas was quick to grab her fist.

"You're stupid," he snapped. A gust of wind blew into her midsection, throwing her back. "You've never been able to beat me, and now you think you can when you're drunk off your ass?"

Xolia sought that connection to water. It was all too far away. Hidden behind drywall and copper pipes. She didn't have the concentration to pull it out.

Blood, then. Hers. His.

Why can't I focus?

Stymied, she backed up another few feet from him. A triumphant smile broke out over his face, the discoloration of his jaw already receding. "Having trouble?"

"I used my powers, though," she said, voice small. She was afraid and couldn't hide it.

"Before you were drunk," he said, glee evident in his voice. He stalked toward her. "You couldn't put out a candle right now."

Fear shot through her brain. She pulled at a stack of boxes and tried to move them in front of her. Anything to shield her.

Atlas waved a hand, and they flew to the side. Reaching out his left hand, he gripped at nothing. All around them came a rattling noise, and then water burst through the pipes, from the ceiling, the walls. It was a torrential downpour.

"You're going to regret punching me. And tomorrow you're going to tell Peter you changed your mind."

The water swirled into a vortex, rising above the boxes, above her. All she could do was stare. She was both within and without herself, some part of her brain screaming at her to move, to run, to do anything to get away.

Then the water dove into her mouth.

Her nose.

Her ears.

Everything was waterlogged. She choked and gagged until even her lungs were full of water. It was all-consuming. Overwhelming. Xolia lost her grip on whether she was standing or falling, dead or alive.

Were the lights still on? Everything was so dark. And cold. And wet. *I hate you. I hate you...*

Chapter Twenty-One

Her eyes burned. Her throat burned. Every part of her burned. Even her skin, which was covered in damp clothes. Her hair was matted and stuck to the sides of her face and neck. The groan and scream of construction vehicles grated against her ears.

Much of last night was a blur. Unfortunately, she remembered every detail of her fight with Atlas. Not that it'd been much of a fight. He had decimated her in between her slow blinks and half-coherent musings. It was worse than humiliating. She cracked open an eye to find the lights were still on in the warehouse, even though sunlight streamed in through small windows at the top of the eastern wall.

Fighting through the stiffness and pain in her limbs, she sat up, looking around for any sign of Atlas. There was nothing. Bracing herself against one of the fallen boxes, Xolia stood up, hating the way the obruo still kept her from fully healing. She hated everything.

This will never happen again, she vowed to herself. *Nothing will ever catch me by surprise again. No one will cross me.*

She was done living in complacency. Done living off the words of others. Walking as silently as possible, she found her way to the door that Atlas had led them through. Her hand paused on the handle. *I feel like I was supposed to remember something.* She struggled to think back through the night, but it was gone. Whatever she was trying to reach was lost in the gaps of her memory.

The door opened easily, and the sun hit her face. The air might've been mild, but in her damp clothes, she was a shivering mess. Construction workers milled about, focusing on the parts of the building covered by the scaffolding. Not wanting to be seen, she ducked her head and made quick work of leaving the property.

People walked along the street, some giving her a passing glance, but in a city as large as Ris, she would hardly be the most interesting or out-of-place character walking in the streets. With that as her only comfort, she made her way home.

SHOWER. *Sleep. Warmth.*

Xolia repeated those words over and over in her head like a mantra. They were all that kept her moving forward. It had been over two hours since she started the trek home, and she was woefully close to curling up on a dirty street corner when she rounded the final block to her apartment building.

Not even on the day she'd moved in had she been so happy to see the nondescript five-story building. She clutched her house key which had blessedly managed to stay in her pocket. The elevator was still broken. *Just these stairs.*

Grunting, she pushed herself onward. Thirty more steps.

Twenty. Fifteen. She made it to her door, in all its chipped-paint glory. The key slid smoothly into the lock. Too smoothly. Normally, it had to hit the tumblers just right for the handle to turn.

Using the last dregs of her strength, she pushed open the door, ready to face whomever had broken in. Nothing was touched. There was a head of black hair poking up over the back of the couch, however. Soft snoring filled the apartment.

"Adonis?" she asked.

His head whipped around, revealing a slightly disheveled Adonis. At the sight of her, his eyes lit up and he leapt off the couch and ran to her. "Xo, what happened?" His hands skated over her body, and he frowned when he encountered her wet clothes.

His caring demeanor snapped what little composure she had been still clinging to. She allowed herself a shuddering breath before collapsing against him. A heaving sigh escaped her, the solidness of his body was so far removed from how afraid she'd been. Atlas had demolished her pride in the span of minutes.

"I came here as soon as I could. I called at least fifty times," he said in low tones, his hands still not leaving her body. They caressed her filthy hair, trailed along her jaw, her shoulders. His touch was just as consuming as the fear.

"My phone broke," she croaked out. There was no way it had survived that much water damage, though truthfully, she hadn't even thought to check it. Leaning on him for support, she let him lead her into the bedroom and then the bathroom, where he turned on the shower. Once the temperature warmed up, they stripped their clothes and Adonis got into the shower with her.

"What happened?" he asked. She shook her head, still struggling to hold herself together. He didn't push for answers, and instead, he carefully massaged shampoo and conditioner into her hair. She sighed as the tension coiled underneath her skin slowly unraveled.

Once her hair was clean of product, she turned to him. With him standing a head taller than her, it was hard to make herself intimidating to him, and Sel, she was so tired, but she pulled herself up into a haughty pose all the same. "Adonis," she said. "It's either me or Helen. You're my... partner completely or not at all." Even under the comforting thrum of hot water, goosebumps prickled at her skin as she waited to hear what he would say.

He didn't answer right away. It was the worst type of torture, her so vulnerable next to him in his domineering silence.

"Did you know that when FAR released variants from the barracks, they never removed the Variant Service Act from law?"

A non answer, but his words were discomforting, nevertheless. If FAR hadn't revoked the Variant Service Act, then it was still too easy to make variants little more than slaves in the eyes of the law. Something that was against FAR's foundations. She raised her eyebrow, unsure of how that tied into his relationship with Helen.

"I told you I met Helen at a bad time." Adonis sighed and lifted a hand to her shoulder, almost like he was seeking comfort from their proximity. "I was embezzling money from Persion, and we had started to get closer. I trusted her, and she used that to trick me into signing a contract invoking the Variant Service Act. I'm bound to her for life now."

Adonis lifted his head, his features pulled back in a grimace. "I can only escape her if one of us dies."

"Why haven't you killed her?"

"And condemn myself?" Adonis asked. "She's dangerous, not just to me, but to Ris. Her own father would thank you if you removed her from the equation. Helen is desperate for power, and the fights are full of desperate people looking for something to believe in. They already love her for what we've built the last seven years. If Helen died by accident or assassination, they'd sanctify her, and I'd lose everything. If she were beaten by a worthier opponent, their loyalty would be swayed."

"You want me to kill her?" Xolia asked. Was this his plan the whole time? She'd never premeditated a murder before, everything had always been in the heat of the moment. On a battlefield or in a cage.

"She's never without the twins. I can't do it on my own." Adonis licked his lips. "Please."

He's terrified of her, she realized. She didn't think he would ever admit it; it was the same kind of pride that kept her from admitting how much Atlas terrified her out loud. *We're the same.* "I'll help you."

They got out of the shower, and Xolia recounted what she could remember of the night. Adonis didn't look pleased that she'd so willingly taken the obruo but refrained from remarking on it. After she finished her incomplete recollection, Adonis offered to get them food. She nodded, though as soon as he'd left, she collapsed into her bed and slept until nighttime.

She woke up, finding that the blankets had been pulled up around her, and the light of the living room filled the small crack at the bottom of the bedroom door. Her stomach growled, and she got out of bed to find Adonis sitting on her old couch, watching the news on her secondhand television she'd picked up after Marshall left. A group of variants had attacked a bank, stealing over \$100,000 according to witnesses. The journalist interviewed the witnesses, and they were all similarly scared and worried about the lax legislation around suppressants after variants completed their court-mandated dosages. The attack hadn't happened in Atalia but in Fortuna, a city that was almost as large as Atalia and sat on the southern edge of the country. It was the city that Atlas had come from.

"Are you hungry?" Adonis asked her.

She nodded; her eyes glued to the replaying security footage of the assault playing on the news. It was brutal. Fast. Terrifying, if she were human. Xolia clicked her tongue, this was the last thing they needed if they were going to settle century-old prejudices.

"It just happened," Adonis said, moving over on the small couch. "A group is taking responsibility. The Underlings."

"And they think this will fix things? Do they not understand what's at stake?" she asked turning off the TV.

"I don't think they are particularly concerned with what the general population thinks," Adonis said.

She supposed he was right, which was why it was all the more important she and Adonis enacted their plans as quickly as possible. She and Peter had plans for the following—they would start interviewing potential staff members, and they were to finalize their schedule for the campaign circuit. Already the political pundits were gearing up for the interviews and rallies and were taking polls as to who would be next to cast their name in the race for chancellor. Not many of them had picked up on Peter's deliberate disuse of Atlas as vice chancellor in the promotional material they were circulating.

"Do you think Ris will ever find peace?" Xolia asked. It was disheartening but unsurprising that one variant attack would be enough to convince an entire human population that they were unsuited for society. *If only you could bring the humans to heel. This wouldn't be a problem.* Xolia clenched her jaw, banishing the thought.

Adonis leaned back against the couch, throwing an arm on the back. "If I don't believe it, what's the point of anything we're doing? What's the point of anything Silas did?"

Xolia shrugged. Once upon a time she'd been so convinced that everything had a point and would find itself fixed once the rebellion was over. Those few fleeting moments from the sight of the Gornne Administration surrendering to learning Silas was detained were the best moments of her life, before reality came crashing down.

"We're doing what we can right now," Adonis said, standing up to hand her the take out he had bought. "Everything is going to work out, Xo." He pressed a soft kiss to her forehead before leaving her for the night. Despite his open offer, she was still stubbornly attached to her shitty apartment, and with Marshall not in any rush to return, it felt a little more like just hers.

Chapter Twenty-Two

Sweat dripped down into Xolia's eyes. "Again," she demanded. Her muscles trembled from exertion, but she wasn't ready to give up.

Adonis stood on the other side of the training room. He was decidedly less covered in sweat, but his brows were drawn in concern. "Xo."

She shook her head. "No. I need to figure out how to do this. You figured it out, so can I."

Since 6 a.m. they had been at the gym, fully empty courtesy of Adonis, and they had been trying to coax from Xolia the ability to create water from nothing by trying to jump-start her self-preservation instincts.

Adonis would attack without water in the room for Xolia to try and defend herself with. Her only line of defense was to push him back through his blood. Xolia had suffered multiple burns to her cheeks and hands already.

"It took me years," he said.

"I don't have years," she argued. "Again."

He looked only slightly put out before nodding. "Fine. But I'm going to go harder."

"Fine. Just do it."

He clenched his jaw and rolled his shoulders, heading over to the sideboard where the gas fireplace burned steadily on. It was a gym tailored for variants, the owner was an older variant who had been in the barracks but whom Xolia had never met. Xolia waited for him to take up the flame along his arm where upon he would launch into a violent assault. He was punishing in his fighting strategy, there was no finessing or skirting around an opponent for him, just a full-on attack.

That didn't happen. His back was still turned to her when screaming bullets of flame shot at her. She dodged two on her left but leaned right into a third that punctured her shoulder. It tore through skin and muscle, and she grunted at the burning pain of it.

Brandishing a sword of fire, Adonis turned on her, advancing quickly. Pain continued to lance through her shoulder, her fatigue slowing down the healing process. "Come on, Xo," he said. He brought the sword in a long arc, and Xolia reached down within herself, searching for any intrinsic feeling of what to do.

She tugged at the pit in her stomach she always associated with her powers. Nothing budged. There was no dam breaking, no revelation of power. Barely jumping away in time to avoid the edge of Adonis's sword, she ran to the other end of the court. Her blood thrashed in her veins, begging to be released to protect her. To fight back. She refrained from the temptation while Adonis advanced once more.

With his left hand he sent another barrage of bullets her way. They flew low, aiming at her legs. *Come on, come on, come on,* Xolia pleaded with herself. If she could just break past whatever hidden barrier kept her from accessing the full amount of her powers, she could—

A bullet grazed the side of her ribcage, burning and cauterizing the skin in tandem. She faltered in her step, and a moment later Adonis was above, with his sword raised above his head. She closed her eyes, screaming at herself.

The heat from the flame dissipated, and Xolia snapped her head up. Adonis was halfway across the court, his face turning blue. Xolia breathed deeply, trying to regain control. Disappointment coiled low in her stomach, and she severed the control she had taken over his blood.

Limping, she made her way to Adonis and offered him a hand to stand back up. "I'm done for today," she snapped. "And I'm sorry," she added. "I didn't mean to do that."

"Don't apologize," he said. Adonis grabbed the tops of her arms and surveyed the various burns that littered her body. "I'm sorry."

Xolia shook her head. She had asked him to do it. "I just can't get it to work."

"I know you want it to happen right away," Adonis said. "But it takes time."

"What worked for you anyway?" she asked. He had never discussed it, just that it had been years of self-exploration before he was able to summon the flame.

He pulled a small lick of flame to his palm, growing it until it covered his entire hand, stopping at his wrist. "I started with my fingers. One knuckle at a time. Then the whole hand." With his unlit hand, he made a chopping motion. The flame snuffed out. "I did that daily until I managed to make a flame. It was so hot it melted the knife, the metal from the knife stayed burned into my skin for almost a month even though my hand grew back. It's old magic, Xo, it doesn't work the same."

"You tortured yourself?" To have enough concentration to do that, to that extent, was a marvel to Xolia. She would throw herself into danger, but there was a distinct difference between someone else inflicting immeasurable pain on you and doing it yourself.

He shrugged. "Who would I have told?"

Xolia conceded the point. If she didn't have him, she would have to resort to drastic measures too. "I'm sorry you had to do that to yourself."

"It worked, didn't it?" He offered a lifeless smile. "But even that took months. You'll figure it out, just give it time."

Time. The thing she didn't have. They were just over a month away from her official announcement as Peter's running mate. Everything would change. "I know," she said, tired of the subject. Complaining about it wasn't going to bring it about any faster. "Let's leave so I can heal before I see Peter."

XOLIA WALKED through Peter's wing of the Presidential Palace with a slight limp. The cauterized cuts would be healed by dinner time, but they persisted into the early afternoon. Peter was adamant about her starting to build her staff, she would need help with the ensuing media frenzy the minute the news broke, or so he said. She didn't remember much of what the media was like when Peter and Atlas were inducted as chancellor and vice chancellor. *And whose fault was that?*

All she remembered was the large amount of speculation about the sudden shift from a presidency to a chancellorship.

Xolia wasn't sure she understood every decision that had gone into the political shift, but she knew the presidency had had a democratically elected senate, while Peter filled his Senate with his own picks.

Lana brought Xolia to a different part of the palace. This part of the building started to look more familiar to her. Lana opened the door to an octagonal office, a wide wall of windows letting in copious amounts of sunlight and showing a breathtaking view of the perfectly pristine grounds. They sprawled for over an acre, taking up space in a city that had little to give. She could have fit her apartment building six times over in the span of the Presidential Palace's gardens. Nestled among trees, but hidden from view, was Atlas's home.

Peter sat behind a desk that was adjacent to the wall of windows on the right side, giving him an easy view of both the door and the outside. On the left side were bookshelves covered with old and heavy tomes, all first editions of works by prominent Risian historians or scholars, she assumed, and couches that she recognized from more than one photo that had made its rounds through the media. Peter sat behind his desk, sun ghosting over him. The room was bordering on unpleasantly warm, but even with that and the sun, Peter shivered. Xolia hoped it was a trick of the shadow over his face that his lips seemed blue.

Once she and Lana were fully inside, Peter opened his eyes and swiveled around to them. "Xolia, I'm so glad you've made it. Lana and I spent all morning preparing candidates who could be your chief of staff. Whomever you choose, you'll come to rely on heavily. They will coordinate your daily schedule and events that you must attend, politicians you'll have to lunch with. It's not an easy decision, so please, choose carefully."

"I understand," she said. While she did, she still couldn't understand why Atlas seemingly had no staff, no guards, no one around him at any time. Peter didn't look well enough to be heavily questioned by her, however, so she kept her mouth shut and took a seat next to Peter behind his grand desk.

"You don't need to make the decision today. We have over twenty candidates to choose from, we'll only be seeing five today."

Xolia bit back a grimace at the thought of sitting through four sets of interviews. *It's part of the job. Get used to it.* Xolia still hoped that the first interviewee would be good enough for the job, though, and she nodded to Peter. She was ready.

The first option was atrocious. So was the second. And the third. All humans who had passable knowledge of the government. While impressive, they either talked down to Xolia or completely misunderstood her. They lacked the ambition and drive she needed to make this campaign successful.

After a small intermission of food and tea and brief discussions between Peter and Xolia, the fourth hopeful chief of staff was admitted. At first, Xolia was ready to write her off. She was middle-aged, human. Her experiences were perfectly acceptable and perfectly bland. Nothing stood out, it was all written just so to get her in the door. When the woman walked in, Xolia's eyes narrowed in suspicion.

Smile lines and crow's feet betrayed her age, but there were no other signs of aging. No scars. No piercings. Nothing permanent in her appearance except the effects of time. She double checked the paperwork. *Human.* Her birth year would put her at forty-seven. Which could be believable, except Xolia had never seen a human make it almost half a century with no permanent changes to their appearance, whether by choice or illness. Even Peter weathered the burden of being human, and he was only ten years older than the interviewee, Bridget Halding.

Xolia glanced at Peter to see if he suspected anything. His smile was perfectly cordial, his eyes warm. Not an ounce of suspicion lurked beneath. She shouldn't have been surprised; she'd never known a human to second-guess one of their own. It was why they were so adamant about variants being registered as such, even in the post-Gornne world.

"Thank you for your interest in this position." For the first time that day, Xolia took the initiative in leading the conversation.

She could almost feel the pride radiating off Peter, and she sat up straighter, both wanting to bask in his approval and see if she could be certain of Bridget's identity without raising Peter's suspicion. If she was somehow unregistered, like Helen, but without the help of an influential father, she was worth having around.

"Thank you for having me here today," she answered.

Xolia had a few filler questions in mind after listening to Peter's succinct way of interviewing three other people. She was still trying to figure out how to ask what she wanted to know. She asked about prior job history, how her skills were transferable to this job, if she was prepared for such a huge workload. Bridget had extensive work experience to pull from for each answer. And they were high-profile jobs as well. So she was ambitious too. That boded well for Xolia. She raised a brow and thought of her next question to ask.

"Which of FAR's policies is closest to you?" Xolia asked.

Bridget smiled. *Perfect teeth*, Xolia noted. "During the Wright Administration there was a particularly violent string of protests between humans and variants. Variants wanted more rights; humans were comfortable with things as they were. Until hundreds of them died. My father lost his life during those protests, but variants were given their own schooling in the barracks. I'll never forget that. How could I lose something so special to me, while an entire group of people were given something just as precious? I want to spend my life giving to people without taking from them. It's the only way forward."

Xolia leaned back in her seat, soaking in Bridget's words. President Wright governed Ris almost forty years ago. Which Xolia knew because of the schooling she got while in the barracks, in between the countless hours of drills and patrols. She had never been taught that their access to education was something that had been so recently given, though, not during her primary schooling or the secondary schooling she got after the war and her time in solitary confinement.

"The loss of a loved one is something we never quite get over," Peter said. Silas came to Xolia's mind. Unbidden. Unwelcome. "Why did you wait until now to try and work in the government?"

Xolia snapped out of her thoughts to stare at Bridget, hoping she would betray something of being a variant.

"I didn't think I had anything to offer," Bridget said. "Now I do."

It didn't give Xolia any further clarity. *But I can wait for that.* "The job is yours," Xolia blurted out.

Peter started next to her, giving her a wide-eyed stare of horror.

Even Bridget appeared surprised, her eyes darting between the two of them.

"Wait," Peter said, suppressing a wracking cough. "Could I speak to Xolia for a minute? Alone?"

Bridget graciously left the room, and Peter whirled to Xolia, well, as fast as he was able. The coughing fit returned, and this time he made no move to hide it. His entire body shook with the force of each stomach-deep cough. Xolia could do little more than look on in terror. She had never known an illness like that, something that would turn your own body against you. With Peter's slight frame, she worried he'd crack a rib.

Once he calmed down enough to drink water, he drained the small cup that sat next to his arm on the desk. Wordlessly, Xolia slid her own untouched glass over to him, which he also drained.

"I know it's sudden, but she's the only person I'll work well with," Xolia said, preemptively assuming what he wanted to talk to her about.

Peter cleared his throat. "I don't want you to rush into anything. We haven't seen half the candidates."

"I know." Xolia debated between pleading with him and just asserting her choice. "This is my decision, though. I want to trust that you trust me enough to make the right decision."

Peter's eyes softened. It was a paternal look that tugged at Xolia's heart. No matter how frustrated they were bound to get with one another throughout the race and beyond, he would be the closest thing she had to a parent. The closest thing to a *good* parent. *For how much longer?* She would not forget his cough or bloodshot eyes anytime soon. "I trust you, Xolia. If you think Bridget is the best option; of course we can hire her. I know you didn't want this, and I can't tell you how proud I am to see you fall into the role so naturally."

Tears threatened to fall. It was so different from Grant

Howard's words all those weeks ago. That she could never be a leader. "I listened to people who convinced me this wasn't what I wanted. Thank you for not giving up on me."

Peter reached over and gave her a hearty one-armed hug. Xolia leaned into the comforting touch. There was an undeniable safety in it. "Okay, let's go get Ms. Halding hired and on the payroll."

Xolia left Peter's embrace and opened up the door. Bridget was patiently waiting outside. Glancing back at Peter, who was staring at the table, Xolia gently closed the door behind her. Bridget looked up at her, a question in her gaze.

"What's your element?" Xolia asked, the barest hint of a command in her voice. She wanted to work with Bridget, but she needed to confirm what she already knew to be true.

Bridget hesitated, her eyes shifting between quizzical and guarded. "Air."

"You're not 47."

The older woman shook her head. "157."

She was older than the oldest registered variant. She was also almost the same age as Silas. He'd made it to 180 before his murder. If she wasn't careful, that line of thinking could send her down another spiral. "Did your dad die during the protests?"

She shook her head. "Not during those protests. He was also an unregistered variant. He left my mom when she started to show signs of aging. He died over a hundred years ago, and I've been in the shadows since."

"A century?" Xolia asked. "Why did you wait until now?"

"What good would I have done? I was left alone in a world that didn't know I existed. I didn't have the resources to change my records or forge documents. But I had the time to learn."

Bridget stood up from the small bench she had been sitting on. "I want to help you, Xolia. Variants are divided about FAR right now. Half of them believe in Chancellor Bellevue and Vice Chancellor Campion, and the other half despise them. None of them know you're planning on running. It's going to divide the community even more. You need help, I can provide that help."

"Variants are really that divided about FAR?" Sure, Adonis had talked about it, but she hadn't really believed it. Who else could the variants turn to?

As if noticing the lost look, which Xolia was sure was written all over her face, Bridget placed a hand on Xolia's arm. "This isn't the time to discuss that. That can come later. I'm sure Chancellor Bellevue is wondering where we are."

Xolia nodded, her mind still swimming. She wanted to go to Adonis, to get his opinion on everything. Despite the lingering lack of trust that she couldn't shake, his opinion mattered most to her. She wanted to awe him. She wanted to be the best everything to him.

Back in the stateroom, Peter called in Lana to get Bridget officially hired and then to run through a list of background checks Bridget would need to pass. Xolia side-eyed Bridget, wondering just how good of a forger she really was, but she seemed unconcerned about the whole affair, just nodding and signing at the appropriate moments. She would start within the week, with Bridget spending her time between working with Lana and working with Xolia. Lana handed Xolia a schedule for the following three months, starting with the official announcement and running up until the first official debate, when all candidates would start their campaigns at full throttle to win over the populace.

Giddy satisfaction ran through Xolia once she got over the

initial swarm of being overwhelmed. It was so different from her menial work at the bureau. It was so different from the barracks, where assignments had-been handed to her on a need-to-know basis. The war had been the most similar, but with Silas running everything and keeping all of his meetings secretive there was little to no true leadership on Xolia being the one to order everyone around. Everything she had to do had been given to her already planned and figured out. Despite this current inflexibility, there was a certain amount of freedom in the power it provided. She could share her voice. It would be her influence lending to Peter's campaign. What she would do from here on out would actually matter. Xolia decided it was worth the security and the staff that would come with it.

Chapter Twenty-Three

Xolia woke up to an arm slung low across her waist and Adonis breathing deeply into the tangled mess of her hair. She'd spent the previous night at his apartment, in anticipation of trying to sell herself as the long-awaited Selermine of the Rheathian Church. Nerves pooled in the pit of her stomach. It was such a far-fetched idea, and yet. . .And yet, she couldn't let it go. It had taken root in her mind, leaving her no peace until she saw it through.

Moving as much as her living restraint would allow her, she glanced at the clock. It was time she started getting ready.

"Adonis," she said, trying harder to move away from him.

He huffed something unintelligible and curled in closer to her. His mouth ghosted the juncture of her neck and shoulder. Desire coursed through her, something that was so unlike the many monotonous mornings spent near Marshall. It was just further confirmation that this was right. This was where she was meant to be. She was on the right track to go after the VC position, it was right to be with Adonis.

"Wake up." She turned around in his arms, pushing at him to wake him up.

"No," he whispered, tugging her closer to him.

Xolia brushed his hair away from his face, betraying his eyes that were scrunched shut and a lazy smile on his face. "We need to get ready for church."

He groaned, finally pulling away from her and throwing the arm that had been wrapped around her over his face. "I know. I know."

Throwing the blankets back from both of them, Xolia pulled herself from the comfort of the bed. "How did last night go?"

"Poorly." Adonis got out of bed and walked over to the walk-in closet. "The twins are fairly confident in the amount of support Helen will get from announcing her candidacy."

"They don't even know she's a variant." Xolia huffed. "And no one outside of the fights knows who she is."

"Once she reveals herself to be an unregistered variant, word will spread and so will the support," he said. "There are more unregistered variants than we know about."

He was right, but that did little to temper the anger coursing through her. It wasn't fair that Helen could sit back with having the right father and money and try to take what Xolia had fought for. What was supposed to be hers.

"How much evidence does she have on you?" Xolia ventured to ask. No matter his answer, it wouldn't change his end goal for Helen or Xolia's part in it.

Adonis stilled, his hand still outstretched toward a button-down shirt. "Enough to put me away for a long time. And being a variant? No judge would hesitate to try and put me away for life."

Xolia nodded. "You really think taking her out in front of other people will sway them? Won't they just turn against me?"

He tilted his head at her. "The fights are about who is the strongest. If we are going to get anywhere in this country, we need to be unified by following the strongest of us. We'll make sure they know that."

Malaise settled over her with the lax way she had just talked about planning someone's death. It was different from war—everything was for survival, a greater purpose. Everyone involved knew they were facing death, it was all a matter of who was faster, stronger.

"We need this," Adonis continued. "The country needs this. If we let her have her way, humans will lose their rights. And what will that lead to? More chaos. More death."

"I just don't want them to turn against me," Xolia admitted. *Why should I care about one life in the face of an entire nation?* Helen wasn't planning to die. But she needed to. Too much was at stake for her to care about one person. *It won't feel any different.* She had been so ready to kill her opponent back in the fighting ring the first time she went. In the heat of the moment, the only thing that had mattered was her coming out on top.

You need the practice for Atlas, anyway. She knew it was only a matter of time before she and Atlas would be reduced to fighting one another again. Whatever he was planning, she was in the way. He was in her way.

"They won't. I'll make sure they won't."

Xolia nodded. Whatever it would take, that's what she would do. *It's for peace. It's for a united Ris.*

He went back to dressing, and Xolia made her way to the guest room, which had really become a large closet of Persion clothes that Adonis supplied her with, and pulled together an understated ensemble. The outfit itself was unassuming, all black with just a hint of luxury, except for the coat. Structured like her old military uniform, it exuded power and control. The lapels were embroidered in the Persion crimson. The small detail wouldn't be visible from far away, making it feel all the more intimate.

They met again in the kitchen, Adonis taking his time to give her a thorough once over. "You look divine." He winked on the 'divine' and Xolia rolled her eyes.

She grabbed his arm, pulling him towards the elevator. "Thanks."

ADONIS DROVE INTO DOWNTOWN ATALIA, where the First Church of Rheatha stood tall and proud. They drove past pedestrians, all unaware of Xolia watching them. She wondered about their lives and if they took their anonymity for granted. She felt the death of her anonymity like a weight dragging her down, slow yet inescapable. It wasn't that she was upset to lose it, she just dreaded the necessity of security and the scrutiny of her every move.

She tried to relax as Adonis pulled into the parking lot. Despite the fluctuations in attendance over the years, the church held an immense amount of power and wealth. It was one of the oldest religions in Ris, though the country had three national religions. The other two had been instituted after the fall of the variant monarchy.

Who's to say I'm not the Selermine? I care about variants, and humans. That's more than Atlas could say, or Helen or John. Xolia kept trying to convince herself she was fit to be the Selermine as she and Adonis walked to the front doors of the church. When they stepped inside, she was once again struck by the intensity of all the paintings. Every brutal war scene was a testament to what variants had overcome. It was a whisper of confidence. This was where she was supposed to be. This was who she was supposed to be. Everything was going to turn out okay.

Xolia thought about how mercilessly Atlas had bested her back at the museum. How woefully pathetic her attempts at self-preservation had been. There was no room for second-guessing. She had to be the Selermine. She had to be better than him. He didn't deserve to make decisions for the country when he was only looking out for himself. He didn't deserve Peter's trust or his mentorship. Atlas had seen Silas up until his death. That wasn't fair either.

Righteous rage burned through her veins. *Peter trusts me. This is what I need to do to help him.*

"That's Caius, the first Selermine," came Adonis's low voice behind her. She was standing in front of that painting again. The one of the man with the flaming sword held aloft, just the angry tilt of his eyes visible above his muscled arms.

"Really?" Xolia turned around to see Adonis nod. A slow, indulgent smile stretched across her face. Faith was hard to come by, but she had just managed to find some. That kinship she felt to Caius had to mean something. "Let's go."

Xolia grabbed Adonis's wrist and dragged him inside the chamber, where the stained-glass windows cast shades of color around the room, contrasting against the flickering flames in the sconces around the perimeter. Up at the altar stood a quartet of priests, all donned in the shapeless robes of gray. Their heads were shaved, and their hands were covered by white gloves.

Many of the pews were already full. Xolia was mildly surprised at the amount of people in the congregation, some were clearly human. Children sat with their parents. The sight of it made Xolia jealous. She didn't wonder about her parents often, but she would think about how little they must have cared about her to send her away as a toddler. How could they have been so disgusted with her very existence that they'd dropped her off at the barracks without so much as a goodbye? Were they really so afraid of her?

A comforting hand settled on her thigh. Adonis looked at her with concern, and she shook her head. There were more important things to worry about than her parents. Only one priest spoke, while the other three remained at the top of the room, standing in silent solidarity with the speaker. The sermon made metaphors of shepherds and sheep. Xolia had no knowledge of farming, but the metaphors weren't too difficult to parse out the meaning. It was just as Adonis had explained. Rheathians believed variants were on earth to govern and guide humans who, in turn, were to govern and guide the land.

Xolia found herself nodding along at certain points, though she couldn't help but think about Peter. There was no one else as suited to hold the title of chancellor as him. There was no one who cared as much about making a united and functioning country as him.

Once the sermon was over, Xolia was quick to get to her feet. Adonis was close behind her as they made their way to the thin walkway between the rows of pews and made their way to the front podium, where the priests stood to receive their congregants in closer conversation.

A priest, who had the beginnings of crow's feet at the corner of her eyes, became available when another couple thanked her and pulled their school-age child away. The child and Xolia made eye contact, the young boy's eyes bright and filled with a hope that she had never gotten to feel. *Am I really jealous of a child?*

She pulled herself up to the priest.

"Ms. Stone," she said. "And Mr. Person. How can I be of service to you both?" She folded her gloved hands into the arms of her gray robes.

Xolia's mouth dropped open. It was still disconcerting to have everyone in the church know who she was while she had no inclination as to what their names were.

"Priest Rhodes." Adonis bent his head deferentially. "Xolia and I need to speak with the head priest, if he's available."

She smiled. "Of course, Priest Irvine always has time for such a generous benefactor. Follow me." She led them out of the main chamber and down the same hallway Xolia had walked through just a couple weeks prior. Eventually, they made their way to the solitary red door.

Priest Rhodes knocked twice before the door opened inward to reveal Priest Irvine. His eyes lit up at the sight of Xolia and Adonis. Xolia wondered if Adonis would be writing another substantial check to the church by the end of the day. She exhaled, slowly, to try and calm the increasing stuttering of her heart. They had planned on bribery, but wouldn't it mean more if she was actually the Selermine? It would change everything for her.

At the head priest's insistence, they stepped inside the office, and Priest Rhodes closed the door behind them. "I was expecting to see you again, Ms. Stone." Irvine gestured at the waiting chairs and both Xolia and Adonis sat down.

Adonis focused on the reliquaries and books with unrestrained interest. Xolia would have to ask him later if he had been in this room before or if they kept most of the treasure troves of ancient texts in other parts of the church.

"It's good to know your name," Xolia said. "You never told me last time."

Irvine smiled. "It wasn't important then. Besides, you learned something about me today, and I'm sure I'll be learning something about you today."

Xolia inclined her head. This was it. Her chance to secure her worth and power. "I believe myself to be the Selermine." She let the statement stand on its own, throwing the full force of her belief into it. He needed to know she was sincere.

Irvine betrayed none of his emotions, save for the brief flash of his eyes. "You read the book I gave you?"

She nodded. She's briefly skimmed it and had Adonis's account of the origin of the religion. So it wasn't a complete lie.

"We haven't had a Selermine in a thousand years."

"I know." Xolia furrowed her brows. "I didn't know if I believed it at first either, that such a person could exist, but now I know."

Adonis gave her a furtive look. She answered him with a slight nod. Maybe he didn't believe, but he believed in her, and that would have to be enough.

"And what do you know?" Irvine asked. His face was still inscrutable.

"I was put on this earth to serve," Xolia said, because it was true. Her happy ending wouldn't be in living for herself, quietly tucked away in domestic comforts. Seven years of failing had proven that. She was made to make things right. She had to be the arm of justice where others reveled in injustice. "Ris needs help, someone to look up to. To shepherd them." She echoed the words of the sermon, hoping that might instill some confidence in Irvine.

The neutral mask cracked, and he smiled. "I hope you are, sincerely. As I said, the church was removed from the fighting, but we were watching constantly. There's only one way to know for sure."

"And how is that?" Adonis asked. Xolia knew how much it had always irked him that there was nothing of the Selermine trials in any of the texts he had read.

Irvine's smile widened. "I can't say, it's one of our most closely guarded secrets, though after Xolia's test, I fear it will be a secret no longer."

"What does that mean?" she asked.

"The test happens in front of the congregation," Irvine explained. "With today's technology and with this being such a historic event, someone will record it, no matter how much we might wish otherwise. You will be the last Selermine to be kept in the dark."

"Or," Xolia countered, "I could be the first to know what will be expected of me."

"If you truly believe yourself to be the Selermine, you have nothing to fear," Irvine responded, a hint of amusement bleeding through his even tone.

She couldn't refute that. Nor did she want to admit to any lingering feelings of doubt she might be harboring about the whole ordeal. It was too important to back out.

"When will she go through the trial?" Adonis asked. Xolia wondered if she would need to tell Bridget about this. *Probably.*

The woman had already started looking for every available opportunity to put Xolia in front of the public eye leading up to the announcement.

"Sel killed Lamina on the shortest day of the year. We are fortunate that that date falls two Sundays from today. Let it be then, to appease the spirit of Sel by uplifting a new mouthpiece on the day of their sacrifice."

Two weeks. Xolia's heart skipped a beat at the thought. Two weeks until she would go through whatever the church deemed appropriate for a Selermine trial. Three and a half weeks until the break of a new year, when she and Peter would stand side by side and announce her as the VC pick and would begin campaigning in earnest. In under a month Xolia would have little of her old life to cling to in the small moments of loneliness and doubt. She wanted Krista, wanted to hear her quiet reassurances and the way she could temper the warring emotions inside Xolia.

But what if Krista wouldn't approve? She had been so adamant that Xolia only wanted a position in government because Silas had wanted it. Would she see this path as a regression on Xolia's part? Xolia couldn't go back to how she had been living before. She would rather die than sit in the dingy cubicles of the bureau and wonder what Rowan was doing on the third floor in her private office with windows. She couldn't let Atlas do whatever he was planning. She couldn't let him win.

"That will be fine," Xolia said, her blood writhing under her skin. She somehow managed to stay in control enough to stop herself from feeling outwards to the other bodies in the room. "I'm ready now, and I'll be ready then."

"I know you will be," Irvine said, standing up. "I will be honored to present you as our Selermine." They shook hands, the gloves cool and soft under Xolia's skin. She and Adonis were quiet, both contemplative, she guessed, as they made their way back to his car.

The entire drive home, she couldn't tear herself away from her thoughts. Everything was happening all at once, and it was beautiful and terrifying. It was everything she dreamed, but not at all how she'd ever thought it would happen. Peter was sick. Atlas was impossible to read. All around her were other, more worldly and informed, political rivals. She understood Adonis more than ever, the feeling of being a renter in one's own life. Her home wasn't hers. Her money wasn't hers. All these opportunities were gifted, and no matter how much she wanted to believe she was entitled to them, gifts could be revoked. Love could be revoked.

Adonis held the door to his apartment open for her, and she grabbed at his shirt collar, pulling his lips down to hers and crashing into him with teeth. She nipped at him and sucked on his bottom lip. He returned the kiss with equal passion, dragging his hands through her hair and pulling her body flush against his. He bit at her jaw and neck.

It was a fight. A taking of control. She pushed harder against him, all rough touches, and steadily led him to the bedroom. He vied for control, but not with the desperation of Xolia. He seemingly knew what she needed, how she needed to have this, because of course he would. He was her first kiss, her first relationship. He was the one who had seen through her complacent haze of mediocrity at the gala. He understood the only thing that would make her happy and didn't judge her for it.

"Xolia," he whispered into her hair as he opened the bedroom door with a hand behind his back. They pushed into the room, instinct taking them to the bed.

"Mine." She put a hand on his flushed chest. "You're mine."

Hair in all directions and his eyes dilated to the point of being black, he nodded. "Yours." They lost themselves in each other, Xolia clinging to the simple pleasure of touch. The immediate relief of control. The safety in knowing that she had an ally. She had opportunity, all springing from Adonis's arms.

Chapter Twenty-Four

Xolia stood in the kitchen, her left palm splayed against the marble countertop, a knife in her right fist. She'd gone to Adonis's apartment after another failed attempt to create water in the gym. He had assured her it would just take time, after all, no variants had probably managed to do this in over a thousand years. *But he had.* Xolia needed to catch up. Her hand wavered. *Am I really going to do this?*

She clenched her jaw. She raised the knife.

Sel, you just have to do it.

Right when she was about to let the knife swing downward, the trill of her phone broke that careful stream of concentration. She couldn't stop from sighing, both her hands shaking even as she told herself she wasn't affected by what she was trying to do. How Adonis had managed this day in and day out for months was a mystery. Still, she couldn't deny that it had given him the desired results. If she could stop being so weak, she'd be able to manage it.

Flexing her left hand, she dropped the knife in an undignified clatter and grabbed her phone, swiping right to answer the unexpected caller.

He didn't say anything, and silence settled between them. Her stomach somersaulted. What was she supposed to say to him? Sorry? Was she sorry? Was she not sorry? Marshall reminded her of everything she wasn't and had tried to want to be. He reminded her of easy mornings and ignoring problems. She'd have to confront him to overcome him. "Marshall."

"Xolia." His voice was rough, like he hadn't slept.

"What do you want?" She leaned against the counter, running a finger along the sharp edge of the knife, the tip puncturing the pad of her finger. A drop of viscous blood beaded along the cut before it closed seamlessly.

A sigh came over the line. "Can we talk?"

She rolled her eyes. "We're talking right now, aren't we?"

"No. Like, in person."

Xolia tempered her reaction. They needed to talk. The apartment would need to be cleaned out, and it would be nice if he could hear from her, not the news, that she was to be the next VC. "We can meet at Windmere." Windmere was a spacious park in the north side of Atalia. Not far from the variant museum, it spanned over multiple city blocks and had been a significant point of interest both while Xolia was in the rebellion and after.

"By the old mausoleum?"

"Yes," came her quiet reply. No one knew who was buried there anymore, or even if there was a body entombed in the slate-gray stone. There were no other gravestones marking the space as a cemetery, just a single shrine to a single person in the middle of a green field and ancient trees and winding sidewalks. "Two hours enough time?"

Marshall consented and ended the call. Xolia put her phone on the counter, exhaling heavily into the quiet space. So much had changed since she'd last seen Marshall, since she'd thought she would spend the rest of her life living by his side. She grimaced at the thought. Something in her would have snapped eventually. He couldn't make her happy, any more than she could him. If she could make sure he understood that, maybe she wouldn't feel so guilty about hurting him.

Two hours later, Xolia was standing outside in the cool autumn air, with the sun shining down over the mausoleum building. She was wearing one of her favorite coats, which Adonis had gifted her from Persion. It resembled their old uniforms, structured and with double-breasted buttons. The shoulders were square, there was nothing soft or demure about it—it was all power. She stood up straighter when she saw Marshall's familiar and unbothered gait heading toward her.

He stopped a good distance away. With so few pedestrians out, there was nothing in between them. They regarded each other, Marshall's eyes shadowed with distrust. Xolia clenched and unclenched her jaw. If she had changed during their short separation, so had he. Gone was the soft-eyed lover. This was a shell of a man, someone lost and barely holding onto reality. While Xolia found herself more each day, it seemed he was the opposite. His clothes were disheveled. The barest hint of facial hair contrasted with his sallow skin.

"Hello," she said, her voice only carrying the barest hint of uncertainty. *What happened to you? Is this my fault?*

"Afternoon." Marshall nodded in one quick, terse moment.

Years of history filled the twenty feet that separated them. She'd once craved the way he saw the best in her, but now the thought of him seeing her at all was almost unbearable. Xolia closed the distance between them, pausing briefly by Marshall's side to cue that they should start walking. He followed, and they trailed through the familiar walkways, having the majority of the park mostly to themselves.

"You called me," Xolia said, breaking the heavy silence. "What did you want to talk about?"

She turned her head to look at him, right as he furrowed his brows, hurt stretching across his features. "Does our breakup bother you at all?" he asked.

Xolia scoffed, a nervous gesture to cover up the multitude of conflicting emotions inside of her.

Before she could answer, Marshall started again. "I was ready to spend the rest of my life with you. I really didn't think you were serious."

"Do you think we would have been happy if we'd stayed together forever?" Xolia stopped walking, forcing Marshall to stop and look at her.

"I didn't know you were unhappy."

Xolia turned to face the grounds—the yellowing grass and the bare trees. Everything was either dying or dead. "It wasn't just you. I was unhappy with everything." Another invisible weight lifted from Xolia's chest. The truth was setting her free.

"And you're happy now?" he asked.

A slow smile spread across Xolia's face. "Something like that."

Marshall stuffed his hands into his pockets and started walking again. Xolia rushed to join him.

"Rowan's worried about you too."

Her smile disappeared. "I don't care what Rowan thinks."

"Xolia, you were friends for years. She still cares about you. Doesn't that mean anything to you?"

"Marshall," Xolia warned. Her blood burned, but she wouldn't lash out at him again. No, she could control herself. She bit at her lip to stifle the way her blood writhed. "I will never be who you or Rowan want me to be. Who Krista wanted me to be. I'm focusing on helping Peter now." She was afraid and thrilled at what she left unsaid—that she was still too much of Silas's protégé to ever really move on. He'd taught her about power and without that, she was nothing remarkable. Nothing special. Nothing that she wanted to be. Even with Silas's untimely murder, he would be remembered long past any of their lifespans.

"I didn't want you to be anything other than who you were."

"You don't mean that," Xolia scoffed. "You wanted a certain idea of me. I can't pretend that I didn't want that too. It just wasn't real."

A broken gasp of breath escaped Marshall. "Was any of it real?"

Xolia thought back to the twilight years after the war had ended. How desperate they all were to fit themselves into the neat little boxes of freedom they had fought for. She thought of how desperate she had been to make it work and how no matter how hard she'd begged and tried, there'd were always been cracks in the façade. Always some insurmountable feeling she hadn't been able to overcome. "We had real moments. I thought I could wish it to be real enough that it would be." Tears pooled at the bottoms of her eyes. "Sel, Marshall, for so long after the war, I was alone. You didn't spend time in solitary, but I did. So when Rowan and you came back into my life, it was a lifeline. It's just one that I can't hold onto anymore."

"Why couldn't you tell me?"

Xolia wanted to laugh. "You were so perfect. Both of you

were. I don't even know if you still think about the war, but the war is who I am. I can't not be myself anymore. I am who I've always been. I'm the Xolia you knew before the war, and during the war. Why should I pretend to be anything else?"

"This isn't you!" Marshall exclaimed. "Before the war ended, yes, but after you got therapy, you got better. Is this because of Silas dying? You don't have to be who he wanted you to be. He can't control you. You're allowed to change."

"Maybe I don't want to." Sel, he was infuriating. This was who she was at the core of her being. This was who she needed to be to help Peter, to help Adonis. This was who she needed to embrace to embody the Selermine. If she'd ignored who she was, she'd still be pushing pens at the bureau.

Marshall leveled her with a cold stare. While Xolia knew she had changed on some level, there hadn't been a good baseline for comparison. This was one, however. Good, sweet Marshall who always looked at her with stars in his eyes was completely removed from the disappointment they now carried.

"I can't afford the apartment on my own, and I know you can't either," Marshall said, turning his glassy eyes away from her. "I'll call to have the lease broken. When can you get everything moved out?"

"Give me a week." There wasn't much she'd have to move out. Her engagement ring was still in her nightstand drawer. Photos of her and Marshall were still on the walls in their frames. "Are you moving in with Rowan?"

Marshall nodded. "Where will you stay?"

She hesitated. There was no way this would end well in an otherwise civil meeting. "I'm staying in Juthian Heights."

Marshall's eyebrows rose to his hairline. "How?"

Xolia suspected he would regret asking the question when he learned the answer. Still. . ."I'm staying with Adonis."

He choked on a strangled laugh. "Right."

The satisfaction Xolia thought she would've gotten from his discomfort was strangely and frustratingly absent. They took a few more aimless steps deeper into the park. "It's not—" she started, not really knowing why she spoke or what the next word leaving her mouth would be. "He's just helping me as a friend." *Idiot.* When would she stop feeling this way? She was supposed to be meeting with Bridget soon, setting up public appearances and getting ready for the VC announcement, but she couldn't stop herself from dealing with this. A broken heart and the fallout that ensued. It was something so normal, something that transcended humanity or being a variant. Something that could accost anyone regardless of job or class. It was frustratingly humbling, and she hated the way that still having to deal with this made her feel lacking for the opportunity before her. Silas had never once been out of control and she was spinning blindly, waiting to catch something that made sense.

"Right, and did you sleep with him 'as a friend'?" Marshall asked. Even back in the barracks during the war, when Xolia and Adonis had started dating, Marshall had hated him. Maybe it was because, even then, the two of them couldn't have been more different if they'd tried.

"Marshall," she said, unwilling to provide any further answer, though that itself was an answer.

Marshall shook his head. "I wanted to be good enough for you, Xolia. Every therapy session, every schooling session in rehab, I thought of how you and Silas made it happen. If you hadn't led the war, I'd still be babysitting politicians. When Rowan reintroduced us, I swore it was fate. But I don't think I'm not good enough for you anymore. You're not good enough for me. Goodbye, Xolia."

He turned and walked away, his frame slowly shrinking against the backdrop of the skyscrapers. Xolia remained rooted to the spot, something ugly unfurling in her gut. Bile rose to her throat, burning the whole way up. She hated feeling this way. She hadn't even been strong enough to tell him her news. She shouldn't feel this way, it was weakness and would need to be exorcised before she took her place by Peter's side.

Chapter Twenty-Five

Xolia didn't try to cut off her hand for the rest of the week. She fully devoted herself to moving what little she owned into Adonis's guest bedroom and working with Peter and Bridget. While the forefront of FAR's policies always revolved around variant equality, they were also a party dedicated to strengthening the country's middle class. Xolia grimaced slightly when she saw all the proposals for heavier taxes on the country's elite, that would be a hard sell to Adonis. Though she did bring up the fact that the Variant Service Act was still in effect and demanded to be at the forefront of removing the act from law.

Friday morning found Xolia alone in Adonis's apartment, her schedule for the day was empty as she needed to prepare for the fights. She needed to prepare for Helen. Xolia pushed away her breakfast, something about knowing she needed to kill unsettled Xolia, and it took away her appetite.

Without breakfast to take up her time, she stared at the knife block on the counter. Perhaps if she could jump-start these abilities, she'd be more confident for the fights. Licking her lips, she grabbed a butcher knife, the edge sharp and glinting under the lights. Taking a deep breath, Xolia spread out her left palm on the counter, the marble cold under her skin.

Maybe this is the Selermine trial, she thought, though she didn't really think the idea had much merit. Sel had sacrificed much more than a hand. Still, if she could do this one thing, then she would be more sure about the trial. It loomed over her every thought, and the days kept disappearing with frightening speed.

"Just do it," Xolia begged herself. Fear settled in her stomach, and she held her right arm aloft. Try as she might, she just wasn't strong enough to commit. *If Adonis could do it, you can do it.*

Xolia tried to dredge up any childhood competition between them that would give her the ambition to cut off her hand—because she feared the first few attempts would result in a missing hand. She wasn't that naïve as to pretend she could master such an archaic use of power on the first try, though she hoped it would be enough to stop the decpaitation.

Sweat slipped down her forehead to her nose before splattering on the marble countertop. *Come on.* She needed this. Surely on the campaign trail there would be a need to protect herself or Peter, and it wasn't like they would be speaking around large amounts of water. Xolia had never even left Atalia, except for the barracks and her brief visit to Dresden Bay, what was she supposed to expect from the rest of the country?

Sure, Peter had his bodyguards, and she would have hers soon enough because Peter didn't believe her strong enough to defend herself, but maybe she could show him just how capable —she screamed.

Blood spattered everywhere, the sight almost comical if she

hadn't been in so much pain. Her fingers, which had been splayed out straight, were now limp and bent. Her arm ended in a nub, blood gushing from the wound.

So much blood.

So much blood.

And she had done nothing to stop it. Not a thought. Not a plan. Nothing. The pain ate away at her conscious thought, but she couldn't let Adonis find her passed out on his kitchen floor, blood and a severed hand waiting for him.

With the last dregs of her control, she reached out to her blood and stanched the bleeding. She needed to close off the wound for a short time while the bleeding stopped on its own and the skin and bone started replicating themselves, stitching together a new hand. Although going to the hospital would help with the speed and pain of regrowth, there was no way she'd open herself to that kind of questioning. *Please heal by tonight.*

Xolia panted from the effort of keeping the blood inside her body. *Sel, that was awful.* She leaned toward the sink, jerking her right hand to the faucet and turning on the water. She leaned her head underneath in a completely undignified action, but she needed water. She guzzled down as much as she could before promptly throwing it up.

Maybe it would be best if she sat down first. Xolia made her way to the living room couch on shaky legs. It didn't matter how many times she was injured, the pain never grew manageable. Recovery never got easier. She wondered how humans managed their brief lives, full of the same hurts but without the promise of a healing flawlessly. It'd drive her insane.

She sat on the couch, precariously oscillating between consciousness and unconsciousness for what felt like hours until the lightheadedness subsided and her heartrate slowed down to something resembling normal. Xolia was halfway to the kitchen, ready to try drinking water again, when the elevator door opened.

Xolia grimaced. This was the worst time for Adonis to come home. "Xo." His rich voice rang through the apartment. "I thought we could get lunch." He stopped in the kitchen, his eyes immediately drawn to Xolia's unattached hand that was now in the throes of rigor mortis on the counter.

"Fuck." His eyes widened at the horror of his kitchen. The hand, the blood, the vomit on the floor. "Xolia, what did you do?"

"It didn't work," she said, voice scratchy.

"This is marble, Xo."

"Wait." She swallowed while trying to process his words. They were so far from what she had been expecting, a strained laugh bubbled out of her. Even though it physically hurt to laugh, it felt good to feel light in the face of everything else.

Adonis turned his wide-eyed stare on her. *He must be wondering if I've gone crazy.* Maybe she had.

Once Xolia managed to settle down, she spoke to him. "I just thought you would be worried about me."

"I am, you idiot," Adonis said. "But I also know that you'll heal. The counter won't. Sel, what were you thinking?" He ran past the mess to her.

"I'm tired of not being able to do it," she admitted. "You did, I figured I would imitate you."

Adonis gingerly grabbed her mutilated and healing arm. He was careful not to touch anywhere close to the flayed skin and bone slowly building itself back together but ran a gentle thumb up and down her forearm. "Xolia, you don't have anything to prove. You're strong. People will listen to you.

They'll follow you. You're the Selermine. The first in a millennium."

"You don't even believe in it, though."

"I believe in you."

Xolia embraced him with her good arm. "Thank you," she whispered against the warm skin of his neck. Her eyes fluttered closed at his comforting presence.

"Hey." He pushed her back, softening the movement with a kiss to her forehead. "We need to do something about the... hand in the kitchen. And then we need to get ready for the fights. After, we can celebrate your win tonight."

She smiled at him, putting her hand in his. He believed in her. She would figure out how to expand her powers later. Everything would be okay.

By evening Adonis had already called someone to repair the countertop. The knife had scratched the soft marble irreparably, and even after the bleach, there was still the faintest stain of red. She had apologized profusely, but Adonis shrugged it off.

Xolia's arm wasn't fully healed. Her palm was nearly done regrowing, though there was no break from the burning pain as her fingers started the meticulous process. Xolia's nerves exploded as Adonis drove them to the old barracks for the fight. Xolia's partially reconstructed hand was wrapped up in black fabric, and she planned to hide it in the pockets of the Persion sweatshirt she wore. She was dressed head to toe in Persion athletic-wear with lightweight shoes that would allow her ease while fighting against Helen.

"Why aren't there ever raids of this place? It can't be safe to always have the fight in the same location," Xolia mused.

"The barracks are private property now," Adonis said. "Helen owns them, and she pays the police enough to not look here too closely."

While the barracks couldn't have been the most desirable property in Ris, they were a substantial amount of land that couldn't have been cheap. Helen's hold over every aspect of Adonis's life came into focus. Not only did she have damning blackmail, but she had wealth that he couldn't match even while his parents controlled all of the Persion family assets.

The barracks materialized outside the city. The ill-kept buildings loomed ahead of them, the knowledge of what she needed to do settled like a weight in her stomach. Xolia had never planned nor successfully executed a killing before. When she had served under the Gornne Administration, she'd always been in the city, protecting important people or patrolling the streets for petty thieves and criminals. There was no premeditated murder.

The war had been different. Silas would dictate her orders. Killing had always been in the heat of battle, an act of self-defense, really. It'd been her or her opponent. It had all been justified. Cut and dry. This was muddy. Helen didn't plan to die at the fights though Xolia had no doubt Helen planned to kill anyone who stood in her way. Unfortunately for Helen, Xolia was thinking the same thing.

Xolia studied Adonis. His dark hair fell to the sides of his face, hiding his eyes but highlighting his nose. *Are you worth killing for?* It was for freedom. For their future. Xolia wasn't well-versed in romance stories, but Rowan was a romantic. She'd regale Xolia with stories of love-struck couples and their declarations that the other was worth dying for. But to kill for someone? Adonis ran his right hand through his hair and must have caught her stare because he turned to her and smiled. Xolia smiled back at him.

Unlike when she'd come to the fights with Atlas, who had stopped at the main gates to open them, Adonis drove around the perimeter of the fencing, the SUV running over dirt. Near the back of the complex, the fencing had been removed, allowing for straightforward access to an old garage that had housed all the vans they'd used to drive around, to and from the city.

There were no more decrepit white vans, but instead, a multitude of cars that ranged in make, model, and price tag. Adonis parked in a reserved parking space, next to a car that rivaled his in expense. Xolia angled her head to get a better look at the car.

"It's Helen's," Adonis said. Xolia tore her gaze away, embarrassed that he'd caught her staring. She didn't respond, but she did allow herself to grip the corner of Adonis's elbow a little tighter than normal once they started making their way to the main training center turned fighting ring.

Guards, overly muscled and hulking, stepped aside at the sight of Adonis. "She's been wondering where you were," the one on the right said.

"I'm here now," Adonis answered, tugging Xolia through the open door. Rather than going down the hallway to the locker rooms, Adonis took her into the upper levels of the building. They had been gutted from the classrooms, which once had lined the main arena, to create open space that let in cold drafts of air. Xolia suppressed a chill.

"She'll be through here," Adonis said. One classroom had

been left intact, with screens and monitors along the walls and a small group of people in the center. Pictures of the fighters with their numbers were lined up, and one of the men sitting on a metal folding chair was inputting information on a spreadsheet. Xolia peered closer through the window. *Betting information.*

Adonis opened the door, drawing everyone's attention. Helen stood in the center of the room, her hair swept up into a tightly coiled bun. Dressed in clothes similar to Xolia's, she looked ready to fight tooth and nail. Two familiar and identical people were conversing silently behind Helen. "Tanzin? Lilith?"

The twins locked eyes with Xolia with unnerving synchronicity. "Xolia," Tanzin said. He looked much the same as he had during the rebellion, though now his black hair was completely shaved off. He was still thin and willowy like his identical twin sister, Lilith, whose hair was in a cropped bob that ended just below her ears.

They had been under Adonis's command during the days of the Gornne Administration. Back in the days of the rebellion, the three of them had been inseparable, their friendship forged and strengthened by the constant fear of death. Adonis had never specified what went so wrong between them, and even though she knew their relationship was fraught, it was strange feeling the tension radiating from the three of them. Underneath her grip, he tensed.

"It's been a long time," Lilith said, sticking out a limp hand.

Xolia raised her eyebrow, while trying to decide whether the blasé handshake was a blatant sign of disrespect or just who Lilith was as a person. Xolia gripped the woman's hand and shook. "Lilith. Helen." Xolia nodded her head in Helen's direction.

"Xolia Stone." Helen sucked in through her teeth, a strained smile completed the disingenuine greeting. "How kind of Adonis to bring you tonight."

"Tonight is going to be historic," Adonis said. "No one will want to miss it."

Helen's smile didn't falter, but she glanced between the two of them. "Can I steal Adonis from you?" she asked Xolia, grabbing at Adonis's free arm.

He pulled away from Helen. "Let me escort Xolia to our seats."

"Tanzin can take her," Helen said.

"I won't be long." Despite the apprehension in the room, Adonis didn't hide the contempt in his voice.

Xolia winced internally. "It's fine. It'll give me time to catch up with Tanzin." She squeezed Adonis's arm, trying to convey that everything would turn out alright. If the lingering essence of Sel was in her veins, it would have to turn out alright.

Adonis leaned down and brushed his lips against the shell of her ear. "Be careful. I'll find you as soon as I'm done" he whispered.

Xolia nodded against him. If she had to immobilize Tanzin, she would. What was one more body in the pursuit of peace? From Xolia's memory, the twins were at a disadvantage in one-on-one combat without the other to cover their weak spots. As if reminding her of how untrue that statement was, Xolia's arm burned as her hand continued to repair itself under the tight bindings. She bit back a groan and adjusted the end of her arm in her pocket. "I'll see you soon," she said to Adonis and gave a cursory nod to Helen and Lilith.

Separated from Adonis by the thin door, Xolia gestured with

her right hand for Tanzin to start walking. "Helen tells me you've gotten close to Adonis again," Tanzin said.

"We got reacquainted with each other at FAR's annual gala," Xolia said. "I'm surprised I never ran into you or Lilith at one of them."

Tanzin shrugged and stuffed his hands into his pockets. "Yeah, well, FAR is not the only party for variants."

He led Xolia into an elevator, which she was surprised still worked, to lead her to the third level. Xolia figured he was taking her to the room on the top level of the building which overlooked the arena. It was where Silas and other high-ranking and elder variants had supervised the younger generations during their sparring matches. The people who'd watched up there had made the decisions as to who would be grouped together and what assignments they were to receive. As far as seats for high-paying spectators went, it was one of the best places to be.

Having a decent enough memory of the layout, Xolia decided to pry into Tanzin's loyalties. "You think Helen could lead a better party?"

Tanzin scoffed while they walked through the wide and empty hallway. It looked exactly the same as in Xolia's memory, but now there were places where the white paint was faded and chipped against the cinder-block walls. "Something needs to change, Xolia. I'm not sure what Adonis has told you, but you'll want to be on Helen's side." He said Adonis's name like it disgusted him.

Xolia hummed, needing to know what had gone so wrong between them. "What does she know of being a variant?"

"It would help if you had a conversation with her rather than just listening to everyone else." Tanzin rounded on her, blocking her. "Though I guess you were always better at listening than making your own decisions. Did you hear the news about Silas?"

Shame burned through her. With just a few barbed words, Xolia was transported back to that last day in Krista's office. It wasn't fair. She had only been a child during the war, but so had Tanzin, and it he wasn't like he'd acted with any more autonomy. "I did. And I don't recall you ever acting on your own orders back then."

"I didn't, but I also didn't act like I was better than everyone else, either. You were always riding Silas's authority, everyone could see through it."

Xolia swallowed down everything she wanted to say, to shout at him. She resisted the urge to fight him. "Well, he's dead. I'm not the same as I was during the rebellion, I'm not planning on blindly following orders."

"'Not the same?'" Tanzin laughed and turned around again, resuming their walk. "Please. You are FAR's biggest puppet. Though your speech this year at the dinner didn't seem to go so well."

"You watched it?"

"Anyone with a stake in politics watches it."

Xolia seethed, nothing she could say would sway him. He must've known the same because he didn't say anything more. They were both hurtling toward their inevitable conclusion. She stepped into the room, which had a few other people, some visibly human, milling about. There was a bar set up to the right, with large screens above the bartender. Pictures of the fighters were presented, along with past fight statistics. Everything set up for bets.

There were no whispers of Helen's ambitions for the evening though Xolia already knew that was set up to be more of a surprise than anything. Tanzin didn't enter the room, he just saluted tersely to Xolia and strode away. It only increased her curiosity, while she'd had no strong opinions about the twins in the past, she wanted to know everything that had happened to them after the end of the war.

"How lovely of you to join us," someone said behind Xolia.

She turned to find the weathered face of Jordan Davenport, the senator of finance for Ris. He had aided Peter during the rebellion, using his role as treasurer to embezzle funds to FAR. Once the rebellion had ended, Peter rewarded his loyalty by naming him senator of finance. He had a reputation for being an upstanding member of the Risian government and Xolia was surprised to see him here, so brazenly.

"Senator." She nodded deferentially.

"Please, Ms. Stone. None of that is needed here." He waved her away and took a sip of his drink.

"I just wouldn't have expected to see you at someplace like this," she admitted. She had only met him once, at the end of the rebellion when she was still searching for Silas.

He lifted a brow. "Even senators need something to do in their free time. And I was persuaded by the variant Persion boy to give the fights a chance. Of course, I haven't been able to get the legalization of the fights past the Senate floor, but all the taxes on the bets get paid so I find it's easy to turn a blind eye." He winked at her.

She lifted the corner of her mouth in return. "I hear tonight is going to be extra. . .entertaining. Is everyone else in here part of the government?"

Senator Davenport shook his head. "Business mostly. Much of the government is far too fractured to engage in mutually secured destruction. FAR has changed a lot of things, Ms. Stone."

It was no secret that the Gornne Administration, and many before it, had been corrupt. Peter had fought voraciously for FAR to escape such low levels. Everything was run above board. Everything was transparent. Xolia looked around at her surroundings. She was not above board. Though neither was Atlas. "Do you think Peter has a good chance at re-election?"

"I couldn't say. This is the first election we're having in this form of government, and the first one in over ten years. Unfortunately, there are a lot of humans that are stuck in the old ways."

"But surely they've seen what Peter has accomplished. What he still wants to accomplish," Xolia pressed. It was at that moment that she realized the full weight of what it meant for her to become the vice chancellor. It would be power, true power. It would mean something. She could mean something again, not just to herself, but to the country.

"Chancellor Bellevue hasn't been polling highly, and neither has Vice Chancellor Campion," Senator Davenport said. "Though without any other official candidate announcements, we don't have much to compare them to."

In the background, the announcer called the first fighters, and the other attendees gathered closer to the large window to look down at the masses of low-level spectators and the two fighters in the small cage. Adonis was still gone.

Xolia pushed all that to the back of her mind as she continued to push for more insight. "What do you want to happen?"

"Of course I want FAR to stay in power. If Chancellor Bellevue goes, I won't be too far behind him. A new candidate will want to fill his Senate with those loyal to him and who helped get him elected." Senator Davenport shook his head. "Tonight isn't about politics, though, let's enjoy the entertainment."

Xolia nodded and walked next to him. Down below, the fight was in full swing. The smaller of the two variants wielded rocks, while the larger wielded water. Xolia had missed what type of fight it was, though the two of them used the elements in their raw states. No weapons of any kind formed in their hands.

It was over when the earth wielder landed a large chunk of rock across the other's head. They crumpled in a heap, and the announcer called the winner after ten tense seconds. Two people in gray uniforms rushed to unlock the cage and dragged the unconscious variant out. Xolia pulled back to see some of the people on her level with smug grins. A small sigh escaped Senator Davenport.

Chapter Twenty-Six

Adonis entered the room during the fourth match. Xolia stood alone, having drifted away from Senator Davenport at some point during the second match. She had placed herself near the back of the room, preferring to study the people in the room rather than the fighters down below. Xolia was confident almost two-thirds of the room were humans, leaving only a small portion of variants.

Adonis's face was harried, and his usual suave demeanor was replaced with frantic movements and a jerky tilt of his head to draw Xolia over to him. "Is everything okay?" she asked under her breath.

"We need to get you down there now," he whispered. "The twins are going to be a bigger problem than I thought."

A shiver ran through Xolia. This was really happening. A quick look around the room confirmed everyone was still focused on the fighting below. Xolia tried to flex what had grown back of her hand and thumb, but sharp pain shot down her nerves. "Let's go."

Adonis rushed her through the hallway and pressed the

elevator button no less than ten times before the doors slid closed.

"Adonis." Xolia used her right hand to grip his chin and force him to look at her. "It's going to be okay."

He breathed in deeply, closing his eyes for a moment, before exhaling. "I've been working toward this for so long. I think the twins are suspicious."

"What happened between you?" she asked.

"They were my closest friends in the whole world." Adonis shook his head. His eyes had a glazed look, as if reliving long buried memories. "But they chose Helen."

"Maybe she has blackmail on them too." Xolia tried to reason.

"No. They believe in her."

Xolia furrowed her brows. On one hand she knew that even amongst variants there was division. On the other hand it was illogical to think that an entire group of people could feel the same way about something, but that didn't stop her from thinking that they *should* have the same opinions, even more so if those opinions aligned with her own. She just wanted what was best for them, they would see things from her point of view once she'd proved her ideas held merit.

They just don't know your ideas yet. That's why you're doing this. "Where will all of this go once she's gone?" Xolia waved a hand to indicate the general area they were in. "Her father?"

"Helen decided to give a white-collar criminal full control over her finances." Adonis scoffed. "If she would've bothered to read the fine print, then she'd know ownership of all of her assets passes to me in the event of her death."

He didn't elaborate further, instead he pulled their focus to cutting through the throngs of eager spectators, who were waiting for the next fight to start. Helen was on the other side of the space, though the crowd parted for her at the behest of the twins in front of her, making use of their ability to wield air to push others out of their way.

Helen climbed into the cage, the bouncers taking a protective stance on each side of the open door. Helen adjusted a small mic affixed to her shirt and called for everyone to quiet down. The rising din of confused murmurs decreased with her clear and magnified words.

"My fellow Risians, my countrymen." It wasn't fair how melodic her voice was. "I stand before you today, in the midst of our entertainment, as a part of the forgotten few of this country. While our government has pretended that variants are equal in today's society, our time here proves otherwise. Variants are still hiding, they are still forced to take suppressants, and not all of them are known to us."

Xolia shifted her gaze to Adonis, whose body was drawn taut. His jaw was clenched. She reached out to give him a comforting touch.

"So many variants have lived and died in this country with no recognition. They were forced to hide who they were for fear of being sent to the barracks. Then peace was promised, and were these variants able to claim their true identities?" Helen paused, and not a single other person broke the silence. "No. Variants who aren't registered with the Census Bureau can face up to three years in rehab and seven years in prison. How is that fair? How is that just? It's time for us to take a stand, and I start by standing in front of you, telling you that I am a variant. I have been hiding for over two decades because the peace I was promised never came."

"Chancellor Bellevue has given us nothing but empty

promises for seven years. And what of his supposed competition? John Clemont? The man who was President Gornne's largest supporter? No. It's time for things to change."

The energy of the room shifted, the tension snapped, and around Xolia, people leaned in to listen to Helen's words. *No. No. This is all wrong.*

Xolia nodded at Adonis. It was time. She needed to make things right. She needed to show people how wrong it was to believe in Helen. For the first time in her life, Xolia let go of the self-control that had been so embedded into her system. She allowed herself the conscious thought to reach out to someone else's bloodstream and took control with delight rather than as a last ditch-effort at salvaging her own safety. The whispers and pull of Helen's blood were delicious, and she sank into them with a reckless abandon. All she had to do was tug once. Helen's easy and gilded words faltered and the whites of her eyes showed. She struggled to stand upright. The twins popped up from the sea of people, their gazes roaming as they pushed through the crowd, seeking the culprit. The guards moved away from the cage door, aiding their search.

Adonis gave her a gentle push toward the cage, and Xolia ran. She took her left hand out of her pocket, no longer caring if anyone saw the lack of fingers, and pushed through the guards to get into the cage. She pulled on their bloodstreams, forcing them to the ground. Commotion erupted around them. People stood up and shouted, everyone in a frenzy.

Outside of the cage, Adonis confronted both twins. Flame from the torches in the cage quickly surrounded Adonis while the twins fashioned weapons, the faint pulse of air the only thing visible. The twins attacked as one, providing no quarter as Adonis struck and parried.

Xolia tore her gaze away, she couldn't focus on that right now. She stalked over to Helen, who was still fighting against Xolia's hold, and ripped a small mic affixed to her shirt, holding it close to her lips. "Stop," she commanded. Her voice didn't lilt in soft cadences like Helen's. She hoped it carried authority at least.

Though Adonis and the twins continued, everyone else appeared to give into a macabre sense of curiosity. That, or they were trained to listen to anyone with a mic. Xolia needed to take her chance. "Helen doesn't care about you. She didn't fight in the war. Not like me. And not like you. Even if there are other unregistered variants out here tonight, she didn't share your childhood either. She's the daughter of the most influential general in the country. You think she knows your suffering?"

The words flowed easily from Xolia's lips. Goosebumps erupted along her arms. This felt different from her speeches at the annual gala. This felt different from rattling off Silas's orders. This was her. It was who she was supposed to be. "What can Helen know of peace when she sacrificed nothing to achieve it? She doesn't want to help us—not like I do. Not like I've proven myself to do."

Xolia walked up to Helen, grabbing her by the hair. She pulled back on her control, just enough to give Helen the ability to breathe easier. Helen's lips were tinged blue from the lack of blood pumping through her system. "This is the face of someone who would let you all die if it meant she got what she wants."

"That's not true," Helen spit out.

Xolia turned back to the crowd of people. "I've worked with Silas. I've worked with Chancellor Bellevue. Change does not happen overnight, but we are on the right path. Give me the chance to prove it to you. Let me spare this country another war."

In the corner of her vision, Xolia caught sight of Tanzin landing a particularly nasty strike against Adonis, sending him flying to the ground. She let her control—physical and mental—over Helen go slack. The other woman didn't hesitate to fly after Xolia, tackling her to the ground.

Shouts erupted from the crowd, though it was all too slurred to tell if they were rooting for Helen or Xolia. Helen looked up, a sinister smile pulling at her lips. She grabbed the microphone from Xolia. "I think it's only fair if we settle this in the same way our ancestors did. A fight to the death. Sel will guide the stronger candidate to see the winning path."

Xolia tilted her head, this was too easy. It was too similar to her own plan. Helen stepped away from her, throwing the small microphone to the ground. Xolia followed suit while Helen gave a small nod to the twins, who were holding Adonis up from either side of him, his head lolling forward. They dropped him.

The crowd was riotous in the stands. Their shouts so like the first fight Xolia had been in, when she had been the enemy to the uncontested crowd favorite. Now, she thought she heard snatches of her name beyond the general roar.

I don't even know Helen's element. The woman held out her hand and a vortex of wind swirled around her body.

Xolia wanted to roll her eyes. Of course, she would have the same domain as the twins. Seeking out the water, Xolia focused and pulled as much as she could around her; wind users were annoying in how they generally blew every weapon or foothold away from their opponent. And, in this fight, she was sure Helen would have no qualms about taking cheap shots.

You shouldn't either. Xolia warred with herself. She'd

already manipulated Helen's blood, but Silas had hated it when she used her blood manipulation more than strictly necessary. Winning this fight like any other variant might further endear her to everyone watching. *But you're not just any variant.*

Xolia yelled her frustration and pulled a fraction of the water away from her body to form a sword. The short reach would make it harder for Helen to separate Xolia from it though it would be harder for Xolia to get close to her.

Helen tried to push Xolia off-balance, but Xolia remained standing. Xolia pushed a wall of water toward Helen, forcing her to the edge of the cage.

Xolia ran at her. Helen blocked the strike. She formed her own melee weapon, hard to see but for the small ripples in the shape of a sword.

They struck, parried, circled one another, and struck again.

Xolia took the offensive again, swinging at Helen. Right when Xolia was about to land a strike across her midsection, Helen knocked the sword from Xolia's right hand, and without her left to help grip, there was no resistance as it flew to the side of the cage, spraying water on the twins and Adonis.

Helen smiled. "My father used to talk about you constantly. I can't really see what all the fuss was about."

With her left hand, Helen funneled a torrent of air, which knocked Xolia to the ground. Instinctively, Xolia braced against the fall with her hands, sending sharp shooting pains through the regrowing nerves and tendons of her left arm.

On the ground, Xolia turned to Adonis, who watched her with wide eyes. She couldn't let him down. She couldn't let Peter down. *I can't let myself down. I'm better than this.*

Taking a deep breath, Xolia closed her eyes and channeled all of her focus onto herself. She was so tired of losing. She hadn't been able to beat Atlas. She still had to prove herself to the church. There was no guarantee Peter would win. And if he didn't win, it would all be for nothing. Every choice she'd made since the gala would have been worthless. Her easy life with Marshall was gone. This was it for her. She needed to act like it.

Xolia's eyes flashed open, and she let herself go. Blood seeped from her pores and over her left wrist until there was an approximated hand. Before Helen could level her with a killing blow, Xolia rolled away, adrenaline coursing through her. She stood and pulled more blood up to the surface of her body, coating her arms, and she punched Helen across the jaw.

The satisfying crack of bone buzzed through the air, and Helen took a wobbly step back. Her eyes flashed; this was the first substantial hit Xolia had gotten on her. Helen tried to push Xolia to the wire wall of the cage, but Xolia ran from her.

The shouts of the crowd urged them on. It almost felt divine, the deadly dance between the two of them—the way their elements clashed and battled for dominance interspersed between the punches and kicks.

Helen mis-stepped. She tried to kick Xolia but overextended her leg and dropped to the ground. Sweat dripped down her unblemished skin.

Xolia drowned out the fears of using her blood manipulation and pulled on Helen's blood. She pushed her against the ground, making it impossible for Helen to move.

Brushing sweat-plastered hair out of her face, Xolia leaned down to pick up the wireless microphone, which had sustained some damage from their fight. Her heavy breaths still reverberated around the room; it worked well enough. "I know that some humans would have us back in the barracks. I know that we still have laws that are only in place to hurt us," Xolia said. "But I know that I can change it. FAR can change it better than Helen DuBois or John Clement can."

Xolia locked eyes with Adonis, a small smile on his lips, and nodded at him. "I know it's hard to have faith but believe me. I made it better once; I'll make it better again." She dropped the mic and sucked in a shuddering breath. Xolia looked up at the top level, the angle of the glass made it impossible to see inside. Was Senator Davenport still watching? Did he agree with her? Would he turn her in?

She looked at Helen, still pressed to the ground. Tears and sweat pooled around her eyes. There was nowhere else for Helen to go, no way to escape. Xolia took a step toward her. Then another.

All the fear and apprehension about what she had to do melted away, only to be replaced by the fear and apprehension of having people watching. There were so many of them, it would be impossible not to trace it back to her. If this leaked, it would derail all of her careful plans. Atlas hadn't hurt her with his own hand at the fights, and when he had made a direct move, it had been under the cover of night. She could do that too.

Her heart thundered against her chest. Xolia knelt in front of Helen. "I win."

Helen strained against the invisible bonds, a vein in her forehead throbbing. If Xolia had to guess, Helen was trying to harness the air without use of her arms. She smirked; Helen wouldn't be able to do anything.

Xolia whipped her head over to Adonis and the twins. Before the twins could retaliate, she jerked an arm out and latched onto their bloodstreams. The strain of holding three people wasn't sustainable, but Adonis jumped into action right away, directing those loyal to him to grab the twins and Helen. The clamor of the room picked up, shouts and cheers and clapping.

It started hazy and indefinite, but within a minute the sound clarified into the three distinct syllables. Xo-lee-a. *Xolia. Xolia.*

A smile stretched across Xolia's face. They were actually cheering for her. They believed in her. She had won. Variants were standing behind her. Adonis stepped into the cage with her and swept her into a tight embrace that she quickly reciprocated.

"We need to take care of Helen and the twins," he whispered.

"Now?" she asked.

He nodded, his cheek brushing against hers. He pulled away and lifted her right arm up in triumph to the cheers of the crowd. "Do you think this means something? Or is this just part of the night's entertainment to them?" Xolia asked through a wide smile.

"I'm not sure," Adonis answered. "I have faith it means something." He squeezed her wrist. Xolia bit back a retort, faith was priceless when people had it.

Xolia and Adonis stumbled out of the cage. The crowd pushed in against the pair, with more of Adonis's people filing in around them. They walked them back through the hallway and up a flight of stairs to the room full of monitors and screens. It was empty except for Xolia and Adonis.

Xolia stared at the chaos unfolding down below with a giddiness she hadn't felt since she was a child. There was no guarantee this would work, but it felt like things were going in her favor. It felt right. She was finally getting the recognition she deserved; her efforts were being rewarded. This was the purpose, the meaning, that had been missing from her life. Nothing Marshall could say would ever compare to people looking up to her for guidance. She couldn't quell her shallow breaths.

Adonis looked at her with half-lidded eyes for half a second before he moved. His hand wrapped around the back of her neck and his lips met hers in a fierce kiss. "You did it," he mumbled out in between their shared breaths. "You were incredible."

Xolia clawed at him, trying to eliminate any space between them. "You were amazing," she said, breathless. Their lips met again, hot and punishing. Bruising. "Holding off both twins at once? Amazing."

The reminder of the twins and Helen had them pulling away from each other, adjusting their clothes and hair. Xolia couldn't stop her cheeks from heating up when she looked at Adonis.

"Where are they?"

"Come on," he said while grabbing her hand. They walked through the arena building and out the back door they had entered through.

Adonis led her over cracked sidewalks and between darkened buildings. He stopped when they reached her old barracks. There were five barracks stationed in the complex. One of them had been for the young children where they all started, there they received basic education and an introduction into how to use their powers and what they could expect for the rest of their lives as Ris's most prominent and elite law enforcement. The one Adonis stopped at existed much more recently in her memory.

It was the building she'd called home from twelve to seventeen. On the seventh floor there was a single room that was barely wide enough for her to extend her arms out on either side. A twin-sized bed had taken up half the space and then a small dresser unit, where she'd kept her clothes and toiletries and stolen trinkets, took up another quarter. There'd been countless nights when either Adonis or Rowan had sat with her while they'd talked about what a future of freedom might mean. What they would do if they didn't have to live under President Gornne's oppressive leadership.

For the first time since she'd left that room, Xolia thought her younger self might be pleased to see her. A younger Xolia would be ashamed that she'd ever stopped fighting for what was right. A younger Xolia would hate that she didn't have the public acclaim she'd held under Silas's leadership. An older Xolia pushed the worry down that she didn't know which was more important to her now.

"Why are we here?" she asked, pulling her hand from Adonis's.

"It's where I had them take everyone," he said.

"Really?"

Adonis nodded. His sense of nostalgia was odd, in an endearing sort of way. "Let's go, then." Xolia took a deep breath and walked in through the front door. Unlike the arena, there was no electricity in the building, just a faint white glow slipping from a closed door, off to the left of the lobby, that once was the entrance to the laundry room.

Even in the dark, Xolia could make out the traces of decay and chipped paint. Despite that, there was still the same overwhelming sense of sterility to the place she'd always associated with it. There was nothing of individuality to the building at all.

Together, they slipped into the one illuminated room. Two

men stood in the back corners watching over the bound and gagged trio. Snot and tears leaked from noses and mouths. A small pit formed in her stomach. This wasn't self-defense anymore.

But they can't stay alive. And really, if I was fighting them, I'd just keep them immobile anyways. This isn't any different.

She half-believed herself, and that was enough to go through with it. Standing shoulder to shoulder with Adonis, she faced them, looked them in the eyes, and killed them.

Chapter Twenty-Seven

THE RIDE BACK TO ADONIS'S APARTMENT WAS QUIET. XOLIA stared out the tinted window, lights flashing in and out of focus. Her mind didn't linger on the event. It'd started and then it'd been over. Less fuss than a full-on fight, and the cleanup hadn't fallen to her. It had been clinical. Without danger.

Something dark lurked under Xolia's skin. An uncomfortable feeling of guilt. Maybe they shouldn't have killed them while they were bound and gagged. Maybe they should have forced Helen's surrender rather than killing her. *She wouldn't have stopped. Peter is relying on me, I can't let him down.* But would he be okay with murder? Xolia bit her lip and tried to rein in her thoughts. They wouldn't stop their cyclical spiral of guilt and justification.

"Will this come back to us?" she asked, leaning over to watch Adonis. The jut of his neck bobbed as he swallowed.

"No." He loosened his grip on the steering wheel and brought a hand to rest on her thigh. "We weren't the only ones who wanted Helen out of the way. They'll make sure this gets buried. Part of her plan was to open the borders, you know? We did the right thing."

Xolia blanched. Ris only had one neighboring country on the southern border and had isolated its borders for as long back to the earliest days of the monarchy. Even the presidents had kept the borders closed. *What was Helen thinking?*

Xolia leaned back against the headrest. "We need to figure out what Atlas is planning."

"Once you're in the public eye constantly, he won't be able to go after you anymore," Adonis reasoned.

"That's not what worries me," she admitted. "I'm more concerned that he hasn't come after me again. I feel like I've missed something."

She placed her hand over his, seeking any amount of comfort from him. "I think that he knew Silas better than I did." The words stung. Silas had always pushed her further, pushed her to want more, and if she had been nothing more than a disappointment to him, what was the rest of this? She would've been better off pretending she was happy with Marshall and working under Rowan.

"Don't say that." Adonis flipped his hand, so their palms met. "We don't know that for sure. If Atlas knows anything more about Silas, or whatever he was planning, we can figure it out."

The full weight of everything they had done, and everything still to be done crashed into her. "He saw him before he died. Multiple times. The last time I saw him, we were supposed to help FAR, and that's what I did. It's what I've done for seven years, Adonis, I can't let Atlas have this."

Coasting to a stop at the apartment's underground parking

lot, Adonis turned to Xolia. "He won't. Silas trusted you for a reason. He would be proud of you, Xolia."

Xolia let Adonis lead her to the elevator and into his room, where they slowly took off each other's clothes, and he lavished burning kisses all over her body. He whispered praises along her skin that Xolia wished she didn't need to hear so badly. She clung to him in the late hours of the night, hoping that she could wake up without the all-encompassing blanket of fear.

A WEEK PASSED, and there was not a single story about the general's dead daughter. Xolia obsessively checked the news at every point in the day, whether it was working with Bridget and Peter, while they planned public outings for Xolia, or organizing their campaign.

By Friday, Xolia had stopped worrying so much and was instead focused on carefully applying mascara to her dark lashes. She and Adonis were going to a highly publicized charity event that night, suggested by Bridget and funded with Persion money. The cause of the evening? Raising funds to rebuild some of the decimated residential buildings that had been damaged before the final battle and had been left to further decay in the years since. It had been a nice neighborhood. While it hadn't been as elite as Juthian Heights, it had been more expensive than the neighborhood she and Marshall had lived in.

She slid into a floor-length carmine gown and left her room, needing Adonis to zip up the back. He was standing in his large walk-in closet, adjusting a silver set of cuff links on his suit.

She didn't need to ask—their eyes met, and he nodded. She turned around, and his fingers grazed her skin as he pulled up the zipper. He dropped a soft kiss to the base of neck. "Ready?" he asked.

Xolia nodded. Parties were easy. She knew how the evening would go, what to expect from the people around her, and what they would expecte from her.

They made it to the elevator before Adonis spoke again. "By the way, my parents will be there."

"What?"

Adonis shrugged, the tense set of his shoulders betraying his true feelings. She didn't know the last time he'd seen his parents, but she knew how he felt about them.

"I'm sorry you'll have to see them," she said, placing a hand on his forearm.

"Don't be. We were overdue for a visit, and even as their CFO, I can't give to any charity without their approval. I just wanted to give you the heads-up."

"You won't have to deal with them alone. We're partners," Xolia said.

Adonis nodded and tangled his fingers with hers. They walked through the lobby to the sleek limousine waiting for them in the cold, the driver already standing by the back door, ready to let them in.

CAMERAS FLASHED as Xolia and Adonis made their way up the red-carpeted steps of the Risian Museum of Art, the rented venue for the evening. People she didn't recognize made polite small talk at the front entrance while event planners ushered them inside, where all the exhibits were open for guests to meander around until the dinner and speeches started later in the evening.

Xolia had never been inside of the Museum of Art before. During the war there'd been no reason to, not even Silas had wanted to destroy a millennium of art, whether it was created by human or variant hands. Afterward, it hadn't really been the sort of thing she, or Marshall and Rowan for that matter, was drawn to. Now, she dragged Adonis from painting to painting, waiting to see whether any of them had such an effect on her like the one at the church—that tether that ground her to the spot while she stared at a figure immortalized in oils.

She was enraptured by a series of paintings that had come out right around the end of the variant monarchy when Adonis pulled away from her.

"Mother. Father." His voice was brittle, and Xolia's heart hurt for him. Every day, she was glad that she had resolutely rejected any form of reunion with her parents.

"Adonis," greeted his mother. Her voice was low and raspy. Xolia snapped her head away from the painting and slipped her arm through the crook of Adonis's elbow.

Even from the first glance, she could see the similarities between Adonis and his parents. He had his father's jaw and his mother's nose. They had both given him his dark hair and green eyes. Despite the animosity between them, the familiarity struck her. Biological family was such a foreign concept to Xolia it almost held no weight to her, but now, looking at this trio of people who shared blood and a name and facial features, she realized they could never fully sever their connection. Not with all of them left living anyway.

No wonder Adonis was so desperate to overtake them. Persion

had always been his birthright, and it should've been given happily, along with their love. Their protection. Xolia didn't understand how someone could look at a piece of themselves and throw it away like it meant nothing. She gripped Adonis's arm tighter.

"Please introduce us to your friend," his father said, staring down at her in a way that wasn't unlike Adonis. Though where Adonis had a fire behind his eyes, his father's stare was cold. There was nothing but icy hatred and feigned civility.

"This is Xolia Stone," Adonis answered stiffly. "We've known each other since we were children."

Xolia held out her hand for them to shake. Both immediately wiped their hands against their thighs. "Are you enjoying the evening so far?" she asked.

"Quite," his mom said. "It was a tragedy that so many innocent Atalians were displaced by that ghastly business. And even more so that we can't rely on our government to fix it."

Xolia had nothing to say to that. All she could do was restrain her anger with shallow breaths. Did his parents believe humans were the only ones who'd lost something during the war?

Silas had always made it a point to evacuate the area of civilians before they would attack. Xolia had always believed in that; those humans in the apartment buildings hadn't been in the army, they hadn't deserved to die, but looking at Adonis's parents with their frigid postures and demeanors, Xolia couldn't help but wish Silas hadn't spared civilians. They had been complacent, after all. Their hatred had burned just as much as the army's, as the government's. It wasn't like there had been thousands of humans clamoring to join their cause. It had just been them.

Xolia couldn't voice that, though. People like his parents

would never understand, and it'd only hurt her own end goal to ostracize them. "Naturally."

"Perhaps we should find our seats for dinner?" Adonis segued the conversation, and their quartet, to the main hall, which had tables and displays of ice sculptures and fountains of sparkling wine stacked in delicate flutes.

On a stage, performers danced in sequined costumes. It was excess to a degree that any FAR event could never hope to match. Xolia clenched her fist. Why was it fair that these people had so much when she'd grown up with so little? They could've rebuilt the apartments five times over with the amount of expenses they'd thrown into renting the oldest museum in the country and all the pageantry they'd stuffed into it.

Adonis had told her that plates started at $15,000 per person. Insanity. A small fear weaseled its way to the forefront of Xolia's mind. What if these people had more power than Peter? They threw their money into whatever project they deemed important, stuffing their faces all the while. The general's party hadn't even been like this.

Xolia shook her head. She had never felt this vitriol toward money before. *They can take everything away from me with a word. A check.* Nothing she worked on would matter if they shot her down. *Why did Bridget suggest this?*

"You go to the table, I need to get some air," Xolia whispered to Adonis.

He stopped and pulled them discreetly out of the way to put a hand on the back of her neck. "Are you okay?"

She nodded. "I'll be right back."

Adonis kissed her brow and gave her left hand a gentle squeeze. Everything had regrown—bone, tendons, skin. Since her disastrous experiment, she had been back to training every morning with Adonis in the gym. She hadn't managed to create water yet, but she hoped she was getting closer.

With a last caress against his skin, she slunk through the halls until she reached the front entrance and slipped outside, where her arms erupted in goosebumps from the early winter chill. All the photographers and journalists had cleared out, and the red carpet that had been rolled out to induct all the illustrious attendees lay in the cold, all the dirt finally noticeable on the shag. Xolia hung her head in her hands, the solitude of the night was the permission she needed to let her guard down. *What the hell am I doing?*

Every time she tried to make the right move, something else popped up that made her doubt. What was the point of anything if there was always someone with more? More power. More money. She didn't understand how Adonis had survived a life like this right after the war.

The air shuddered around her, something like wind, but too controlled and sudden to be natural. Xolia lifted her head to find four figures shrouded in darkness and heavy coats. Large hoods obscured their faces from view, though their breaths were visible as small white clouds.

Xolia tried to track who was controlling the air but couldn't make out such a subtle movement. She grounded herself with a deep breath, waiting for the right moment to make her move. They couldn't know she was a variant or they wouldn't have been so rash in their decision to flaunt their power.

"You've gone somewhere you shouldn't have," one of the figures ground out.

Xolia snorted. "The front entrance of the museum?"

None of her uninvited companions thought her retort was funny. There were a few scattered scoffs. The wind died down, and the flicker of a lighter broke against the cool cast of the street lamps.

"Who are you, anyway?" Xolia asked, her chill momentarily forgotten as she straightened her stance. Her weakness was not for other people to see.

"Do you know how long variants have begged for funds for housing? How many of us live on the streets?"

She was only too aware of all the problems that continued to plague variants. It'd been her constant companion at the bureau. For every one variant or variant family she helped, there'd been three more added to the waitlist, in dire need of assistance.

"You're happy to let us die and suffer, but the minute a family of humans decides they don't have enough housing options already? You flock together to fundraise."

Another member of the quartet stepped up when the first speaker's voice cracked. "Humans will reap what they have sown. This is the promise of the Underlings, and you will carry our message."

Flaming bullets shot toward Xolia, and the airy graze of a wind-made spear brushed against her cheek, drawing blood.

Xolia's blood sang at the sudden surge of adrenaline. In a dress, she didn't have the same reach or flexibility, but she didn't need it. She coaxed her blood free of the veins along her wrists and formed curving blades along both of her forearms.

There was a moment of hesitation from her opponents, and Xolia took advantage. She swiped left, drawing a harsh, jagged cut along the leader's chest, and kicked the figure that had lit the lighter.

The other two dissipated their weapons. "Xolia?" asked a woman's voice. The woman lowered her hood, but Xolia didn't recognize who it was.

"Am I not who you expected to see?" Xolia asked, almost upset at their easy surrender. "What could the Underlings possibly hope to gain from being here?"

"Justice," the leader said from the ground. He held a hand to his chest, Xolia's cut was shallow as they'd been too far away for her to do substantial damage, but it had covered a wide portion of his chest.

Xolia sneered at them. "All you're doing is making sure humans have a reason to hate us. You're no better than them."

"You have to understand—"

Xolia lifted her arm so her bloody blade rested it along the soft skin of the woman's neck. "You don't understand. You don't make decisions for variants, but I can. I know what's best. I'm working on what's best." Xolia hadn't even been thinking when forming the words, they'd flowed out of her, and the moment she said them, she believed them. She was the Selermine. She was the voice of her god and no one knew better than her. *Why did I ever doubt myself? All the money in the world cannot stop me.* She pushed harder against the woman's neck. *Nothing can stop me.*

The action drew a soft whimper from her, and her other standing companion rushed toward Xolia. With a look, a thought, and a subtle hand gesture, Xolia grabbed hold of his blood stream and pushed him back. He flew into the street. Xolia panted slightly at the exertion from such a large movement.

Behind her, blazing yellow light distracted the assailants. "Xolia!" Adonis yelled. A flaming ball hurled past her and hit the already dazed man, lying still in the street. In another moment Adonis was next to her.

She couldn't let this woman get away yet. "Are there more of you Underlings?"

The woman nodded.

"Are any of you the leader of the group?"

She shook her head. Flashing red lights lit up the otherwise quiet street. Law enforcement had arrived. Xolia cursed and pushed the woman away from her. She knew what detainment meant for a variant and didn't need to make an enemy of the Underlings. The woman scampered away.

"Are you okay?" Adonis asked.

Am I okay? Xolia turned away from Adonis and tried to ignore the approaching officer. What had she said to that woman? Nothing felt as right, nothing as true to herself. But dear Sel, that wasn't what she was trying to do, was it? It wasn't as if there was no one else who could help her people, just that she was the most qualified. In two days, she would be the Seler-mine. That was as good as royalty. It was royalty. Her phrasing just needed a little work, she decided. It was a communication issue, the message itself was sound and justifiable.

"I'm okay." She smiled at Adonis and allowed the officer to run down his list of questions about her assailants. Xolia answered as vaguely as possible and lied when asked if any group had taken responsibility for the attack. She shivered when the officer walked away, so that he could confer with his partner. Adonis placed his suit jacket over her shoulders, and the warmth and scent of cedarwood wrapped her up.

"This feels vaguely familiar," she said with her eyes closed. Without their surroundings, and just the feel and scent of his jacket, it was easy to imagine herself back at the gala.

"I do like the change that my jacket will end up in my closet at the end of the day." Adonis nudged her with his shoulder. "Who knows what happened to it while you were slumming it?"

Xolia huffed out a laugh. "I think we're still slumming it compared to some of these people."

"Very much so."

In the wake of the flashing lights of law enforcement, their imbecilic staff taking pictures, and Xolia talking to Adonis came the even more smothering vans of the press.

"Bridget couldn't have planned this night better if she tried," Xolia said as reporters and cameras made their way toward the pair.

"Maybe she did," Adonis quipped.

One reporter walked up to the pair. The woman was strangely familiar. Xolia furrowed her brows trying to place where she had seen her before.

"It's Violet," Adonis whispered to her.

Xolia's eyes widened as she made the connection. Violet had always been drawn to the public aspect of their rebellion, helping to hijack newscasts and spreading the word of the variants' plight to the country.

"Xolia, Adonis," Violet greeted. "I'm sorry we have to be reunited in circumstances like this. Would you be willing to give a statement?" Violet waved over her accompanying cameraman, the camera a large contraption that rested over the man's shoulder and almost completely obscured his face.

"Of course," Xolia said.

Violet cued up a smile that looked more practiced than sincere and stood with a microphone held just below her chin until some unseen cue spurred her into action. She introduced herself to the Risian National News viewers and gave a brief overview of what had occurred.

"I'm here with Xolia Stone, a variant who helped spearhead the Variants' Revolution and the same woman who was just attacked outside the museum. Xolia, can you tell us what happened?"

The microphone was thrust into Xolia's face. Xolia tried to opt for a more genuine smile. She couldn't afford to offend variants or humans. This was for everyone. They needed to know they could rely on her. "I don't consider myself a victim of a targeted attack. Everyone is scared right now, and it can be easy to lash out. I hope that the variants who were so misled understand that I cannot side with variants or humans more than the other. I put aside my prejudices the minute *FAR* freed us. I urge all of Ris to do the same."

A hint of sincerity crept into Violet's expression. "How do you feel about the increase of variant-led attacks on humans? Do you think this is related?"

The question made Xolia squirm. Seeing the abused wealth in the museum would have sent Xolia into a tailspin if she were a variant who had been led around by the bureau for years with nothing to show for it. "Again, I urge Risians to find common ground as citizens. I can't say I'm familiar with any violence from variants."

"Thank you," Violet said. She said a few closing remarks and directed viewers back to the main anchors. "That was fantastic, Xolia. Much better than your last gala speech."

Xolia curled her lips. "You watched?"

"Every journalist watches the PAN." Violet lowered the microphone and handed it off to the cameraman.

"We're loading up in ten," the cameraman said as he grabbed it from Violet.

Violet nodded, and the man lifted the camera from his shoulder and turned back in the direction of the van.

"Violet," Adonis said. "You look well. I didn't know you were running your own segments."

"I'm not," she answered. "I'm filling in, normally I'm just on the writing staff."

"You sounded very natural," Xolia said.

Violet smiled. "Thank you. This story was actually a great opportunity for me to get in front of the camera. I'm still sorry you were attacked, though."

"It's okay," Xolia said, wiping away the small smear of blood from her already healed cut. *This is why I have to make sure things stay right. FAR is working, I just need everyone to see that.* Violet looked happy. She was doing better than she'd been before. Seeing her strengthened Xolia's resolve. Nothing would deter her from her path.

Chapter Twenty-Eight

Nerves woke Xolia long before her alarm was set to go off. She lay in bed, listening to the steady inhale and exhale of Adonis's breath. A hint of snow flurries brushed across the window of the high-rise apartment.

The first snowfall of the year on the shortest day of the year. It was unnatural for the snow to come so late, but for it to come on the day of her Selermine trials almost felt intentional. Xolia yawned, giving up any hope for another hour of unaffected sleep.

She got up to shower, spending longer than necessary under the scalding spray. She wiggled her fingers around, forming little shapes that resembled animals out of water. The small act reminded her of her childhood. In the barracks they'd been prohibited from having any toys. It had been a constant influx of puzzles, tasks, and schooling. As children, she and her comrades had had to make their own toys, and it became a status symbol among the children—who could make the most shapes and hold their forms the longest while they played amongst themselves.

Xolia wasn't anything like that little girl anymore. The shapes came easier, and they pranced around her head and the shower, but there was no laughter behind the action. No joy. Just an imitation of fun. Xolia dropped her hands, letting the animals splash down into the drain. She made sure all the soap was rinsed off her body and hair was clean of conditioner before shutting off the water and launching herself into the rest of her morning routine.

By the time she left the shower, Adonis was gone from the bed, and the sweet aroma of syrup drifted into the open door of the bedroom. Xolia slipped into the pressed trousers and sweater that both hung in the closet and twisted her hair into a low bun.

In the kitchen she was greeted not only by Adonis but also by Bridget, who held a spatula in her hand and was serving three plates of pancakes. Xolia blinked. "Bridget?"

Bridget raised an eyebrow, wrinkles forming above the arch. A strange sight; Xolia still wasn't used to seeing a variant who aged. There weren't many around. "I saw the news. I think you undersold the other night."

"I didn't think it was that bad," she said, sitting down at the bar next to Adonis. She hadn't even known he had any food in the kitchen, as they never cooked.

"Regardless, it was probably the best possible outcome of the evening. Your name is everywhere, and you really sold human-variant unity," Bridget said, settling into a stool to dive into her own plate.

Xolia scoffed. "You're not even going to ask if I was alright afterward?"

"You fought in a war," Bridget said. "And you're a variant; if you're alive, you're alright."

"Do you want to be coddled?" Adonis teased.

"No." Though the first part of the question stuck in her head. *Do you want?* She did want, but she didn't want to want. This feeling hadn't been supposed to follow her once she left Marshall and the bureau. This feeling of wanting more, always more. She had a void in her soul, and the job with Peter was supposed to be enough to fill it.

Each bite was a struggle, and she stayed quiet while Adonis and Bridget made idle small talk. Xolia had only cleared away a quarter of her breakfast when she noticed the time. "We have to leave."

Both Adonis and Bridget sobered, and Bridget cleared away the plates. "It's going to be okay," Adonis said, grabbing her hand and giving a comforting squeeze.

"I'll be there, too, since I can't trust you to stay out of trouble. I talked to the church, and we've arranged for security to meet us there," Bridget said. "There are going to be more reporters and bystanders."

Xolia nodded, thankful for the support. She drew in a deep breath. Together, they stepped into the elevator and descended into the parking garage.

The drive to the church was silent until Xolia spoke. "Does Peter know?"

"Of course he knows," Bridget said. "What happens to you affects everything."

Xolia thought about Peter's cough and how it wracked his body each time he fell victim to a fit. He didn't need to spend time worrying about her too. "I won't let him down again."

Adonis slid into a parking spot right behind the ancient building. The spires appeared even sharper than they had the last couple times Xolia had been there. The shadows around the scaffolding were somehow darker. It felt malevolent for the first time. Xolia shivered.

Adonis came around to open the door for her, and she placed her hand in the corner of his elbow. Bridget trailed behind them. Xolia hadn't asked whether Bridget was religious or not. It didn't really matter anymore, she supposed. She was there to support Xolia and that had to be enough.

Upon entering the building, that sense of evil dissipated and calm settled over Xolia. She found the painting of the first Selermine, the one she felt such a palpable connection to, and tried to pull strength from him again. *It's going to be okay. This is right. This is the right path.* She tightened her grip on Adonis when Irvine entered the antechamber.

"Xolia." He dipped his head. Xolia, Adonis, and Bridget responded in kind. Rather than the gray robes she had come to associate with the clergy, Irvine was in pristine white robes. Just like the white of FAR's uniform at the end of the war. Her chest tightened. That day hadn't ended well. *Please let me not get shot today.*

Xolia realized Irvine probably didn't know who Bridget was. "This is Bridget Halding. She works with me."

Irvine nodded. "I talked to her earlier. She arranged for you to meet with your new security detail here."

"They're from the Presidential Palace?" Adonis asked.

"Yes. I understand you'll be working closely with him soon. Nothing is more important to the clergy than the protection of our Selermine and government," Irvine explained, holding Xolia's stare.

Xolia had let go of her reservations about having a constant guard. If it was the price of being in the public eye, it was a price she had to pay. "Lead us to them."

"A guard will give you freedom," Bridget said. "Peter chose this team from his own personal guard."

Freedom is admitting to what makes you happy. The first time she had been here, Irvine had told her that. Something twisted in her gut. *What if nothing makes me happy?*

She buried the thought and followed the small party as they walked down the side hallway. Rather than going into the office she had sat in before, Irvine led them to a large classroom. A set of windows overlooked the east-facing parking lot, where congregants were parking and talking in small groups. The room had a few round tables with chairs; one of the tables had three people sitting around it. Two men and one woman in casual dress, though one of the men had a handgun protruding from the pocket of his jeans.

"I've had the honor to talk to them before you arrived." Irvine folded his gloved hands into the folds of his white robe. "Allow me introduce you, unless you'd like to do the honors." Irvine gestured to Bridget, who shook her head.

"This is Jareth." Irvine gestured to the tallest of the three. He was broad-shouldered and had a short beard and bushy eyebrows, which made him the most rugged man in the trio. His skin was free of any blemishes, and there were no wrinkles around the creases of his eyes or by his mouth; he was a variant.

"And Isiah." Isiah was shorter, but rivaled Jareth in bulkiness. He was clean-shaven, though he had a scar through one black eyebrow. Human. *Interesting.*

"And your final guard, Emily." Emily had cropped red hair. Recognition sparked for Xolia.

"We were in the same barracks," Xolia guessed.

Emily nodded. "We were. I look forward to working with you again."

Xolia nodded. She turned to the two men. "It's a pleasure to meet you both. How did you come into this line of work?"

"I fought in the rebellion, just not in Atalia." Jareth held out a hand, and Xolia shook it. While most of the fighting had been concentrated in Atalia, there had been other cities that'd seen uprisings against the status quo.

Isiah held out his hand. "My brother was a variant. I never got the chance to meet him or protect him."

Xolia clenched her jaw. She wasn't used to seeing humans express regret for variants' suffering. *I shouldn't judge him before he's had a chance to prove himself.* "I appreciate your dedication to helping, though I hope I won't have to use your services."

"The Palace and the Church are in agreement—you'll have one of them with you at all times," Irvine said. "The safety of our Selermine is paramount. Nothing is ever going to be the same for you again, Xolia."

Xolia couldn't stop from glancing at Adonis. He looked at her and nodded reassuringly. *This is the right thing to do.*

"The service will be starting soon; we should get you ready." Other priests entered the classroom to guide Bridget and Adonis out, and Jareth and Isiah followed them. Emily remained by her side, shoulders straight and head held high.

"Follow me," Irvine said. He strode out of the classroom, folding his hands into the robe sleeves.

Xolia followed him and Emily followed behind her. The hallway was empty, and the darkness weighed down on her even though the flame torches still burned violently against the old stone. Xolia could barely breathe. *Why is it so hard to breathe?*

They reached the antechamber, and the pressure on Xolia's

chest only increased. Even looking at the first Selermine didn't give her any of the usual comfort. She had no idea what to expect. What if she failed? Everything was dependent on this working.

Sel, it was so hard to breathe. A pair of acolytes entered the antechamber through the main doors. One carried a polished wooden box in his gloved hands. "For you, Priest Irvine."

Irvine lifted the lid, on well-oiled hinges, to reveal a solid gold pendent of a moth with flaring wings. Rather than a moth's body there was a dagger. The symbol of the Selermine. Irvine lifted it from the velvet and placed it around his neck. He turned to Xolia and said, "I told you once before this was the mark of the Selermine. It hasn't been worn in a thousand years. I'll wear this as I'm administering your trial. Should you be successful, it will be my honor to give this to you."

Xolia nodded. She didn't trust herself to speak. This was more nerve-wracking than the war. More vulnerable. There was no Silas. No Adonis. It was just her. The acolytes opened the doors to the grand room. Light spilled in through the stained-glass windows, illuminating the stone altar at the foot of the podium. Flames danced around the walls, and each and every pew was filled with people. Xolia didn't have the mental capacity to try and guess whether they were variants or not.

Somber notes of an organ filled the silent room, and Irvine walked down the aisle, with her following, and behind her the rest of their growing procession. She kept her head held high and refused to deviate from looking straight ahead. It was too late to show weakness. Irvine took his place behind the altar, and the two acolytes positioned her slightly behind him. Off to her right, Adonis was waiting in a small alcove. Relief washed over Xolia, though she didn't let her shoulders slouch or even look over at him. She couldn't, not when everyone had their eyes on her.

Irvine opened his sermon. "It's been a thousand years since a Selermine has last walked among us. It's been even longer since we've seen a trial. But on this auspicious day, we have a chance to change history for the better. This is our time to restore the rightful hierarchy that Sel wanted for us."

The acolytes brought a set of white robes to Xolia. They were identical to Irvine's. Xolia lowered her head, and they placed the thick wool over her head and pulled down. Xolia slipped her arms through and let the rest of the garment fall to the ground. Heat enveloped her, and sweat began beading around her forehead and down her back. If only she could look at Adonis.

Irvine kept talking, and the acolytes moved away from the dais before returning with another box. It was the same polished wood as the one that had carried the Selermine pendant, but it was larger. Narrow and long. Xolia tried to puzzle what could be in there. It wasn't more jewelry.

"Xolia Stone stands before us and Sel. She is a variant who spent her childhood fighting for variants. She spent her days under the tutelage of Silas. She humbles herself before the church to be named this generation's Selermine." Irvine turned away from his congregation to her. He held out a hand, hidden away by the white glove. Xolia took his hand in hers, and he led her to the altar. "Please kneel before the Altar of Sel. It is against this rock that Sel took the life of their sibling for *us*. For their creation that they so loved. And it is against this rock that every Selermine has laid to offer themselves to Sel."

Xolia clenched her jaw but did as she was told. Dropping to her knees, she scooted up to the altar and placed her elbows over the carved stone, holding her palms together in a picture of prayer. Her heart thudded against her chest. She stopped trying to breathe.

"No, my child. Arms at your side, and hang your head over the stone." Irvine opened the latch on the box.

Xolia wanted to know what was inside, but she also wanted the trial to be over and done with. She moved her body along the stone. The harsh ridges of the carvings were dulled by the thick robe she wore.

A thick gasp swelled from the congregation. Panic gripped Xolia. Something was wrong. She couldn't hold off any longer; she turned her head to where Adonis was hidden away from the rest of the congregation. He wasn't looking at her. His gaze was beyond her, eyes wide with fear. He made to run toward her, but gloved hands pulled him back.

"Sel." Irvine's voice boomed from behind her, paralyzing her to the altar. "It is your blessing we ask for. Your guidance. We know that a variant's limbs grow back. We can withstand extreme temperatures. Poison and illness cannot take us."

Xolia twisted her head the other way, trying to see what made Adonis so afraid. In Irvine's hands was a sword. The blade glowed red bright in the low lights of the church, and it had a wooden handle with a ruby resting in the pommel. Chills ran down Xolia's spine. A sword was a weapon of a human, no variant needed steel to inflict damage, though this didn't seem like a normal human weapon.

This isn't right. She turned back to Adonis, who was now on his knees, still restrained by acolytes. All around the room the flames flickered in and out.

"It is only through separating the brain from the heart, or stopping both, that a variant will meet an untimely demise. And it can only be through the will of Sel that one can survive such an act." Irvine moved toward her.

Beheading? Why couldn't Xolia move? She was going to die. She didn't want to die. *No, please—*The cold bite of metal stung the back of her neck. Sel, she couldn't breathe. What the hell was happening?

Slowly, like moving through syrup, she tried to turn her head once again, to see Adonis one last time. But nothing happened. She was weightless.

Blank.

Warm.

Floating.

In the abyss a moth flew around her. Well, not her, there was no corporeal body. Her soul, maybe.

And then there was another moth. Another. Another. Until her awareness was eclipsed by wings and antennae. The fluttering wings crescendoed into a buzzing. A droning. A screaming. And she was on fire. Burning and in agony.

She opened her eyes; blood flooded her vision and the iron bite of it filled her mouth. Choking. She was choking. If only she could move. She stared at the ceiling—Wait. *I'm on my back?*

She had been on the altar, last she knew. She shored up her energy and courage, she moved her head to the left. There was the altar. Crimson blood dripped from the stone. It steadily poured down to the floor where she lay. Her body felt like it was melting from the inside out. Her hands shook so badly she could hardly make sense of how to move them.

Somehow, they made their way to her neck, which sported a jagged rejoining of flesh. The tendons and veins and bone fused back together, sending jolts of electricity arcing through her body with each atom that snapped back into place. Time ceased to have meaning. *I shouldn't be healing this quickly, not from a wound like this.*

A white-robed figure stepped in front of her, the hem drenched in blood. *Her* blood. *Irvine,* her mind supplied. The priest was standing in front of her. He lifted his gloves, now red, toward the heavens, though her ears were ringing too loudly to hear whether he was talking. Something touched her shoulders, a heavy, steadying weight that eased some of the terror and grounded her to reality.

Too afraid to move her neck, she put a bloodstained hand on top of the weight. It was another hand. Adonis dropped to her side. Out of the corner of her eye, she saw his mouth moved, but she still couldn't make sense of anything. He lifted her up, ducking his head under her shoulder.

Once she was off the floor, Xolia realized all the candles and chandeliers that had lit up the chapel were out. It was dark except for the window behind them, light streaming down to illuminate the dais. There was no congregation, no pews, nothing beyond the blood. Someone led her to the edge of the dais, where a raucous cheer overpowered the ringing. They stood there, Xolia barely holding onto consciousness, clinging to Adonis, while the torches were relit, candle-wick finding flame. Everyone stood, enraptured.

She reached up to grab Adonis's shoulder. He looked down at her. "I want water." Her voice could barely be considered a voice, it was so cracked and low. She hardly understood herself, and it was she who had formed the words. He must have understood or known that whatever she needed wasn't around the crowds and priests. Together they walked away from the noise and the religious miracle. An acolyte stopped them and led them through a series of hallways to a plush sitting area. Neither spoke. What was there to say when they both needed to process everything that had just happened?

Barely given the chance to be alone, Xolia winced when Irvine and the woman priest entered the room. The woman held a box, her gloves still unmarred and white. Irvine still wore the stained ones. Almost with a sense of pride. Xolia shuddered. Not even she was so depraved.

"I'm so glad Sel found you worthy," Irvine said reverently.

She couldn't tear her eyes away from the third box. What more could they do to her?

"What's in the box?" Adonis asked, his voice was cutting. Xolia relaxed into him further. Tears stung the corners of her eyes. Dear Sel, why had that happened to her?

"No one will forget what they saw today, but she needs to bear Sel's mark permanently. This is just the last step." Irvine grabbed what looked like an ink pot and some sort of gun from the box.

"You're branding her?" Adonis asked. He still held Xolia, and around her, all of his muscles tensed.

"It's not a brand," the woman said. "It's a gift. We need you to leave, Mr. Persion. I know your other companion is asking for you."

"Send her in here, then," Adonis said. "I'm not leaving Xo."

"You must," Irvine said.

Xolia raised a hand to touch Adonis's jaw. She couldn't speak again, but she would do anything for this nightmare to end, and if that meant Adonis needed to leave, then he needed to leave. She nodded once at him, which was enough. Adonis moved her to the soft couch and glared at the rest of them before slipping out of the room.

The low buzzing of the tattoo needle disrupted the terse quiet. Irvine's steady hand hovered over her neck for a brief moment before he brought the needle down to the exact line the sword had passed through.

Unbidden tears sprung from her eyes. Desperately—valiantly—she tried, and failed, to stop them from pouring out. The needle dug and gouged at the barely healed skin, skin that was still reforming over muscle and cartilage. She couldn't even clench her jaw, the pain ricocheted up and down her body, singeing what nerves had grown back. And it would not end.

Chapter Twenty-Nine

XOLIA CRACKED OPEN A SORE EYE, FEELING LIKE SHIT BUT more or less like herself. Her entire body ached, and chills assaulted her insides. Adonis and Bridget sat next to her, both of their faces were scrunched in concern. Adonis had a comforting hand over her own, his thumb caressing her knuckles.

"What time is it?" she managed to eke out with strained vocal cords. She opened her other eye.

Bridget leaned over, picking up a glass full of water. "Drink this."

"It's almost midnight," Adonis said.

Xolia struggled to comprehend. More than twelve hours had passed. She pulled her hand from Adonis's and grabbed the water. As much as she wanted to chug the entire glass, her throat was too dry and drinking hurt. Much of the water spilled around her mouth when a cough assaulted her. Bridget was quick to take the glass back. "I'll go get some more, take your time, Xolia." She slipped out of the room.

Adonis brushed hair out of her face. Xolia closed her eyes. He was so warm against her pallid skin. When she opened her eyes, she noticed Adonis wasn't looking at her face, but right below. *My neck.* Gingerly, she brought a hand to her neck. The skin was raised and puckered.

A sob escaped Xolia. "What did they do to me?" Would she ever sound like herself again? She couldn't stop rubbing her fingers around the raised skin. It didn't feel right. This wasn't right. It wasn't part of the plan.

She raked her nails along the length of the scarring. Her neck burned.

"Xolia, stop." Adonis grabbed both of her hands and pressed them against her chest. "Please stop."

Xolia wept.

She wept harder than she had after the war. She wept the tears she had withheld when she got the news about Silas. She wept until the tears dried away and all she could do was shudder against Adonis. He held her, and that made it worse. They were together because they were strong, and they helped each other be stronger. Now she was changed. Variants didn't scar. This was entirely human. She was both below and beyond her fellow variants.

A knock on the door silenced Xolia. She pressed her lips together and hid her head in her hands, determined not to let anyone else see her like this. Bridget entered the room, a full cup of water in her hands. "I brought more water. Irvine wants to talk to her soon."

"Thank you," said Adonis.

"Of course," Bridget said. There was a small shuffling sound as she moved to put the water down. "Are you okay?"

Xolia whipped her head up. "I'm fine." She couldn't let Bridget know how much it was affecting her. "I want to see it."

"There isn't a mirror in here," Adonis said.

"Then take me to one."

Adonis helped her up. She leaned on him, tingles shooting up and down her extremities. Bridget swiftly moved to her other side, and the two of them offered their support as they left the safety of the office.

The fires of the torches burned low, leaving the hallway almost entirely in shadow. Once they reached the antechamber, Xolia broke away from Bridget and Adonis to go up to Caius. That sense of kinship was back. She studied him again. The anger in his eyes wasn't fully directed at his opponent, Xolia suspected. Some of it was at himself, for having become the Selermine at all. That he would have to bear a scar when he'd not been born to do so. His neck was completely covered by the lift of his arm, but she knew there would have been a red, jagged mark around his neck. Her fingers ghosted around her own neck. She could feel the scarring, where her skin had been rejoined and tattooed over, but the area itself had no feeling. There was a sense of pressure, but that was it. Another tear leaked out from the corner of her eye.

She wanted to fall into the painting. If she could only ask him what made it bearable, how he overcame the garish display of his title, then she could survive it too. Xolia turned around, both Bridget and Adonis were waiting a respectable distance away. Slowly, she walked back to them. They started to lead her toward the main chamber and cold sweat broke out along Xolia's forehead and spine.

"No. I can't go back in there."

"Of course," Adonis said.

"Let's go to the bathroom. They have mirrors there," Bridget suggested. They went through a door on the right of the antechamber and into a restroom. Unlike the rest of the ancient church, this room had been updated to modern standards. Amber electric lights lit up the dark-green room. For the first time in over twelve hours, Xolia looked at herself in the mirror.

Her hair was matted and tangled and crusty with what she knew was her blood. Her skin was wan, and bags rested beneath dull eyes. Xolia bit her cracked bottom lip before letting herself look at *it*.

The scar wasn't as jagged as she thought it would be from touching it. There was a thick band of scarring, though it was a much deeper red than any of the human scars she'd seen due to the tattoo ink, and it was relatively uniform. It was only upon closer inspection that she could see breaks in the uniformity, where the skin pulled itself together to reseal her head to her shoulders. Those, too, were made redder by the priest's careful tattooing.

The temptation to touch it was too strong. No matter how many times she ran her fingers across it, she needed to do so again. Again. *Again.* Each time she touched it, it hurt less. It was just numb. Numb and red. Numb and forever. *Sel, this is never going to go away.*

"It's proof of how strong you are, Xo," Adonis said. Xolia looked at him through the mirror. He didn't seem disgusted or repulsed by it.

"It's ugly," she said. Beauty—the first thing she had once the war was over. And now it was gone again.

"Many humans have scars," Bridget said. "And they are still—"

"But I'm not human."

"You're right." Adonis grabbed her hand from her neck and

laced his fingers through hers. "How many humans could have survived that? Shit, how many variants would have been able to survive that?"

Bridget brought a hand to Xolia's shoulder, the weight of it was simultaneously comforting and cloying. "You don't have to like it, we can get clothes that cover it, right, Adonis?"

He nodded. "What's important is that you have the support of the church, no matter what happens. This will sway the election."

They had a point. She couldn't dwell on the scar, but dear Sel, she hated it so much. It was a pain that went deeper than physical discomfort. "I'm okay. Irvine wanted to see me?"

Just ignore it for now. As long as she could get through this night, she could deal with the rest in the morning.

"I'll go find him," Bridget offered, and she left the bathroom.

Xolia stared after the door. "She's skittish tonight."

Adonis didn't answer right away. Xolia turned around to see if he had heard. His eyes were red and glassy, and it was then that she realized how clammy his hand had gotten. "Adonis—" she began, but Adonis cut her off by pulling her into a crushing embrace.

"You did it. Fuck, Xo. You might've given me enough faith; I thought you died. She thought you died, and she was beside herself. We weren't allowed to see you for five hours after the ritual, and then when we were able to see you..." He peppered kisses all over her face. Xolia's own composure slipped. "When we were able to see you, I still wasn't convinced you would wake up, and when you did. . .I've never heard you cry like that before."

Xolia kissed him. She hated Irvine and hated the church

and hated Marshall for ever having brought it up to her, because once the idea had gotten into her head, there'd been no other place for her to end up than here. This had always been inevitable. The pain and the memories of those harrowing moments were the only places she could ever have gone. It wasn't fair that she was on this path, this cruel twist of fate that made her unable to be happy with a normal, regular life.

They pulled away from each other, their quickened breaths slowly returning to normal. "We've made it this far. Now it's time to finish it."

A knock broke the moment. Xolia opened the door, and Bridget and Irvine were waiting for them. Irvine, still dressed in the blood-spattered robes and gloves, bowed deeply at the sight of Xolia. "Sel could not have chosen a better Selermine, Xolia. I'm glad to see you up and moving."

Even though she had reneged on her earlier deal with herself to not show weakness to Adonis, she would not—could not—show weakness to Irvine. Especially not when he wore her blood like it was something to be proud of. "Thank you."

He lifted the golden talisman from his neck and held it over Xolia's head. She dipped her head just enough for him to lower the moth symbol around her neck. The chain rested below the scar, and while the moth was small and rested against her chest, it felt heavy around her neck, like any wrong move and she'd find herself hanging from it rather than wearing it.

"Jareth is waiting to see you home," Irvine said. "I hope you know how serious we are about you. This isn't something even our more cynical of congregants take lightly. I know your aims lie with leading this country, and every member of the Rheathian church will back you. Ris has been a secular nation for too long, and we've suffered for it. This is the only way forward."

"Of course." Xolia swallowed down her disdain. "This is how we unite all of Ris."

Irvine nodded and led them back to the front of the church. True to Irvine's word, Jareth was waiting by the door, arms crossed over his chest. After everything that had happened, a bodyguard was no longer something she fretted over. The scar was another freedom lost. The church was now her burden to bear. But if it helped Peter win again, it would be worth it.

Irvine bowed to her again. She remained standing tall even as her stomach growled and all she wanted to do was shower and sleep for the next ten years. Jareth opened the doors to the church, and rather than the cold, dead air of one in the morning, there was a swarm of reporters and cameras and microphones all being thrust into the group's faces.

Why couldn't it end? Xolia thought about pushing them all away, but she barely had the strength to hold herself up. There was no way she could hold onto so many people's bloodstreams at once and still have enough strength to push them. Bridget, Adonis, and Jareth shielded her from the onslaught, and they kept yelling "no comment" but that didn't do anything to sate the reporters' curiosity.

Xolia pushed through her small shield and tried to single out individual voices. With her appearance at the forefront of the group, there was a rise in the chaos; cameras snapped, and voices melded together.

"Is it true you worked under Silas during the Variants' Revolution?"

"What have you been doing the past seven years?"

"Do you think that Rheathism creates a larger divide between humans and variants than already exists?"

And on and on the questions were thrown at Xolia without a thought for how she could feasibly answer them all. Xolia couldn't even make eye contact with a single journalist before the next one was vying for her attention. She latched onto a stray mic.

"It's true I was directly under Silas during the rebe—Revolution, though I didn't know of his plans to betray FAR. I fully support Chancellor Bellevue. . ." Xolia rattled off talking points that she and Peter had been discussing day in and day out for the past week. They were the foundations of what she would say at the announcement speech in another week. Xolia pushed away her tiredness and smiled at each of them. Filling the role came easily to her, the words she needed to say popped into her mind like on the night of her attack.

The smile grew forced the longer she had to hold it and the more her answers prompted further questions. Without thinking about it, Xolia touched her scar, which elicited a whole new flurry of questions about her faith and what the Selermine was. She tried to answer those questions, but they were harder. The smile fell away. She leaned further into Adonis.

Jareth started pushing the raucous crowd away from the church steps so Adonis, Bridget and Xolia could inch their way closer to the safety of the car.

Xolia slumped over in her seat. "You did really good today," Bridget said. "I'm proud of you, and I know Chancellor Bellevue will be too."

"Do you think so?" If Peter was disappointed in her, she didn't know what she'd do.

"I do. You should take tomorrow off, or later today, I guess."

Xolia shook her head. "No. I need to be there. I need to talk to Peter."

Adonis got into the car and turned the key. Bridget tried to protest Xolia's decision but was quickly silenced. There was no going back for Xolia, if she had any doubts about what she was doing, it was too late now.

Chapter Thirty

Xolia stared at her closet. The Selermine pendant rested against her skin, falling right between her breasts. The metal remained cool against her, even though she'd been wearing it all morning. Xolia grabbed a long-sleeved cape dress. It wouldn't cover the scar, but she hoped the cape affixed to her shoulders would provide some sort of distraction from her neck. She slid into the garment and left the room to find Adonis, who was sitting in the living room.

The television was turned on to the Risian National News Network, and all the coverage was of her. It showed blurred footage from the actual Selermine trial, which was weird, in an alluring way, for Xolia to watch. Even with the pixelation, she could make out what was happening—the rolling of her head after the sword came down. The anchor shared more footage from last night, and she and the co-host speculated about what it meant for the country and politics to have such a mythical religious figure in their midst.

"Has the news all been positive?" Xolia asked. She stood in

front of Adonis who dutifully zipped up the back of the dress for her.

"It's evenly split from what I've seen. Though the negative press is really bad. Please keep your guard with you at all times."

She nodded. Even if she could hold her own in a fight, there was something intimidating about walking with armed guards. When Peter had had his guard right after the war, it had made him look that much more important—showing that he, above everyone else, was worth protecting. "I think we're as ready as we can be for the announcement."

"I agree."

She kissed him before going down the elevator to the lobby, where Isiah was waiting for her. "Good morning," she greeted. Isiah nodded, and he trailed behind her to the waiting car that Peter sent every day to escort her to the palace. There were no throngs of reporters waiting for her, which Xolia was relieved to find. If she had to answer any more questions about being the Selermine, she would explode.

She was even more relieved when the car passed through the iron and guarded gates of the Palace grounds. She was safe here. The car pulled around to Peter's wing of the building where both Bridget and Lana were waiting for her.

They exchanged greetings and went inside to the heated hallways. Isiah remained a respectful distance behind them. Lana took them up a flight of stairs to get to one of Peter's favorite studies. It wasn't a room used for televised addresses or meetings with the Senate, it was more intimate.

When they reached the hallway, Atlas stepped out of the study room, and he made eye contact with Xolia. They each froze.

"Vice Chancellor Campion, I didn't know you were meeting with Chancellor Bellevue," Lana said.

Atlas forced a polite smile. "It wasn't scheduled." His eyes flicked down to Xolia's exposed neck. "I didn't know you were that religious, Xolia."

She wanted to cover the scar with her hand but stopped herself from moving. *All in.* "I believe in protecting variants and continuing our crusade for peace between variants and humans, just as Sel does."

He scoffed. "How can there be peace when we fundamentally don't understand one another?"

Bridget tried to intervene, but Xolia shook her head. She was tired of hiding from Atlas and tired of losing to him. "Perhaps under your leadership they were unable to understand each other."

Atlas shrugged and checked his watch. "Perhaps. If you'll all excuse me, I have to run to my next appointment." He walked through the small crowd and stopped right by Xolia. He whispered, "Are you still so desperate to act like Silas?"

"What?" she asked, but he was already down the hall, not looking back once. Xolia fumed. He'd still managed to get the last word in, to throw her off balance, and he didn't even need to stay and gloat because he knew he'f won.

"What did he say to you?" Bridget asked.

Xolia shook her head. She wasn't trying to act like Silas. Silas had planned to overthrow FAR. She was working to save it. *You made yourself a religious figurehead to save it. But isn't that exactly what Silas would have done? He taught you to go as far as it took.* Xolia's stomach sank. If Silas was alive, would she be seeking him out, wanting to hear he was proud of her?

Xolia opened the door to Peter's study. He was sitting

against a high-backed chair, behind a solid mahogany desk. Papers covered the desk, and there was a small television on the wall next to the door, where news coverage of the Selermine trial played.

Peter stood near the entrance. His movements were stiff, and he looked older than his years. Frail, losing hair. A dead man walking. She ran to him to avoid him having to move more than necessary. "Peter."

"Xolia, I'm so glad to see you're okay. This video is horrible, did they really do that to you?" he asked, his eyes scrunched in concern. He had a hand on her shoulder that weighed so much less than it should've. It was so far from the firm handshakes he used to give when they'd first met.

In his paternal presence, Xolia doubted whether she would have betrayed Peter to do Silas's bidding after the war. Peter had never hurt her or betrayed her or constantly compared her to Atlas. *But Silas made you who you are.*

"I did it for you," she said, touching her scar. "The church will back FAR no matter what. I'm going to make sure we win this."

"Oh, Xolia, I would never ask you to hurt yourself for the campaign," he said, moving to sit down again. She held onto his elbows to offer extra support to guide him back down to the chair. Once he was seated, she took her seat on the other side of the desk.

"I know you wouldn't. I wanted to," she said. "What's on our agenda today?" If they could focus on work, maybe Peter would momentarily forget his sickness. *Is that how human illnesses work?* It had come on so suddenly, and every time she saw him, he looked worse instead of better. It wasn't right.

Lana and Bridget were quick to sit next to Xolia. Lana laid

out Peter's recent polling numbers. He was evenly matched with John Clemont, which was an issue. There were a few other minor people that had joined, but they fell so far short of Peter and Clemont that they were no threat.

A speechwriter came in and helped Peter and Xolia prepare some opening speeches for the first few rallies of the campaign. They were to spend six months traversing Ris and campaigning in local communities. Other members of Peter's team came and went, offering their suggestions or research as to what mattered most to voters in different parts of the country and how they should present themselves. The information overload kept Xolia's mind off her own life and Atlas.

By the day's end, it was just Peter and Xolia in the office. He coughed twice before it broke out into a full-blown fit. Xolia winced and tried to support him, though nothing she offered or tried the whole day had made any difference.

"Drink some water," she pleaded and held a cold cup of water out to him.

Peter took the drink, spilling a few drops as the coughing subsided. "Thank you, Xolia. It's probably best to wrap up the day anyway. Before you go, I wanted to let you know that I changed the order of succession. If I die—"

"You're not going to die, Peter—"

Peter held up his hand and Xolia stopped. "If I die, you will be named chancellor instead of Atlas."

Something snapped in Xolia. She had never imagined *herself* as chancellor of Ris. She pushed that feeling away. "What happened between you and Atlas?"

"These past few years have been difficult. You were at the bureau; you know how many variants, and the few variant families that have started, have struggled to make ends meet. Atlas and I have very different ideas as to what resolution means for our nation." Peter shook his head. "Him not staying on as my vice chancellor was a mutual decision."

Xolia tilted her head. "But he made it sound like it wasn't his choice."

He smiled sadly. "Your childhood took a lot from you; the war took even more. And despite everything, you both have accomplished so much and the responsibilities you have. . .You are so very young. I don't blame him for our discord."

"You don't think he's. . ."—Xolia considered what word to use—". . .evil?"

"Nobody is evil, Xolia."

Xolia nodded, though she didn't fully believe him. If President Gornne and all of his predecessors hadn't been evil, what had made them treat variants like little more than weapons? How could anyone have goodness in them and so much hatred at the same time?

She considered Peter and all the things she had learned about him since they first met. He was good, truly good. It made sense that he couldn't comprehend evil in someone. "Take care of yourself, Peter. I'll see you for the announcement?"

He nodded. Xolia would keep coming to the palace every day to work with Bridget on her campaign as the vice chancellor, but Peter had other engagements with the Senate for the rest of the week, and doctors' visits, Xolia hoped. They wouldn't see each other until the museum's opening, when they would officially announce her as his running mate. "Be good, Xolia."

WEDNESDAY, Xolia was back in Peter's study, though he wasn't there. It was just her and Bridget finalizing the schedule for Saturday afternoon. She and Peter would arrive together at the museum and deliver their initial remarks, before the building was opened for the first time to high-level politicians and journalists. Lunch would be served in one of the museum's private rooms, and if everything went according to plan, it would be a triumph for the kickoff of FAR's campaign for the election next year.

"The church will be there in an official capacity, correct?" Xolia asked, ensuring Irvine, as well as several other high-ranking priests, was on the guest list.

Bridget nodded. "They were given fifteen minutes of speaking time. I believe Irvine will be the one speaking."

"Has he sent over a copy of his speech?"

Bridget looked up at her, and gave her a slight shake of her head. "I didn't know you wanted to see it prior."

"I do." Xolia needed to make sure Irvine's words aligned with her own, and with FAR's. She needed to show a united front with the church, Bridget of all people should know that. She rubbed at her neck again, it had become a habit. Every hour, she had to check if the scar was still there. Each time she did, it was, and as she ran her fingertips over the cool, dead skin, it became harder to breathe, like her throat was constricting itself repeatedly where the scar was. Maybe her body hadn't healed it correctly, maybe there was something seriously wrong underneath the scar tissue and red tattoo ink forever marring her.

Xolia sucked in a deep breath, trying to regain control over the situation. If only she could talk to Krista. . .None of her old mantras were helping in this new life. Xolia bit at her nails. There wasn't any reason she couldn't see if Krista had time before the announcement. One last session before she went off to gallivant around the country. It couldn't hurt to ask.

"I'll be right back." Without waiting for a response, Xolia slipped outside of the study and scrolled through the contacts on her phone until she found Krista's number.

She answered on the fifth ring. "Hello, this is Krista White, licensed clinical psychologist. How can I help you?"

A shuddering breath escaped Xolia. Her voice was familiar, comforting. "Krista, it's me. I need to see you."

"Xolia," Krista said. She sounded surprised, like she had never expected to hear from Xolia again. "Are you not seeing anyone else?"

"No." Xolia hated how thick her voice was. She was done with tears and crying and vulnerabilities. She wanted it to end. "I need to talk to you, before Saturday."

"Of course. I can squeeze you in tomorrow around nine?"

"Okay." Xolia breathed a deep sigh of relief. She could make it that long and then she could get everything off her chest and everything would be okay again. Xolia held the phone to her forehead, soaking in the precious moments of solitude. Nothing could shake her from her path, not anymore. It was right. It was her destiny. But that didn't make it any easier to stomach. Having someone to talk to would ease the nerves that didn't leave her alone no matter how hard she tried to meditate or distract herself.

Chapter Thirty-One

Xolia shifted closer to Adonis in the large bed. Heat radiated off him while she shivered. Her chest felt hollow; something bad was going to happen, she just couldn't figure out what. She rolled over to check the time, seven-thirty. If she wanted to make it to Krista's by nine, she would have to get up.

She procrastinated for a few minutes before dragging herself from the comfort of bed to the bathroom. Once she was ready, she made her way to the darkened living room to wait for the driver to arrive from the Presidential Palace. Ever since the attack, Peter had been insistent she only be driven in an armored car.

She ate a small breakfast, the thought of anything more unsettled her nerves. What would Krista think of her scar?

Xolia grabbed her coat and buttoned it up, double-checking that her scar was completely hidden from view. She avoided looking at her reflection in the mirrored walls of the elevator. Emily was waiting for her in the lobby, ready to escort her to the car.

The sky above was cloudy and gray, with a freezing chill in

the air. Xolia pulled her coat closer to her body and waited for the driver to open the back passenger door. She slid into the heated seats and Emily followed her. Once the driver was inside, they were off to Krista's office.

Krista's office was in a ward that Xolia hadn't stepped foot in since their last appointment. It was in a neighborhood that didn't know if it wanted to cater to commercial or residential buildings, which resulted in a mishmash of dull office buildings and high-rise apartment buildings that had lost their most respectable tenants a few decades ago.

Children played in rundown playgrounds, their coats shabby and weatherworn. It was hard for Xolia to tell a human child from a variant child. They rarely had scars, and even the most destitute of children she had come across could smile at a small paltry joke. Had she ever been that easy to comfort? Memories of running laps around fields crossed her mind. There had been no baby fat filling out her face, or that of her fellow variants.

Xolia frowned at the children. She hated them, through no fault of their own. She knew she *shouldn't* hate them, and that made it worse because they were helpless and innocent, but she had been that way too and no one had saved *her*. They didn't have much, but they had more than she'd had, and it wasn't fair.

"We're here," the driver said. Xolia came back to herself and realized the car was parked, and Emily was staring at Xolia expectantly with her hand on the door handle.

"Ready?" she asked.

Xolia nodded. Emily slid out of the car and Xolia followed. Some of the kids stopped their games to look at them, but most didn't pay Xolia any mind. She was no more interesting than the cold games of tag or hide-and-seek. Adults paid her more mind, their faces pinched like they were trying to place where they knew her from. Xolia kept her head held high and avoided making eye contact with anyone as she went inside Krista's building.

Krista's office was on the seventh floor. She and Emily entered a crowded elevator that crept past each floor. The stale smell of sweat nauseated Xolia. She had forgotten what the building was like outside the sanctuary Krista's office provided.

She and Emily were the only two to step off at the seventh-floor stop, which relieved Xolia. It wasn't that she was ashamed of therapy, rather that she didn't entirely know the optics of a would-be elected official sitting in a psychologist's office. Would the public worry she was incapable of handling such an important job?

Her scar burned and she struggled to breathe. Xolia resolutely ignored Emily even as she could feel the woman's eyes becoming glued to her. "You can wait here." Xolia gestured to a metal folding chair outside of Krista's office. She knocked and waited half a minute until Krista's familiar 'come in' invited her somewhere safe.

Everything was the same as last time. Everything except for Xolia. Krista was the same—the couch, the desk, the box of tissues on the coffee table. It was disconcerting, much to Xolia's horror. *She* was the odd one out, the thing that didn't quite fit in anymore.

"Xolia," Krista said. "I'm so glad you reached out to me."

"You are?" Xolia sat down, right in the center of the couch. Her spot.

Krista nodded. Xolia's stomach fluttered. If people decided to question her choice to see a therapist, it didn't matter—she had done the right thing.

"I saw what you did on the news." Krista's gaze dropped to Xolia's neck. Krista didn't look awed or inspired by it at all. No, she looked rather concerned. "I'm worried that you're regressing or acting manic."

"Manic?" Xolia clenched her jaw. The flutter turned to lead. "I don't know what you mean."

"Xolia." The way Krista stressed the first syllable of her name made Xolia see red. For the first time in seven years, Krista was treating her with pity. "In seven years, you never once expressed a belief in religion. In fact, you actively spoke against it. Calling yourself a religious leader after three months is something the old Xolia would do. We need to get you back into regular sessions."

"You're wrong," Xolia said. She couldn't stop the heaviness of her breathing. "I think I'm acting like myself for the first time in years."

Krista arched an eyebrow. "And why do you feel that way?"

"Because." Xolia chewed on the inside of her lip. This wasn't why she came here; this wasn't what she'd needed to get off her chest, but Krista wasn't understanding her. "I'm doing something that matters again."

"Being happy didn't matter?"

"I wasn't happy," Xolia exploded. She leapt up from the couch, it wasn't comfortable anymore. Maybe it never had been. "I wanted to be. You don't know how badly I wanted it to be enough. But it wasn't. This is, and you don't even know what I've done to—" Xolia broke off. She couldn't talk to Krista about Helen either.

"What did you do?" Krista uttered.

Xolia's eyes burned. Was that apprehension hiding in Krista's eyes? "You don't understand."

"What don't I understand?"

Everything. "It has to be me. I have to fix things," Xolia said instead. "Have you seen how little has changed? If I don't do something, it's not going to get better."

"Silas put a lot of pressure on you," Krista said. "But you are not in charge of everyone, and it isn't your job to be in charge of everyone."

Not her job? It was the only thing she knew how to do. It was what Silas had taught her every time he'd singled her out or put her in charge of dangerous missions and battles. She'd given her childhood to be better. She would never have the childhood of those kids outside, laughing despite the cold. It was why Peter needed her; if he was ever going to recover, he needed a VC he could rely on. This was the reason she had Adonis. If she lost it, she'd lose him.

Krista didn't understand. She would never understand.

"Change is coming. I'm going to be a part of it." A glass water bottle on Krista's desk shattered, and the water sprayed everywhere. Xolia tried to rein in her emotions and the part of her that was always searching for water or blood.

"I need to call someone," Krista said, her skin becoming pale. "We're going to get you the help you need, Xolia." Slowly, so slowly, Krista moved up from the chair and leaned over her desk where her cellphone lay.

"No." Xolia reached out, literally and mentally, to latch onto Krista's blood stream. The older woman stumbled to the ground. "Shit." Xolia released her but couldn't say sorry. She should be able to keep better control over her emotions than this. Krista was still on the floor, she turned to look at Xolia. *Hurt, betrayal.* Xolia ran from the office.

She slammed the door behind her, trying—and failing—to

take steadying breaths. Emily jumped from the folding chair. "What happened?"

"Nothing." Xolia shook her head to punctuate her point. "Let's just go to the palace."

Emily didn't look sure but acquiesced. Xolia kept glancing back at the door to Krista's office until the elevator door closed behind them. Xolia held her head in her hands. It had been stupid of her to assume any part of her old life would fit in her new one.

Xolia was fortunate that no one else got into the elevator. She had just composed herself enough by the time it reached the ground floor and dinged to signal the end of their trip. Emily left the elevator first, and Xolia followed close behind. The car would be waiting outside for them to get her to the Presidential Palace.

She didn't wait for the driver to get out of the car to open the door for her, Xolia got in, Emily slid in behind her. "Is everything okay?" she asked.

The car pulled out into the street, driving away from the kids and the people that didn't care about Xolia or her problems. "I'm fine." Xolia tugged her coat closer to herself. Krista was supposed to have made the burden easier to bear, not to have added to it. No matter how desperately she wanted to talk to Peter, she refused to do anything that would make his condition worse. He needed to get better, and Xolia would make sure that happened.

When they reached the street of the Presidential Palace, Xolia was surprised at how many news vans and people were clustered around the closed gates of the property. "What's going on?" Xolia asked.

Emily furrowed her brows. "I'm not sure."

The driver twisted in his seat to look back at the two women. "It might be a minute before we get inside the gates. They're sending out extra guards to make sure no one follows us through."

Anxiety twisted Xolia's insides. She couldn't wait in the car. Unbuckling her seat belt as quietly as she could, Xolia kept her focus on Emily to make sure she didn't suspect a thing, then Xolia shot over her to the passenger-side door and fled the car.

Chapter Thirty-Two

IMMEDIATELY, THE MASSES TURNED TO XOLIA AND swarmed her. It wasn't solely reporters like the night of the charity event had been. Regular pedestrians were standing, interspersed with the perfectly coiffed and made-up journalists. Questions were lobbed at her from every conceivable angle.

It would have been easy to get swept up in the chaos of it all, but she was too pumped up on adrenaline and the worry that something had happened to Peter to care about herself. She had a responsibility to him, and it made Xolia straighten her shoulders and attempt to single out questions rather than letting them bleed together.

Everyone was looking at her—to her—for answers to unintelligible questions. She was trying to figure out what a reporter from the Atalian Herald was asking when someone broke through the invisible barrier around Xolia.

"Did you do anything to him?" the man asked.

"What are you talking about?" Xolia asked, unease rolling through her at the use of 'him.' Sel, it really was Peter. Her stomach lurched.

"The chancellor is in the hospital, and now you're coming to the palace? You and the vice chancellor are fucking freaks." Without any hesitation, he landed a solid punch across Xolia's jaw.

She snapped.

Xolia spit out blood and a tooth onto the cold sidewalk and grabbed him by the neck. He was human; small pockmarked scars covered his face. Shrapnel scars. He had most likely been in the army during the rebellion. "I didn't do anything to Chancellor Bellevue, but you just assaulted someone."

The man scoffed. "As if you're a person."

Someone touched Xolia's shoulder. "Let go of him, Xolia. Let me handle him," Emily whispered. Her bodyguard. *Let him go.* She didn't want to let him go, though. Xolia wanted to hurt him. She wanted to make him scream and beg forgiveness.

Still, Xolia let him go, allowing Emily to swoop in and take him away from her. Through the haze of anger, she registered the other thing he had said. Peter was in the hospital.

"What hospital is the chancellor at?" Multiple people answered at once, but they all said the same thing. Meillus Hospital, it was the best hospital in Ris, close to Juthian Heights.

She thought she might say something to reassure the people that FAR was still the strongest party or that Peter would pull through, but words failed her. There was nothing eloquent that came to mind when her jaw was still sore and she was angry. Police sirens wailed. Xolia got back into the car. She waited almost twenty minutes before Emily joined her.

"We need to go to Meillus Hospital," Xolia told the driver. He nodded and backed away from the gates of the Presidential Palace. As they were pulling away, Xolia got a glimpse of Atlas walking out through the front doors, impeccably dressed in a suit and a somber expression on his face. She forced herself to turn away, not wanting to see how he calmed the crowd.

Realistically, the drive couldn't have lasted longer than fifteen minutes with the way the driver cut through the traffic and dared to take yellow lights that were a hair's breadth away from turning red, but it still felt like an eternity to Xolia.

More journalists were waiting outside the front doors, filling the already-crowded parking lot. Law enforcement had put up barricades and now blocked the entrances with heavy guns. Xolia groaned. "Let me help you this time," Emily commented wryly.

Xolia didn't have the energy to argue. She nodded. She and Emily pushed through the thickening crowds and drew the attention of the press.

"Duck your head," Emily whispered. Xolia did as she was told, and the two of them steadfastly ignored the clamor of the reporters. Xolia pulled out her phone to tell Adonis what had happened. Her fingers shook as they ghosted across the phone screen. *Peter has to be okay.* Her stomach rolled around. What if she was too late?

Fueled by her worst thoughts, Xolia picked up her pace, leaving Emily to follow her. Xolia slid through the revolving hospital doors and sped past the security desk. She was only vaguely aware of Emily doing damage control with the guards. All of her focus was on the front desk. "Where's the chancellor?"

The receptionist looked up at her with wide eyes. "I'm sorry, but I cannot divulge that information."

Xolia slammed her fist against the desk, which made the receptionist flinch. "Yes, you can. Tell me where he is."

"Ma'am, I'm sorry, but—"

Without thinking, Xolia reached out for the woman's blood. She jerked upright, her fingers freezing on her computer keys. Her wide eyes widened even further. "I know he's here," Xolia pleaded. "Please, my name is Xolia Stone. Let me see him." She let go of the woman, who fell forward in what Xolia thought was a grossly exaggerated manner.

"What did you do to me?" she whispered.

"Nothing." Xolia looked around. Where was Emily? Where was anyone who could help her? Why wasn't anyone doing anything?

Shouts and clamoring from outside filled the otherwise-calm room as the automatic doors slid open. Xolia turned to see if Emily had anything to do with it, but it was Atlas. His face was set in grim determination, and a retinue of guards followed him.

The receptionist greeted him immediately. "Vice Chancellor Campion, we have a team waiting to escort you to the chancellor." She dropped her voice, like it was a secret that the chancellor was here.

Atlas nodded, only then did his gaze turn to Xolia. They locked eyes, he in his subdued mask, her a barely contained mess of emotions. "Atlas," she sobbed. Tears streamed down her face, Sel, she could barely stand to think about herself, but Peter was worth the humiliation. "I need to see him."

A long minute passed between them. He betrayed nothing. A team of hospital staff and security personnel entered the lobby. Atlas nodded once at Xolia. "She'll be joining us."

Another sob tore itself from her throat. Xolia managed to keep herself upright as she hastily wiped away the tears. Peter couldn't see her like this. Emily ran into the lobby and placed herself behind Xolia. The large group made their way through the wide hallways to a large elevator. There wasn't enough space for the entire party, so half of the hospital staff, Atlas, and Xolia stepped into the first elevator. The rest of their teams would follow.

Xolia shook the entire ride up. How could Atlas stand to be so calm? As much as she wanted to shake him and try to see that mask crack, she couldn't bear to break the silence in the elevator. Up and up, it went in agonizing slowness. By the time it reached the tenth floor—which the doctors explained had been completely cleared except for Peter—tears were already slipping out of the inner corners of her eyes again.

"He's in room 1559," the head doctor explained. Xolia couldn't remember whether he had introduced himself or not. It wasn't that important, she brushed past him and Atlas and everyone else in pursuit of room 1559.

Inside, monitors beeped in a steady rhythm, the only indication that Peter was still alive. Xolia stood frozen in the doorway, taking in a breathing machine and multiple IV lines in his body. She had never been surrounded by so much medical equipment in her life.

Peter lay in a sterile white hospital bed, a mountain of thin blankets covering his prone form. His skin was gray, and his eyes were closed. Xolia's heart stopped. Sel, he looked dead.

"Are you going to go in?" Atlas asked from behind her.

Xolia clenched her jaw. "Don't you care?" She forced her body to move forward. The smell of harsh cleaning chemicals surrounded her. The curtains to the room were drawn shut. Atalia right after the rebellion had looked less bleak than this room.

"Of course, I care." Atlas stopped next to her; he seemed just as fixated on Peter as she was. "Worrying won't help him, though." His voice cracked and Xolia turned to him. Under the unaffected attitude, she found immeasurable sadness in his eyes. "He's been sick for a long time."

"I wish he would've told me sooner," Xolia whispered. If only she hadn't wasted so many years ignoring his many job offers, she could've been by his side the whole time. Maybe she could've prevented this, somehow, some way. "It isn't fair. First Silas and now Peter?"

"Silas got what he deserved," Atlas said.

Xolia stared at him, her face contorted in disgust. What gave him the right to be so bitter? "But you still went and saw him."

He stared back at her, as if daring her to pick a fight. "I did see him and I hated him. Both can be true."

She didn't hate Silas, and she never saw him. How cruel.

"Look, Xolia." Atlas broke eye contact with her and inched closer to Peter, who hadn't so much as flinched at their arrival. "You can't be vice chancellor. You need to step aside."

"What are you saying?" Xolia clenched her jaw. This was hardly the time or place for this conversation.

Atlas sighed—no, deflated. His shoulders sagged, and pure exhaustion radiated from him. Gone was his mask of neutral impassiveness. He was broken. "You didn't know Silas like I did, and what he wanted, what he was planning. . .It. . .I won't let it happen. I can't."

His words crushed Xolia more than his actions ever had. "What do you mean? I knew him longer than you did."

"What does that matter?"

"I. . .it—" Xolia stuttered over herself. What did it matter? Of course it mattered. It did. It had to. Silas was hers. He had loved her. . .*but he favored Atlas more. You know it's true.* She couldn't handle this, not when Peter was dying.

"And you, Xolia, you're more like him than anyone I know. You act like him, Sel, you even think like him. If you knew what he was truly like, you wouldn't try so hard to act like him," Atlas said. He faced her with wide eyes. His hands were splayed, palms up; he was truly pleading with her. "It scares me. I can't let you finish what he started. I won't let it happen."

The room door opened, and Atlas's entourage entered, followed by Emily. "Sorry, Vice Chancellor, the elevator malfunctioned," one of the men said. They flanked Atlas to surround him while Emily placed herself right behind Xolia.

While the men on Atlas's team were professionals, not even they could stop themselves from peeking at the scar on Xolia's neck, now visible with her coat slightly unbuttoned. It burned against her skin with each glance and side-eyed stare. All she wanted to do was to scratch at it until it fell away from her skin, to prove it wasn't part of her, not really.

"I think Peter needs to rest," Xolia said. *She* needed to get away from Atlas's words and the sight of an unresponsive Peter. She stopped in front of Atlas. "I'm not backing down. Peter wants me by his side. I want to help Ris. I've come too far to stop."

She stared, trying to convey the severity of her words to him. Atlas's jaw clicked, but he didn't say anything in response.

Xolia left the hospital room, Emily trailing close behind her. As Emily was hitting the ground-floor button inside the elevator, Atlas rounded out of the room. "I'm not done talking, Xolia."

She scoffed. Atlas opened a hospital room close to the elevator, and Xolia didn't stop to consider her actions before preventing the elevator doors from closing and following him inside. Emily stepped out and started to follow her, but Xolia stopped her. "It'll be fine, just wait out here."

Emily didn't need to speak for Xolia to pick up on her apprehension. Xolia gave a slight shake of her head, a silent plea for her not to speak. Xolia's stomach fluttered when Atlas closed the door behind him. She hadn't been alone with him since the night at the museum. At least with Peter in the hospital bed, there was still another person with them.

Unable to fight off the incessant need to scratch at the scar, Xolia relented and scratched at the raised skin. Atlas watched unabashedly, which only made Xolia feel more ashamed and all that did was make the scar itch more.

"I would really like to go home and try and forget about today," Xolia said and forced her hand back down to her side. Images of Peter's still body flashed through her mind.

"Xolia." The vestiges of Atlas's neutral mask slipped away. "Step aside."

"Tell me why."

A strained puff of air escaped Atlas, and he paced the length of the room. His Oxfords slapped against the white hospital tiles. "Silas was cruel to you. We all knew it. Everyone in the barracks. Except for you. No matter how many times he berated you or told you not to manipulate blood, you loved him."

A lump formed in Xolia's throat. She was loyal, and that was commendable. The way Atlas put it, she sounded weak. Pathetic.

"He was going to kill Peter, you know." Atlas stopped his pacing to level her with a piercing stare. "Peter is so trusting; he wouldn't have seen it coming."

Bile rose in Xolia's throat. "What are you talking about?"

"He told me he was going to do it. If we had killed Peter, humans wouldn't have stood a chance. We could've re-established the monarchy." A tear slipped down Atlas's cheek. Xolia couldn't stand it. Who was this in front of her? She hated Atlas, and Atlas hated her. They didn't cry in front of each other. "If he had done that, you know what he was going to do to you?"

Xolia couldn't respond. She couldn't do anything more than listen to him in horror.

"He would have followed the old ways. He was so disgusted by you, Xolia."

She shook her head. That couldn't be true.

"He hated you but knew he wouldn't have won the war without you. You were useful, but once the war was over?" He scoffed. "Silas was going to kill you. Any variant that was able to manipulate blood was killed in the old days. Did the church tell you that? Did the priests tell you the first Selermine commanded all four elements and killed someone like you?"

"You're lying," Xolia insisted, but the words were weak against her tongue.

Atlas shook his head. "I had to stop him, Xolia. Don't you see? It was the only thing to do."

"You fought him?" Things she had never stopped to think about slid into place. Why hadn't Atlas been a part of the conversation with Peter in the tent? She had assumed he had been in the medical tents, not trying to save the country right after *she* had saved it.

He nodded. "I almost had him, but I wasn't strong enough. It took me seven years, but I made sure he could never hurt anyone. *I* did that, Xolia. *I* sacrificed and *I* worked with FAR. Peter can't see what's in front of him, but you're going to do the same thing as Silas."

It was too much. How could Atlas tell her how disgusted Silas was by her and then turn around and say she was just like him? He kept ripping her heart out of her chest with each sentence he uttered.

"I'm not him. And I'm not you. If you care about Peter so much, why are you abandoning him?"

"I'm not abandoning him." For the first time that day, anger poured from Atlas. "I was done. I served my country, and I was ready to do something else, but then he chose you. He's always had this soft spot for you. I had to fight back. I'll admit I was rash, but come on, would you have done anything differently?"

Bile rose in Xolia's throat. She wanted to yell, run. Something. She balled her hands into fists. Or *something* indeed. For the second time in her life, Xolia punched Atlas.

He groaned in pain. Anger flashed in his eyes. "I should have tried harder to kill you," he snarled and launched at Xolia. They fell in a tumble of fists and kicks. Hospital equipment clattered to the ground as they pulled away and reconnected from each other in a furious and violent dance.

Even if fighting sans elements was crude and very human, there was a certain catharsis to the base depravity of it. Xolia's lip was busted, and at least one of her ribs was broken, but she leaned into the pain, allowing it to push her punches just a little further. Just a little less restrained.

Suddenly, hands were pulling her away from Atlas, and his entourage of suited men were pulling him off her. Xolia tried to shake Emily off her, but the woman had a viselike grip.

"Let go," Xolia demanded, trying to shake Emily off of her.

Atlas was similarly protesting his people manhandling him and yelling curt commands. Emily dragged Xolia from the hospital room and threw her against the wall of the elevator. "Sel, you didn't have to do that." Xolia struggled to her feet and rubbed at her tailbone. She winced and moved to coddle her ribs instead.

"Are you stupid?" Emily hissed. "Do you think Peter would be proud of you for getting into a fistfight with the vice chancellor?"

"Don't talk to me about Peter." She crossed her arms and tried to control her breathing, but it came out as more of a wheeze than anything. Xolia was aware she was pouting like a child, but it was hard not to act like one when that's what Emily was treating her as. "Just get me home."

Chapter Thirty-Three

Xolia sat on the living room couch in complete darkness. Relatively speaking. Once she had gotten home, she'd slipped into her Persion hoodie, dragged the hood over her head, and pulled on the drawstrings until she was cocooned in a soft and peaceful darkness.

Emily was somewhere in the building, and Bridget would turn up soon enough with more plans and public appearances for Xolia to show her face as if it wasn't all meaningless. Had Silas really hated her that much? She didn't want to believe it, but she couldn't deny that it made sense. The picture of Silas and Atlas in Atlas's home was proof enough. There was nothing she could have done that would have impressed Silas enough to throw his arm around her shoulder and take a picture with her.

Xolia groaned and fell onto the couch, kicking her feet off the ground and lying down against the moderately uncomfortable cushions. She had almost killed Peter for Silas. Sure, Peter had forgiven her, but was that enough? Atlas was wrong about one thing; she wasn't going to continue what Silas started. She wasn't taking the vice chancellorship for the sake of her own power but because the country needed her. No one else was suited to the job.

The sound of the front door disrupted the oppressive silence of Xolia's solitude. Xolia suppressed another groan. She wasn't in the mood to talk to Bridget, or in the mood to talk at all. Warm hands grabbed her shoulders. "Xo, I got your text. Are you okay? Were you able to see him?"

Adonis. Half of her relaxed against him while the other half couldn't stop from repeating Atlas's words. *Everyone knew how Silas felt about me.* Did that everyone include Adonis? With lethargic limbs, Xolia pulled the hoodie back to re-emerge into the real world.

He brushed tangled hair away from her face and frowned. "How bad is it still?" Xolia asked. It hadn't been more than an hour since she and Atlas had fought. Some of the more superficial bruising would be gone, but Atlas hadn't held back in his punches.

"It's bad," he said softly.

Xolia sat up, wincing. She grabbed at her ribs again, and Adonis immediately dropped to his knees to assess her. She brushed off his hands. "Did Silas really hate me that much?"

Adonis stopped and looked up at her, his brows furrowed.

"Atlas said everyone knew. Was it obvious? Was I really that stupid?"

"Xolia. . ."

"Never mind." Xolia shook her head. "I don't want your pity."

"I'm not pitying you." Adonis pulled at her wrist and helped her stand. "You told me that I shouldn't be ashamed of my family's history. You shouldn't be ashamed of being loyal to someone. I think he loved you, in the way he knew how." He led her through the living room to the bedroom. Bridget would be here any minute, she didn't have time to rest.

"I was loyal to someone who didn't deserve it," Xolia refuted. *I didn't even realize it. How can that be anything other than weakness?*

Adonis arched a brow. "You're right."

Xolia scoffed and bypassed the bed for the windows that had once so entranced her and now were commonplace. The people on the street below were small, so far beneath her. Did Peter ever feel this way? That the weight of his responsibilities was the very thing that vaulted him above everyone else? Had Silas?

She slammed an open right palm against the glass while her left hand felt for the scar along her neck. *Sel, why can't anything just work out? Why can't I make things work? Why can't I be happy?* She clawed at her neck. It was the scar's fault. It made her less than she should be. She scratched until the burn of ripped skin calmed her frayed nerves.

That and the strong hands of Adonis ripping her hand away from her neck. "Stop." He spun her around until she was facing him. "What the fuck is wrong with you?"

Xolia pushed him with her free hand, but he didn't budge. "What am I doing, Adonis? Silas was everything to me, the closest thing I had to a father, and I lost him. He was horrible."

He leveled her with a look and guided her to the bed, gently laying her down with extra consideration for her ribs. "You're not the only one with a shitty dad."

Xolia blanched. Of course he understood an unloving parent. A biological parent at that. Silas was never a real father to her, and they both knew that, even if Xolia wished she didn't. Adonis pressed a soft kiss to her jawline.

"You're not going to turn out like Silas."

"How do you know?" Xolia asked. She closed her eyes, trying to drown out all the doubts and fear. What would it take for her to be over them? She was *supposed* to be over them.

"Silas wasn't as strong as you are. He wasn't the Selermine." Adonis kissed the scar. Lightly. Reverently. Her shallow scratches had healed, though she felt the phantom grip of pain ghost around the press of his lips.

She couldn't separate herself from the events of the day. From Peter. How he'd looked. But neither could she bring herself to tell Adonis to stop. It was only in the safety of this bedroom that she could let her guard fall.

The loud bang of a door being closed made the two of them flinch. "It must be Bridget." Xolia pushed Adonis off her. The pain in her ribs was slight when she rolled off the bed to walk out into the apartment's foyer.

A frazzled Bridget greeted her and Adonis, who had followed her. "What were you thinking?"

"I wasn't." What else could Xolia say? Bridget wouldn't understand. She'd call her young and shortsighted.

Bridget *tsk*ed. "No, you weren't. Sel, things are all muddy right now. The Senate is convening tomorrow, and both you and Atlas need to be there."

"What?" Xolia stepped back. Was it because they'd gotten into a fight? Or had Peter. . .? She couldn't finish the question, though it didn't stop her chest from growing tight.

"Peter changed the order of succession, but not all the senators agree with it. And they want to know who the chancellor will be if. . ." Xolia wondered if the horror she felt was so clearly written across her face.

"He's still alive?" asked Adonis.

Bridget nodded. "He's still unresponsive."

Xolia sagged against Adonis's solid frame. *He's still alive.*

"I can get a meeting with General DuBois tonight," Adonis whispered against the crown of her head.

"I've been working with Peter every day," Xolia said. "I know his policies and all the campaign plans. He named me as his successor. What power does the Senate hold over that?"

"You need the Senate as your ally," Bridget countered. "Peter picked every one of them, and they still stall his plans. We don't know Atlas's relationship to any of them either."

Did any of them know the truth about Atlas? He was so much better at talking than her, and they already knew him. Xolia stared at the floor thinking; if she could talk to General DuBois, she might get an idea of how much of the Senate supported Atlas. Maybe she could sway the general to back her; as one of the most powerful men in the country, other senators would be sure to follow his lead.

"Set the meeting with the general," Xolia told Adonis. He flicked his eyes briefly at Bridget before nodding and walking away from them. "What should we prepare for tomorrow?"

Bridget pulled her tablet from her bag that she used for anything pertaining to Xolia's political career. "We need to stress how much Chancellor Bellevue wants you to succeed him as well as how closely your values align with his."

"What happens if they choose Atlas to succeed him?" Xolia asked.

"Then you pray to Sel that Peter lives."

Xolia stood outside the Armistice, though this time she was next to Adonis and they were meeting the most acclaimed general in Ris. Warm lights spilled out onto the darkening street whenever some well-to-do person exited the building.

Apprehension trickled down her spine. The last time she'd been here she had snorted the obruo and had one of the worst experiences of her life. Beneath the high-collared coat she wore, her scar burned.

Sel, it was annoying to have such a visceral reminder of her insecurities. She caressed the scar along the side of her neck with the backs of her fingers.

"It's going to be okay." Adonis took her free hand in his and gently squeezed. Hand-in-hand, they made their way to the bouncer and listed off their names. The bouncer nodded at them and checked their IDs before opening the door.

Xolia stepped through the entryway first, no longer an easily passed-by patron, she was now garnering stares from everyone in the room. Some tried to hide their interest in what the Selermine was doing in a politicians' bar, while others stared blatantly in her direction. She didn't deign to make eye contact with any of them and focused on the warmth from Adonis as he tugged on her wrist to lead her to the back of the bar where a dark hallway beckoned them.

The hallway was dingy compared to the rest of the bar, just one pale lightbulb in the center with a frayed string to turn it on or off. Several doors lined the hallway, painted black and chipping along the corners. Adonis entered the first door on the left.

A small coffee table took up most of the room, and four chairs were placed around it. The farthest chair from the entrance was occupied by General Hugh DuBois. A legend more than a man. Another pale and uncovered bulb lit up the room, much like the hallway. *They don't care much for ambiance back here.* Xolia settled into the hard chair and tried to imagine General DuBois taking all of his meetings here in a room that looked like it belonged more in the Hannith District, one of the poorest parts of Atalia, than the Armistice.

"Adonis. Xolia," General DuBois greeted them. His hand rested against a sweating cup of some dark alcohol. The sight of it made Xolia's stomach churn.

"You need to vote for Xolia tomorrow," Adonis said, leaning forward and placing his fist on the table.

Xolia raised an eyebrow, she didn't expect such an up-front strategy.

The general didn't seem to be put off by the behavior. "Why should I do that?"

"You know what I did for you," Adonis said, voice low.

Xolia's brow raised further. What had he done?

"Yes, and I paid you for that favor. Will you pay me for mine?"

Bribery? The best strategist in the country would stoop as low as bribery? "You don't need money," Xolia said. "You don't need power. What do you need?"

"I need someone I can trust running the country. Atlas is too concerned with buying the barracks to give a shit."

Atlas is trying to buy Helen's property? She glanced at Adonis. *The property that now belongs to Adonis.* Getting Atlas out of the picture was shaping up to be something that was at the top of Adonis's list. Atlas was probably a higher priority than Adonis's parents.

"Even when we were on opposite sides of the war, I respected you," Xolia said. "I want what's best for Ris, the same as I've always wanted. I know all FAR's policies—"

"We don't need another Peter," the general interrupted. "That hasn't worked. We have a terrorist organization hiding right under our noses. Peter refuses to believe it. Atlas doesn't want to risk upsetting anyone to do anything about it. What would you do, Xolia?"

He must be talking about the Underlings. The variants that were tired of being under human rule. Under the weak protection of the bureau. Xolia was back on the street the night of the charity dinner, listening to how they didn't care for her or what she stood for. After all she did for them. "I will do whatever it takes." Xolia's resolve hardened. Should Peter live, she would make him see the truth. Terrorist groups, human or variant, couldn't be given an inch of space in a modern-day Ris.

"She has the backing of the Rheathian church," Adonis added. "They will follow her anywhere."

General DuBois sipped deeply from the glass. The only sound was that of a large ice cube clinking as he sat the cup back on the table. "I saw the video. Is it truly real?"

Xolia clenched her jaw and nodded. *That* day was by far the worst of her life. The general's eyes settled on her neck, and fighting back no small amount of shame, Xolia pulled aside the top of her coat, revealing the jagged scar made redder with the tattoo ink.

"So what, are you divinely destined to rule?" General DuBois asked, but the question was buoyed with a slight breathlessness.

"I'm the Selermine. My path is true and will not lead me astray. If I am to rule, I will not lose." Xolia felt that conviction that flowed through her when she needed it most. She *was* the Selermine. This was *her* right.

"Ris has been a secular nation since the fall of the monarchy," the general mused. "But you'd be hard-pressed to find anyone who can deny *that*." He rubbed his chin with his fingers. "I'll cast my vote for you tomorrow, but you will let me make decisions as I see fit when it comes to leading the military and dealing with domestic terrorists."

"Naturally, a man of your talents should hardly be restricted."

Adonis stood. "You'll explain the situation to Senator Davenport, won't you?"

The general smiled without joy. "Of course, son."

"It was good to meet with you, General," Xolia said, standing. "I look forward to tomorrow."

"And you as well." The general bade them goodbye with a tip of his drink in their direction before downing the rest of the liquor.

They were back in the warm glow of the main room of the Armistice when a loud boom broke the soft whisper of conversation. Xolia's body immediately loosened into a defensive stance. Adonis did the same.

There were three beats of utter stillness before a gust of wind knocked out the windows of the building and car alarms sounded up and down the street. Adonis and Xolia met each other's eyes while the rest of the room descended into chaos.

Xolia raced out of the bar to find cars pulled over and people holding their ears. From their parked car, Isiah jumped out and ran to Xolia, his eyes wide with panic. "Xolia!"

"What happened?" she yelled at him. Emergency sirens wailed. Above the ancient courthouse a plume of smoke overshadowed the twilight sky. It was southwest of their location. Xolia's heart raced. Juthian Heights was southwest, and so was Meillus Hospital.

"No." Her breath stopped, she stumbled to the ground. Adonis caught her, and together they toppled against an empty car with the blare of the alarms still ringing in her ears. "Peter."

"We don't know it was the hospital," he said. He held his forehead to hers, trying to get her to look at him, but she couldn't do it. His voice was unsteady; he knew he was lying.

"Xolia." Isiah reached them, he pulled at her arm trying to get her to stand. "We need to get you both out of here. This could be another target."

Xolia put her hands over her head. This had to be a nightmare. She needed to wake up now. Now. *Now.* Two pairs of hands pulled her into the dark SUV. Around her, warbled voices spoke and lapsed into silence. The car moved in choppy bursts of speed and stillness.

Sel, please. Xolia prayed, harder than she ever had before in her life. Was there enough faith in the world to spare Peter's life? What would she do without him? All these plans were supposed to be simple contingencies. She hadn't even gotten to say goodbye. Same as with Silas. A low sob broke free from deep within Xolia's soul.

"Xolia. Xolia," a voice repeated itself. The longer she tried to ignore it, the more insistent it became. Xolia pulled herself up from Adonis's lap. Adonis had been the one speaking to her, using her full name.

"The apartment's windows were blown out, Xo. The entire block is closed off." He brushed sweat-stuck hair away from her face and behind her ear.

"It was the hospital?" she croaked out, so overcome that she didn't care who saw her in such a pathetic state.

She didn't know why she'd asked. She knew the answer before Adonis nodded. Her heart plummeted, a meteoric fall to her stomach. Peter was. . .*Peter is dead.* They would never talk again. He wouldn't be the chancellor again. Burning tears ran down her cheeks, what had been the point of it all if she was only going to lose him?

Adonis rubbed her back, though it was hardly a comfort in the face of such tragedy. "We can't let them get away with it, Xo. We need to find out who did this."

Adonis was right. Xolia wiped the tears from her face, letting the anger swallow the sadness. Peter's death would be in vain. His killers couldn't live without punishment.

She sat in the back seat, her head in her hands, while she took gulping wet breaths. Isiah reached back to hand her a tissue, which Xolia gratefully accepted to wipe away the snot and tears. "Has anyone taken responsibility for it yet?"

Isiah nodded. "The Underlings have. They released a statement right as the bombing started."

He handed her his phone, a video paused and waiting to play. She pressed play, and a masked figure with a heavily distorted voice spoke. "Citizens of Ris, for too long, variants have suffered under human rule. FAR has been no exception. Every one of your ilk who pretends to care about variants will die, starting with Chancellor Peter Bellevue." Xolia put the phone to sleep and handed it back to Isiah.

"I will kill them all. They declared war on Ris when they killed him."

"Almost nothing is known about the organization," Adonis said. "Helen wanted them to back her during her campaign. She couldn't find anything."

Xolia clenched her jaw. Once the Senate instated her as chancellor, she could pivot much of the military's resources to ferreting out the identities of the Underlings. "Is the Senate still going to wait until tomorrow? We should go there now, before Atlas can try anything."

Adonis nodded. With a few quick words to the driver, they were on their way to the Presidential Palace. Press swarmed the gates with armed guards standing along the entire perimeter, all armed with automatic weapons that would shred through flesh and bone. Xolia shuddered at the sight of so many guns.

Once they made it through the sea of people, they were carefully ushered behind the iron gates of the property and led to a fortified garage. When they got out of the car, Lana was there to greet them. Tears glazed her eyes as she led them to the Senate Hall.

Chapter Thirty-Four

The Senate Hall had once been the throne room. The opulent thrones of millenniums past had been replaced with a podium, now flanked by FAR's flag. Raised seats had been placed in a circular fashion, twenty for the Senate in the front and groups of seats behind for their aides. To the right of the podium was an ornate box seat for the chancellor and vice chancellor.

Xolia was seated near the front of the room, in a folding chair, the same as the rest of her party, though Isiah stood protectively behind her. Senators straggled in. Bridget ran through the entrance to Xolia, pulling her into a tight hug.

Surprised, Xolia let the older woman hug her. "I'm so sorry," Bridget whispered in her ear before pulling back. Her eyes were heavy. "I know how much he meant to you."

Xolia nodded, knowing if she spoke, the tears would start falling again. General DuBois entered the room. He nodded at Xolia before taking his place next to General Perrin. Both were dressed in their highly decorated ceremonial uniforms, though

General DuBois had more honors affixed to his. It settled Xolia slightly. No matter what General Perrin thought of her, it was General DuBois who carried the military's influence.

Once everyone was in their correct places, Lana stood behind the podium. "Tonight, our beloved chancellor was murdered in a terrorist plot to destabilize our democracy and send Ris back into war. Normally, the vice chancellor would immediately succeed a fallen chancellor, but we are in a unique situation. Chancellor Bellevue did not want Vice Chancellor Campion to act as his successor, nor as his running mate in the upcoming election. He has been guiding the nation's first Selermine in a thousand years, Xolia Stone, to take up the mantle of leadership. It's up to us to decide who will ascend to the chancellorship tonight so that we may face the upcoming election under a united front."

Xolia took note of Lana's eloquence. Peter had clearly chosen Lana for her quick intelligence and ability to control a room. Xolia regretted that she hadn't spent more time getting to know the woman in her weeks spent in Peter's confidence.

No sooner had Lana cleared the podium than Atlas took his place at the front of the room. His suit was disheveled, as if he'd thrown it on in haste. Xolia steeled herself for whatever vitriolic words he was sure to say.

"I've faithfully served Chancellor Bellevue for seven years. I am no stranger to war. These terrorists must be dealt with but not at the detriment of citizens' everyday lives. Peter would not want to send the country back into such dark times. I am prepared to lead this country through an election and then spend the next seven years bringing the arm of justice down on any who spurn the ideals Peter had spent his life upholding. I want what's best for Ris, and I will work nonstop to ensure peace." He nodded at the Senate and stepped down from the podium.

Xolia wiped away any lingering tears before standing and going to the podium. She took in each of the faces that stared blankly at her. Some were more familiar than others. She caught General DuBois's eye who leveled her with a critical stare.

She swallowed. "Like Vice Chancellor Campion, I, too, am no stranger to war. I am well acquainted with the horrors of humans and variants." She gripped the stem of the thin mic. "We cannot allow such an act of savagery go unpunished. The country needs to know that their government will protect them. The enemy needs to know that they cannot act with impunity. Ris needs strong and decisive action to ferret out the enemy. If we don't treat these rebels with the full weight of our armies, everything Peter stood for will fall."

"You're suggesting war," interjected General Perrin. He stood, facing his fellow senators. "We cannot allow Ris to fall into civil unrest. If we seek out the Underlings with war, we will be met with violent protests in the streets."

"There are already protests in the streets," Xolia said. Her scar burned. Though it wasn't from anxiety or insecurity. No, it was a reminder. The pieces slotted into place. Her hardships, the losses, they were all pre-ordained to bring her to this point. "I am the divinely appointed Selermine, I will lead variants and humans down the right path."

One of the senators scoffed. "You were appointed by a variant religion. One that holds no sway over me."

Senator Davenport spoke up. "We all saw the video. No normal variant could survive a beheading."

"It's not natural," another said. Xolia couldn't make out who was talking. "I've played nice for seven years. Why do we have to have a variant rise to the role of chancellor at all? A vice chancellor was fine, but we need a human to lead a human-majority country."

Yelling sprung up around the room. Everyone had something to say, and the shouting only increased with each barbed jab.

None of them were listening to *her* anymore. None of them were even looking at her anymore. Xolia ground her teeth together. The Senate needed to come to a decision. Peter's body was nothing more than ash and the hospital was still burning. Hundreds of people had died in an instant because no one else had been strong enough to do what needed to be done. Terrorists were furthering the divide between humans and variants, and the governing body couldn't even come to a decision.

"Xo," Adonis called to her from her party's small corner. Xolia turned to him. He looked at her with wide eyes. She furrowed her brows at him, then looked down at her hands. Water dripped from them. Big droplets formed at her palms, the back of her hands, her fingertips. She lifted her hands up and watched as the water slowly dried up, leaving her skin dry to the touch. Exhaustion fell over her all at once. Somehow, she had managed to create water. Xolia could scream. She couldn't possibly replicate it consciously. Unaware of her revelation, everyone continued their screaming matches.

There was a way she could grab their attention. Shoring up the remaining dregs of her energy, Xolia's fingers twitched into a familiar pattern, and she felt for their bloodstreams. For all the pulsing life thrumming through their bodies. She took hold of it, pulling it towards her, sending the room into immediate silence. All eyes snapped up to her.

"This infighting won't solve anything," Xolia said, releasing her hold on everyone. She leaned against the podium for support. "Peter's body, and who knows how many others, lie rotting in the rubble of the hospital. Lana, would you please start the vote?"

The woman in question nodded and quickly made her way up to the podium. Xolia staggered to her seat next to Adonis, who leaned over to whisper in her ear, "I'm in awe of you."

She wanted to melt under his praise, but now was not the time. She did allow herself to lean into him slightly. As a thank you. An acceptance.

"The voting for our next chancellor will now commence," Lana said. "When I call your name, you may cast your vote for Atlas Campion or Xolia Stone."

"General DuBois."

"Xolia Stone."

"General Perrin."

"Atlas Campion."

Down the list Lana went. Three senators withheld their votes altogether, leaving Atlas and Xolia tied by the time Lana made her way to the senator of finance, Victor Davenport. She held her breath, waiting to see what he would say. With everything happening so suddenly, she doubted General DuBois had had time to talk to him, but with the general already having cast his vote, surely Davenport would follow suit.

"Senator Davenport."

The man in question stood, certainly knowing that whatever he said would change the course of history for the country.

"I cast my vote for. . .Xolia Stone."

Xolia's breath escaped her.

She had done it.

She could avenge Peter.

Lana opened her mouth, but before she could speak, General Perrin stood and ripped off the four-pointed-star-and-halo badge on his uniform. Throwing it to the ground, he said, "Xolia Stone is no chancellor of mine. I stand with Atlas Campion."

Xolia turned to Atlas, who was also standing, his chin raised. Xolia's stomach plummeted; he must have been planning for this.

"You're a traitor to the country," General DuBois said. The two generals turned on each other, and Xolia wondered if this wasn't something that went deeper than their choice of chancellor. It looked too personal, almost like how she and Atlas would fight. There was a deeper hatred that went beyond political differences.

Something crashed into her, sending her and her chair flying to the floor. "I did warn you to back off," Atlas cried. Panic made his voice waver, like he was truly afraid of her.

Sel, she didn't have the energy for this. She had made it; the job was hers. Atlas brought his hand back and curled it into a fist. How stupid she had been, to think Atlas would let her win. Nothing between them could ever be so easy. Xolia was preparing for sudden and brutal pain, but it never came.

Adonis pulled Atlas off her, and his hand lit up in a blaze of red flame. He punched Atlas across the jaw. Atlas yelped and shied away from Adonis. Xolia got to her feet, ready for Atlas to launch another assault.

Guards stormed into the room while senators yelled. Both generals were shouting conflicting orders at the guard, sending the room into further chaos. Meanwhile, Adonis and Atlas connected again, Atlas pushing Adonis back with large torrents of air. Adonis, while agile, was strong and able to hold his own better than most. When Atlas's attack died down, Adonis would launch his offensive and the two would throw punches and block before Atlas pushed him back again.

Xolia ran to General DuBois. "We need to secure the palace. Get General Perrin and Atlas arrested." If they could secure the palace, they would have the upper hand.

Something slammed into Xolia's back. She pitched forward, but General DuBois was quick enough to catch her. She turned around to find the senator who hated the idea of a variant chancellor.

He didn't say anything, but his eyes widened, maybe in shock that she was still standing. His act of violence would mean nothing. Hatred poured out of Xolia. She groaned through the searing pain and saw the long knife that came standard on every Palace guard piercing through her ribcage. He must have slipped it from one of the fallen men in the chaos.

Xolia pulled her blood to her arm, pushing it against the confines of her skin until she formed a blade of her own. It pulsed with the frantic beat of her heart, and she relished that the man's eyes grew even larger, practically popping out of their sockets.

She removed his head from his shoulders and groaned again as his body fell limp against the ground. He had managed to get the knife deep between her ribs, and she was sure one of her lungs was punctured. Without medical care, she could expect hours of coughing up blood while her body healed and purged itself.

"Chancellor Stone," General DuBois said. He gripped her

arm, and she let her blood sink back into her body. "We need to get you out of here."

"Not until Atlas is gone," she said. Violent coughs wracked her body, and sure enough, blood spilled over her lips. She wiped it away and focused on staying upright.

"I can call in a team that I know is loyal to me," General DuBois said, his brows furrowed at the carnage unfolding around them. He pushed Xolia behind one of the fallen solid oak seats and crouched. "We can't trust anyone else. Not until we find out who is loyal to General Perrin."

She breathed shakily. "See that it's done."

General DuBois nodded. He pulled his phone from his pocket and made a call. Xolia coughed again. More blood. If she could just close her eyes for a moment. . .Xolia jerked her head back up.

Adonis was flung against the wall, his head bouncing against the stone, and his body crumpled to the floor. Isiah ran for Atlas, already shooting, but his bullets were unsuccessful in hitting him.

If Xolia was exhausted, Atlas had to be wearing thin too. She only had to last long enough for General DuBois's team to make it to the palace.

Xolia took a deep breath, as deep as she could with blood steadily filling a lung. She thought about the pain of cutting off her own hand—the anger and panic that had overwhelmed her on the podium—and smoothed it over with the reminder that she'd already won. She just had to last longer than Atlas. She clenched her hands into fists, visualizing the flow of water forming into blades. At first, nothing happened.

Then water poured from her palms, crystalizing and lengthening into twin blades. She stifled a cough and charged at Atlas.

He was unprepared for her assault and barely managed to avoid getting skewered. He pushed at her with wind, but it lacked conviction. She planted her feet and leaned forward.

She pushed forward again, this time forcing Atlas to reach out and pull ancient granite from the wall to act as a shield. An act of sacrilege.

Xolia charged and swung, keeping him on the defensive. Over and over again. He smashed the stone against her left wrist, shattering bone and her blade. Xolia tucked the broken arm to her chest and continued forward with her right hand.

Swing.

Block.

Repeat.

One well-aimed cut at his chest forced him to drop the rock to the ground. Atlas stumbled over a body.

Xolia let her blade disappear, overtaken by the sheer amount of energy that she had used up. She was running on the fumes of adrenaline. *The general's people better get here soon.*

Supine, Atlas could do no more than look up at Xolia. She planted a foot on his chest, breathing hard as she struggled to speak.

She held her thumb to her forehead and ran it down her face and then across her throat. "I am the Selermine. I am the leader of the variants. I am the leader of all. Not you. Not the Underlings. You will all fall in line."

"I will die before I follow you," Atlas ground out, pulling a gun from the fallen guard and slamming the butt of it against her ankle. She fell to the ground at the same time an explosion broke through the wall of the Senate Hall.

Despite the shock, her body seized. Was it another terrorist attack on top of everything else? More armed guards stormed the area, and Atlas, holding his hands to his ears, got to his feet and ran.

Xolia choked on another mouthful of blood and turned onto her stomach to spit it all out. She laid her head on the ground; it was wet and sticky with her blood, but she hardly cared. There was no more strength in her. She closed her eyes.

Chapter Thirty-Five

Xolia awoke to voices talking over and around her. She was on her back, still in the Senate Hall. Smoke drifted across the ancient stones of the ceiling. Medical personnel had a blood pressure cuff strapped to her arm, and on the other side of her, there was a single IV drip in the pit of her elbow.

Xolia tried to sit up, but something was restricting her movement at her midsection. A nurse caught her. "Chancellor Stone, you need to stay still."

"I'll be fine. Let me up." She moved her arms, trying to free herself from the medical devices. The pain in her chest was more of a dull ache, and she could breathe uninhibited—for the most part.

"Chancellor—"

"I said, let me up."

The nurse obeyed quickly, carefully removing the long needle from her arm, uncuffing her from the blood pressure monitor, and unstrapping the supportive restraints that had prevented her from getting up herself. The room was in a state of chaos, medical staff were tending to the wounded while dead bodies were carried out of the room in haste by soldiers.

Xolia unsteadily stood. Using the railing of the gurney to guide her, she stumbled over to General DuBois, who had made it out of the fray with only a grazed shoulder and a cut to his cheek.

"General."

"Chancellor."

"Where's. . ."—she coughed into her arm, a few spots of blood adding to the filth of her sleeve—"Where's Atlas?"

"He escaped during the explosion, along with General Perrin. Twelve senators are dead, including Senator Davenport."

Those losses were staggering. "Of those left, how many support us?"

The general shook his head. "We have them all detained right now. And, Xolia? The reports from the Meillus explosion? At least 1,500 people died."

A sharp pain emanated from her stab wound, and Xolia struggled to breathe. 1,500 people dead? This wasn't how she'd wanted to start her term. One terrorist group killing civilians. And now there was Atlas and his actions to contend with. It was treason. Unforgivable.

"Has news of the Palace attack leaked?"

General DuBois nodded. *Of course.* It'd been a naïve hope that this had all been somehow contained under the shadow of the hospital bombing. Of course, if the press was owned by the state, they would have been able to suppress the news a little longer. Xolia breathed in slowly, ignoring the throbbing in her side.

"Do we know anything about Perrin or Atlas?"

"I have my men searching for them."

"How much of the military will follow Perrin?"

"I don't know."

"Find out." Xolia exhaled, trying to straighten out her body. "Where's Adonis?"

"He suffered eight fractured ribs, a snapped spinal cord, and a severe concussion. He's in a coma right now."

Xolia winced. That kind of injury would take almost a week to fully heal, and she needed Adonis by her side now more than ever. She couldn't delay in leading, no matter how much she wished she could. With two attacks from two enemies in such quick succession, the entire country was vulnerable. The irony that she had now started two chapters of her life with such violence and loss was not lost on her. Last time, she'd lost Silas. This time, Peter. There was no one to guide her now. No steadying or comforting presence to either push her or comfort her.

"We need to bring in some of the press," Xolia said. "And I need Bridget."

FOUR HOURS LATER, Xolia was surrounded by Jareth and Emily; Isiah had been one of the casualties of the Palace attack. They sat in the octagonal office that Peter had used for official addresses and meetings. His ghost lingered in the small photographs on the eastern-facing wall and in the small handwritten notes that were still on the desk from his last televised speech. She ran her fingers over the lined paper, hoping to draw comfort from this small piece of him.

Alas, it was just ink and paper. A final remnant immortalized in such scraggly penmanship that she could never hope to read it. A single tear slipped down her cheek. She wiped it away before either of her companions could notice it. Xolia buried her sadness and sat down behind the desk, Emily and Jareth flanking her at either side. On the wall behind them, FAR's flag stood next to a flag with the mark of the Selermine, representing both sides of her. Xolia was grateful to be dressed in clean clothes, though she was constantly aware that her scar was exposed. It took almost all her mental strength to avoid scratching at it.

A knock sounded at the door. Xolia licked her lips. "Come in."

Bridget peeked her head in. "I've got Violet with RNN here for you."

"Send her in." Violet was the only journalist Xolia wanted to talk to. Violet was the only person she trusted to share the events honestly and faithfully to the country. With a fractured military, a huge death count, and a slaughtered Senate, Xolia needed to make sure everything she said gave off the assurance of her capabilities as a leader and as a figure that would set the country back to order.

Bridget fully opened the door and Violet entered. A small team of four followed behind her. One man held a camera, and the other three carried various mics and lighting equipment. "Xolia," Violet greeted.

"Violet, I'm so glad you were able to meet with me." Xolia flashed her a joyless smile.

"I'm honored you wanted me to meet with you," Violet said. "Though I do wish we could meet in less dire situations."

"I wish so too." The woman in charge of the mics asked to attach a mic to the collar of Xolia's coat. As she made sure it was secure, her hands brushed across Xolia's scar. Xolia flinched.

"I'm sorry," the woman said.

Xolia grit her teeth. "It's fine." It really wasn't fine, and Xolia's heart pounded against her chest. Bright lights switched on and Xolia blinked.

"We're ready," the cameraman said to the room at large. He mounted the camera to a tripod and turned to his viewfinder, holding up a thumbs up when he found the angle he wanted. Violet sat next to the desk, not quite behind it where Xolia sat, but not quite in front where she would look misplaced on camera.

The cameraman held up a hand and counted down from five on his fingers. As soon as he held up a fist, Violet spoke in a clear and assured voice. "Breaking news from Risian National News. My name is Violet Smith, and I'm here with newly appointed Chancellor Xolia Stone in the wake of not one, but two attacks on our country. One of which tragically took the life of our beloved Chancellor Bellevue. Chancellor Stone, what can you tell us?"

Despite her nerves, healing body, and fear, Xolia faced the camera. *This is what it's all been for. I won't let Peter down.* "It's true that Chancellor Bellevue and many other innocent Risians were killed in a terrorist plot to destabilize our hard-earned equality between humans and variants. This is a cowardly group operating under the name of the Underlings, and myself, and my administration, will not rest until each of these terrorists are brought to justice."

Xolia paused. She, Bridget, and General DuBois had decided to speak about Atlas's betrayal as well, in hopes to bar him from garnering any more support and to bring in the public's help in finding him. If Atlas was smart, he'd be out of Atalia by now.

"It is with a heavy heart that I have to say that Chancellor Bellevue's ideals have not only been betrayed by the Underlings, but also by former Vice Chancellor Campion. Atlas Campion refused to accept Chancellor Bellevue's pick for succession, and actively rebelled against the country when he attacked the Presidential Palace. This comes as a devastating blow, but not one that will overwhelm FAR or the people of Ris. I promise to guide us all through this dark night to the morning that awaits us." Xolia's scar burned. "I trust in Sel, so should you all trust in me. Together, we are Ris, and we are united."

Acknowledgments

I don't think this book would exist without Daniel Radcliffe's H**** P***** skit in SNL in which he plays an older H**** P***** trying to relieve the glory days of his youth while the rest of the characters had moved on to living their lives in quiet domestic bliss. Just one silly SNL skit that I've never seen again, but it has shaped and warped this obsession I have with young heroes thrust into fame and greatness during their most impressionable years and then expected to fall back into anonymity once they become adults. Real life is certainly less dramatic with lower stakes, but I always related to that burgeoning ingenue with the good grades at minimal effort and constant fawning over my potential from adults to falling out of grace during my teen years. School actually got hard and my studying skills were sorely underdeveloped. I wasn't picked out amongst my peers any longer, I was just one of many. I couldn't imagine that on a larger scale.

Except, I do imagine it. Constantly. I can't get it out of my mind. That's where the first inkling of Xolia and her story was born. The rest of it formed with my obsessive love for The Hunger Games. A story of a young girl, thrust into greatness, and by the end she goes back to District 12 to live quietly. Raise a family. Disappear into anonymity.

While, I do love a happily ever after, I just couldn't put

down the idea of a young girl trust into greatness. Wins. And then is expected to settle down into some form of a functioning adult, but finds herself completely unable to do so. Power corrupts, even if it's given with good intentions. It was always important to me that Xolia's story started at the end of that arc. Because we've all seen that story before. We all know what to expect from the plucky young hero who is expected to win the wars of people decades older than themselves. We all watch them grow from unsure and naive to confident and worldly. And while that journey is riddled with obstacles and moments of moral decline, they always end up on the 'right' side. I wanted to explore the after.

So, thank you to Daniel Radcliffe and the writers at SNL. Thank you to Suzanne Collins who created a story that I'm obsessed with to this day.

Thank you to my mom who always encouraged my creative dreams, even when others were quick to tell me that writing wasn't fiscally viable. Thank you for the hours you spent listening to me have mental breakdowns over the phone and crying when I didn't understand a simple software issue and helping me fix it. I wouldn't be half the woman I am today without you.

And thank you to Dale, who supported me through the many long hours I spent locked away working on this book during all my spare moments.

Thank you to all of the wonderful writing friends and critique partners and beta readers, etc. who've I've met through various social media platforms and have formed beautiful friendships with, even if I've never seen your face. Thank you Seth, Kiva, Caylie, Peter, Mekenzie, Loren and everyone who read messy early drafts, helped clean them up and made sure I switched all my semi-colons to commas. Thank you Britney, my editor, who helped me find a clear vision for this story instead of it branching off into 500 different directions.

About the Author

Maddi Bluhme is an author and content creator. After graduating with a BFA in Creative Writing she has devoted herself to improving her craft and focusing on strong character driven stories. *This Cruel Fate* is her first novel.

www.ingramcontent.com/pod-product-compliance
Lightning Source LLC
Chambersburg PA
CBHW030117310726
48970CB00004B/1296